KU-470-099

The Red Rockingbird

By Ann Marlowe and published by New English Library

THE WINNOWING WINDS
THUNDER IN THE KERK
THE RED ROCKINGBIRD

The Red Rockingbird

Ann Marlowe

Shetland Library

Ann Marlowe

The red rocking bird

083175

6517

SHETLAND LIBRARY

WITHDRAWN

NEW ENGLISH LIBRARY

Copyright © 1984 by Ann Marlowe

First published in Great Britain in 1984 by
New English Library, Mill Road, Dunton Green, Sevenoaks, Kent.
Editorial office: 47 Bedford Square, London WC1B 3DP.

All rights reserved. No part of this publication may be reproduced
or transmitted, in any form or by any means, without permission
of the publishers.

Typeset by Hewer Text Composition Services, Edinburgh.
Printed in Great Britain by Biddles Limited, Guildford, Surrey.

British Library Cataloguing in Publication Data
Marlowe, Ann
  The red rockingbird.
  I. Title
  823'.914[F]   PR6063.A/

ISBN: 0 450 04748 2

for
the real Addie's real Gran
UNA HUMBERT
with a daughter's love

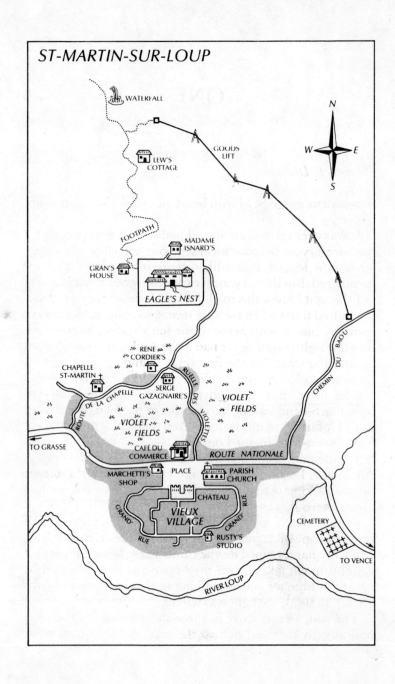

ONE

ACROSS THE gorge St Martin burst into view, as breathtaking as ever.

It was over three years since I had seen it, time enough for the memory to become idealised. But somehow the *village perché* now looked, if anything, more impressive than I remembered. But then, I wasn't expecting to see it, not just yet.

I thought I knew this road. Jay and I must have travelled it a hundred times when we were teenagers. But we had always come by bus or with Serge in the inn's station wagon if we timed it right. Gran never had a car. So I was seeing it from behind the wheel for the first time. Climbing from Nice on the coast to Vence and heading west, I kept thinking I was almost there. But the road twisted through the pine-clad hills, one S-bend leading into another in unending succession, until I lost track of the distance. And then, all at once, there it was – Saint-Martin-sur-Loup.

I pulled on to the shoulder and switched off the engine. Anxious as I was to reach the inn, I could not resist a minute or two looking across at the village. And this view, we had always agreed, was the best.

Automatically my eye began framing a shot, picking out a bit of foreground, judging the effect of the telephoto lens, while my hand groped for the camera case behind my seat. I caught myself and curbed my impatience. There would be plenty of time for photographing in the weeks and months ahead. Besides, the light was wrong.

The sun, setting early in these shortest days of the year, had already dropped behind the hills, so the ancient stone

1

buildings missed the warm glow of Provençal afternoon light. But the dusk emphasised the village's solidity, the houses that rimmed the gorge huddling against each other in a curved phalanx that must, in medieval times, have been impregnable. Fingers of deeper shadow reached up along the sheer rock face of the promontory from where the river Loup far below plunged unseen toward the Mediterranean. Backlit by the last daylight the jumble of rooftops and chimneys converged at the top of the Vieux Village on the square crenellated tower of the château. A new flagstaff rose from the tower, where a tricolor hung limply in the stillness of dusk. So the restoration had been completed; the château was now the *mairie*. Things had changed in St Martin.

Suddenly I realised why this view surprised me. It too had changed. Now it was uninterrupted, where before it had been partly blocked by the big white sign with its bold red letters proclaiming

LE NID DE L'AIGLE
— sa vue panoramique
— sa piscine
— son calme
— sa cuisine
2500 m à droite

Monsieur Isnard would not, I thought, have given up that sign without a fight. It was situated to lure tourists through the village with its competing hostelries and up the hill to the Isnards' aptly named Eagle's Nest. But perhaps the French, belatedly awakening to visual pollution, had clamped down on billboards.

Well, if the sign was missing, the inn at least was still there. High above the village I could see the tight row of cypresses that bordered the gardens and, rising above their pointed tips, the traditional round corner tower of the *mas*. The smaller dependent buildings of the compound were screened from view but I knew they were there too. And I knew that just beyond was Gran's house, empty and waiting for me.

Empty. I did not want to think just how empty it would be. Always before the house had been filled with the bright presence of Gran, resolute and vigorous even at eighty. But Gran was dead now. Dead like my father and mother –

I pushed the thought firmly aside. Tonight I would stay at the inn, wrapped in the warmth of the Isnards' welcome, cosseted as they had always cosseted me.

Time enough tomorrow to open the house and face the ghosts.

I stopped a second time at the edge of the village and headed for the phone booth, fishing in my pocket for a half-franc. Flipping the Michelin guide open to the place marked by the red ribbon, I ran a finger down the page to the entry for the Eagle's Nest. There it was, the name of the hotel followed by the little red bird on its rocker, symbol of seclusion and tranquillity.

ST-MARTIN-SUR-LOUP 06 Alpes-Mar. 84 ⑨. 195 ㉘ G. Côte d'Azur – 2 188 h. alt. 375 –
✉ 06140 Vence – ○ 93.
Voir Vieux Village* . Peintures* de la chapelle St-Martin
Paris 934 – Grasse 21 – ♦Nice 28 – Vence 9.
🏛 **Le Nid de l' Aigle** ⌂· ☎ 59.43.85 , ≼. ⊐. 🐎 – 🚽wc ☎ Ⓟ
fermé 15 fév au 17 mars et dim soir du 15 sept au 31 mai – SC : **R** 45/135 ⌂ – ⌷
14 – **11 ch** 120 – P 195 bc/230 bc

The number was what I remembered and I dialled it carefully, but when the clicks and beeps cut into the start of a recorded message I didn't wait to hear it through. I shrugged, retrieved the unused coin, and folded myself back into my little car. In a few minutes I would be there anyway.

The late afternoon traffic in the village was heavy enough to afford me a leisurely look as I inched through. Everything seemed much the same, the butcher's shop with its plastic streamers in the doorway, the estate agency, the antique shops. No, that crêperie was new, and the metalworker next door. And the lights. The Route Nationale that ran through St Martin was now, the week before Christmas, strung across with five-pointed stars trailing comets' tails, blazing in the

3

deepening dusk. There were lights over the square before the church too. I had time for a good long look there. As usual, traffic was snarled in front of the Café du Commerce. That much about St Martin hadn't changed.

Finally I was through the village, past the spread of new *mas*-style villas, over the bridge.

I almost missed the turn. Again, I was expecting a sign-board that wasn't there. I stamped on the brake, slewed into the narrow road and stalled. Then I sat for a moment, staring to my left while my hand groped for the ignition.

Funny about the sign. I could understand the other one being taken down, zealous municipal fathers prettifying their tourist town. But the one that had stood here was not an advertisement, it was an announcement of arrival. Now there was only the highway department's standard black-rimmed, black-lettered rectangle identifying the Route de la Chapelle. Nothing to indicate that the Eagle's Nest lay above.

For the first time I began to wonder whether it really did, whether the Isnards were there as they always had been. Not that I had expected an answer to my hasty aerogramme. My plans had been too last-minute for that. But I had tried to call twice from Nice, this morning from the airport and later from the used-car dealer, and again five minutes ago, and each time received the same recorded response, a tinny intimation that the number I had dialled was not in service.

Nonsense, I told myself. France's so-called telephone system had always been cranky and it was not likely to have changed.

I coaxed the engine back into life and lurched forward in a mashing of gears. Puffing and protesting, the little Citroën laboured up the unpaved track. I knew that its designation of 2CV – *deux chevaux*, two horsepower – referred to the braking capacity, but as the grade steepened to one-in-four I questioned whether it might not also apply to the engine. I also questioned whether my new car, or to be accurate my rather old car newly acquired, had been such a canny purchase. But I had bought it outright for what a late-model sedan would cost to rent for a week. Besides, 2CVs were reputed to cruise at seventy miles to the gallon. On the flat, that is.

4

As I urged the little Citroën up the slope, the Route de la Chapelle reached the junction with the even steeper Ruelle des Violettes, and the pervading earthy-sweet smell of violets, the smell of St Martin, rolled through the open windows to fill the car. It filled me too, as nothing else could have, with the sense that I was truly back in St Martin, that I was coming home. Slowing, then stopping, I watched the light fade over the neat fields of flowers and the village roofs below. The violets had roofs of their own, sheets of clear plastic spread over the cages of sprinkler pipes that alternately provided water and weather protection. Now, in the height of the growing season, the lush green rows were thick with purple blossoms.

No wonder, I thought with a pang, Gran spent the last twenty years of her life here. How could anyone not love a place that existed for the sole purpose of raising violets? St Martin might have a one-product economy, but in this age of noise, speed and pollution, as Gran always said, it was a product that was hard to improve on.

Tomorrow, I promised myself, I would take some violets along when I went to the cemetery. I could do that after I opened the house to air, and before I visited the *notaire* and the bank and the butane dealer and whoever else wouldn't wait.

Tomorrow, in fact, looked like a long day and I was tired already. I never could sleep on aeroplanes, and though it was not yet noon in New York, I had gone almost thirty hours without sleep. And for the last hour I had been driving along half-forgotten roads in an unfamiliar car. The prospect of an early dinner and an early bed at the Eagle's Nest was over-whelmingly attractive.

I shifted into first and was about to forge up the next steep section when I realised I was being hailed. Just below me on the Ruelle des Violettes a young man was approaching, trailing an empty burlap sack from one hand and waving at me with the other.

'*Ma'm'selle! Vous montez au Nid de l'Aigle?*'

The idea of a hitchhiker didn't appeal, but there was

5

something about his voice, a telltale flatness of vowels, that made me lean over and open the far door. 'That's right. Want a lift?'

'Hey, you're American! Far out! But how did – oh, is my accent still that bad?'

I grinned. 'Dead giveaway. And you look American too.' He did. He had curly reddish hair and a beard to match, gray-blue eyes the colour of mine, and he was taller than the average Frenchman. He had trouble wedging himself into the little Citroën.

'So do you. But the car's local. You live around here?'

'I've got a house up there.' I gestured in the direction we were now mounting.

'No stuff. I thought I knew all the foreign set in St Martin, especially the girls.'

'I haven't been here for three years. I just got back.'

'Yeah? Well, I'm glad you picked now to do it. I wasn't looking forward to the hike up. It'll be a bitch just getting back down with a load of rocks on my back.' He flicked the burlap sack on his lap. 'I'm bringing down some chunks of native stone. Not really the best stuff to work with but I hack some quick things out of it that the tourists like. Pays the bills.'

'You're a sculptor?' It wasn't a very bright question.

'Depends who you ask. My father says I'm a bum. But at least I'm a self-supporting bum. A couple people think I have talent. You an artist too? Everybody around here is.'

'Not really. I write, but not fiction. I'm going to grad school next year, Columbia Journalism. Meanwhile, I figured I'd take a working vacation – do some text and photographs of the area. I might sell something to a travel magazine, even *National Geographic* if I'm lucky. St Martin's a perfect subject.'

'Right on. Look, since you're going to be here for a while, come down to the studio. It's right on the Grand'rue, just ask anybody for Rusty's. Or if I'm not there, I'll be at the Commerce; it's where everybody hangs out. Great bunch – very laid-back – you'll like them.'

Maybe, I thought. Right now I didn't feel laid-back; I felt

6

ready for laying out. I was glad to see we had reached the end of the road.

Rusty the Sculptor climbed out and, with a casual wave of thanks, plunged off at an angle into the underbrush. He didn't seem to have a flashlight, or to need one. Probably his cache of rocks was close at hand. It must be, because it was a strange hour for – never mind, I was too tired to figure it out.

I put the car back in gear and swung gratefully through the arch bearing a black iron eagle and the wrought-iron legend *Le Nid de l'Aigle*.

The car park looked uncharacteristically empty for an hour when most travellers were off the road. And the garden which, at least on summer evenings, had always been lit by giant floodlights, giving the cypresses and mimosas a faintly oriental air of mystery, was dark now. There was, however, a light over the steps.

Hauling my flight bag out of the car, I locked the rest of the luggage inside and ran up the steps. The double doors to the main hall pushed open easily and I raised my hand to wave, ready with a greeting for Monsieur Isnard. But the words of fast-returning French remained unsaid. No one stood behind the bar that doubled as a reception desk; no one sat in the cosily grouped chairs.

Frowning, I went on to the dining-room. Though the tables gleamed with silver and crystal on crisp linen, it too was unoccupied.

Faintly from the back I heard a voice, and then music. A radio. I banged on the swinging kitchen doors and said, 'Hey, where is everybody?'

A stout, grey-haired woman stood at the stove, peering into a soup pot. She turned, peered at me instead, let the pot cover clatter on to the stone floor and swooped toward me.

'Mademoiselle Addie!'

I returned her bear-hug, then held her off at arms' length. 'Easy, Mathilde,' I laughed, 'let me breathe.'

'But, *ma petite*, where have you come from? Why did I not

7

know? Here let me look at you! Ah, you are truly a grown woman now.'

'That's right, Mathilde. I'm twenty-one years old and at least six inches taller than you. Don't you think it's time you stopped calling me your *petite*?'

She snorted. 'And what else should I call you? Haven't I known you all your life? The first time your parents brought you here you could barely walk. Didn't I teach you your first words of French? And later, when you and your blond giant of a brother would come alone, you were always slipping past Madame Isnard and in here to me. Those summers it was impossible to fill you up. I taught you to cook in self-defence, or I would have spent all my time feeding you. Don't tell me you don't remember?'

'I remember, I remember! I must have been here at the Eagle's Nest almost as much as at Gran's.'

The old cook's round face was suddenly solemn. 'Ah yes, your grandmother, such a loss. Everyone loved Madame Addison. I think you will be missing her greatly.'

'I do, Mathilde. I know it won't be easy at first, to live in that house without her.'

'You have come to live in your grandmother's house?' Mathilde seemed surprised.

'Yes, for six months or so.'

'Six months.' She sighed. 'Oh, to be young again. For you, anything is possible. But surely you are not going there now?'

'Not tonight. I planned to stay here, if there's room. I wrote ahead, but there wasn't time for an answer.'

'There's room all right. But I know nothing about a letter. Ah well, not surprising. Nobody tells me anything here any more. But there is no entry in the reservation book either.'

'It doesn't matter. The mail's awful nowadays. Even if the Isnards didn't get my letter, I thought they'd find someplace to put me.'

'The Isnards – then you don't know?'

'Know what, Mathilde?'

The old cook spread her hands. 'The Isnards no longer

own the inn. Monsieur Isnard, may God rest his soul, died at the end of March. And Madame – well, Madame Isnard planned to continue running the place herself, but after only a month she suffered a stroke. They had no children, you know, so she had to sell.'

I let my flight bag slip to the floor and sat heavily on a straight-backed chair.

'My God! How terrible, and all happening at once like that. Poor Madame Isnard. What ever happened to her?'

'She's up there,' Mathilde waved vaguely in a direction behind the inn, 'in her own house. Better than she was, but still not good. I go every day. Of course, I cannot tell her how things are, and I pray no one else does. She and Lucien Isnard gave their whole lives to building up le Nid de l'Aigle. It's better that she doesn't know.'

'Yes, I suppose so,' I murmured. I was still absorbing the first shocking news and it took a while for Mathilde's words to sink in. Then I said, 'But I don't understand. What is it about the inn that would upset her?'

Mathilde folded her arms. 'Everything,' she said grimly. 'That Scotto is hardly ever here, it's a mystery why he bought the place. And his wife might as well not be here, she's an invalid, or crazy, or both. The only responsible person is her nurse, "companion", whatever she is. At least *she* gives some orders once in a while. Not that she would deign to do any actual work. That is all left to Marie and me, and you know Marie. We have no proper staff, even the laundry is sent out. Nobody cares about the guests. Nobody even cares,' she concluded, red-faced with indignation, 'whether there are any!'

'Oh dear,' I said weakly, 'I see what you mean. I did think it was strange about the signs down on the highway.'

'The signs are gone, the telephone number changed. It's a wonder he doesn't barricade the road, that Scotto, and have done with it. Then no one could find the place.'

I did not answer right away. 'Do you think, Mathilde – I mean, with things as they are, maybe it would be better if I went somewhere else?'

9

'Nonsense,' she said roundly. 'You will stay. You have as much right to be here as anyone. Certainly more than that foreigner Scotto!'

An hour and a half later I was climbing the winding staircase up the tower of the *mas* for the second time, replete and ready for sleep.

It was like Mathilde, I thought with a smile, to insist on putting me in the tower. 'You shall have the bridal suite,' she declared. 'If they do not like it, too bad. They never tell me what to do and what not to do, so they cannot complain.' She also insisted on feeding me before the other guests, serving me herself, then sending me up to bed with a solicitous, 'Run along, *ma petite*. You need all the rest you can get if you are planning to put that house into shape.'

I did not suppose the job would be as daunting as Mathilde implied. Gran was a good housekeeper and her talent or taste for homemaking seemed to have descended down the maternal line. Naturally there would be a certain amount of dust and mould and fallen plaster after two years of disuse, but I thought I would whip the house into some sort of order fairly quickly.

Mathilde was right though about my needing sleep. The climb to my rooms took all the energy I had left. I knew why the Isnards had dubbed these tower-top rooms the 'bridal suite'. They found that the winding staircase, for all the charm of its wrought-iron banister and wall sconces, did not delight guests who were much over thirty.

Still, the rooms were worth the climb and they were more inviting on a second look. At some time during my meal Mathilde had come up, or sent Marie, with a vase of flowers that stood on the round table between the chintz-covered chairs. And in the bedroom the chintz bedspread had been turned back on the oversized double bed.

I looked at it longingly but forced myself to take a shower.

Wrapped in virtue and an immense bath towel, I padded across the little sitting-room to the quarter-circle of flowered

10

drapes, parted them, and pushed open a pair of casement windows. The night smells of Provence, wild thyme and rosemary, cypress and pine, blended with the earthy-sweet scent of violets filtering up the hill. I folded my arms on the sill and leaned out.

Below, the garden was dark except for the pool of light that spilled from the dining-room. Down the hill a ragged line of pinpricks led to the diffuse glow hovering over St Martin. On either side was blackness.

If the moon were out, I thought, I could see Gran's house off to the right, just beyond the garden of the inn. At ground level the cypresses formed an effective screen, but from up here I could see through the treetops to the sloping tile roof, to the improbable, whimsical tile-capped chimney pot. Gran loved that chimney pot with its silly hat. She said it was half the reason she bought the house.

Gran, Gran, I lamented. Gran with her girlish enthusiasms, her unflagging optimism, her gentle voice and quiet wisdom – Gran who brought life and soul to that unseen house beyond the garden. She had died two months before my own parents, but somehow now her death was the fresher, the more unresolved. Was it because until today I had not had to accept it? But I was back in St Martin now, back where Gran should be, and the reality of her loss was growing with every minute. How long would I have to live in that house before the pain gave way to happy memories?

I pushed myself up from the sill and was closing the drapes when the moon came out. It was feeble at first, still half veiled in cloud, turning the blackness into scarcely distinguishable shapes and shadows. Off to the right Gran's house was just a dark mass beyond the treetops.

Then it came out fully and I could see. I leaned again on the windowsill, straining forward, seeing but not believing.

The chimney pot, Gran's beloved chimney pot, was tilted at a crazy angle. And below it, where the front half of the roof should have been, there was a great gaping hole.

11

TWO

THE ROOF looked no better in the morning, by sunlight. The only difference was that I could see the damage more clearly.

The sun, in fact, was well up in the sky before I was able to take a close look. I had slept fitfully, only dropping off just before dawn, so I was late getting down to breakfast. Mathilde, serving as well as presiding over the kitchen, was too busy to talk until I started my second cup of coffee. Then I asked her:

'Mathilde, do you know where the keys to the house might be? I suppose Gran's are with the *notaire* who always looked after her business affairs. But I think she used to leave an extra set here with the Isnards.'

The old cook paused. 'Could be. I can ask Madame Isnard. You want them right away?'

'If it's no trouble. I'd rather open up the house before going down to the village.'

'Mmm, well, I'll be seeing her as soon as the dishes are done. Which is to say,' Mathilde resumed shuffling cups and plates on to a tray, 'as soon as a certain lazy – '

'Okay, okay.' I gulped the rest of my coffee and got up from the table.

Out in the car park I collected the rest of my luggage and dragged it up the steps. I had better resign myself, I knew, to paying whatever the Eagle's Nest now charged, at least for a few days. Despite my original plans, I could not stay in Gran's house until it had roofing, however rudimentary or provisional. This might be the glorious South of France but it was also December.

12

The hall, I saw as I nudged my suitcase across the tile floor, was no longer deserted. I dropped my typewriter and camera case on to a chair and approached the reception desk cum bar.

At one end lounged a youngish man, alternately sipping a small black coffee and a larger brandy. He was French, judging by his clothes and colouring, and probably in business or the civil service by evidence of the standard zippered portfolio under his arm. The French part at least was definite – his dark eyes were appraising me openly. At the other end a stocky couple were turning to leave, the man pocketing his change, the woman crooning in baby-German to the pair of toy poodles she held. Behind the bar stood a woman of perhaps thirty-five.

This, I assumed, must be the nurse-companion of the ill or insane Madame Scotto. Her thick black hair was swept into a roll at the nape of her neck, the tinted glasses that obscured her eyes were set in simple round frames and she wore a neat black skirt and white blouse. But despite the nun-like sobriety of her dress, she did not have the air of a servant. She looked coolly self-possessed, and chic.

She looked up and smiled faintly. 'Good morning. I regret that I was not here to welcome you last evening. I hope you slept well.' Not waiting for an answer, she reached below the counter and placed on it a printed card and a ballpoint pen. 'Perhaps you would be good enough to complete this now.'

I picked up the pen and obediently began to fill in the familiar *fiche de voyageur*.

Nom: Forrester. *Prénoms*: Anne Addison. Date and place of birth. *Profession?* I started to write 'journalist', then decided on the more modest 'student'. *Domicile habituel?* Another problem. Gran's house was not yet my residence, permanent or otherwise. I settled for the old one, Vassar College, Poughkeepsie, New York. After all, it was only ten days out of date.

Now the back. Piece of identity, passport. Like every seasoned traveller, I had the number memorised. But date and place of issue? Boston, April –

13

'Excuse me,' I said to the woman behind the bar. 'I have to get my passport from my room.'

I started out of the hall, then decided I might as well take some of my luggage with me, and picked up the typewriter and camera case.

The young Frenchman appeared beside me. 'Hold on, let me get part of that for you.' He lifted my suitcase.

'Well – thank you, that's very kind.' I returned his smile, more tentatively. In the absence of a porter, it was true that I could use help. And he looked harmless, even rather nice. The fact that he was a solitary morning drinker, I told myself, did not mean that he was depraved, merely Mediterranean. His smile now, indeed, was decidedly charming.

He accompanied me to the tower and up the winding stairs. Though he was a couple of inches taller than I and athletically built, he puffed exaggeratedly under the weight of the suitcase. 'What is it you have in here, bricks?'

'Not a one. But there are some books. Sorry.'

'No, no. My pleasure.'

He waited while I unlocked the tower suite and followed me in. Locating the luggage rack he deposited the suitcase on it, then looked around with frank interest.

'Very nice. Are you rich, as well as beautiful and accomplished?'

I stared at him.

He waved his hands in one of those expressive Gallic gestures. 'It's obvious. Plenty of tall blondes come to the Côte d'Azur, but they bring bikinis, not books, typewriters and professional-sized cameras. So you read, write, and photograph, and you do it seriously. *Voilà.*'

Rummaging in my flight bag I mumbled, 'You're half wrong. There is a bikini in that suitcase, it just weighs less than the books.'

'All the better. The pool below needs adornment.'

I straightened, passport in hand. 'Anyway, I'm not rich. I'm simply an old and valued client of this hotel.'

'Valued, that I can believe.' He cocked his head. 'But old, no. You can't be much past twenty.'

14

'And that,' I said firmly, 'is how many years I have been coming here. Shall we go down?'

He let me precede him on the staircase but did not let himself be silenced. 'Then you'll have known it in the days of the previous owners. Have you been back since it changed hands?'

'No. I've been in America. I didn't even know Monsieur Isnard had died.'

'They were here, the Isnards, ever since you started coming here?'

'Longer. They were marvellous people. Perfect innkeepers, too. Always ready with a welcome, but,' I added with slight emphasis, 'always respecting one's privacy.'

I couldn't tell whether that had any effect, as he was behind me. Anyway, we were back on the ground floor. I took my passport to the bar and completed the registration card, while my volunteer helper finished his brandy.

The woman behind the bar coughed discreetly. 'Excuse me, mademoiselle, I had understood from the cook that you would be with us for one night only. But I see – ' She gestured towards the tower where my luggage was freshly installed.

'Oh, that.' I smiled, winningly I hoped. 'I'm afraid my plans have become rather unsettled. If it's possible, I'd like to stay some few days more.'

'We shall be pleased, of course, except – ' She moved her hands in a sort of helpless flutter that, I thought, did not seem natural to her. 'That is, perhaps it would be better if you could be more precise. We are not, as you see, fully booked now. But for the weekend we expect quite a large party, and I doubt whether – '

'What?' The young Frenchman injected himself uninvited into the conversation. 'You can't mean, Régine, that you'd send her away when she's just arrived? She's the best thing that's happened to this place all month. Besides, if your "large party" is another of those all-male conference groups, the tower suite won't be in demand by them. They're too grim and intent on business. So you may as well let – '

15

He reached for the registration card on the bar, flipped it over and read it unabashedly.

' – let Mademoiselle Forrester stay where she is. Every tower needs a fair young maiden. You're more likely to want my room. You won't turn me out will you, Régine?'

'But no, Monsieur Bertrand! Of course it is understood that you stay here as long as you wish,' the woman Régine assured him earnestly. She seemed not to catch his bantering tone.

'Well.' He tucked his zippered case under his arm. 'I'm off to work.'

Régine removed his empty cup and glass from the bar and was again trying to pin me down on my length of stay when a bell, long and insistent, shrilled from the east wing of the inn. It was followed by a series of muffled crashes and a thin, querulous voice calling, 'Régine, Régine!'

Her mouth tightened and her brow contracted slightly, but when she spoke her voice betrayed no annoyance. 'Excuse me, I must go. We shall discuss it another time.'

'Of course. In a couple of days,' I said, choosing a convenient French formula, 'no doubt everything will arrange itself.'

And I sat down to wait for Mathilde.

The path from the Eagle's Nest to Gran's house was overgrown, but I scarcely noticed the weeds as I pushed through. My mind was busy with the problem of getting into the house.

Mathilde had been apologetic about the keys. 'Poor Madame Isnard, her memory is so undependable now, I didn't want to distress her by insisting. She remembered you, though, and she made me promise to bring you to see her. You'll come, won't you? You need not stay long. In fact, it's better if you don't.'

'Gladly, Mathilde, tomorrow or the next day. And don't worry about the keys. I can manage without them.'

I thought I could, too. Jay and I had discovered many

summers ago that with the proper manipulations – if I could just recall them – one of the ground-floor windows would open from the outside.

Emerging from the path into the small neglected garden, I stopped for a first close look. From here the damage to the roof was barely visible and the walls of rough old honey-coloured stone rose as strong and solid as ever. But still the house had an alien air. Though the lines were the same, the life was gone. With the door locked and the shutters fastened, the façade somehow resembled the face of a dead person whose eyelids have been closed for ever.

The image made me shiver. I would have to change it, and opening the shutters was the first step. These shutters here, midway along the west wall.

Something thin and strong was needed. I felt in my pocket. My passport, that would do. I slipped it spine-up between the shutters and jerked it upwards. The latch fell over with a metallic clank. The louvered panels swung wide. I put the passport back, thinking it was a particularly appropriate open-sesame.

The window now. Which side was it that fitted loosely? I tried to picture Jay's hands. He had done the manipulating then, for he was older and taller, as tall at thirteen as I was now. Palms against the frame, pushing down at the bottom, in at the top. Yes, the upper catch sprung free. And then the same process in reverse.

I hoisted myself on to the sill and slithered inside in a cloud of dust.

After the Mediterranean dazzle outside I could hardly see. I circled the ground floor, throwing the windows open and the door, which worked from the inside without a key.

Then it was time to explore.

The bathroom was neat and surprisingly clean, perhaps because it had a close-fitting door. In fact, it was the only room in this open-plan house that had a door at all. And it was Gran's great pride. She might have seen no need to install electricity – got along perfectly well without it, thank you – but she spared no expense in plumbing. Her daily ritual with bath salts and lotions – always remember, Addie dear, a girl must take care of her skin! – consumed a good hour and was performed amid the most modern of blue porcelain fixtures surrounded by the most lovely and traditional of Provençal tiles.

I turned on a tap. The water ran rusty, then clear.

The kitchen, separated from the living area by a serving counter, took up the rest of the space under the sleeping loft. Here was the dust I expected, soft grey house dust, reddish earth blown in under the door, white powder sifted down from the plaster ceiling. It blanketed the floor and work surfaces, mounting in the corner like tiny snowdrifts. But otherwise the kitchen too was neat. On the day before Gran's funeral, Mathilde told me, she and Madame Isnard had come to clean it as a last loving service. They knew their friend would go unquiet to her grave if her kitchen were not spotless.

Still, two years had passed. The refrigerator, its door propped open, housed the architectural efforts of countless industrious spiders. The copper pans hanging along the tiled wall over the stove were tarnished to a greenish brown. In the sink two beetles lay on their backs, their legs shrivelled.

I washed them hastily down the drain and pulled open the louvered doors under the sink. Everything I needed was there: ammonia, metal polish, scouring powder, an unopened package of sponges. I wanted to plunge in, to start bringing Gran's house back to life, room by room.

But that would have to wait. The roof was the first priority.

Passing into the double-height living-room without really looking at it, I scrambled up the ladder to the loft. Now I would see how bad the damage was. Probably the beds and chests were intact. Their sturdy oak would withstand more than falling roof tiles. And there was no other furniture, except for some folding screens. The loft – the 'campsite', Gran called it – had been used only by youthful visitors, chiefly Jay and me. Grown-ups stayed at the Eagle's Nest.

18

My head came even with the floorboards. I clutched the rungs, appalled.

Of course I knew much of the roof had fallen in, but somehow I had not visualised this shambles. Two of the sloping beams had cracked cleanly in the middle and dropped to the floor. Others on either side hung splintered in mid-air. Chunks of terracotta roof tiles and white mortar lay everywhere, ranging from the shards that littered the floor and furniture to great slabs that still clung to the broken beams. It looked as though the roof had not just collapsed, but had been struck by a meteor.

It also looked as though any disturbance would bring it tumbling down.

Once I had adjusted to the initial shock, I decided there was no need to investigate further. I could judge the situation well enough from the ladder.

Admittedly it was awful, but perhaps not as hopeless as it looked at first glance. To begin with, the ridge pole was intact and the crucial two-storey-high living area still roofed. That was already a plus. And since I had noticed no cracks in the kitchen ceiling, probably the floor of the loft was sound too. That would all have to be checked, but barring unseen damage, the only major expense would be the roof over the loft itself.

Expense. I didn't want to think about that. Jay and I had agreed that the money Gran left would be set aside. With any luck the interest would cover taxes and upkeep on the house, so we would always be able to come here. But now it seemed I would have to tap the principal right away.

I backed down the ladder into the living area.

Slowly I wandered through the big room, aimlessly fingering familiar objects, idly tracing the spines of Gran's books on their dusty shelves. My thoughts were on the unwelcome prospect of coping with builders' estimates and contracts. I looked at but did not really see the empty rocking chair where Gran had always sat, the day bed where she slept, the round oak table where we ate our meals, played cribbage and did jigsaw puzzles.

19

Suddenly it all seemed futile. The house would not be the same without Gran.

If only Jay were here to take over the business affairs or simply to keep my spirits up, it would be different. But Jay was in Costa Rica, five or six thousand miles away, and I had not seen him since July.

If only I could pick up the phone, as I had in my first year of college, and know Mother would leave her sewing or Dad the editorial he was working on, to talk my problems into perspective. But my parents were dead now, dead two years almost.

If only —

Voices and footsteps. The voices were masculine, two of them, and the footsteps came up the flagstone path and through the open door. The man in the lead did not knock. He took a folding rule from his pocket, measured the thickness of the wall, and dictated the result to his young companion. Then, his eyes on the ceiling, he moved forward into the house.

I cleared my throat. 'Good morning. May I help you?'

The man's eyes lowered to my level. 'Ah, good morning, miss. Didn't expect to find anybody here. You must be seeing about the furniture. We won't bother you if we go ahead?'

He didn't wait for an answer. Surveying the ground floor quickly, he swung on to the ladder and mounted towards the loft, relaying his observations to his assistant as he went. He must have been training an apprentice, for he commented not only on the dimensions of the house, but on its solidity and general condition as well. When he paused, I cleared my throat again, more forcefully.

'Excuse me, are you sure you have the right house?'

He looked down at me in mild surprise. 'No question about it. The abandoned house just beyond le Nid de l'Aigle, the one with the caved-in roof. This is the place.' He went back to his scrutiny.

20

I tried again. 'In that case, perhaps you would tell me what you are doing here?'

He didn't look down this time. 'Contractor's estimate.'

'Oh!'

My relief was as great as my depression had been minutes before. Everything I had been worrying about, all the business details, were being taken care of. It must be Monsieur LeClerc's doing. I knew from Mathilde that the roof had gone in a big storm last month, the middle of November. And already before my arrival, without even knowing that I was coming, the *notaire* was taking steps. He was safeguarding our interests, Jay's and mine, as he had always done for Gran. Bless Monsieur LeClerc!

I waited until the man on the ladder descended, then said happily, 'You must have been sent by the *notaire*.'

'I wouldn't know about that.' He stuffed the folding rule into a back pocket. 'I'm just the foreman. Boss says make an estimate, I make an estimate. When d'you think you'll have the furniture cleared out of here?'

'Cleared out? But surely that isn't necessary. I suppose I can move part of it into the kitchen, if you'll tell me your requirements. But for the things on the far wall, I would have thought,' I searched unsuccessfully for the word for dust-covers, then said, 'that putting old sheets over them would be enough.'

The foreman stared at me. 'Sheets?'

'Well, yes. Of course, I don't know whether the floor of the loft is sound – you're the expert, please tell me – but if it is, I think it should protect everything else sufficiently until the débris from the roof is taken away.'

'Certainly it would, but what's the point of that? If there's anything in here you want, you better get it out – and I mean anything, furniture, plumbing fixtures, the works – before we bring in the heavy equipment.'

'But, but – I don't understand.' The pit of my stomach did, though my mind wouldn't. 'Isn't that a little drastic? Just to repair a roof?'

The foreman turned away from me and when he spoke his

voice was resigned. 'Lady, I don't know who you are, but there's plenty you don't understand. We're not being hired to repair any roof. We're being hired to pull the whole damn house down.'

The little 2CV bucketed down the hill at a far greater rate than it had mounted. But when I got to the village, the traffic was worse than usual. It was market day. Though my car was the smallest model on the French roads, it still took me ten minutes to find a barely plausible parking space and wedge it in.

I would have preferred to go straight to the contractor and demand to know what, in the name of all that was holy, was going on. But the contractor's offices, according to his foreman, were in Vence, while the *notaire* was right here in St Martin. I would have to see Monsieur LeClerc soon anyway, and perhaps he could enlighten me. So here I was, forging through the crowds in the square in front of the church.

The curé, basking in the late morning sun, nodded to me sleepily. Heads turned as I passed the groups of old men occupying the stone benches and the knots of black-clad, gossiping women. Some heads turned more than once before I was placed. I did not know most of these villagers by name, and I had been away a long time, but they knew who I was. St Martin, after all, was a small town.

Eventually I got through and found myself standing before the brass plaque that said *J.-L. LeClerc, Notaire*, pressing the bell with my thumb for the fourth time and wondering what exactly he had always done for Gran.

I knew a *notaire* was some sort of lawyer, but he also seemed to embrace the functions of a notary public and an account-ant. To an American it was all quite mysterious, though I had an idea that the distinction between *notaire* and *avocat* was roughly parallel to the British system of solicitors and barris-ters. Which was exactly no help.

The bell was not answered on the fourth push or the fifth.

22

I turned away, thinking that I had better enquire next door at the Marchettis' produce-and-fine-groceries store, when Madame Marchetti herself appeared outside, a weighing pan from the scales in her hand and a customer in her wake.

She saw me. The weighing pan was dropped into a crate of oranges, the customer forgotten. She surged forward.

'Mademoiselle Addie!' she cried. 'What a delightful surprise! My God, how long is it since we have seen you, it must be since – oh, my dear, I must extend our condolences, such a very nice lady, your grandmother – and we thought you would now not come back to us any more. And your brother, the great handsome Jay,' – she pronounced it Zhay – 'he is here with you? No? In Costa Rica! Whatever does he do in such a place? Ah, how marvellous, he will be a great success, an ambassador before he is forty, I know it! And you, you will not fly away like a pretty yellow bird, you will stay with us for some time?'

I said I would and I also saw it would be 'some time' before I could steer the conversation. Madame Marchetti's forceful questions overrode my answers as soon as I could voice them, and her almost Italian French, exaggeratedly pronounced, rising and falling wildly, drowned my half-forgotten Parisian phrases. But at last I was able to inject a question of my own.

Madame Marchetti laughed hugely.

'LeClerc, that *salaud*? If you want to see him, you're looking in the wrong place. He won't be back in St Martin, not for a good long time!'

'But where has he gone?'

'Where every *notaire* ends up, or ought to, sooner or later,' Madame Marchetti told me with relish. 'He's in jail.'

That was the beginning, and the day only got worse.

Madame Marchetti could not tell me who was looking after LeClerc's affairs during his enforced absence, and by the time I tracked down someone at the *mairie* who could, it was well past noon. Which meant I had a couple of hours to kill. The bank in Vence would be closed until two thirty and most offices until three. It was supremely frustrating.

But there was one thing I could do, one visit which could be made without regard to the Mediterranean midday close-down. I bought a big bunch of violets and drove to the cemetery.

It was situated on a bluff just across the gorge from the Old Village, and as I passed through the gates, I thought that Gran could not have a better resting place than this one, with its sweeping view of St Martin. If she knew, she would be content.

No one was there to direct me and it took a while to find the gravesite. But finally I stood before the wrought-iron cross with the simple inscription *Anne Lowell Addison*, the dates of birth and death, and the letters RIP.

I knelt and placed the violets at the base of the cross.

In the midday peace, with no sound but the occasional birdcall, Gran's presence seemed to come close to me. Curiously, her memory was not painful here as it had been in the house. I remained kneeling for many minutes, thinking of the remarkable woman after whom I was named, and hoping that I might be able to draw on her indomitable character as well.

Gran, I vowed, you will be remembered with love as long as Jay and I live. And you *can* rest in peace. I don't know who is trying to take away our house, but I will find out and I will stop them. That's a promise.

At opening time I was camped on the doorstep of the bank.

The bank manager could not have been nicer. He beamed at me from across his desk, and when he had called for the records on the account, he hovered over me while I studied them. His solicitude puzzled me, until I realised I was wearing an open-necked shirt. But I decided I could not afford to get huffy and smiled back. In due course he assured me all was in order and I could draw on the money Gran had left whenever I needed it.

24

The contractor Aumale was charming too, but not so helpful.

He heard me out, then said he was frankly mystified. 'When Monsieur Scotto consulted me,' he said, 'I was given to understand he had recently purchased le Nid de l'Aigle together with certain adjoining property. He wishes to make alterations. The demolition of the abandoned house is only to be the first step, preparatory to the renovation and expansion of parts of the inn itself. It will be an extensive project and I cannot think a man of Monsieur Scotto's business experience would undertake it without proper documentation. So you see, what you tell me is rather unexpected.'

'If it's unexpected to you,' I said, 'you can imagine how unexpected it was to me. I arrive in France planning to live in my grandmother's house, and I find that not only has it been damaged without my being notified, but someone else is claiming it and about to tear it down. It's outrageous! That house was willed to my brother and me. It does not belong to anybody else, particularly not this Scotto!'

Aumale was silent a moment. 'Actually, now that I recall his words, he did not say it did. What Monsieur Scotto said was, "an abandoned house which stands on my property". Perhaps that distinction is suggestive.'

'I'm afraid I don't follow you. What does it suggest?'

'That the title to the property, when your grandmother bought it, may not have been clear.' Aumale spread his hands apologetically. 'After all, your grandmother was a woman of another era, a widow unused to business dealings and a foreigner. She may perhaps have been misled.'

'Nonsense! Gran was extremely intelligent and capable.'

Even as I leaped to her defence, I was busy considering Aumale's suggestion. It was not altogether implausible. Gran, for all that she was bright and forceful, could be a bit scatty. But about something that important? No, I told myself. Gran was not *that* scatty!

'Besides,' I pursued, 'Gran knew the Isnards – the previous owners of le Nid de l'Aigle – for twenty years. They weren't just neighbours, they were friends. If there were any question

25

of title conflict or boundary claims, it would have been discussed and settled right at the beginning. There simply can't be any problem.'

'My dear Miss Forrester, for your sake I hope not.' Aumale sounded genuinely concerned. 'But you must see my position. I cannot risk losing a client as substantial as Monsieur Scotto on the basis of your unsupported assertion. In fact, I can offer you very little help.'

I looked at him steadily and waited for him to continue. At least he was offering something.

'Only a bit of time. My firm could not undertake the work, in any case, until after the holidays. So you will have a chance to look for support of your claim in the public records. I suggest, Miss Forrester, that you seek legal advice without delay.'

'Thank you, Monsieur Aumale.' I rose. 'That is precisely what I intend to do.'

If Monsieur Aumale was not very helpful, the *notaire* Rénaud was less so. And he wasn't even charming.

I followed the directions the village clerk in St Martin had given me and found Rénaud's office in the twisting Old Town of Vence just before four o'clock. His secretary took my name, went into the inner office and returned to her typewriter while I waited on a hard straight-backed chair. I was prepared to wait; I had no appointment. But as time passed and it became clear there was no one with Rénaud, I began to be annoyed. Eventually he condescended to see me.

I had had some practice telling my story in the course of the day and I did it succinctly. But Rénaud tapped his foot and tapped his Gitane on the lip of his ashtray until I came to the end. Then he stubbed out the cigarette and leaned back.

'It is true,' he said, 'that I have access to the files of this LeClerc.' He did not, I noticed, call LeClerc his colleague. 'For the protection of his unfortunate clients, someone must. But I was never in any way associated with LeClerc and I have not undertaken to represent his clients, together or singly. I have my own practice, which occupies me fully. You must, my dear Miss Forrester, understand my position.'

By now I was a bit tired of being called somebody's 'dear' and told I had to 'understand his position'. I was also down on lawyers. So I said:

'On the contrary, my dear Monsieur Rénaud. It is you who must understand mine.' I managed to sound almost as pompous as he did. 'I grant that your strict duty only requires you to open LeClerc's files to any lawyer I may choose. But would it not make more sense, since you already have access to the files, to do it all yourself? I can't see that a simple title search would take very long. And even if I *am* a foreigner, I can assure you I have solid bank references. So you don't have to worry about getting your money!'

Rénaud had the grace to look abashed. He shook another cigarette from the crumpled pack on his desk, then put it down again.

'Miss Forrester, my duty extends further than you see. If, as you tell me, there is a disagreement over the ownership of your grandmother's property, it could develop into an adversary relationship between you and Monsieur Scotto. In that case I would be unable to help you.'

He picked up the cigarette again, and this time he lit it.

'It is my duty to inform you that I am already the legal adviser of Monsieur Joseph Scotto.'

By the time I got back to the inn, the fading twilight was as dim as my spirits and I was bone tired. But the Eagle's Nest, which had beckoned like a safe harbour twenty-four hours ago, had become the stronghold of my enemy. It was too much to face just yet.

I skirted the outbuildings, pushed along the path to Gran's house, and climbed through the trick window. Inside the darkened living-room my sense of solitary helplessness grew. This was *my* house and I didn't even have a key. I was reduced to entering like a common burglar. One final indignity to cap the day.

Since my arrival nothing had gone as expected – and I had no idea how to begin putting things right.

Well, there was no point in standing here in the dark. I roused myself to check the gas, and felt slightly cheered. The butane bottle in the kitchen was attached and fairly full, and so were the little blue cylinders that fed the hurricane lamps. I set them blazing and decided a cup of tea might help.

While the water heated I prowled the familiar living-room. Gran's rocking chair was still too much her own for me to sit in. But I had often sprawled on her day bed, and now, in an instinctive search for consolation, I stretched out on it.

The bed squeaked under me. The springs, I thought, must have got rusty. No wonder, in two years.

The squeaking continued.

Odd. My mind was fuzzy with fatigue, but it seemed the noise should have stopped when the springs rebounded from my weight. The bed was still moving too. Not much, just a gentle undulating motion, but definitely un-bedlike.

I rolled off cautiously and watched, fascinated, as the bed continued to ripple and squeak.

Reaching for the hem of the bedspread, I took it in both hands and peeled it steadily back. The ticking of the bare mattress emerged, intact at first, then rent by a yard-long raggedly chewn hole.

In the hole were scores, even hundreds, of baby mice!

My hands seemed glued to the bedspread as I wondered wildly what to do next. Scream? Faint? Clamber on to a chair like a Victorian lady in distress? But that would only work with one mouse, and a man around to deal with it. Here I was faced with a whole nest of wriggling newborn rodents. And there was not a man in sight.

I yanked the bedspread back into place, hoping to keep the mice underneath, and opened the front door wide. With a shudder I dragged the mattress off the bed and across the floor – bedspread, mice and all. The mattress stuck in the doorway. I tugged at it, half cursing and half moaning.

Suddenly the squeaks from the mattress were overridden

by a chorus of shrill excited yaps and a deep-pitched British voice.

'Might I help?'

I turned and saw a tall, lanky, dark-haired man setting a bundle of books and newspapers on the ground and slipping a rucksack from his shoulders, while two little dogs danced around him.

'Please, would you? I can't get it through the door.'

Together we got the mattress dislodged and into the middle of the garden. The dogs, terriers of some kind, circled the mattress in a frenzy. I pulled the spread away and they dived for the hole in the centre, while baby mice scurried in all directions. My companion stuck his hands in his pockets, threw back his head and laughed. 'I say, this is quite wonderful!'

'You wouldn't think so,' I retorted, 'if it had been you who lay down on that bed and felt it wriggling and squeaking under you. I'll bet you'd have been as spooked as I was.'

'No doubt. But look at the dogs, do. They've not had such a marvellous time in ages. They're in pure heaven.'

They *were* comical, I had to admit, chasing every which-way as the mice escaped into the shadows. I began to laugh too, but my laughter sounded forced and then hysterical.

Before I knew it I was sobbing.

Try as I might, I couldn't stop. My companion watched in irresolute embarrassment, then put a diffident hand on my elbow. 'Come along, you'd best sit down.'

He steered me into the house and settled me in a chair. It was Gran's rocker, but I didn't protest.

'Now, what you want is something to drink. I wonder –'

'Oh, the kettle! I forgot.'

'Sit still, I'll get it.' He went to the stove, turned off the flame, and began opening cupboard doors. 'No, dash it, tea won't do. Wait, I'll be back in a tick.'

He disappeared outside. I heard him whistle and call, 'Dylan, Caitlin!' Then he was inside again, this time with the rucksack and the dogs. 'Here we are.'

From the rucksack he produced a bottle of Scotch, from

29

which he poured me a generous three ounces, neat. Again I didn't protest.

'That's better. Now tell me, do all American women come unstrung at the sight of mice or was there more to it?'

'It wasn't just the mice,' I told him. I didn't say any more, but he waited patiently, pouring out a drink of his own and installing himself in an overstuffed chair with the dogs at his feet, looking perfectly at ease. He asked no more questions, just watched me with a quiet smile and steady blue eyes until I found myself telling him the whole story.

When I paused he said, 'Good Lord, you've not had a pleasant day, have you? Still, at least you know now what you need. One, a new mattress. Two, a full-grown cat with a healthy appetite. And three, a good lawyer.'

'Sure, but where do I find one? The only lawyer I *did* go to turned out to be already in the other camp. All I accomplished was to tip my hand thoroughly to the enemy. And I don't know who to ask for advice. I don't suppose you – '

'Not me,' he said cheerfully. 'I've been lucky enough not to need a lawyer here. But if I did, I'd go straight to the British Consulate. You've got one here, haven't you, in Nice? Why don't you ring them?'

'That's a good idea. Better yet, I'll drive down tomorrow. It might work better than over the phone.'

'Might indeed. I'll be interested to know how you fare. I say, why don't I come by tomorrow about the same time? I'll give you drinks and dinner and you can give me a report. If you're not busy, that is?'

'No. I mean, I'm not busy, but – if it isn't too nosy of me, do you always invite girls to dinner without even knowing their names?'

He laughed. 'Now that you ask, I don't. Since I already know half your history, you might as well give me your name to go with it.'

'It's Addie Forrester. Actually it's Anne Addison, after my grandmother, but I've always been called Addie.'

'And I'm called Lew. Llewellyn Rhys-Owen. Obviously a Welshman – but not, like Taffy, a thief.'

As he gathered his things, stowing the whisky bottle in the rucksack and pulling out an oversized flashlight, I thought I could believe him. I knew nothing of Llewellyn Rhys-Owen, neither who he was nor how he came to land on my doorstep, but I thought he was the sort of person who could be counted on.

If I had promised tomorrow evening to Lew, tonight I was to dine with Jean-Marc Bertrand. He was in the lobby of the Eagle's Nest when I got back.

'Ah, the fair Mademoiselle Anne!' he called from the bar. 'Come join me for an *apéro*.'

I didn't want another drink, and it was almost time for dinner anyway, but I accepted a tomato juice. It gave me a chance to straighten out the business of names. Also it allowed me to cultivate the acquaintance of young Monsieur Bertrand. If he had been staying at the inn since the beginning of the month, as I inferred, he might be able to tell me about the new owner. And that, I thought, was a subject I had better explore. Fast.

Jean-Marc was willing enough to be cultivated. But being a young French male, he tended to begin every second sentence with '*moi, je*', so for a while I learned mainly about Jean-Marc Bertrand. He was, he said, employed by the tourism ministry, and he was currently vetting restaurants in the area. Apparently this only involved dropping in at odd hours, not dining, for Jean-Marc seemed to have dinner here at the Eagle's Nest regularly. He stayed here, he said, because Mathilde cooked like *un ange*. There I had to agree with him.

Somehow we were automatically seated together in the dining-room. Mathilde was in top form and our conversation, lively until then, subsided in favour of serious eating. Eventually the roast veal gave way to a platter of cheeses and I broached the topic of Monsieur Joseph Scotto.

'Him!' said Jean-Marc with easy contempt. His dark eyes gleamed and his mouth twitched. I could see that I was about to be treated to some Gallic gossip. A national trait of the French is to talk about their neighbours. It is not invariably malicious, but it *is* invariable.

'Scotto,' said Jean-Marc, 'is as unlikely an innkeeper as you can imagine. I've been here almost a month and he has shown up exactly four times. Not what you'd call a firm hand at the helm. Of course, the fact that his wife lives here permanently may explain it.'

I pretended to misunderstand. 'You mean that he leaves the running of the place to Madame Scotto?'

'Hardly! I mean he prefers to forget she exists. Which I gather is understandable enough. Madame is said to be "in delicate health", and you know what that means. In all likelihood her illness is located in her head. Not that I've seen her; nobody does except Régine. But I've heard her, and that's enough. I don't know how Régine stands it.'

I glanced across the room to where Régine sat, alone and aloof, at a corner table. I did not think our low-pitched voices could carry that far. But Jean-Marc followed my glance, and rose. 'Why don't we move somewhere less public?'

In the lobby he went behind the empty bar, set two glasses on a tray and took an unopened bottle of cognac from the top shelf. He scribbled on a notepad. It was proof, I thought, if I needed any, of how little actual running le Nid de l'Aigle got.

'Your room,' he said, 'or mine?'

I raised an eyebrow. I had assumed we would stay in the main hall. But Jean-Marc had a point; it was as public as the dining-room and I wanted privacy. Though not, truth to tell, the privacy of the bedroom of a man I had scarcely met.

'Mine,' I said promptly.

After all, I told myself as I followed him up the winding tower staircase, the reputation of Frenchmen had been discredited ages ago. And if he didn't behave I could always pick up the telephone and hope someone answered the switchboard. Or I could simply rely on the few lessons in self-defence Jay had given me. There are advantages to being five-eight and athletic.

Still, when we entered my sitting-room, I closed the door to the bedroom before pulling the quarter-circle of curtains shut. A subtle hint which couldn't hurt.

Jean-Marc commented again on the poshness of my eyrie, but I didn't let myself be distracted. While he splashed cognac into the snifters, I answered:

'It was Mathilde who gave it to me. I'm sure Régine wouldn't have, but luckily she wasn't here. I gather she's the one who runs the place, more or less?'

'Mostly less. She's supposed to be Madame's "companion", but she doesn't seem to spend much time accompanying. She isn't even here most afternoons. I generally get back before she does. But I suppose Scotto is satisfied. They have, shall we say, a "close relationship". Or so it sounds from the bits of telephone talk I happen to have overheard.'

I let that go, in favour of the main point. 'What sort of man is he, this Scotto?'

Jean-Marc shrugged. 'What you'd expect. He has plenty of money and that appeals to women like Régine. He doesn't have any sense of humour that I can see, but then neither does she. He's all business. Like those cronies of his, who come in a group for a "weekend conference". My God, they're a sombre bunch, dark suits, dark faces. But what can you expect from a Corsican?'

'Corsican?' I echoed. I didn't give the word the shading Jean-Marc had, but I understood it. And I understood too why Mathilde had called Scotto 'that foreigner' in just the same tone of contempt.

To their mainland compatriots, Corsicans are a profound embarrassment. Though Corsica is a department of metropolitan France, the islanders are regarded as a breed apart, incomprehensible in speech and in conduct – a swarthy, stocky race of brigands forever going about in bandannas and gold earrings, brandishing knives and guns, conducting interminable vendettas, kidnapping people, throwing bombs. Their elevation to Frenchness, a year before Napoleon's birth, failed utterly to endow them with the virtues of honest work and thrift, let alone the slightest vestige of culture. To

33

this day, a considerable proportion of French children believe that Corsicans wear the skins of wild animals.

'Well, that explains a great deal,' I agreed.

'It explains why his wife went round the bend, if that's what you mean. Though she must have had a screw loose to marry Scotto in the first place – even with all his money. What it doesn't explain,' said Jean-Marc, 'is why he chose to dump her here. It makes no sense from either angle, personal or business.'

'No, I can see that. If he wanted someplace quiet in the country for her, why not a private house instead of a public inn? And if it was an inn he wanted, why leave her here to disrupt it? Maybe he was just killing two birds with one stone.'

Jean-Marc puzzled over the English idiom, which apparently didn't translate, then nodded. 'Maybe. But what did he want with a hotel in the first place? As far as I can see, he's letting the whole operation run to seed.'

'Some sort of tax write-off?'

Jean-Marc looked blank.

'I mean, he might want to show an operating loss to balance profits from something else, for taxes.'

This time Jean-Marc understood, and he laughed uproariously. 'My God, is that what Americans do? No wonder you have such a reputation for being naïve. Every Frenchman is born knowing how to evade taxes, and the system is built accordingly. It's all done by bargaining. No Frenchman would ever, *ever* lose money on purpose!' He laughed some more.

I had to laugh too. 'Sorry, bad guess. But then why would Scotto neglect the place?'

'Who knows? Maybe he just bought it because the price was right and he's hoping for a quick resale.'

'No, I don't think so. I heard in town today that he's planning a lot of work, alteration and expansion.'

Jean-Marc looked up sharply. 'Who told you that?'

'Oh, I don't remember.' I kept my voice casual; I thought I had aired my private affairs to too many people already

34

today. 'But it could be true. This place has lots of possibilities. As it stands, the Isnards built it into a paying operation. What would it bring in, do you suppose, in a year?'

'Don't ask me,' Jean-Marc said carelessly. 'I don't know the first thing about the tourist business.'

This time it was my turn to look up sharply. But Jean-Marc was busy refilling his brandy snifter. 'That's enough talk about Scotto,' he said. 'Let's talk about you.'

THREE

I WAS up early in the morning. Early enough, indeed, to be leaving the dining-room when Jean-Marc appeared for breakfast. From across the lobby he raised a hand in greeting.

Aware of Régine behind the reception desk, I returned his wave with a coy and intimate flutter of fingers. There, that would fix her! Damned busybody, standing in her starched black and white like a censorious magpie – let her think the worst. I didn't care a sou for my reputation (if girls in France or America still had such things) as long as Régine, the eyes and ears of the Great Scotto, imagined I was safely sidetracked by lust. And she would. From what Jean-Marc said, she was none too innocent herself.

The sober truth was that Jean-Marc hadn't even made a pass at me. Though he was flatteringly attentive the rest of the evening, enquiring about my background and ambitions and tastes and opinions, he left before midnight. He did leave the bottle of cognac behind, saying it would give him an excuse to call on me again soon. And when I extended my hand to shake, he kissed it instead, not perfunctorily. But that was all. Probably, like me, he felt it was enough on twelve hours' acquaintance. Still, I expected I would be seeing more of Jean-Marc Bertrand.

As it happened it was sooner than I thought. Twenty minutes after breakfast I was back in the lobby, heading for the reception desk and muttering in frustration. The telephone was occupied but as I approached Régine said into it, 'Can't talk now, call me back later,' and hung up. She looked at me expectantly.

'I'd like to see a directory, the Yellow Pages. Or maybe you can tell me if there is a Citroën garage nearby? I'm having trouble with my car.'

'What's the matter?' asked Jean-Marc, emerging from the dining-room. 'Nothing much, I'll bet; nothing ever goes wrong with a *deux chevaux*.'

'Something has with this one. It won't start.'

'Let me have a look. Me and my brothers, we used to take them apart at weekends for fun. About as complicated as a model aeroplane.' He headed for the door, leaving Régine staring after him with a telephone book in her hand.

Behind the wheel, he tried the starter and listened a moment to the complaining whine. Then he went to the hood, opened it up and dived into the engine. 'Okay, try her now.'

The little engine coughed and caught. I flipped the window open and called, 'Jean-Marc, you're a wizard.'

'Nothing.' He came to the side, wiping his grease-stained hands on his handkerchief. 'Someone had just been playing games with your distributor. Typical teenage prank. Funny, I didn't think there were any kids up this way. But I suppose you find them everywhere.'

'I suppose,' I said without much conviction.

'Off you go then. Have a nice day!'

'And so,' Lew asked, 'you then proceeded to Nice, as they say, without further incident?'

It was evening again and Lew was back in the same over-stuffed chair in Gran's house, the terriers at his feet, drink in hand. The only difference was that he had dragged the chair closer to the fireplace. He had the fire going, in fact, before I arrived. I had found him lolling before it, scribbling away in a notebook.

'But how,' I had demanded, 'did you ever get in?'

'Simple. I came down from the rooftop like Saint Nick. I wanted a look at the damage anyway and it wasn't hard to get up there. I've done a bit of mountaineering – Snowdonia and all that, you know – and those rough stones form pretty good handholds. Then once I was up, I saw I could slide right into the loft. I thought you might be glad of a fire.'

I was. I was less delighted by the thought of Lew on the side of the house like a human fly or pinned by a collapsing roof. I told him about the trick window, in case he contemplated further housebreaks.

What did delight me was Lew's idea of 'giving me drinks and dinner'. He intended to do it right here in Gran's house. Or, as he insisted, in my house. If I proposed to fight for my rights, he said, the first step was to dig in. Possession being nine-tenths of the law and so forth. Besides, it was psychologically sound for my own sake.

It was certainly restful. I needed no persuasion to put my feet up and recount my day. Now I answered him.

'Well, not quite without further incident. But I was lucky. I decided to stop on the way out of St Martin at that Aral station and top up the tank. I figured it wouldn't take more than twenty francs' worth, but I was curious to know what sort of mileage I was getting.'

'And?'

'And it took a full tank, the whole twenty-five litres. I would have run dry long before I hit the coast. Someone must have siphoned the tank down to the last centimetre.'

'Charming. I take it you don't buy this fellow Jean-Marc's theory of child vandals. Then what's the motive? General harassment?'

I considered. 'That sounds too random. I think the idea was to slow me down, keep me from racing off here and there stirring up trouble. And it might have worked.'

'Not for very long, just for today at most.'

'Maybe that was enough. I have a feeling Monsieur Joseph Scotto will be turning up in the flesh any time now. Meanwhile someone did his best. I wish I knew who. Somehow I don't see Régine messing with engines and siphoning gas tanks.'

'Never mind, it didn't stop you getting to Nice. Now tell me how it went.'

This was the good part of the story. Retelling it to Lew, I

wiggled my toes contentedly in front of the fire and thanked my lucky stars for steering me to Consuelo Ortiz. Connie was a doll.

She even looked like a doll. Ushering me from the pamphlet-filled Consulate waiting-room into an inner office, she barely came up to my shoulder. She was pert and perky, with clear olive skin and lustrous dark eyes fringed by thick dark lashes. The skin around the eyes crinkled when she smiled, which was often. She spoke in a breathless rush, more at the speed of Spanish than English, but perfectly clearly and with infectious verve.

'I'm Consuelo Ortiz,' she said. 'Super name for this business, isn't it? Almost sounds like consul. Actually I'm just a vice-consul, which isn't all that lofty, but I'm afraid the boss is out of town, so I'm as high as you get. Still, maybe I can help. What's the problem?'

While I told her, she frowned, jotted notes, interjected questions and poked a pencil through her sleek dark hair. She stirred her hair some more after I finished, then raised an eyebrow and said deadpan, 'Must have been a swell place in your grandmother's day. But then this Corsican moves in and – there goes the neighbourhood!'

I caught my breath, saw the sparkle in her Puerto Rican eyes, and we both wound up laughing.

'Seriously, though,' she went on, 'you better not waste any time. The first thing you'll need is a preliminary injunction to – oh hell! I forgot. The *first* thing is, I'm supposed to tell you the State Department doesn't give legal advice. So okay, I've done my duty, I've told you. But of course we do give advice all the time, we can't just leave people hanging, it's just that it's unofficial, right? Except that in your case it almost is official, with the protection of property rights and – ' She flung the pencil on the desk. 'But still, any way you slice it, you're going to need a lawyer who really knows French law. Can you pay?'

'Yes. Some.'

She nodded decisively and punched a tab on her address/ phone book. While she dialled, she said, 'I think Robert's

39

just the fellow to help you. Don't let his manner put you off. He's really quite harmless, and one of the sharpest legal minds in –

'Robert Mercier, please . . . Roberto, darling, it's Connie Ortiz. How's the last of the great lovers? . . . Ah? Listen, Robert, I have a client for you, absolutely made to order. Damsel in distress, tall, blonde, leggy, perfectly gorgeous. Shall I send her around? . . . I know, you always are, but there's a fairly urgent time factor involved, so if you could . . . Super! Oh, and one other thing, Robert. The rich American is an outdated myth. Don't charge her any more than you would me . . . No, I didn't mean *that*! Give my love to Liette. Bye now.'

She scribbled an address on a memo slip and handed it to me. 'Just turn left out the door and left again on Victor-Hugo. It's about three blocks. When you're through, come back and fill me in. If you make it by twelve thirty, we can have lunch together. Good luck!'

I did make it and over lunch I told Connie, as I was now telling Lew, my impressions of Robert Mercier. They were good. So was the lunch.

We ate in an Italian restaurant on Rue Masséna, Connie's choice. 'I hope you don't mind,' she said. 'Sometimes I get homesick and Italian food tastes more – well, American. If you know what I mean.'

I grinned. 'Sure, but here even the Italian food is better. The French wouldn't stand for that glop made from canned tomato paste that they throw at us back home. Say what you like about the French, they have their faults, but they know how to eat.' I dug my fork happily back into my *risotto ai funghi*.

Connie speared a strand of her linguine, wound and waved it at me. 'You are in a good mood. Could this be due to my buddy Robert?'

'It could, it certainly could. He's just like you said. He must be marvellous with dowagers in furs, great bedside

40

manner. But I guess lawyers have to generate confidence the same as doctors. Your Roberto sure got mine.'

'Grand. But what did he *say*?'

'He said that since I was in the right – and I must be, or he wouldn't take the case – I should act as if I hadn't a qualm in the world. With some prudent precautions, of course. He takes the precautions, I do the acting. Such as openly moving myself into the house PDQ.'

'Seems a sound idea. Can you?'

'Well, I can't sleep there until I get something done about the roof. But at least I can make it my base, spend my spare time there, cook meals and so on. That part's no problem – it's the paperwork that's such a headache.'

'Some trouble with the will?'

'Oh no, it's on file, leaving everything to my brother and me. When Gran died, Dad flew over from Massachusetts and took care of things. But then –' I bit my lip and stared off into space for a minute. 'Then that winter my parents were killed in a car crash. All their assets were sold off – the newspaper, the house. My brother was executor, so I don't know what happened to Gran's papers, whether he left them in a safe-deposit box or with some lawyer up in Springfield, or even what they are. I guess I'll have to phone him this afternoon. I don't want to call from the inn, obviously, and the PTT in St Martin closes before five, and with the time difference to Costa Rica I'll be getting him out of bed in the middle of the night. He's going to love that!'

'Nonsense, he won't mind. That's what brothers are for.'

'I hope you're right. And then there's the problem of getting his signature on that power of attorney thing. It'll take for ever unless – I wonder, Connie,' we were on a first-name basis by now, but still I hesitated, 'would you do me a favour?'

'Sure, if I can. Name it.'

'It's just that, with the house having two owners, Robert wants my brother to sign a form. authorising me to act for him. But with the mail the way it is, it could take a month, or even get lost. If I gave it to you, could you send it by diplomatic pouch to the American Embassy in Costa Rica? Then he could have it witnessed and get it back to you the same way.'

She cocked her head. 'Sure, Addie, regulations are there to be bent. I can send it all right. But he may have trouble at his end, talking them into sending it back.'

'No problem. Jay works right in the Embassy. He's a junior political officer, a diplomat type like you.'

Connie's jaw dropped. 'Addie! You don't mean to tell me you're *Jason* Forrester's sister?'

'And after that –'

'I can imagine,' Lew said drily. 'This Connie sounds even worse than you. The pair of you must have been talking nine to the dozen.'

'You bet we were. Connie said she – am I boring you?'

Lew just grinned.

'Well, it turns out Connie and Jay were in Foreign Service school together. He's a couple of years older, because he already had his master's, but they were in the same class. They even dated for a month or so until graduation. She said she *knew* there was a reason she took to me right away, I must have reminded her of Jay. It's funny she didn't make the connection, I even look like him. She couldn't get over it. It really is a small world, don't you think?'

'I think,' Lew said, stirring the fire and chucking another log on, 'that it's odd you didn't tell Connie who your brother was, straight off.'

'That's what Connie said. Here she was doing her best to help me, like any citizen off the street, when all the time the house was half owned by Jay.' I spread my hands. 'Honestly, it didn't occur to me to mention it. If I'd said I had a brother in the Foreign Service, it would have sounded like I was asking for special treatment. But Connie says it makes quite a difference.'

'How so?'

'To start with, I don't have to tackle the international

42

telephone system. Connie said it would be her personal pleasure, as soon as working hours were over, to raise Jay by telex. She could tell him all the details and have a chat at the same time. They're probably clacking away at each other right now.'

Lew set the poker at the side of the fireplace and turned slowly.

'But Addie, you should be there. Surely you didn't come back to St Martin just because of me? I'm truly sorry.'

I laughed. 'Nonsense, Lew! Connie'll do much better without me around – she may even manage a little long-distance rekindling of old flames. I'd rather be right here. But if you insist on feeling guilty, I'll let you make amends.' I held out my glass. 'You can freshen my drink. And then I'll show you where the pots are, and you can cook me that dinner you threatened.'

I was late getting back to the Eagle's Nest. Lew and I lingered over coffee – my sole contribution to the meal – until I realised it was nearly eleven o'clock, when the door would be locked.

The lobby was deserted, with just one small light burning. There was not a sound in the inn. I got my room key from its hook behind the desk and went quietly along the corridor. My hand was already on the wrought-iron banister of the spiral staircase when I heard, from the private apartments below the tower, a choked wail. I paused.

'Hush, Régine, for pity's sake!' The male voice was sharp and authoritative, with a markedly sibilant accent. It dropped then, so that only disconnected phrases were audible. 'Why in God's name . . . utter stupidity . . . can't even trust . . . entire days . . . do everything myself . . . happen at a time like this, when I need all the . . . let anyone interfere with . . . tiresome female . . .'

The voice, I deduced, could only be Scotto's.

It dropped too low to hear. I stood a moment longer, wondering what 'tiresome female' had provoked Scotto's disgust. Régine or perhaps his wife? An uncomfortable intuition suggested it was neither. I started up the stairs.

Where I almost collided with Jean-Marc Bertrand.

He looked as startled as I, and a shade guilty. He must have been up to my quarters; the staircase led nowhere else. But I had not heard his footsteps descending. That was unlike Jean-Marc. Normally he made his presence felt, acting as though he owned the world.

'Ah, there you are. I've just been up looking for you. Couldn't phone, the switchboard isn't working tonight. Naturally Régine can't be bothered since her *patron* showed up.'

'I know,' I said and immediately wished I hadn't. Jean-Marc might guess I'd been listening at the foot of the stairs, but there was no point in admitting it. I stammered on, 'That is, I saw a big black Mercedes in the parking lot that looked like it might be his.'

Jean-Marc laughed. 'Sure, the one with the blinds on all the windows. People are funny. They think they're protecting their privacy, when all they're doing is attracting attention. Typically *nouveau riche*. Look, what I wanted to ask, would you like to have a nightcap with me?'

He meant a nightcap in his room.

I hesitated only a moment. 'Not tonight, Jean-Marc. Sorry, but I'm absolutely wrung out.'

He nodded and stood back to let me pass.

Once in the tower, I peeled off my clothes, flung them on the nearest chintz-covered chair and turned the shower to full hot. The stinging spray eased the knots in my back muscles and the vapour wrapped me in a soft soporific cloud. In minutes I was ready for sleep.

Now where was my nightgown? I had unpacked only this morning and already I couldn't seem to find the simplest thing. Not that I am obsessively orderly – I think a few items scattered around give a lived-in look – but still. Probably it was Marie, tidying up what I had left unstowed. Mathilde must have browbeaten her into doing a thorough job for once. The drawers seemed neater than I had left them.

44

The nightgown turned up under the pillow, where I should have looked first.

I scooped up my discarded clothes, stuffed them into the laundry bag, then pulled them back out and started going through the pockets. I was so tired I had almost thrown away Connie's home address and phone number. While I was looking, I came across Robert Mercier's card as well. It would be a good idea, I decided, to file them both in my address book before I lost them altogether. At least I knew where that was. It was in the sitting-room on the writing table, under a stack of books.

But it wasn't.

I tipped the stack over, frowning. The address book was new, a bon voyage gift from my college room-mate, but it had gotten bent from being stuffed into the flight bag and I had piled on to it my half dozen hardcover books to try to straighten it. Now it was almost at the top of the stack. Why would Marie – or *was* it Marie? Over the years I had seen her desultory dusting and she never moved anything.

Shrugging I opened the address book, tucked Robert's card and Connie's memo slip under the appropriate letters and snapped the clasp. Then I saw what I had missed on entering.

Just inside the sitting-room door, a white envelope lay on the floor. It was addressed to 'Mlle Forrester' in a vertical Gallic script. From Jean-Marc, I thought, opening it without much curiosity. But inside, instead of a brief note, I found a full sheet of flowery French phrases, ending

> I beg you to receive kindly, mademoiselle,
> the assurance of my most distinguished sentiments.
> J. Scotto

I went back to the top and read with care.

Scotto said that, having learned of my arrival from business associates, he had formed the unhappy impression that we might be in conflict over certain matters of interest to us both. Unwilling to permit this distressing circumstance to prolong itself needlessly, he proposed that, if it was agreeable to me, I should wait upon him at eleven the following morning in his office, at which time he was confident matters would arrange themselves to our mutual and full satisfaction. Meanwhile . . .

Another reading told me no more, so I tossed the sheet on to the table on top of the address book and crawled into bed.

It was not to sleep.

The fatigue that had overwhelmed me was chased by visions of Scotto. I had never seen him, so the figure that danced on my closed eyelids was just a vague dark-clad shape, formless and featureless. It advanced and retreated, always with one hand extended, beckoning. The other hand was behind the back, holding – what? In the kaleidoscope of my half-waking fantasies it held a sheaf of documents, a bunch of violets, a grimly lethal weapon. Then it was just a hand, with the fingers crossed in the childish gesture that nullifies the telling of a fib.

Finally I must have fallen into an uneasy sleep, for the dark figure of Scotto became . . .

Régine lifting her sober black skirt to dance a jig in the village square of St Martin before the church with . . .

Monsieur le Curé in his long black priestly skirts partnering her to the horror of his parishioners gathered for Mass and the milling villagers and Madame Marchetti and all the shopkeepers fusing into . . .

An enraged mob chasing Régine and then somehow chasing *me* up the hill alone except for . . .

Rusty the Sculptor running with me and shouting California hip words of encouragement before he veered off into the underbrush and . . .

Jean-Marc standing before the inn and calling to me to stop, except he had a briefcase and a bottle in his two hands and no hands free to stop me and I ran and ran to Gran's house and then I was somehow inside and safe and leaning against the big heavy door watching . . .

Lew clattering pots in the kitchen and wearing one of Gran's old aprons and looking for all the world normal and

46

saying, 'Would you find the pepper?' and everything was all right until Lew in the apron changed into . . .

Gran in the apron looking frail and helpless and reaching out to me and pleading, 'Find the papers, *the papers*!'

I woke. My pillow was wet with tears.

FOUR

Friday, 19 December

IN THE morning the interview that really shook me was not,
oddly enough, the one with Scotto. It was my courtesy call on
Madame Isnard.

Mathilde was there before me, for which I was glad. I
had purposely avoided breakfast at the inn, only ducking
into the kitchen by the back door to have a quick word with
Mathilde and filch a couple of croissants. I took them along
to Gran's house. There I boiled a kettle for instant coffee
and ate standing up, looking over the house and deciding
what to do first.

Probably nothing could be done about the roof, at least not
right away. Even the contractor Aumale, who was perfectly
willing to knock down the whole house on Scotto's orders and
proceed with a large and lucrative deal, was too busy to start
just yet. So nobody would be tripping over himself to do a
small roof repair. I would have to arrange it, but in the
meantime – hmm, maybe the answer was tarpaulin. That
would close off the loft and make the ground floor snugger. If
I could get hold of an extra-long ladder and some capable
hands – Lew's maybe? – the place could be made livable for
the interim. Even sleepable in.

That brought me back to the question of locks. I wasn't too
eager to sleep here with the keys to the house God-knows-
where. I would have to get a locksmith up from Vence for
refitting. Which, again, would take time. Until then I thought
I could wedge the door well enough. I might also add a
padlock outside; I could pick one up in the village this
afternoon. It wouldn't deter anyone with a toolkit, but it just

might give pause to someone with a door key. More important, it would make him assume I had one too.

The trick window would remain my secret, and Lew's now. Perhaps I shouldn't have . . . no, it was unlikely he would tell anyone else, and as for Lew himself, my instincts were all for trusting him. Besides, he had shown he could get in through the roof any time he liked.

I finished checking the cupboards, scribbled a shopping list and rinsed my mug. Then I made sure the snap-lock was off and headed down the path to Madame Isnard's, leaving the house standing wide open. If Scotto wanted to come here with me later, that was the way he would find it. I had nothing to hide and nothing to fear. Robert Mercier would approve.

At the Isnard house I found Mathilde waiting for me halfway up the flight of stone steps.

'We won't go in for a moment, *petite*,' she told me. 'Madame isn't ready yet. She wants to look her best – not for me, I come every day, but you're a special visitor, so she's nervous and she keeps fussing at Lili. Poor Lili! You do remember her?'

'Is that Serge's sister?' I remembered Lili as a shy slender girl of fourteen who helped at the inn in summer and for Sunday lunches.

'That's right, Madame Isnard's grandniece. A pity Madame has no children to live with, but at least she has her house. They got a proper nurse for her for the first few months and now Lili has come to stay. Poor child, she tries really quite hard, but I fear it is too – here's Lili now.'

The slender girl in the doorway still had the look of a skittish colt, but she must now have been in her late teens, and she was almost my height. She said nothing, just nodded and led us in.

After the sun outside it was hard to see, so by the time I located the old woman in a cocoon of blankets and pillows I already had a warm smile prepared. That was a good thing. I knelt beside her chair and kissed her on both cheeks.

'Madame Isnard, I was so sorry to hear all that has happened. Please accept my condolences. And Jay's too.'

49

The old woman peered at me as though her eyes could not penetrate the inches that separated us. She plucked nervously at her covers and repeated, 'Jay? Jay?'

'Yes, madame, my brother. Jay is not here now, but I know he would want me to give you his sympathy and love.' If my voice faltered, it might have been natural emotion.

'Lili, who is – ?' Madame Isnard sighed and fell silent.

Behind her Lili exchanged a quick glance with Mathilde and leaned over the chair. 'This is Addie, and her brother is Jay. You remember, Tante Irène, Addie and Jay are the grandchildren of Madame Addison, your American friend, your friend Anne.' Lili's tone was carefully matter-of-fact, though she spoke slowly.

'Addie, my friend Anne's granddaughter, yes. Anne is my neighbour. She has been my neighbour for many years. Addie is her granddaughter. Why does Anne not come to see me too?' She looked from me to Lili and back.

I could not speak, but Lili answered.

'Now, Tante Irène, don't worry yourself. You just talk to Addie and Mathilde, while I go and make you a nice tisane.' She hurried from the room, with relief I thought.

Mathilde settled herself in a chair across from Madame Isnard and tried to interest her in other topics, but the old woman could not seem to fix on anything. She had nodded off before Lili came back. Lili saw that she was asleep, put the tisane on a spirit lamp to keep warm, and poured coffee for the rest of us.

Lili was sorry, she said, that I had found her great-aunt in one of her bad spells, usually she was at her best in the morning, really she was doing much better, it was just that sometimes she was a bit . . . forgetful or . . . irritable perhaps.

Of course, I said, I understood.

Dear God, I thought, I don't understand. If this is 'much better', what must she have been like? This sunken shape in the cocoon of blankets, with no memory, no will, no power to do anything for herself – this was not Irène Isnard. It was too cruel to be called a 'trick' of fate. How lucky my grandmother had been! Over eighty vigorous years and a swift death. Her

50

friend Irène was nowhere near eighty and here she was spinning out useless days. Worse than useless, for every day was stolen from the young life of Lili.

Mathilde rose and I followed gladly. I would come back another day, I told Lili, and hope to find Madame more rested.

But the old woman roused then, blinked rapidly and shook her head. 'Lili? Lili? Ah, you've served our guests, that's a good girl. Do you have a cup for me?'

Lili brought her the tisane and steadied her arm while she drank.

'Thank you, dear, that's enough.' She waited while Lili took away the cup and straightened her pillows, then said, 'Well, Addie, it's good to see you again, and looking so grown-up. Mathilde tells me you plan to stay for six months, is that right?'

I was almost too surprised to answer. 'Yes, madame.'

'And you'll be in Anne's house. That's nice, the place needs to be lived in. Tell me, have you managed to get anything done about the roof?'

'N-no, madame, not exactly, but – '

'Now listen to me, Addie, if you have any problems, you must go to Serge. I meant to tell Mathilde, but now you're here yourself, it's better. You know Serge could always arrange things, he knows everybody. And he'll be glad to help you. You were always so fond of each other. There was even a time when I hoped – but then, Sabine is a lovely girl. You did know Serge and Sabine were married?'

'Oh, yes, madame! They were married in summer, four years ago last summer, so I was at the wedding.'

'Of course you were, how could I forget? You looked so pretty in your long dress all printed with big yellow flowers, and a matching band on your straw hat, and your long blonde hair falling down. I remember Anne bringing the pieces of that dress, so she could use my sewing machine. She had to wait. We were doing a lot of sewing just then.'

Madame Isnard smiled and leaned back against her pillows. 'I love garden weddings, and I've always thought

51

the garden at the Eagle's Nest as perfect as you'll find. I do hope, Addie, that when you're married, you'll choose it for your wedding.' She sank further back and smiled again. 'We shall do it all in yellow and white flowers, to match the bride. Lucien knows a florist – '

I looked at Mathilde in alarm. Lucien was the late Monsieur Isnard.

'And Anne,' the old woman went on, 'will be so proud!'

Mathilde nodded to me and we both stepped back to let Lili take over.

'It will be lovely, Tante Irène,' she said, 'but now it's time for your nap. Your friends will come back tomorrow.'

We slipped quietly outside.

As the door closed behind us I heard a plaintive voice. 'But, Lili, why doesn't Anne come to see me?'

On the steps I murmured a word to Mathilde and fled. I couldn't bear to talk about it, even for the two minutes it would take to get back to the inn. Instead I ran to Gran's house.

I sat in Gran's chair and rocked for a long time, not thinking, trying not to think. What had happened to Irène Isnard was too awful to think about.

My mind wandered, and when it came to rest, it was on the sudden realisation that I was in Gran's chair. Not involuntarily, as when Lew had sat me in it two nights ago, but naturally, as if I belonged there. I wondered if that was somehow significant.

I rocked a while longer, enjoying the quiet of the house. Odd – the house was causing me so much trouble and turmoil and yet when I needed it, the house brought me peace.

At ten to eleven I got up reluctantly and went back to the Eagle's Nest. I wouldn't have time now to call Connie before seeing Scotto, but that was just as well. Going through the switchboard was practically an invitation to eavesdrop, and I had no idea whether Régine spoke English. With luck I could get down to the village and call from the Commerce before Connie went to lunch. Anyway, she would probably want to know what Scotto had to say.

I was getting a bit curious myself and a bit apprehensive too. Robert had done his best to prime me, but it was one thing to sit in Robert Mercier's office discussing a theoretical situation, and quite another to face the actuality alone.

The lobby was deserted, so I went into the powder-room and killed a couple of minutes brushing my hair and picking the burrs off my jeans. That was another thing I had to do – get out Gran's garden tools and hack the weeds back. I debated going upstairs to change into something more sedate. No, Scotto would see me in jeans or not at all. Besides, jeans had been the height of chic in Europe for twenty years and were going stronger than ever. He'd probably think I dressed up for him.

At eleven sharp I stood outside the door marked *Bureau*. Now remember, I told myself. One, you are completely in the right and cannot conceive how Monsieur Scotto has been so sadly misled. Two, you really do not speak French at all well. I hoped the first was truer than the second. I knocked.

'*Entrez!*'

I swung the door wide and entered with what I hoped was assurance. Behind his desk Scotto half rose. I made him come up the rest of the way by extending my hand to him, just out of reach. 'Monsieur Scotto? I'm Anne Forrester.' The name sounded strange to my ears, but Addie was for my friends; for Scotto I would use my grandmother's name.

'*Enchanté, mademoiselle.*' He gestured to the chair across from his desk.

I took my time, looking around the office. Then I sat, allowing Scotto to do the same. I wanted him to notice that, even without my high-heeled boots, I was the taller. I decided the jeans were a fine idea. Leather with metal studs would have been better.

Scotto must have weighed a good two hundred pounds. He had broad shoulders and, though his conservative dark suit was expertly cut, he was obviously just as broad at the waist. His face, too, was heavy and square. I could not form a clear impression of his features, for he sat with his back to the window. If I had the advantage of height, he had given himself the advantage of lighting.

I reached into my bag and got my sunglasses. While I was at it, I took out cigarettes and matches as well. I seldom smoke, but this seemed like the right time.

Scotto lit my cigarette, then leaned back in his executive-model chair and began to speak. His voice was deep and, despite the sibilance of the Corsican accent, it had an edge of hardness which he could not quite conceal. When I had heard it last night, charged with authority and anger, it had been less pleasant.

'Mademoiselle Forrester,' he said, 'I am delighted you are here, and at the same time distressed. It is good that we can discuss this matter. Yet I fear you may regard me with – mistrust, and feel you have not been – um, fairly dealt with.'

It would be dishonest to protest, blunt to agree. Instead I said, 'Please, monsieur, could you speak more slowly?' I was following just fine, but it was true that his Corsican accent didn't help.

'Ah, my apologies. We must of course understand one another. Fortunately, I already appreciate your position. My legal representative, Monsieur Rénaud, telephoned me after your visit and related your conversation in detail.' I'll bet he did, I thought, as fast as he could dial! Too late for regrets about that. 'And now I should like to explain my own situation in turn.'

By all means, I thought, and make it good.

'By all means,' I said.

Scotto paused to light a cigar. It was large and noxious, but I was already smoking, so he was within bounds. I began to wish I had read Stephen Potter for more than amusement. Monsieur Joseph Scotto knew plenty about upmanship.

'Some months ago, when the Eagle's Nest came on the market, it was suggested to me as a reasonable investment. I had no experience of hotels and the price seemed high, but – well, I am sure you will understand – once I saw it I had to have it. I simply fell in love with the place.'

54

Scotto sounded almost convincing. I had to remind myself he was hardly ever here, so his love must be the sort which thrived on absence.

'So I bought it. But I am after all a businessman and I could not fail to recognise that the inn needed expansion if it were to be a truly profitable venture.'

Now he was sounding more like the real Scotto.

'Given the terrain there could be only two directions for expansion. North, where the house of Madame Isnard stands, and west, where your grandmother lived. I hoped, in time, to acquire both properties. In fact, I have arranged that Madame Isnard's house will pass to me after her death. But that time may be long in coming, as we must all pray.' Now Scotto was trying piety. It was noticeably forced.

'You bought Irène Isnard's house *en viager?*'

'It was the only way she would sell.'

'Good for her.' The custom of selling *en viager* was a peculiarly French one, wherein the buyer bought not the property but the right to inherit it. He made a down payment and thereafter paid an agreed amount monthly to the seller, who continued to enjoy the use of his property along with a steady income. On the seller's death the title devolved and the 'mortgage' payments ceased. Occasionally the seller outlived the buyer. The whole arrangement was a triumph of hope over hard logic.

In this case, though, it looked like Scotto had gambled wisely.

'Since I could not purchase Madame Isnard's directly, I turned my attention to the other adjoining property.'

'Yes indeed, mine,' I said vigorously. 'If I follow you correctly, I understand your interest. What I don't understand is why I'm only now hearing of it.'

'Ah, but that is what I must explain. I fear we have both been badly served, as your grandmother was before us. And by the same agency – the wretched *notaire* LeClerc. I cannot say whether he was corrupt or simply incompetent in this case. Certainly he was corrupt on at least one occasion.'

I smiled. 'Yes, I'm told he's been given a long vacation at

the expense of the government.' I spoke haltingly, partly for effect, partly to judge Scotto's reaction. 'As a taxpayer, I must approve. Only the threat of prison keeps many people honest. A sad reflection on human nature, don't you agree, monsieur?'

Scotto agreed, and smoothly. But he seemed to have lost the thread of his narrative.

'And how,' I prompted, 'does LeClerc come into this?'

'For my part, only indirectly. When I learned he had represented your grandmother, I approached him about buying the property. He told me it was not for sale, but when I pressed him he gave me the address of the executor and suggested I enquire directly. I later realised he could have done no less, for the information was in the public record. In any case, I wrote to the executor, a Mr Jonathan Forrester of Massachusetts. I believe, mademoiselle, that was your father?'

'Yes. But my father died two years ago and I'm sure LeClerc knew it.'

'Perhaps, but I did not. I waited for a reply. After several months my letter was returned. By this time LeClerc was no longer available. It mattered little, however, for I had meanwhile learned that what I sought was already largely my own. I learned, that is, that your grandmother had been living on borrowed land.'

I raised an eyebrow. 'Borrowed? My grandmother *bought* that property. In the twenty years she lived there, no one doubted her ownership – not her neighbours, nor the *mairie*, nor the tax assessors!'

'As you say, everyone agreed. Except the surveyor.'

Scotto went on while I listened in growing consternation. The land, not just the inn and environs but the whole hill, had for centuries been Isnard property, he said. The holdings had dwindled, but until well into this century the part I thought of as Gran's had stayed in Isnard hands. After the war Lucien Isnard, the last of his line, had converted the *mas* that was the family home into an inn and eventually sold off the adjoining property when it became

56

clear he would have no heir. The buyer was my grandmother. The boundaries were apparently not questioned, then or later. Everyone assumed the Eagle's Nest ended at the row of cypresses that bordered the garden, and the rustic plot beyond with its quaint old stone house belonged to Gran. Nobody cared to enquire, for nobody wished it otherwise. Until Scotto.

His assured speech now became almost confidential.

He could not have been more surprised, he said, to learn how matters really stood. His plans for expansion were contingent on buying Gran's property. But routine examination of his title proved he had bought not just le Nid de l'Aigle; he also owned a good few metres to the west. The property line, in fact, cut Gran's land almost in half!

I was too taken aback to say anything. Scotto continued.

He still wanted to buy the rest of the land, he said. It was no longer urgent, since he could expand on what he already held. And yet, he was glad I had come so we could set our affairs on a more 'regular' footing. He was prepared to offer a fair sum. He thought –

I held up my hand. 'Please, monsieur. Could you go over it all again? I'm not sure I understand.' I understood too well, but I wanted time to think.

He repeated everything while I tried to make sense of it. Could everyone have been so careless, Gran, the Isnards, LeClerc? The *notaire* could have been, and culpably so. The Isnards, as Scotto said, had no reason to care. Gran? But she would have relied on LeClerc, wouldn't she?

Of course, Scotto could be mistaken. Robert Mercier might find Gran's title perfectly in order after all, and I would have nothing to worry about.

But if it were true – what could I do?

Sell? No, this was Gran's house, bound up with memories of her, of childhood, and dreams for the future. I had vowed it would not be taken away from us. No matter what the interloper Scotto offered, it was out of the question.

Buy out Scotto's half, then? But I doubted Jay and I could meet Scotto's price. Assuming he would sell at all, which was unlikely. Anyway, if I even suggested it, it would imply that his claim was valid. Robert Mercier would not approve one bit.

Simply hold on to what I still had? But that would not stop Scotto's expansion plans. My six months of peace would vanish while construction went on. And ultimately the house would stand cheek by jowl with the new hotel wing. Everything would be gone – the view, the garden, the privacy that gave the house its charm.

It was a depressing choice.

'You are of course at a disadvantage,' Scotto was saying. 'Even had the boundaries lain where you believed, it is not a large parcel of land. The house is now uninhabitable. And at its best, it was – forgive me, Mademoiselle Forrester – small and quite primitive, worth very little.'

I was too indignant to dispute him. How dare he – this oily overfed Corsican in his black silk suit, this parvenu with windowblinds in his overpriced car, this smug, self-satisfied creature who kept his crazy wife and his humourless mistress under the same roof – how dare he make slighting remarks about Gran's house? He wouldn't recognise taste if he tripped over it!

'However, I wish to be fair. While your property would find no other buyer, it is still of value to me. As neighbours,' now Scotto assumed an almost delicate tone, 'we should avoid the unpleasantness of haggling. Your disappointment is already great, without the addition of severe financial loss. A quick settlement will be best. We both have plans to make. So I propose, for your share of the property, the price I would have offered for the whole.' He named the figure. 'Provided only that you accept directly.'

Scotto waited while I took another cigarette and considered my answer.

Accepting was the last thing I wanted to do. But I could not afford to refuse either. If Scotto turned out to be right, I wanted his handsome price to fall back on. And if I could contest his claim, I didn't want him rushing into legal manoeuvres before Robert Mercier could marshall my own. I had

58

to convince him that I was harmless, helpless and gullible. Which might prove all too easy.

Also, I needed time.

'Monsieur Scotto,' I said slowly, 'you've been very understanding and generous, and you deserve an immediate answer. But I'm afraid I cannot give one. I must ask my brother. Now that my parents are dead, I depend on his advice. In fact, everything hangs on his approval, as half-owner of the property. But he is in Costa Rica, so there might be some delay – '

'Yes, I see, naturally you must ask. You could not, perhaps, hazard a guess?'

I pretended to think. 'Jay's more practical than I am. He might want to accept. I don't think he's so emotionally attached to the house. To me, it's valuable for its memories. That's why I came here. If it were left to me, even with the property cut up, I'd still want to live in the house.'

'Surely you're not thinking of moving it? If it were feasible, which I doubt, it would be ruinously expensive.'

'Move it? Move the house?'

Scotto shrugged. 'It can't stay where it is. The property line cuts right through it. And I intend to begin construction in January.

'Of course, I could leave standing the part which is on your land. But I doubt, Mademoiselle Forrester, that you would want to live in a house with only two walls.'

I went down the steps to the car park feeling, all things considered, not too depressed.

True, Scotto's claim was about as sweeping as it could be, but it was not unexpected. Robert Mercier had told me not to be discouraged. I still had plenty of legal recourse. The important thing was Scotto's attitude, and that could not be better – whatever his motives, he brimmed with solicitude and sweet reasonableness. I was more than happy to go along. As long as it was a battle of charm, I might hold my own.

In fact, I won a concession. Scotto said he understood the wrench it would be for me to lose the house. He had no objection to my using it as much as I liked until things were settled.

I didn't even mind when he called me his 'dear Miss Forrester'; at least he 'understood my position'!

The little 2CV started without complaint this morning. I drove down the hill to the intersection with the Ruelle des Violettes and pulled off beside the house of Serge Gazagnaire. Serge was out, as I expected, but Sabine was there. She greeted me without surprise – she must have heard from Lili, I supposed – and with apparent delight. Serge would be dying to see me, she said, and he'd be in from the violet field at twelve thirty. I'd have to have lunch with them. No, it was no trouble, she'd just set one more plate. I was not to say another word.

So I didn't, except for thanks-see-you-then.

In the village I found, for a wonder, a parking slot right in front of the Commerce. The café terrace was crowded with pre-lunch drinkers. As I threaded my way through the tables, I heard my name called.

'Addie, over here!' It was Rusty the Sculptor, waving from a group of perhaps a dozen seated at two tables pulled end to end. 'Come join us!'

'Can't for a minute, have to make a phone call,' I answered. 'But I won't be long. Order me a coffee, will you?'

Inside the café was as empty as its terrace was full. I got through to Connie right away and recounted my meeting with Scotto.

'Then he strikes you as a reasonable sort to deal with?' she asked.

'Ha! I think he'd trample his own grandmother to get what he wants, let alone mine. But at least he seems to care about his image. Probably he's worried I'll run all around St Martin blackening his name. He bent over backwards to justify himself.'

'Well, that's something.'

'Maybe. Now tell me, how's my big brother?'

'Simply super! You know, Addie, even over the telex he sounds just like himself – relaxed and natural and as capable as four other men. It seemed like we'd been talking only the day before, it was all so – '

'Connie,' I said patiently, 'you can skip the testimonial. I've been crazy about Jay myself for twenty-one years. Did you happen, somewhere along the line, to discuss anything concrete?'

'Oh sure. He said to send the power of attorney thing. He's not so clear on your grandmother's papers, they're in a safe-deposit box in Massachusetts and he'll have to get somebody to open it, but he'll get right on it. I'm supposed to call him back tonight. Meanwhile he said to tell you not to worry, and to give you his love, and to take care of you. He said he wants us to be friends because, um – '

I laughed. 'Never mind, Connie, you can skip the tender parts too. Have a nice chat with Jay tonight and give him my love in return. Now I think I'd better call Robert Mercier.'

I did but he had already left. Robert Mercier evidently enjoyed a longer lunch break than Connie. His secretary told me to try again after three.

Back on the terrace I found my coffee and an empty chair next to Rusty the Sculptor. Apart from his casual, 'Hey, everybody, this is Addie,' nobody bothered about introductions.

Rusty's circle seemed to be an arty-crafty crowd. St Martin had always attracted artists and artisans, French and foreign, ever since I could remember. But the colony must have expanded – assuming these café-sitters were only a sample, and some were actually at work. The ones who were here, even before I tuned in on their conversation, looked like a sort of club. They almost had a uniform. Their hair – some clean and some not, some straight, some kinky – hardly ever came within range of scissors. A couple of the girls wore long cotton print dresses, like flower children left over from the Haight-Ashbury era. All the others were dressed in the style Tom Wolfe liked to call Low Rent.

I felt subtly out of place. My hair, falling long and straight down my back, was too freshly brushed and its ripe-wheat colour, though natural, might have come from a bottle. My jeans and Jay's baggy old sweater were all right. The leather pouch over my shoulder was not. It matched my boots too well and it didn't look handmade, at least not aggressively so. It just looked middle-class. I sipped my coffee and listened.

The conversation centred on the upcoming show they were all putting on in the old château, now the *mairie*. It was due to open next week and run through the holiday season into January, but there were some last-minute snags.

Interestingly the appeals were all addressed to Rusty. Though the nominal organiser of the show, a girl named Camille, was present, she tacitly deferred to him. Rusty was not the senior member of the group, not even the senior male. Still he fielded the questions.

– Rusty, we've got a problem with Leon, he says he's bringing in five. I know the limit's five per exhibitor but, Christ, five of *Leon's*, that's practically five whole *walls*! Couldn't you tell him . . .

– I distributed the posters where you said, Rusty, but wanna hear something great? The printer threw in fifty extra. Free, gratis, his contribution. So where do we . . .

– Look, Russ, you better talk to Jenny, she's bitching again about the crafts getting the short end. I thought we agreed the artists should have the whole upstairs, we need the exposure. I mean, they all have their shops on the Grand' rue. They want two galleries each, when we don't have any? Like, St Martin's not so big anybody walking through could miss . . .

– Hey, Rusty-o, give us a hand with the media? We've got *Nice-Matin*, they're sending Nicole What's-her-name and a photographer to the opening, but I can't pin down the *Trib*, and we could use the English coverage. You know Jeremy Arlington, maybe if you called him and . . .

– About the lighting, Rusty, can you scrounge another . . .

Even when the subject was not the show, the focus was on Rusty. If someone had unexpected visitors, Rusty had the keys to a vacant house. If someone had surplus furniture, Rusty knew who needed it. He advised on shopping too. For an offbeat purchase, when every merchant had ritually intoned *ça n'existe pas en France* in mock sadness, Rusty could tell where to find it. And for standard items Rusty's source was cheaper. He was the all-purpose authority for St Martin's arty set.

He wasn't arrogant about it, though, just nice to everybody. At one point, when he was explaining to me something about the show, a shadow fell between our chairs. A weedy, undernourished youth stood on the sidewalk shifting from foot to foot until he had Rusty's attention.

'Hey, man, you got anything for me?'

Rusty replied, 'Ho, Mike, no sweat. Come by my place about five, huh?'

The boy's hangdog expression changed to puppy-devoted. He shuffled his feet again, muttered 'Thanks, man,' and went away. I wondered what he was looking for – a message, a handout, an offer of casual work or, as seemed quite possible, a bag of marijuana. Whatever it was, Rusty had once more come through.

He turned back to me. 'We're all having lunch today at Camille's. Want to come along?' He didn't trouble to ask Camille, who sat at the end of the table.

'Thanks, but I've got a lunch date. In fact, I'd better get going if I plan to walk.' I pushed back from the table and threw some coins beside the coffee cup. Rusty got up too and so did the others.

Rusty crossed the pavement to my battered 2CV. 'What's the matter, don't you trust the old heap to go very far?'

'Sure, I just need the exercise. Don't make cracks about my trusty chariot. I've had her for three whole days and she's only broken down once.'

' "She", is it? How come, because she's temperamental?'

I scowled. 'Because *la voiture* is feminine, you Male Chauvinist Pig.'

'Lighten up, sweetheart. She puts me away, really.' Rusty kicked the nearest tyre. 'What's her name?'

'Name? I haven't thought about it.'

Rusty pretended horror. 'But that's awful. She may die

any moment, without being baptised.' He raised his hands. 'Hey, everybody, think time! Addie's car needs a name, gender feminine, no offer too low.'

The others circled the car, ready to play Rusty's game.

'A *deux chevaux*, eh?' said a Canadian girl. 'How about The Wonderful Two-Hoss Shay?'

'I love it, I love it! Let's hear more,' Rusty urged.

'Not as fast as a Rabbit,' offered a scruffy-bearded German, 'but she gets there. Maybe she's The Tortoise.'

'Too quiet – this one's a rattler,' said a Texan. 'What do you say to The Sidewinder?'

'In Holland,' a blonde girl said, 'the 2CVs are always called Donald Ducks. So she could be Daisy or Marguerite in French.'

'A flower? Wrong smell, for sure. We always called them Garbage Cans,' Rusty said. 'I'm for La Poubelle.'

I laughed. 'We called them that too. But it's a bit strong. Why don't we just make her Peu Belle?' Which meant not-very-beautiful.

Rusty's game was over. But as his friends drifted across the square toward the Vieux Village, I got the feeling I had been admitted to their formless group. They couldn't have measured me against their standards, if they had any. I must have been accepted as Rusty's friend – even his latest girl-friend. That might explain the faintly hostile looks from the girl Camille.

Rusty hung back. 'How's it going? Shooting lots of pretty pictures for the glossy travel mags?'

'Not yet, I'm afraid. The house is taking all my time.'

'Yeah, you've been away quite a while. But look, if you need anything – introductions or supplies or good darkroom work – let me know, maybe I can help. Okay?'

'Sure, Rusty, thanks.'

'Anyway, you ought to take it slow, get your head together after all those ivied walls. Don't sweat it. You making the scene Monday?'

'Monday?'

'You know, the opening. The party'll probably go on all

night. I'll wangle you an invitation. Where do you get your mail, at the Eagle's Nest?'

I nodded and Rusty was gone in the wake of the others. It wasn't until I was halfway up the Ruelle des Violettes that it occurred to me to wonder how he knew that. So far as I could remember, I'd never even told Rusty my name.

If Sabine had gone to no extra trouble, then the children always ate in the kitchen, while she and Serge had their midday meal in the parlour at a round table with flowers and a tablecloth. The flowers, I noted, were not violets.

Sabine had things well under control when I arrived. She handed me a glass of wine, told Serge and me to have a good gossip, and went back to the kitchen. But somehow, between serving the twins, spoonfeeding the baby and stirring the pots on the stove, she always managed to be in the doorway when anything interesting was under discussion. This alone was a feat; with her waistline swelling again, Sabine did not have much clearance between the stove and the highchair. I hoped that Serge's fields were as good at producing violets as Sabine was at producing little Gazagnaires.

Soon Sabine was putting the baby in his crib while the twins crawled over Serge's knees. I admired them dutifully and tried to talk to them, but they were not yet three and I had never mastered baby-French. So I was glad when they too were settled for a nap.

Over lunch Serge and Sabine tackled my problem. Occasionally they asked me a question, but mostly they conversed in the rapid-fire shorthand of a well-attuned married couple.

'But if anyone questions the – '

'Don't worry, I'll call Uncle Louis. After all, it's not – '

'You're right, it's her own house. The only thing is, it being so close to Christmas – '

'All the more reason. They'll come. And old Jeannot will let us have whatever – '

After a while I gave up trying to follow. Whenever I

opened my mouth, Sabine just gave me more food to put into it. I couldn't complain. She must have sautéed the chicken with a whole kilo of mushrooms. The result was not only exquisite but endless. I was still working on it when the door burst open to admit a middle-aged man, small, wiry and dishevelled.

'Serge, this doesn't do, you'll just have to – oh, excuse me.'

'Come in, René.' Serge got up imperturbably, set another chair and wine glass, and introduced me. The newcomer was René Cordier, a neighbour and fellow violet grower. 'Have you eaten?'

'Thank you. Worse luck for me, my old woman's not like Sabine, not for cooking or – ' He glanced at me and hastily changed his tack. 'What I came to say was, there's going to be a general meeting tomorrow night, and you have to come. Enough of this fence-sitting.' His actual phrase was more colourful, something about accommodating the nanny goat and the cabbage, but I got the drift. 'If you're not with us, you're against us, that's what people will think.'

'Easy, René, I'll come. I may not wave flags and burn torches – or vice versa – but I'll come.'

'And never mind the sly remarks about my politics, either. This is something else, a local matter. You'd think you were a dirty rich bourgeois, instead of one of us. You have to realise we growers won't get anywhere unless we're unanimous. United we stand – '

'Sure, sure, I know. "Workers of the world, unite!"' Serge grinned and turned to me. 'Our friend René is a flaming Communist. Still, he's not a bad sort. He just tends to see things in black and white. And red.'

René started a retort, then laughed. 'Say what you like. Just so you come.'

'I will. And I promise you one more thing. I may oppose you on some points, but I'll stand with you for majority rule. Whatever the vote is, that's what we all do.'

'Good enough.' René stood. 'Now I'd better get back to the posies. You too, Serge old buddy, it'll be dark in a couple of hours.' He nodded at Serge and Sabine and, to me, raised his hand as if tipping a cap. It was, I thought, an oddly feudal gesture coming from a Communist.

Serge watched him go and sighed. 'He's right. Why does God always send us the most work on the shortest days of the year? I'm off. Save me a piece of the *tarte*, love.' He bent to kiss Sabine. 'Sorry to run, Addie. Come again soon, and make it after seven when the kids are in bed. Meanwhile, we'll see what we can do for you.' And he too was gone.

I helped Sabine clear the plates and persuaded her to save the whole *tarte* for supper. 'The last thing I need is dessert. Three days in France and already I can feel it.'

'Say what you mean, Addie, *I* don't need it. I'm as big as I was when I was carrying twins. Good Lord, you don't suppose – '

I laughed. 'You'd be glad to have triplets, and you know it. Now let me do this, Sabine. You just pour the coffee.' I got the dishes out of the suds and into the draining rack, and finished polishing the glassware while she checked on the children.

By the time I joined her, the parlour had been transformed into a flower grower's workshop. Panniers of violets covered the chairs, buckets of leaves stood on the floor, and the table, except for the corner where Sabine had put my coffee, held both flowers and leaves as well as a sheaf of evenly cut lengths of green string. Sabine waved me into the one empty chair and set to work.

'You don't mind? It's such a busy time, right before Christmas, we all wish we had four hands.' She picked up a bunch of violets, two or three dozen wound with a string into a clump, from the pannier brought from the fields. She caught up a handful of leaves, nestled the blooms into a collar of green and wound a second string around the stems. The finished nosegay went into a wooden tray. The whole process took about ten seconds.

While she worked I sipped my coffee and watched. Presently I shoved the cup aside and reached for violets and leaves. It looked easy enough.

67

'Addie,' Sabine protested, 'put those down. You're a guest.'

'I'm not, I'm a friend. Anyway, this is fun. Just tell me if I'm doing it wrong.' I wound the string, much slower than Sabine but fairly neatly, and started on another bunch. 'This is the first winter I've come here, you know, so I've never seen the growing season before, just a bit of planting. Funny, after all the vacations I've spent in St Martin, I don't know the first thing about raising violets.'

'You do now,' Sabine laughed. 'You know it takes more time than talent. Violets aren't really that fragile, but they're so darned *small*. Every year about now I catch myself envying people who raise gladioli.'

'I can believe it.' We went on winding and reaching and winding again until I was doing two bouquets to Sabine's three.

When I had settled into a rhythm, I asked, 'What's all this about mass meetings and joint action?'

'Don't ask *me*. Our neighbour René says I don't understand because I'm a woman. Serge just says I don't understand. I don't think he does either. I don't think any of them do.'

'Who? The local violet growers?'

Sabine nodded. 'Here in St Martin, and over in Tourrettes too – which is to say just about every violet grower in the known universe – they're all up in arms. Naturally René is one of the ringleaders. He only has to hear the word "exploitation" and he's off. But it wasn't his own idea, he just caught it the way you catch a germ. And no wonder – it's spread through the whole area like an epidemic.'

'The violet growing area, you mean?'

'I mean everywhere up and down this coast where flowers are grown for the perfume industry. It's got to the point where – hold on, I think I still have that issue.' Sabine left the room and came back with a copy of *Nice-Matin*. She riffled through the pages, folded the paper raggedly, and passed it across the table.

The article was a long one. I read the lead paragraphs and scanned the rest, then asked Sabine whether I might take it home with me to digest at leisure.

'Sure. Keep it. Of course it's not the whole story.'

'No, there must be a lot of little factors. But on the surface it looks almost like a classic strike and lockout situation. The flower growers say they won't supply the perfume makers in Grasse unless they get a better price. And the perfume makers say they'll shut down indefinitely rather than pay what they can't afford. I suppose there's some justice on both sides.'

'As there generally is,' Sabine agreed. 'The flower growers are suffering from inflation, the same as everybody. Even some of the bigger operations are marginal now. They do need more money.'

'But can they get it?'

'Certainly nothing like what they're asking. The owners of the perfume works are squeezed too. They just can't pay much more. And they're organised through their syndicate even better than the growers are. They won't cave in.'

'So the growers must know they'll have to compromise.'

'And that's why it makes no sense. In the past everything arranged itself without any fuss. The perfume manufacturers need the growers – even with modern chemistry there's no substitute for fresh flowers. And the growers are even more dependent. Where else but Grasse can they sell their jasmine or mimosa or orange blossoms?'

'Or violets,' I added.

'These?' Sabine swept a hand at the trays of finished nosegays. 'Oh no, we're not in the same case at all. These don't go to Grasse, except maybe a few, and a few more to the confectioners who candy them for decorating cakes. These go to florists. What the perfume makers get from us is the leaves, which we cut for them once a year when the blooming is finished after Easter. It's practically a sideline for us.'

'Then I don't see the point of joining the growers of other flowers, even if they stand to win.'

Sabine sighed. 'It's nice to know I'm not the only one who doesn't understand. Even the other growers, over Grasse way and further west, are crazy. But at least they're squaring off against the right opponent – suppliers versus buyers. Our group will only be dealing with the perfume works in Grasse once, months from now, and the current price for leaves is five francs a kilo, so even if they got double how much could they possibly gain? But to listen to them talk, they're being exploited worse than medieval serfs. And they've got themselves so worked up, they're ready to take on their own wholesalers now.'

'The wholesalers of cut flowers, you mean?'

'That's it. The ones who distribute to Paris and wherever. And that's the stupidest idea of all. Those dealers buy all sorts of flowers every day, and it's strictly according to supply and demand. How can the local violet growers fight the whole economic system?'

I thought. 'Well, they do have a monopoly.'

'Sure, but it's not like cornering the market in sugar or coffee. Flowers are a luxury item. If violets are too high, people will buy freesias instead, and the violet growers can whistle.'

'But if you're right, Sabine, there's no way they can win. None of them can, whether they grow for the florists or for the perfume works. It's just a lot of disruption and dissension for nothing.'

Sabine tossed a finished nosegay on to the top tray and folded her hands across her swelling waistline.

'Well,' she said finally, 'maybe I'm just imagining things, the way they say pregnant women do. But sometimes it seems to me as if the Devil himself has come here and stirred his pitchfork in every plot of flower-growing ground. *Something* is causing all this mischief and I wish I knew what it was.'

I could bear to know myself. My journalistic thumbs were pricking.

Somewhere here, I told myself, there is a story.

On the way down the hill I kept turning it over, and the more I thought about it, the more it seemed to suit my purposes.

Not that I intended to drop the photographic end. Even

70

now I was intentionally walking back to the village the long way, by the Route de la Chapelle, scanning the adjacent slopes with half my attention for scenes that might come out well on film. I wasn't worried about getting enough good shots. The South of France was one big picture postcard. And with cameras like the Canon and the Hasselblad that had been Dad's, an ounce of talent was plenty.

The actual writing didn't worry me either. I was practically born with printer's ink in my veins. Dad had me doing re-writes in a little cubbyhole off his editorial office by the time I was thirteen. And I was the only kid in town who got paid to attend her own school's sporting events. It wasn't much, but it did cover the pizzas afterwards.

My only problem now was *what* to write. The standard travelogue format might do for a magazine like *National Geographic*, but if I could find a hook to hang a long feature article on, it would open up the market considerably. And I just might have one.

Idly I started composing heads, florid phrases like ALL IS NOT ROSES IN PERFUME INDUSTRY or perhaps THORNS OF DISCORD IN RIVIERA FLOWER FIELDS.

Silly. I didn't even know whether there was a story yet. It could turn out to be only a spontaneous and futile revolt. But if there was a political angle or some financial power play in the background, I was in a good position to find out. My neighbours were flower growers and the perfume industry in Grasse was less than twenty kilometres away. I'd be working right in my own backyard.

That was all to the good, I decided. Thanks to Monsieur Joseph Scotto, I couldn't afford to be idle. His claim had torn my budget to shreds. But until it was settled, I intended to stick as close to Gran's house as work would permit.

The Route de la Chapelle was steep enough, even walking downhill, to tire me. Or maybe it was the sun, or the weight of Sabine's lunch. When the chapel appeared at the bend in the road, it looked a welcome spot to rest.

71

Besides, I meant to check into its photographic possibilities.

The little Chapel of St Martin had always been a favourite of mine. Removed from the centre of the village, it was seldom visited by tourists. It was not old by European standards, only a century or two, and was architecturally undistinguished inside and out. Its windows had no stained glass, nor were they large enough to admit much light. The rough altar and straight-backed chairs were painted a homely yellow. And yet for me the chapel was a place of unfailing charm.

It was the murals that did it. They rose behind the altar and marched around the walls in an unrestrained joyous expression of primitive art. No doubt the painters in Rusty's circle would turn up their noses, but those murals had entranced me as a child and I was sure they still would.

Funny, just as I thought of him, there was the red-bearded sculptor emerging from the chapel. I lifted an arm and called, 'Rusty!'

He was squinting against the sun after the dimness inside and seemed not to see me. Before I could call again, he hurried off towards the village, obviously checking his wristwatch.

Just as well, I thought. I'd rather have the chapel to myself.

I did, too, for almost ten whole minutes. First I sat and looked above the altar at the oversized Christ, bearded and toga'd, surrounded by a host of angels in traditional local peasant dress and carrying baskets of violets. Then I followed the vivid murals around the walls from one delightful anachronism or incongruity to another. I'd just reached my favourite scene, the one where St Martin, also in beard and toga, was blessing a troop of uniformed Boy Scouts around a campfire, when the door scraped open.

Heels sounded on the stone floor and Régine came down the aisle.

She seemed to welcome the encounter no more than I did, though we greeted each other civilly. She took a chair at the rear and said after a minute:

'Don't let me interrupt your sightseeing, please. I only

72

want to sit for a while. I like to come here when I can for a little – peace and quiet.'

I glanced at her suspiciously. But her words sounded direct and simple. Perhaps she meant just what she said.

Perhaps, too, my first impression of Régine was unfair. It could not be easy, keeping her composure every day through the outbursts of the Scotto woman, who was ill or mad or at least very neurotic, and then facing a tirade from Scotto himself when he showed up. No doubt she could use a refuge. I had one in Gran's house – for the time being, anyway. She had none.

'I was going, really,' I told her. 'The shops will all be open now. I'll leave you the place to yourself.'

On the way down to the village, though, I couldn't help resenting Régine's intrusion. Not for usurping the chapel – I could go back any time. But for recalling to me the topic I had briefly succeeded in forgetting, my troubles with Monsieur Joseph Scotto.

The topic kept recurring as I made the rounds of the village shops. Wherever this particular grapevine had its root – Mathilde, Lili, Jean-Marc – it had already crept clear around the square. I was given forceful views on Scotto's parentage and probable end by the butcher, baker, greengrocer, dry-goods dealer, hardware merchant, pharmacist, news-vendor and café proprietor. Also the village priest.

My first stop was the café to call Robert Mercier. He counselled patience.

'These things always take time and it's worse around the holidays. Today is Friday and next week even the people who *are* in their offices won't be working. Don't count on anything really solid for ten days.'

'Okay, but what do I do meanwhile?'

'Meanwhile you go on as usual. Oh yes, one thing you might do. It wouldn't hurt to get a line on Scotto's other interests locally. Could be he's susceptible to a little – how do you say? – horse-trading. Or even some naked pressure.'

'But, Robert, do you really think we should – '

'For heaven's sake don't start getting nice-minded! You said yourself Scotto is the sort that takes advantage of widows and orphans. With him, you deal any way you can. Provided, that is, that you want to win.'

As I hung up, I had to concede Robert's point. What was right and what was legal did not always square. Still, I did not have to like it. Robert Mercier might be a charming fellow, but he couldn't be all good. He hung around with lawyers too much.

Jacky, the café proprietor, had listened to my end of the conversation unblushingly. He said that nothing Scotto did would surprise him.

'People like that, they come into a town and do just as they please without any thought for the local ways. No matter how other people's lives are messed up, they don't know or care. But what can you expect? Foreigners!'

Others echoed Jacky. None of them, oddly, seemed to want to pin the foreigner tag on me – nor on Rusty and his circle. The arty young set might be a trifle bizarre but, French or not, they lived and worked and shopped in St Martin. It was Scotto the Corsican who was the outsider. His Corsican-ness was deemed sufficient explanation for bad manners, bad morals and questionable mental health.

As to local interests, Scotto apparently had none beyond the Eagle's Nest – and that, according to one and all, was already too much. Scotto had not exactly endeared himself to the village merchants.

'I used to send up crates of produce every day,' said Madame Marchetti. 'Hundred-kilo sacks of potatoes, everything. Now they might call me once a week if they run out of salad.'

'Look what they've done about the laundry,' said Madame Viret next door. 'My cousin Laurette used to go up to the Eagle's Nest every morning. Now they use a linen service, which can't be any cheaper, and Laurette's out of a job.'

The fishmonger said, 'Either they aren't serving fish, or it's not fresh, because they don't get it from me any more.'

Only the baker still supplied the Eagle's Nest, but he said the order was down; clearly the inn was doing less business than under the Isnards. And no wonder, with Scotto as landlord.

Everyone commiserated on my problem. Madame Marchetti had the most original comment. 'Scotto would never have dared try it,' she said, 'if your grandmother had been alive.' I wondered – and wondered too how Gran would have handled him. No one had any constructive ideas. Several suggested prayer.

To my amusement, Monsieur le Curé did not think of that. He smoothed his cassock, gazed thoughtfully heavenward and recommended direct legal action.

I resolved to have a longer talk with the priest soon, but it was now getting dark and my shopping was not done. A stop at the hardware store yielded more gossip, plus a hasp, padlock and screwdriver. While I was stowing my purchases in my little 2CV, Lew appeared beside the car with his laden rucksack, the terriers at his heels.

'Might I hitchhike as far as the inn? If you're going up now, that is.'

'Sure, if you don't mind being seen in my rattletrap.' I slid behind the wheel while Lew shoehorned the rucksack and dogs into the back and himself into the other bucket seat. 'She has a name now, by the way. Peu Belle. Rusty and his gang persuaded me this noon that she should be christened before her imminent demise.'

Lew groaned. 'How about that – the Pied Piper of St Martin and his rat pack, scaling new heights of frivolity. God, they weary me! Talk, talk, talk. They sit around a café table all day piffling about Truth and Beauty and Immortal Art. If I did that, I wouldn't get any writing done either.' He slumped back in his seat.

I concentrated on driving. It was not up to me to defend Rusty's circle. And I was reluctant to ask Lew what sort of thing he wrote, in case I ought to have heard of him – at least by his own lights.

Finally I said, 'It must be the French air. Talking's the

75

national pastime here. It took me two hours to do twenty minutes' shopping, and now it's dark. Lew, why don't you let me drive you home? You've got quite a load there. Where do you live anyway?'

'Nowhere you'd want to take a 2CV. Even a jeep – look, could you stop a minute at the chapel? I have to pick up some things there.'

While I kept the car running, Lew ducked into the chapel and came back with his giant flashlight and a handful of books. Before his door shut and the dome light went off, I saw a well-used guide to Mediterranean plant life, a novel, a slim volume that might be poetry and a spiral-bound notebook.

'We've been for a ramble,' he said as I drove off. 'Whenever the weather's fine, I like to find a new spot, settle myself for a bit of reading, then scribble a while. Dylan and Caitlin don't mind; they chase butterflies while I grope for metaphors. Today we've been up there.' He indicated the next hill to the west. 'So on the way into the village I dropped off the extra weight. Nobody'd nick anything from the chapel; nobody even comes.'

'No? You're the fourth person I know of, today alone. It's just the villagers who don't come. But you were starting to tell me – '

'Oh yes, where I live. It's not so very far from your house. But it's almost straight up, and the old logging trail isn't really passable any more. You pretty well need a compass and crampons to get there. Which is why I bought it. I don't have to worry about neighbours dropping in.'

Shifting into second, I clashed the gears. 'I beg your pardon. I certainly wasn't angling for – '

'Good Lord, I didn't mean *you*, Addie. I just meant – '

We broke off, started to speak together, stopped again. I drove and Lew shuffled the books in his lap.

'Look, I don't mind showing you my place, truly. But it'd better be in daylight so you won't break your neck. I can come by and take you up some morning.' Lew seemed to gather enthusiasm as he talked. 'There's a nice spot by a waterfall

76

just above there for a picnic. We could do it tomorrow, if you like.'

'Whoa! I'd like to, but not tomorrow. It's a work day, and I'll be charging around the countryside interviewing people. High time I did something constructive, *n'est-ce pas?*' I smiled in the darkness and added, 'Otherwise you'll think I'm one of those café-sitters.'

'You're not like them, not a bit.'

Lew made it a flat statement, but I wasn't so sure. Rusty and his circle were open, relaxed, witty and with-it, gregarious and generous among themselves and to others. I wouldn't mind sharing some of those qualities. Did Lew think them all so inconsiderable? Perhaps he was basically anti-social – or was he simply independent?

He was certainly persistent. 'What about Sunday? Do you go to Mass?'

We established that we were neither of us churchgoers, at least not here in France, and agreed he would come for me on Sunday morning. By this time we were in the parking lot and unloading the car. With packages up to our ears and the dogs underfoot, we skirted the inn and went along the path to Gran's house, Lew leading with the flashlight.

At the house Dylan and Caitlin bounded ahead and in through the open door. Lew expostulated but was too burdened to stop them. When we got the gas lamps lighted, we found the dogs already settled at the foot of the overstuffed chair they regarded as their master's. Lew stood over them and sighed.

'Come along, you two. You've got a home of your own, you know.'

The terriers looked back at him unmoving.

I laughed. 'You're outvoted, Lew. That's what you get for bringing them here three days running. No wonder the poor beasts have misunderstood your intentions.'

Lew mumbled something inaudible. His face looked ruddier than usual, but perhaps that was just the lamplight. He whistled. This time Dylan and Caitlin got up and pattered out after him.

I stood for a minute staring at the empty doorway. Then I shrugged, found the package from the hardware store and set about installing the hasp.

When that was done, and the refrigerator cleaned and running, and the visible kitchen surfaces swabbed off, it was well into the dinner hour. I gave myself a quick wash, locked up, and went straight to the Eagle's Nest dining-room.

The place was full. Half the room had been given over to a banquet table seating perhaps fourteen. The other tables were crowded together. I was about to leave and go into the village when I saw Jean-Marc waving and beckoning me to join him. He flagged Marie down as well. Surprisingly, everything he ordered appeared on the instant. A contest between Marie's laziness and Jean-Marc Bertrand's charm was evidently no contest at all. He had the girl eating out of his hand.

'Welcome,' he said, pouring me some wine. 'I am enchanted to have your company again. It makes the difference between feeding and feasting.'

I raised my glass to him. 'Likewise, I'm sure. Though I wonder, given the competition, how much of a compliment that is to either of us.'

Jean-Marc sputtered. 'Addie, you're a snob. You're right, though, the clientèle tonight is definitely not *le tout Paris*. Our Régine sits in her corner like a sulky child. As to that "businessmen's conference" Scotto is hosting – well, I told you what to expect.'

'Uh-huh. They're not your typical Rotary Club meeting.'

'They're more like a convention of undertakers.'

Jean-Marc's description was apt. The men at the long table wore sober suits and sober expressions. They barely conversed while their plates were being cleared away by a burly fellow in a white linen jacket that strained at his shoulders. I indicated him to Jean-Marc. 'Where on earth did that specimen come from? Almost any man at the table could pass for an Italian waiter. But the one serving them looks more like a bouncer.'

'Or a bodyguard. He comes with Scotto, ostensibly as his chauffeur.' Jean-Marc raised an eyebrow.

'Oh, swell. Tell me, what are two nice people like us doing in a place like this?'

We laughed together, but a minute later I was not laughing. Régine had left her table and was standing beside ours, twisting her napkin and shifting from foot to foot.

'Mademoiselle Forrester, I fear there has been a mis-understanding. We had expected you to check out this after-noon. As I told you on Wednesday, we are fully booked for this weekend. Of course I shall be glad to help you find other accommodation. But when you had not returned at five o'clock, we could wait no longer. Your baggage has been packed and is waiting for you in the lobby.'

At first I could not speak. I simply stared at Régine until she turned and left the dining-room, the napkin still trailing from her hand.

It was hard to know what made me most furious. The thought of someone packing my bags was high on the list, particularly as the person who handled every book and brassière was undoubtedly Régine. But the underhand way it was done was at least as galling. I had seen Scotto this morning and Régine as recently as mid-afternoon; neither had said a word. Had something made Scotto decide at the last minute to turn me out? Still, he might have faced me himself instead of leaving it to Régine. He was both a bully and a coward, and probably a good deal worse, and I could not wait to get out from under his roof.

If I could not speak, Jean-Marc could. He vented his indignation along every line I had thought of, and a couple besides. He appointed himself my champion and declared he would do anything to help me – including blackening Scotto's eye, if that was what I wanted. His language became highly inventive. Just listening to him took the edge off my own fury.

When he wound down enough so I could get a word in, I

told him he could indeed help. He could play porter for me again, at least as far as my car.

Between the two of us, we managed everything in one trip. Jean-Marc heaved the suitcase on to the back seat. 'Where are you going now? Evidently not to your grandmother's house.'

'No, it's not fit for sleeping.' It wasn't the lack of a roof that ruled it out so much as the lack of a mattress for the bed, but I didn't feel like explaining all that. I didn't even feel like thinking. I sat down on the low stone wall rimming the parking lot. Jean-Marc sat beside me. For a minute we watched the lights of the village below and listened to the silence. Jean-Marc put an arm tentatively around my shoulders.

'Addie, you're cold!'

He slid along the stone wall, closing the little distance between us, and pulled me toward him. It was rather touching, I thought at first, and amusing too, that Jean-Marc meant to warm me with just his two arms. But as they tightened around me and his mouth sought mine, I forgot to be amused. Before long, I even forgot to be cold.

In between kisses Jean-Marc murmured words, probably encouragement and comfort, but I wasn't listening. I was busy discarding the popular notion that Frenchmen are really lousy lovers. Another stereotype shot to shreds.

Presently I began to hear Jean-Marc: 'This is no hour for you to go looking for a hotel. It's senseless, Addie. You'll stay in my room tonight. They don't have to know.'

He didn't give me a chance to answer right away and when he did I wasn't sure what to say. I stood up slowly. 'I don't think so, Jean-Marc. It – it's too risky.'

'Why?' He stood too. 'At the worst Scotto can just throw us *both* out.'

My laugh was shaky. 'It wasn't Scotto I was thinking about. Not just this last little while, anyway.'

'Oh.' Jean-Marc's smile was lopsided, but he looked mostly pleased. 'Well, I wouldn't want you to think I was *that* harmless. But honestly, Addie, I promise I won't – '

' – do anything I don't want you to do. Sure.' I reached out and ran a finger along the line of his jaw.

That was just what worried me. Everything I had learned about Jean-Marc Bertrand – that he was twenty-eight, and came from Lyon, and had three brothers, and liked Mireille Mathieu and skiing and the St Etienne football club, and could tear down a car engine, and preferred Burgundies to Bordeaux – wasn't enough. I knew there was at least one way I couldn't trust him, any more than I could trust myself. When Jean-Marc was kissing me, any hope of rational thought went up in smoke.

'Sure,' I repeated. 'But I think, even so, I'd better stay with local friends tonight. Female friends.'

Lili could not quite hide her surprise when she answered the door. I realised that almost nine must be on the late side at the Isnard house, and said so.

'Not really.' Lili pitched her words low. 'She doesn't go to bed for an hour yet. It isn't easy for her to sleep, especially now with . . . especially now. She'll be glad to see you.' Lili went ahead of me into the living-room, switched off the television and said brightly, 'Look who's here, Tante Irène, it's Addie!'

Madame Isnard looked up from her cocoon of blankets and tilted her head. She was so wrinkled now that I could not tell whether she was frowning. I could not tell whether she knew me, either.

All she said was, 'What time is it?'

'Almost nine. I'm sorry to come so late, madame, but – '

'No, no, you're always welcome, my dear. My friends must come to me nowadays, so I cannot complain when they do.' She sounded a bit querulous, I thought, or perhaps the stroke had thinned her voice. 'Still, at such an hour – tell me, what's the matter, Addie?'

Madame Isnard's directness made me doubly ashamed of my thoughts. Briefly I told her and Lili how it happened that I needed a place for the night. I left out most of the story, including criticism of Scotto.

'Sleep on the sofa? Nonsense, child! There are two perfectly good beds in Lili's room. Is the spare one made up, Lili?' The girl nodded. 'That's settled, then, it's yours for as long as you want it.'

'Bless you, Madame Isnard! I won't be a bother, I promise. And perhaps by tomorrow I can have Gran's house ready –'

'Not another word. I'm just happy I can help.' The old woman leaned back on her cushions. 'Sometimes I'm afraid I'm not as sharp as I was. But it was easy to guess something was wrong tonight. Otherwise you wouldn't be calling on a shut-in, you'd be out with some young man. That's only natural.'

Lili, hovering over her great-aunt, paused in straightening the coverlet and I saw a shadow cross her face.

On impulse I said, 'Perhaps you're right, madame. But I have plenty of time for that. Tonight I'm here, so why shouldn't it be Lili's turn to go out?' The girl started, and I thought again how like a colt she was. 'It's only nine. We can chat for a while and go to bed when we like and let Lili stay out with her friends. Can't we?'

Lili looked up with a flash of hope in her dark eyes, but she would not add a plea of her own. She waited for Madame Isnard to speak.

'Why, that's a lovely idea, Addie, and how sweet of you to think of it. Lili dear, do you suppose you can arrange for someone to come and fetch you? I don't like to think of you walking down alone.'

'You could take my car if you want,' I said quickly.

'Thank you, but I'm sure I can . . . I'll just . . .' Lili dashed to the telephone, started to dial, then with an apologetic murmur picked up the instrument and moved it around the corner. From the hallway we could hear her soft voice indistinctly.

Madame Isnard chuckled. 'I'll bet it's not her brother's car we'll hear in five minutes, but the motorcycle of the Marchetti boy. He's here twice a day delivering groceries. When I tease Lili, she just says she forgot to order something. She doesn't fool me – she's not a *bit* disorganised about anything else.'

I smiled and Lili was smiling too when she came back. It struck me for the first time that she was really quite pretty.

82

She took me into the kitchen to show me where things were, and when she finished explaining about Madame's bedtime drink, I said, 'Lili, I think it might be better after all if I stayed the whole weekend. Now, about tomorrow – I want to go to the growers' meeting, but I should be back by eight. So why don't you go ahead and make a date for tomorrow night too?'

Lili protested only once, not forcefully, caught my hand in a brief squeeze of thanks and dashed off again for a last-minute session with her mirror.

The next hour was quiet, at least after Lili had departed to the predicted snarl of engine and squeal of tyres. I turned the radio at Madame Isnard's direction to France Musique and soft chamber music filled the lulls in our conversation. Madame Isnard was content to let them occur. She asked me first about my brother. As I recounted Jay's impressions of Costa Rica and his anecdotes about embassy life, her attention seemed to stray. But just when I thought she had nodded off, she wondered aloud why Jay was sent to Central America when his Spanish could hardly be as fluent as his French. I said, thinking of Connie Ortiz posted here in Nice, that bureaucratic logic was often hard to follow. After a comfortable silence, Madame Isnard asked me about my own plans. I told her a bit about the graduate programme in journalism at Columbia and how, now that I could no longer look forward to taking over Dad's paper back home, I hoped eventually to get on the staff of the *Trib*. Madame said she knew the *International Herald-Tribune*, had often seen it lying around at le Nid de l'Aigle, and it looked like a respectable paper for me to work on, not like those British tabloids that were no better than *France-Dimanche*. We discussed French newspapers for a few minutes, until I saw that she was really too tired to talk any more.

In the kitchen, waiting for the kettle to boil, I admired Lili's tidiness and wondered whether I would ever achieve anything like it, then brewed Madame's tisane and some super-strong coffee for myself. It would be welcome. If it kept me awake, so be it.

By the time I got Madame Isnard into bed, my admiration for Lili was higher. The old woman refused to be carried, but could walk only if her weight was totally supported. While she was no longer paralysed, she had no strength at all on the left side and not much on the right. Lili, so slightly built, must find her Tante Irène almost more than she could handle. When I finally had her settled, a night light burning and her bell at hand, I was ready for sleep myself.

I nearly didn't go down to the car. It seemed too much trouble to root through luggage packed by somebody else, in the cramped back seat of a 2CV, just for a nightgown and toothbrush. But everything would have to come up in the morning, I reminded myself, so I might as well get the suitcase and flight bag now. Wriggling back into Jay's oversized sweater, I checked to see that Madame was asleep and let myself out.

A light mist had gathered and the moonlight was pale and watery where it penetrated the scraggly pines. I waited at the top to let my eyes adjust before cautiously negotiating the long flight of irregular stone steps that led to the car park of the Eagle's Nest. The shadows were deceptive and I missed my footing more than once.

With all my purchases today, I thought, I might have had the sense to pick up a flashlight. Lew's looked like the right sort; I must ask him where he got it.

The car park was crowded. Régine's claim that the place was full might be true enough. It was not hard to guess which cars belonged to Scotto's group of 'businessmen' – they were relatively high-priced and absolutely black. There seemed to be one car per conferee. Either the men all came from different places, or not one of them trusted another's driving. I was glad now that my car was cheap, old and metallic grey. Somehow in this setting it looked more respectable.

The 2CV occupied a slot against the east wing. I dragged my suitcase and flight bag from the back seat and was just locking up again when the double doors to the main hall opened. A dark figure stood for a moment under the dim naked bulb then sauntered down off the stoop. The crunch of his footsteps on the gravel carried sharply through the mist.

Instinctively I drew back into the shadows.

It was not fear that made me hug the rough-hewn stones of the *mas* wall, but some vague uneasiness tinged with embarrassment. Technically I was an intruder here. No longer a guest of the inn – having left, in fact, without paying my bill – I had no right to use the parking facilities. My presence here might be viewed with suspicion. Worse, my departure by car might be viewed in the same light. Either way, I was not in a comfortable position.

Besides, I did not know who was out here with me. A hazy glimpse by dim light and the sound of his tread indicated only that he was male. His steady crunch-crunch moved first in one direction, then another, paused, resumed. Through the mist a cigarette lighter or match flared briefly.

The stone of the *mas* wall was cold, too cold for Jay's old sweater to keep out, and I began to shiver. It was foolish, my common sense argued, to risk pneumonia for the sake of some unformed anxiety. I should pick up my bags and go back to Madame Isnard's. I would. Just as soon as that man was a little further away.

Behind me a voice rang out sharply. I turned, one hand to my mouth, the other pressed against my unbreathing chest.

Where was he? Who had called? To my right, away from the dimly lighted entrance, was only the solid bulk of the *mas*, ending in shadow at the corner, and more cars extending to the wrought-iron entrance gates. There was no one to be seen. And yet the voice had been quite close. Was the mist playing tricks on me?

The crunch of gravel sounded again, still on the far side of the entrance. Almost simultaneously the voice to my right spoke, lower than before.

I began to breathe. The voice was coming from a window scarcely a yard from where I stood. Though the drapes were drawn, the window was open perhaps a hand-span. Small wonder I had been startled, hearing that cold commanding voice so close.

A check of the distance to the entrance confirmed that the window would be the one in Scotto's office, just behind his desk.

I started to move away, intent only on escaping with my luggage. But the voice came again, at a hypnotic pitch, and my feet stopped in spite of me.

The language was not French, that much was certain. It sounded more like Italian, but without the melodic cadences of a Neapolitan love song or of grand opera; it sounded thick-tongued instead of trilled. And it sounded, from Scotto's mouth, icily contemptuous. The words meant nothing. Even if I had spoken Italian, I did not think I would understand. This must be the island tongue of Corsica.

A response burst out, impassioned first, then pleading, finally shading into petulance. It was cut off by a word from Scotto.

Scotto shifted then to French. '*Alors, les gars,*' he began, the tone as much as the words conveying that he spoke to everyone in the room. His accent was marked, but not too different from the Provençal I had heard over so many summers, and I had already listened to him for the best part of an hour today. Even without seeing his face, I found I could pick up the words.

Picking up the meaning was something else again. At first Scotto seemed to be running some kind of sales meeting. He made individual suggestions to his colleagues on how to deal with certain parties and which approach would work best. He spoke in vague allusions, comprehensible to those in his office but not to me. There was nothing to indicate the nature of the business or even who was involved.

Before long I noticed that Scotto also avoided names. He might urge 'J-J' to pressure 'those mules in Valbonne' or tell 'Brownie' to contact 'our friend with the rose gardens'; nothing more specific. He almost seemed to be playing a cloak-and-dagger rôle, except that Scotto struck me as someone who would never be less than deadly serious.

Then suddenly he became specific after all, just when I was about to creep away. 'Listen!' he said. 'No more messages to the old address. We have a postbox now. Memorise this: Créations Régine S.A., BP 47, 06130 Grasse.' He repeated the address. 'Anything into the post office by three will be collected the same day. And *no* telegrams. If it's urgent, call Régine here and leave a number. You'll be reached within two hours at most, ten minutes if I'm not on the road.'

Someone asked a question, too far from the window for me to hear.

'No change,' Scotto said. 'But if it comes to that, remember I don't know you and you don't –' The rest of the words were lost in the scraping of a chair.

Under cover of that noise, I finally moved away from the window toward the 2CV and my luggage. My cautious footsteps sounded appallingly loud. They reminded me that the crunch of gravel beyond the entrance had faded and stopped some time while I was listening to Scotto. I peered anxiously to my right through the mist.

But he came from behind me. His arm circled me, pinning me immobile. Before I could scream, before I could even draw a breath, his other hand was clamped across my mouth.

I struggled feebly in his grasp. It was futile, pointless, to try to get away. My writhing was more in angry frustration, as I cursed myself for stupidity. Everything I had done from start to finish was wrong – stumbling down in the dark without a flashlight, sneaking through the car park instead of marching boldly to claim my own luggage, breaking for cover like a startled fawn the moment someone appeared, huddling in shadows, eavesdropping, and finally, when I really had something to act guilty about, compounding it all with care-lessness. I should have known he might be circling the building and coming up from the garden; I hadn't even looked both ways.

His grasp tightened. 'Addie!' he hissed in my ear. 'You big beautiful idiot, what in God's name are you doing here? I thought I had you safely away.' He shook me roughly, then relaxed his grip.

'Jean-Marc!' I pivoted in the circle of his arms and held him as tightly as, a moment ago, he had held me.

87

He covered my mouth again, but gently now. 'Hush, hush.' He rocked me in a steady rhythm, rubbing his hand across my back over Jay's sweater, then slipping it underneath and stroking the tension away until my body nestled pliantly against his own. He let his warning fingers slide off my lips and kissed them into silence.

'That's better,' he whispered. 'If anyone comes, he'll think we're lovers. We're very convincing, aren't we? We're convincing *me*. Could we practise some more, somewhere less exposed?'

Jean-Marc's kisses, for the second time tonight, were making the car park of the Eagle's Nest a less unpleasant place. But it was still the last place I wanted to be.

I nodded at my luggage and again in the direction of Madame Isnard's. Jean-Marc picked up my suitcase while I took the flight bag and, arms twined loosely around each other's waists, we moved off through the mist away from the *mas*. I tried to keep my footsteps light, but still they made more noise than Jean-Marc's. For someone who often clattered around like an exuberant overgrown pup, he could be quiet enough when it suited him. Like last night, I thought, on the tower stairs.

Halfway up the stone steps to Madame Isnard's house Jean-Marc dropped the suitcase and sat down. After a moment's hesitation I joined him. We were far enough from the car park not to be heard and, between the mist and the heavy shadows of the trees and bushes, barely visible even to each other. Jean-Marc edged closer and put his arm around my shoulders again, but he did not kiss me. He just turned my face towards his and studied it. He looked perplexed, and something else too. Worried? Disappointed?

He sighed. 'Addie, don't you have any sense? Of all the crazy things to do, skulking around in the dark, listening under Scotto's window – what ever possessed you?'

'I wasn't skulking,' I said defensively. 'I just went down to get my things from the car. Then somebody came out from the hall and I couldn't tell who it was and – well, you can imagine I don't feel exactly welcome there right now. It seemed better not to be seen, so I just slipped into the handiest dark spot.'

'Handy maybe. But hardly the most innocent.'

'How was I supposed to know that? It happened to be where the car was parked.' This time it was my turn to sigh. 'Besides, I *wasn't* eavesdropping. If Scotto doesn't want to be overheard, he shouldn't talk so loud. You know what I mean, you must have heard him yourself.'

Jean-Marc frowned. 'No, just a few words. What was he saying?' In his interest he forgot he was scolding me.

'Lord knows. Half the time he was speaking Corsican, I guess. And the other half, he wasn't making any sense. He sounded like something out of a grade-B gangster movie. He likes to throw his weight around. After he chewed somebody out, he gave a lot of orders, but it was all in nicknames and code words. He only said one thing I could understand.'

'Yes? What?' Jean-Marc was really eager now.

It was the business about the postbox, but at the point of telling him, a nagging doubt stopped me. Jean-Marc might talk to anyone. So I substituted something he was likely to have overheard too. 'Scotto said if whatever-it-was happened, for all of them to remember he didn't know them. Swell, huh? How would you like to deal with a loyal fellow like that?'

'I wouldn't. I also wouldn't like to be caught listening under his window.'

'Damn it, Jean-Marc, I wasn't listening! I just didn't want to be seen by whoever came out into the car park. If I'd known it was you – '

'But it wasn't me.'

'What?' I choked. 'Then why – if you weren't – '

'Addie, for pity's sake, speak French! Or something co-herent. I don't know who came out this side, but whoever you saw, it wasn't me. I came out through the garden.'

'When?'

'When?! How should I know? Two minutes before I ran into you, more or less. I was looking for cigarettes.'

'In the garden?'

'Hey, what is this? I'm not the one who – all right. *Not* in

89

the garden. In my car. In the map compartment, to be precise.'

'What kind of car do you have?'

'Good God, does it matter?' Jean-Marc sounded disproportionately annoyed by my questions, considering he had so many of his own. 'It's a VW. A brown Rabbit. I can't afford the kind of car Scotto's cronies drive.'

I smiled. 'Brown bunnies are nicer.' I didn't want Jean-Marc's car to be expensive and black.

'Well, anyway, I never got to the car. The minute I hit the east wing, the first thing I saw was you, tiptoeing through the mist like Mata Hari. And then I heard Scotto's voice. Do you wonder that I wanted to get you out of there?'

'No, Jean-Marc,' I said meekly. It didn't seem the time for further protestations of innocence. 'I'm sorry to cause you so much worry. I'll try to be careful from now on.'

This made him, if possible, even more the masculine protector. It was five minutes before he escorted me the rest of the way up the stone steps, and by the time he did, I was not cold at all any more.

In Lili's room I was rummaging through my luggage for overnight essentials when the bell on the night table rang. It was a brief and tentative trill, not an urgent summons. Probably, I thought, Madame Isnard had only brushed against the call button as she stirred in her sleep. But then again, her stroke had left her with no strength; perhaps she could not push any harder.

Belting my robe and shoving my feet into scuffs, I went along the dark hall toward the glow of the old lady's night light. She was listening for the steps. I was not through the doorway when she said in her thin voice:

'Lili, I'm so relieved that you're back! It started again almost as soon as we went to bed. And it was hardly something, you know, for our guest to – '

'It's only me, madame. Lili isn't home yet. But if you'll tell me how, perhaps I can help.'

90

'Addie?' she quavered. 'No – thank you, dear, there isn't –
it's nothing you can – '

'Please. I'd like to try.'

Madame Isnard made a sound that might have been a sigh
or a sob, or difficulty in breathing.

I waited. Finally she said, 'Don't worry, I'm just being a
foolish old woman. Go back to bed, dear.'

She closed her eyes, leaving me no choice. Still, I lingered
in the hall, and as I listened, my uneasiness turned to distress.
Madame Isnard was trying to be quiet about it, but she was
unmistakably crying.

FIVE

SATURDAY HAD been one of those days that seemed forty-eight hours long – or only four, depending on your viewpoint. From shortly after dawn until well after dusk I didn't sit down once, except at the wheel of my rattletrap 2CV. Even lunch was a stand-up affair.

'Which makes your picnic doubly welcome,' I told Lew on Sunday morning.

We were climbing the hill behind Gran's house. It might have been vertical, for Lew's apologetic tone. 'Are you sure you feel up to the climb? If you had such an exhausting day –'

'It'll do me good. Yesterday just proved a person can charge around for twelve hours and still get zero exercise. I have to admit, though, my tongue and ears got a workout.'

'What's the story? If it's not a secret.'

'Hardly. It's the universal topic from here to beyond Grasse. The flower growers' strike. You must have heard about it.'

'Not much.' Lew sounded apologetic again, so I sketched in the background. He listened thoughtfully, then said, 'It doesn't seem to make any sense.'

'I haven't found anybody yet who understands it. All I hear is righteousness and recrimination, even from the biggest growers and from the secretary of the perfume makers' syndicate. Still, I've got some leads.'

The path narrowed then, and Lew dropped back to let me go first. Probably he wanted to be ready to catch me if I slipped. He was burdened with a bulging rucksack, as usual, but he knew the path and he was wearing proper Swiss mountaineering boots, while I had on Adidas that were meant for the level surface of an oval cinder track. I didn't have regulation hiking breeches either. I wondered whether my newest jeans looked as snug from behind as they felt, but Lew's thoughts were on a higher plane.

'Hearing you,' he said, 'it's hard to realise your writing and mine have anything in common. You go out and dig for a story while I sit alone and dream one up. Still, in the end what matters is how the story's told, isn't it?'

I laughed. 'Are you being charitable? I thought all serious writers despised journalists.'

'Then don't call me "serious" please – leave that for the café crowd. They haven't any choice, they have to convince themselves they're too good to be commercial. But as soon as one of them gets published and starts making a living, just see how fast he switches from "serious" to "professional"!'

'Okay, okay.' I raised my hands in surrender. 'Tell me, how long have you been a non-serious writer?'

Now it was Lew's turn to laugh. "If you mean self-supporting, I'm still more serious than I'd like. But it's three years since I've had to crank out advertising copy for Baby-cham and Bovril. By watching expenses, I manage to stay in that happy ground between ulcers and starvation.'

'That's not bad, with three mouths to feed. Where are Dylan and Caitlin anyway? I've never seen you without them.'

'Home, and unhappy about it. I was afraid they'd trip you.'

'They could have come, if I'd known it was this path. My brother and I used to climb up here a lot. There was a tumble-down shepherd's hut we made into a sort of secret clubhouse. I'll show you, it's not far now.'

Lew said nothing. We clambered on up the hill and around a remembered bend. I pointed.

'It's in this clearing here, just over – Lew!'

'I rather thought we were talking about the same place.' He grinned, enjoying my doubletake. The 'tumbledown'

93

shepherd's hut had a chimney now, with smoke coming out of it. Windows too, genuine glazed and curtained windows. On the far side of the building was a fenced garden plot. It was mostly winter-bare, but the leafy tops of root vegetables could be seen and, as if by design this week before Christmas, a cabbage patch with heads alternately green and red.

The terriers gave us a vocal welcome. Lew untied them from the garden fence and let them convoy us, now ahead, now underfoot, to the cottage door. At the threshold they bounded inside. I stood letting my eyes adjust, while Lew pulled down a counterweighted lamp suspended from the roof tree and lit it.

'Place look familiar?' he asked.

'Pretty much.' His offhand manner was too beautifully British for me to match, but I tried. 'Three of the walls haven't moved at all. The roofbeams, either. Of course there are some minor alterations. You've cut a few new holes.' I waved at the windows. 'And plugged up the old ones. And put in that stone wall with the fireplace. And the floor. Nothing terribly radical.'

Lew nodded. 'Same with the furnishing. I liked what I saw, the first time I poked my head through the door, so I kept the theme and expanded on it.'

'Oh no, not that old thing!' Where Lew gestured, I saw with dismay a relic of past summers, the makeshift cupboard Jay and I used to keep our picnic gear in. It was the worse for age, and it had never been anything but curtain-tacked-to-orange-crate. 'It was just a – '

'Just what made me realise this place could be habitable. I kept it as a talisman.' Lew pushed aside the faded floral print to reveal chipped dishes and cups and mismatched utensils. 'It was also in the back of my mind that one of you might some day come back.'

'But how did you know who we were?'

'I didn't.' Lew looked sheepish. 'Being me, though, I made up a story to go with the napkin rings marked J and A. From the housewifely touches – the pine boughs on the floor, the pots of dried flowers and the improvised furniture – I decided you were teenage girls, sisters or maybe cousins. I named you Jeanne and Anne.'

'And my name *is* Anne.'

'But you're not small and dark and French.'

I shrugged. 'You can't win 'em all.'

'You know I didn't mean it that way. And I was right about one thing – you did come back.' Lew snapped his fingers. 'I've just remembered. I saved something else of yours. Your kite.'

A moment later he had reached behind a chest and was holding it out to me. It was much less shabby than the orange-crate cabinet. I said, 'That's a nice new tail you've put on it.'

'The last one got chewed up by mice, if you'll pardon my mentioning the creatures. We haven't any of those about nowadays, though, have we, youngsters?' He was now addressing the terriers, who clamoured at his ankles. 'What's got into you two? You think we're going to go and fly this thing, is that it? Well, I'm sorry to disappoint – '

'Why, Lew? If that's what they want, do we have anything more important to do?'

He saw he was outnumbered. 'Come on then.' We trooped outside and again he offered me the kite.

'Uh-uh. You planted your kitchen garden smack in the middle of my old launch run. You'll have to get it aloft yourself.'

'With the updraughts here, it's never hard. Besides, we're not after altitude. As far as Dylan and Caitlin are concerned, the object is to keep it as low as possible so they can chase it.'

Lew demonstrated. He sent the kite in shallow swoops as the terriers tacked back and forth across the meadow in shrill pursuit. He worked his way around until the kite hovered closehauled a bare few yards above the ground. Slowly he lowered it even further.

'Watch this!'

Just as Caitlin managed to get hold of the tail, Lew let the kite catch the wind. For a moment Caitlin seemed to be winning her tug-of-war. Then she was skidding along in the

95

wake of the filling kite. Dylan raced beside her, barking a frenzy of encouragement. Caitlin herself was silent, her jaws closed tenaciously on her prey, her little legs skittering faster and faster across the grass until, incredibly, she was airborne.

Lew laughed exultantly. 'That's it, my girl, hang on!'

Over the surface of the ground she flew, sometimes touching down for a few steps, sometimes treading air for five full seconds.

Finally Lew let her touch down for good, dropping the kite behind her and running across the meadow to her. She must, I was sure, be too exhausted and frightened to move. But she came to meet him, barking a whole series of messages, and scrambling into his arms with every appearance of happiness.

'I've heard of flying fish,' I said. 'I've even *seen* flying squirrels. But this is one for the books.'

'Hmm, I suppose their game is rather unique.'

'You mean Dylan does it too?'

At the sound of his name, Dylan set up a renewed clamour for attention. I picked him up.

'But of course. He invented it, or at least he was the first to "solo". Though in all fairness I must say Caitlin's the better aviator.'

'She's terrific.' I took her from Lew, nuzzled her and Dylan, and set them both back on the ground. 'Now run along and catch grasshoppers or something, you two. Your master and I have to have a talk.'

'We do?' Lew sat down beside the dogs, selected a blade of grass to chew, then stretched himself out at full length. 'You know, I've never brought a girl up here before. If I knew it meant "having a talk", I might even have waited a bit longer.'

I ripped up a handful of weeds and wildflowers and threw them at him. Most of them fell short. 'Wretch! I only wanted to discuss a simple business proposition, between me and the dogs. If Dylan and Caitlin could talk, we could get along without you altogether – except maybe for handling the kite.'

'Kite?'

'K-i-t-e, kite. Can't you see it? It'll make a fantastic picture

96

story. Even if we don't hit the mass market, there are hundreds of animal magazines all over the world. They may not pay much, but your half still ought to cover the dog food bills for quite a while.'

'My half? What *are* you talking about, Addie?'

'That's after expenses, film and processing and so forth. Honest, it's generous. Most people would offer you a flat fee, but I happen to be fond of those dogs. I just hope they aren't camera-shy.'

'One thing they've never been is shy,' Lew said decidedly. 'Now let me see if I read you – you want to catch the pups' trapeze act on film and turn it into a sort of photo essay, is that it?'

'Sure. It's a natural.'

Lew, though he hadn't thought of it himself, caught on fast. Before long he was talking about 'joint artistic control' – which meant he wasn't eager to have some other scribbler writing about *his* dogs. We agreed that he would have final approval of the format and we would do the text together. This was decided with a tacit trust that was somewhat remarkable in that neither of us had ever read a word the other had written.

Lew got up and said it was time to fill the picnic basket. My pro-forma offer of help was declined, so I spent the time browsing through his bookshelves.

You can tell a lot about a person from his books, and somehow in Lew's case I knew I was going to like what I saw.

Some of the items were old favourites in Britain that aren't seen so much in the States – *The Natural History of Selborne*, for instance, or the works of Norman Douglas. Other veins were more standard. The major philosophers and historians were there, and many fiction classics, though I noted that the most turgid ones were missing. Lew apparently thought great age didn't take the place of a great story. There were a lot of modern novels, some of which I knew, and a handful of modern poets, all unfamiliar. But that was not the shelf which surprised me.

'Lew,' I said, turning toward the tiny kitchen area, 'what are you doing with all these cookbooks? There's no way you can use them. You don't even have a stove.'

'You're wrong there, and I'll show you how in two ticks. But that's not the point. They're like any good books, meant to be read for pleasure.'

I had a closer look. The authors ranged from Apicius with his *De Re Coquinaria* (first century AD) right up through Waverley Root and Alan Davidson, whom my mother had considered among the finer prose stylists of our era. Their recipes, she thought, weren't too bad either.

Choosing solely by title, I started reading a book called *Consuming Passions*. It was by an Englishwoman named Philippa Pullar and it turned out to be a lively history from Roman times of eating and other pleasures of the flesh. I sat crosslegged on the floor, engrossed in an account of medieval aphrodisiacs, until I saw with a guilty start that Lew was standing over me.

He grinned, reached for the book to replace it on its shelf, and hauled me to my feet.

'Come,' he said, 'and see a rustic male-designed kitchen. You will be dazzled by its ingenuity.'

I was, and said so. Lew's fireplace was not just a burning-hole with a flue. Two pothooks allowed a kettle and a cauldron to be swung over the fire. Brackets on the back wall could hold a grilling rack at various heights. And the two side walls were largely metal plate.

'On your left we have water tanks.' Lew opened a spigot and steaming water drained into a bucket. 'Two of them, so we're seldom entirely deprived. And the right side is double too, except there it's a pair of ovens.'

I peered into the cast-iron chambers. 'They're big enough. But how do you regulate the temperature?'

'Build up the fire along that wall to raise the heat. Open these escape vents to lower it.'

'Neat.'

Seeing what Lew had accomplished, I felt markedly un-resourceful. If the problem with Gran's roof had been Lew's to solve, he would have gone at it with a saw and a hammer and a mouthful of nails the very first day.

I asked him what he thought about my idea of rigging a tarpaulin.

'Might work. I'll have a look when we go back down this afternoon. You're planning on moving in, then?'

'Tomorrow, I hope. I phoned a furniture store in Vence yesterday and they promised to deliver a new mattress first thing in the morning.'

'Good. You've found the lawyer and the mattress, now all you need is the cat.'

I was puzzled for a moment, then remembered Lew's prescription the day we met.

'No, no cat yet. I have to see whether I'm going to be evicted before I think of sharing the place with anybody.'

'A point. See here, if things do get sticky and you need somewhere to bunk, you can always come here.' Lew's suggestion sounded reticent in comparison with Jean-Marc's gallant Gallic offer thirty-six hours ago. He added, with that offhandedness of his, 'Dylan and Caitlin wouldn't mind.'

I wondered how effective they would be as chaperones, if that was what Lew meant to imply. Instead I asked: 'How old are the pups?'

'I really ought to stop calling them pups, since they're fully grown. They're almost a year old now. My sister Gwenllian brought them last spring.'

'From Wales?'

'Yes. She spent a week with me, ostensibly on holiday. My own suspicion is that the family pitched on poor Gwennie and sent her out here to make sure I wasn't too under-nourished or out-at-elbows. And the gift of the pups was utterly transparent. I couldn't be allowed to go on living alone halfway up a mountain – mentally unhealthy, that.'

'I'm on Gwennie's side,' I said, 'at least about the dogs.'

'So am I, now.'

Lew handed me a wicker hamper. 'Take this one, will you? It's not as heavy as it looks. What's your preference for music?'

'You choose – nothing too noisy and modern though. Something woodsy.'

'Pipes of Pan, that sort of thing?' Lew crossed to the far bookshelf, studied his rack of tape cassettes and put three in his pocket. Then he whistled to the terriers and we struck off uphill again.

In ten minutes we came to the waterfall. Like the clearing where Lew lived, it was recognisably a place I had known in childhood, and yet unfamiliar. Lew had transformed the pile of stones and rubble at the base of the cascade into a pair of stepped pools, large enough for bathing. Alongside he had cleared and levelled the ground and, obviously some months back, seeded it with a sturdy species of grass.

He unstrapped a rolled blanket from his rucksack and spread it on his almost grown lawn. 'Welcome to Eden North.'

'It looks like a miniature country club. Swimming pool, tree-shaded patio, bar.' Lew had just taken the wine from the rucksack.

'All the comforts,' he agreed. 'I'd have put in a phone, but I'd have been pestered the whole day by my stockbroker.'

We laughed together and even the dogs yapped to share the joke.

When we had the hamper unpacked, Lew put a cassette in the tape-player part of his radio. 'Every country club has Muzak at poolside, right?'

But it wasn't Muzak. It was the pipes of Pan that Lew had promised, or pretty nearly. At least there was a solo flute. It was backed by what sounded like a full symphony orchestra, and yet somehow the flute could distance itself and evoke a solitary shepherd on a rock.

Lew seemed to be waiting for my reaction. He didn't say so, though, and as we ate our way through the small mountain of picnic fare we talked of other things – Lew's family in Wales, my summers here with Gran, our mutual perceptions of the French character. The music ended in a burst of applause and the tape clicked off.

'You recorded that live?'

'Via the BBC. What did you think? Not too noisy or modern?' Lew's question was clearly loaded, but I answered truthfully:

'No, I liked it. It had a kind of ethnic flavour, like the music based on folk tunes that Smetana and all those Bohemians were always collecting.'

Lew nodded approval. 'Right idea, wrong country. You just heard Joaquín Rodrigo's "Concierto Pastoral" in the premier performance by James Galway, who commissioned it.'

'You mean that piece was written in the last ten years?'

'More like five.'

My hands rose and fell. 'I really have to get over all this rigid thinking.'

'If you mean a prejudice against composers who use computers to invent cacophony, you're not alone, Addie my girl.'

'But they say if you understand it, even that – '

Lew snorted. 'You know the story about Tolstoy and Shakespeare, don't you?'

'No, which one?'

'Tolstoy couldn't understand why Shakespeare was supposed to be a genius. He concluded the problem must be in the translation, so he spent seven years mastering English. Then he tried the Bard again. And he still couldn't see what all the fuss was about.'

'Oh. And you think that's what would happen if we studied avant-garde music?'

'I do. Except that when Tolstoy was finished, at the least he'd gained a useful language.'

Lew put in a new tape and began gathering up the picnic leftovers, which mostly meant feeding them to Dylan and Caitlin. I helped. The music was a Baroque horn concerto, brassy and bright.

'Not quite the woodsy music you asked for,' Lew said, 'but it was written by Förster, which has to mean "forester". I crave your pardon on double grounds.'

I waved magisterially. 'Perfectly all right. This is *good* noisy music.' I folded my arms under my head and stretched

101

out on the blanket, my eyes half closed against the sun. 'Anyway, after all that food it'll keep us awake.'

Lew moved the hamper aside and lay prone on the other half of the blanket, leaning on his elbows, inspecting the grass for weeds or maybe four-leaf clovers. 'Talking of noise, were you down in the village last night for the rally?'

'Do bears like honey?'

'You're right, it was a silly question. Lord, it must have been deafening! I could hear the shouting inside the cottage with the windows shut. It even woke the pups.'

'That would have been right at the end. They chose their council by voice vote, then gave a French version of hip-hip-hooray. Most of the time they weren't very moblike. No throwing things, no heckling the speakers – probably because they were already unanimous when they arrived.'

'Did they bring in outside speakers?'

'No, just the local violet growers. But some of them sounded as if they were primed, particularly René Cordier. Do you know René? Quite a firebrand. He's got one of the larger flower fields, next door to Madame Isnard's grandnephew Serge Gazagnaire. René got up last night in his cloth cap and work clothes and gumboots, standing there in the torchlight like a peasant direct from Central Casting, and he waited until they were quiet and then he started playing that crowd. I never saw anything like it.'

'What did he say?'

'Everything, the whole party line. Exploitation of the masses, iniquity of inherited wealth, tides of history, latent power of the proletariat – well, you know the stock phrases as well as I do. But René had the crowd thinking every word of it was original and profound. And he had them believing it.'

'Did he recommend turning St Martin into one vast violet-growing commune?'

'René? Give up his own land? He'd be insulted to hear it, but I think our Comrade Cordier has a secret middle-class streak.'

Lew chuckled. 'Probably does. France's middle class is on the broad side. Most of the "aristocracy" are basically bourgeois, and most of the lower classes are trying to be. In fact, I wonder why so many French profess to be Communists. They've already got a classless society.'

'I never thought of it that way.'

'So far as I know, it's original,' Lew said, not modestly. 'Then what did they decide, apart from electing a council?'

'They decided to show solidarity with the other growers. They set a new price, and if the perfume makers and the cut-flower wholesalers won't meet it, they'll sell the violets themselves.'

'Will they now? To each other?'

'They'll take them to Paris, to the big new markets at Rungis. Naturally, Paris is the sum and the limit of their vision.'

'Naturally. I wish them luck.'

'Me too. But I'd have more sympathy if they weren't dreaming up the whole problem like Don Quixote.'

It was all too remote to worry about on this drowsy sun-drenched Sunday. The plash of the waterfall and the droning of bees were more natural sounds than last night's mob yells. The village of St Martin was not just downhill but a dozen miles away.

I pushed my shoes off and wiggled my toes. This was a mistake. Dylan and Caitlin immediately began nuzzling my feet.

'Hey,' I yelped, 'that tickles! Cut it out, you guys. Lew, call them off.'

Lew turned lazily on to his side. 'Good show, pups. You take the toes, and I'll get the nose.' His hand homed in, brandishing a brushy piece of sprouted grass.

I tried resistance, but I should have known better. The ensuing tussle took all of sixty seconds and ended with Lew pinioning both my wrists and the terriers sitting on my stomach.

'Unfair! Three against one.'

The dogs climbed off, but Lew was unmoved by the protest. 'It needed all three of us. I didn't know a woman could be so strong.'

103

The compliment, if any was intended, was a dubious one. 'Really? What kind of women do you normally wrestle with?'

Lew didn't answer, but he did let go of my wrists. He rolled over and started playing with the radio, switching to a short-wave band, deploying the antenna, tuning. For all his efforts, the reception wasn't very good, but I could faintly make out the announcer of the BBC World Service saying that the time at the tone would be noon GMT. The famous 'pips' followed, and then snatches of news emerging and fading in a background of static.

'Don't bother, Lew, it's too nice a day to – '

'Ssh!'

Lew was evidently someone who kept up on current affairs, and it did not occur to him that even a journalist – especially a journalist – might sometimes like to get away from the constant flood of news.

Obediently I kept silent, scratching Caitlin desultorily and listening with half an ear to reports of British steelworkers striking over pay, British train drivers striking over overtime, British car assemblers striking over their tea break. The next item seemed to concern London traffic being paralysed by six inches of snow. There were man-in-the-street interviews, mercifully submerged in static.

Then suddenly I was sitting bolt upright, straining to hear.

'In Costa Rica early this . . . capital city of San José was rocked by . . . measured at 6.7 on the Richter scale. The epicentre was located . . . miles from the . . . according to . . . for Seismographic Research. Initial reports from the Central American country . . . fragmentary, as all communication lines have been . . . efforts to ascertain . . . British subjects among the victims . . . planeloads of relief supplies already despatched from airfields in . . .'

The voice dissolved in crackling and when it came back it was speaking calmly of race riots in Johannesburg.

I sat staring straight ahead, trying not to move, trying to fight down the nauseating waves of fear.

Jay had to be safe. Of course Jay was safe. Anything else simply could not be.

Lew switched the radio off slowly and came to sit beside me. He reached out a hand, pulled it back.

'Addie, you mustn't worry. We don't even know whether it struck the centre of San José.'

But if it did? I thought. *What about that quake in Algeria the year before last? They said the centre of the town was gone, levelled, in the first thirty seconds.*

'Even if it did, he's bound to be all right. The casualty figures look a lot worse until you start figuring them as a percentage of the population. Then the odds get decent.'

Sure, but the unlucky ones are dead. For them it's one hundred per cent.

'And they're downright good odds for the rich foreigners. I mean to say, at the risk of sounding callous, most victims are poor because the cheap housing in the slums collapses first. Not the kind of construction that goes into an American Embassy.'

But he wouldn't have been there unless – was it early morning British time or Costa Rican?

'Or the sort of apartment he'd live in, either.'

Not Jay. He lived in a native barrio and he ate and drank with his neighbours. He didn't think Americans should insulate themselves from – oh God, why am I using the past tense?

'It may be days and days until he can let you know he's all right. In the meantime there's no sense in worrying yourself into a nervous breakdown. It won't do Jay any good, now will it?'

I stared out across the folds of pine-clad hills to the Mediterranean, and thought how many miles of water separated the Côte d'Azur from Costa Rica.

Finally I said, 'If you don't mind, Lew, I'd like to go back down to the village now.'

When we got to the foot of the path, it was not just down-hill momentum that propelled me. I went past Gran's house with hardly a glance. Something was happening there, some-thing involving a lot of people and commotion and clouds of dust, but I left Lew to find out what it was. He seemed interested.

At her house above the Eagle's Nest, Madame Isnard was dozing in the usual cocoon of pillows and afghans. I slipped past her to the telephone, took it into the hall and quietly shut the door. But I was not alone after all. In the kitchen Lili and the Marchetti boy sat, in total propriety, across the table over two cups of tea. The boy got up when I came in. So did Lili. She said:

'What's wrong, Addie? You look like – like – '

Gesturing an apology, I went into our shared bedroom for my address book and dialled Connie's home number. It took her so long to answer that I almost gave up.

'Addie, hi! Gorgeous day, isn't it? I've been out on the balcony painting flowerpots. Want to help? Only kindergarten graduates accepted.'

She sounded so perky, it was obvious she hadn't heard the news. I tried to tell it calmly, but my voice wouldn't stay steady.

Connie's concern was instantaneous and genuine. Oddly, though, it was all for me. She wasn't in the least worried about Jay; she simply assumed he would come out of it safe and sound. 'But you, Addie honey, you must be worried sick.'

'I am. I keep telling myself he's okay, but then – '

'Sure, I know. Those people who go around saying no-news-is-good-news are idiots. Just let them try living through it themselves. What you need is to *know* he's all right.'

'But they say all the communication lines are cut. It'll be ages before private messages start getting through, won't it?'

'Probably, but Aunt Connie and Uncle Sam can maybe speed things up a little. I'm not promising miracles, but I'll get on it right away.'

'On the telex to San José, you mean?'

'That too, though I don't expect any answer. I meant I'd shoot off a message to the head office. You know, like, Foggy Bottom, District of Columbia, U S of A. They'll hear before anyone else does. I'll call you just as soon as – no, that's

106

a rotten idea. You can't sit around all night in a hotel room looking at the phone and waiting for it to ring.'

Connie and I had not talked since Friday, I realised. She did not even know where I was staying and why. I started to give her Madame Isnard's phone number, but her Hispanic tongue was quicker than mine.

'Look, the best thing is for you to come down and stay here with me. That way you'll know as soon as I do. Just don't go breaking any speed limits, huh? I won't even be back from the office for a couple of hours, and it'll be a lot longer than that before there's any chance of an answer. Come for supper, any time from six on. Okay?'

'Okay.'

My answer was involuntary. Connie talked in such a rush that I had absorbed only half of what she said. But I did know she was going to find out about Jay, and the last thing I wanted to do was delay her.

Connie must have felt the same way. The phone in my hand was dead. I put it back in the cradle and stood looking at it.

'Addie?' Lili spoke diffidently. 'Is there some way we can help you? Please tell us what is wrong.'

Her concern was as genuine as Connie's, but frustrated by a language barrier, so I had to go over the whole thing again in French.

'No, there's nothing we can do,' Lili agreed. Her regret seemed to have an extra dimension. 'Poor Serge! He worked so hard to get everything ready and to surprise you with it before Christmas. And now it couldn't matter less to you.'

Distracted as I was, it took me a moment to realise she was talking about the activity at Gran's house. And she was right. I hadn't even noticed what was going on, or who was doing it. But it would be ungrateful to say so.

'That's not true, Lili,' I said. 'Right now I'm especially glad to have friends I can count on. It really means a lot.' I smiled to let her know she was included. 'Look at the way you and Madame took me in this weekend. And now all that Serge is doing – I must go and thank him properly.'

107

I stopped only long enough to dump everything out of my flight bag and repack it with overnight things. Then I went out past the sleeping Madame Isnard, down the flight of stone steps and along the path to Gran's house.

Lew was watching for my return and hurried to meet me. I told him what Connie had said.

'So I don't have to leave for a couple of hours. Now please tell me, *sotto voce*, what's going on here. Should I just cross my fingers and thank them nicely for the hopeless mess they've made? Or have they actually done any good?'

Lew considered, and decided to grant qualified approval.

'It's only jury-rigged, of course, so it's bound to look a bit unsightly. But it's basically sound, what they're doing. In fact, except for aesthetic considerations, it could last indefinitely.'

We were now at the house, where Lew tactfully turned me over to Serge for the grand tour.

Dutifully I admired what progress had been made, though honestly there wasn't much to admire. Everything was in chaos.

The crew numbered eight – including a cousin of Serge's, his neighbour René Cordier, some villagers I knew and some I was introduced to and, improbably, Jean-Marc Bertrand who said he had come to investigate and stayed to help – and they were swarming all over. They were on the ridge pole, and in the loft with only head and shoulders clearing the broken tiles. They were armed with sledgehammers and shovels and crowbars and a gas-powered chainsaw. The noise of their tools and their own shouts was loud enough, but these were drowned periodically by the crash of débris on to the ground as a chunk of roof was cut loose, passed hand to hand, and chucked overboard. Clouds of white dust accompanied each salvo. I thought how long it would take afterwards to clean up down below, and willed myself to look on it all as an improvement. A roof, after all, would be better than no roof.

About that time things calmed down. No more major chunks came out of the hole in the roof, only buckets of smaller stuff, broken tiles and mortar. Somehow it made me think of the way a dentist attacks a decayed tooth, hacking away with burrs and picks first, and then tidying up before doing the actual filling.

They got to that stage next. After inspecting the sheets of corrugated plastic and the outsized clamps, I left them at it and went over to join Sabine.

Placidly knitting, Sabine sat just outside the zone of up-heaval on a low stone wall bordering Gran's garden and – as I had always thought – her property.

'This is such a peaceful spot,' she said.

A stone's throw away eight men (nine now) were working like a detachment of Seabees, but I thought I knew what Sabine meant. 'Where are the kids?'

'I parked them with Lucie Cordier for the afternoon. Incredible luxury! The best part is sitting here doing absolutely nothing and watching everyone else knock himself out. Is that mean and petty, do you think?'

'Don't worry about it. You'll never get the chance to make it a habit.'

'*That's* true, so I might as well enjoy it now.' She turned her knitting and pointed with the free needle towards the house. 'They're making progress, aren't they? We hoped you'd be here when we arrived, naturally, but it's good this way too. The messy part is just about done.'

Sabine was pleased with everyone and everything this afternoon. I could not bring myself to spoil her mood by sharing my worries.

'I noticed the way the furniture was covered,' I said. 'I'll bet Serge didn't think of that.'

'No, but he thought of all the rest, and organised it too, in just two days. It had to be on a Sunday, of course, because everything's borrowed. People, tools, the block and tackle, the housepainter's dust-sheets, the wheelbarrows, the dump truck –'

'Dump truck?'

'To cart away the débris. You don't think we'd leave it all over your lawn?'

That's exactly what I had envisioned. My face must have shown it, but Sabine was knitting again and did not notice.

'I just hope,' she went on, 'you won't be bashful about telling us what else you want. We only know about the roof, but if the fireplace needs work or something – I mean, the tools are here now, so it makes sense.'

'At the moment I can't think of anything,' I said in all honesty.

Sabine's offer reminded me poignantly of times while I was growing up, times when the folk of our Massachusetts town would pitch in and get the job done. It might be building the community ice rink Dad had campaigned for in his editorials. It might be furnishing a house for a family that had been burned out, or setting up lifelines to people cut off by a blizzard. Whatever it was, the work was shared out by general agreement and nobody angled for credit.

It was the kind of neighbourliness we like to think of as particularly American, a part of our frontier heritage, but maybe small towns breed it everywhere.

This reflection was broken into, appropriately, by an American voice. It was not New England, though, but Rusty's own unmistakable brand of Californian. He had come up to the Eagle's Nest to deliver my card of admittance to the château for the *vernissage* the following evening, he said, but had been told I had left the inn.

'Left?' I repeated wryly. 'I wouldn't use the active voice. It was more of a shotgun departure. Luckily I've got friends who'll give me a roof to put over my head – as you see.'

'Not just see. You can hear the result practically down to the Old Village. But hey, Addie, you should have come to me. Didn't I say, like, anything you wanted – '

'Sure, Rusty, I remember. But Serge and Sabine organised all this as a surprise party. So actually I didn't have to ask anybody.'

'Yeah, I guess.' Rusty still sounded put out. 'It's just that, you know, it's a little funny, all these guys busting their balls to fix up your house and no Americans here. It's not like there's not enough of us in town. Normally we take care of our own. But this – it kind of makes us look, you know, unpatriotic.'

'If that's all that's bothering you,' I said innocently, 'you could go and tell Serge you're a friend of mine and you'd like to pitch in.'

Rusty thought this over. He went, but as he did I heard him mutter something about 'not the same thing'.

It was coming up for the hour, so I reached into the flight bag for my pocket-sized radio. Except for changing the wavelength from WQXR's to Radio Monte Carlo's new classical channel, I had barely touched it all week. Now I switched to the AM band and started running up and down the dial, but no blast of sound seemed more promising than any other.

'Sabine? What's the best station for news?'

She took the radio from me. 'What a marvellous little machine! It's got everything, AM, FM, antenna, jacks for stereo headphones, and it all fits in the palm of your hand. Japanese, naturally. It's simply amazing how they do it.' Sabine's chatter was making me edgy, but through it she went on adjusting the dial. 'There. This is the one our neighbour René the Red is always listening to. For me twice a day is plenty – more, and it stops being news.'

'I know just what you mean,' I said, hardly even hearing her words. I put the radio on my shoulder, like any street youth in New York, and shut myself into a private world.

The radio didn't tell me anything. It didn't even get to Costa Rica until the fifth item, and then it only gave preliminary casualty estimates, not anything specific like where they came from.

Sabine listened too, and understood. 'They don't say just where the damage was, do they? That's not much help.' She thought for a minute, then added, 'There's nothing to worry about, though. It's just an earthquake. It would take more than that to stop Jay Forrester, or even slow him down.'

Jay had that effect on people, I knew. He was so tall and strong and capable and confident that he seemed somehow less destructible than other men. But then, I had thought the same about my father . . .

I got up and, keeping a wary eye on the roof, went into the house.

In the kitchen, I decided the least I could do was provide coffee for the work crew and maybe something cool. While the coffee water boiled, I rummaged in the pantry and refrigerator. Then I loaded bottles and paper cups on a tray, took it out to the stone ledge where Sabine was sitting, and hailed Serge. He said the last clamps were just being fixed, leaving only the cleaning up.

I didn't feel like making conversation, so I let Sabine play hostess and took my cup of coffee along the garden wall to the far corner. From there I could see and hear without having to mix.

The original work crew clustered around the tray of drinks, producing clouds of acrid black tobacco smoke to mingle with the plaster dust and rapidly reducing my limited supply of wine.

Rusty and Lew, each with a bottle of beer, moved apart from the others. Jean-Marc, wavering at first between native villagers and foreigners, followed them. Snatches of their conversation drifted to me. First they all praised Serge, but I got the feeling that both Lew and Jean-Marc, like Rusty, wished they had thought of it and could be the one looking like a knight in shining armour. Next they began a sort of oblique contest over which one had the strongest claim to me. Rusty established that he had actually met me before the others, and invoked his status as fellow-countryman. Jean-Marc with Gallic nuance contrived to suggest a certain physical intimacy while never sounding less than a perfect gentleman. And Lew, who could fairly claim to know me best, artfully made opportunities to stud the conversation with details about me that the others could not match.

At any other time it would have amused me hugely, and maybe flattered me a bit too. Not today. I saw three grown men acting like little boys, exchanging boasts about the new girl on the block. And I kept thinking that Jay was easily worth all three of them, and he was a third of a world away, perhaps lying hurt or dead under tons of rubble.

I turned away so they would not be encouraged to join me.

Nobody's company was welcome now. Except Connie's, of course. Connie knew Jay, so Connie could understand.

Around midnight we began talking of Jay. Until then neither Connie nor I mentioned his name. We did not need to. Every subject led back to him, and every obscure reference was understood.

Connie did her best to make me relax. She gave me a tour of her apartment, which was compact but cleverly furnished. She put a stack of easy-listening records on the stereo. She served a casual coffee-table supper. She encouraged her cat to sit on my lap. But none of it was too successful. Unquiet silences were frequent.

The phone rang at odd intervals. My heart lurched each time, then sank again as I heard Connie speak in French. During the first call I was chafing, too, to think that the line might be tied up with chit-chat when Washington was trying to get through. But Connie hung up sounding well pleased.

'Guy I know, Vincent, staffer at *Nice-Matin*. He doesn't work nights, but he went in as a favour to me and pulled all the stories coming over the wire from Agence France-Presse and Reuters and so on. Not only that, Vincent talked his colleague who's on duty tonight into keeping a close watch. If there's anything at all, he'll call us.'

'But so far there isn't –'

'Just the usual garbage. They must get paid by the word, it's all so vague and padded. Honestly, sometimes I wonder how journalists get away with . . .' Connie let the sentence trail off.

'Never mind, I agree with you. Basically it's a case of supply and demand. With the public so thirsty for news, there are always plenty of people willing to brew it up out of nothing. It's tough on the rest of us, but it's an occupational hazard.'

'Speaking of which, are you getting anything done on that photo piece you told me about?'

113

'It's on the back burner. I've got a new project.'

I told Connie about the flower growers' protest action. She tried to sound interested, but it was clear that she was really waiting, like me, for the phone to ring. Finally we gave up pretending and played gin rummy.

The teletype watcher at *Nice-Matin* called three or four times. Connie listened patiently, rolling her eyes skyward as he read a whole story off the wire, and thanked him. She didn't waste her breath repeating what he'd said. She didn't waste time on social calls either. She just told them she was tied up and would talk to them tomorrow.

Washington didn't call.

Connie got linen out and we made up the couch into a bed for me. Then we sat on it crosslegged in our pyjamas and Connie asked some question about my home town that led us to Jay in boyhood and we didn't stop talking until the phone rang again at 2 a.m. It was only the teletype fellow, but it made us realise how late it was. Connie asked him to hold any more tear sheets until morning, and we went to bed.

Perhaps Connie slept, as she said she would. I didn't.

It was not worry over Jay, strangely, that kept me awake. Somehow talking with Connie about him had calmed me. The more we talked, the more real and fully fleshed he became again, until it was hard to doubt his continuing vitality.

I considered the idea of Jay and Connie together. That didn't bother me either – at least, not beyond a reflex twinge of jealousy. For years it had been axiomatic that no girl was good enough for Jay, but I knew I would have to get over that sooner or later. I could think of a lot worse sisters-in-law than Connie Ortiz. And she was obviously sold on Jay (which I accepted as no less than his due) so the only question was on Jay's side.

I turned restlessly, trying to get comfortable. It was not a bad bed, but it was the third one I had occupied in four nights.

Still, it was decidedly preferable to the alternatives. Even if I had wanted to stay under Scotto's roof at le Nid de l'Aigle, no room was offered – except Jean-Marc's which I did not count. The same objection applied to Lew's place. He was less obviously amorous and more British-reticent but probably, the terriers notwithstanding, just as chancy a roommate. The option of Gran's house – my house – was not open until the mattress had been delivered, which should be tomorrow, and until the plaster dust was swept up, which looked like it could take days. That left Madame Isnard's. And of the several places I could sleep it was the one I least wanted to face.

Cowardice, that was the only name for it.

Today of all days the admission was unwelcome. Here was I, shying away from a harmless old woman's house as if it were haunted, while Jay was in an actual danger zone. Yet I thought he would understand my reaction. Jay didn't have a cowardly bone in his body – physical peril or hardship daunted him not at all – but he became very uncomfortable and tentative in the presence of psychological upheaval. And so did I.

It wouldn't have been so bad if there were some way to tell when Madame Isnard was lucid and when she wasn't. But she would be here one moment and off the next in some era when Lili and I were not yet born. Nor were the transitions always smooth. She might doze off and wake up alert, or she might come out of it fuzzy and fretful. Then she would apologise over and over for being a bother. And over and over Lili would assure her that she was not.

In the daytime it was distressing. At night it was downright spooky.

I hadn't had a chance to talk to Lili about it on Saturday. All day I was in Grasse pursuing the flower strike story, and when I got back after the violet growers' rally Lili was eager to be off on her date. But the same thing happened on Saturday evening as on Friday, so the next morning I had followed Lili into the kitchen and asked her about it while we washed up the breakfast dishes.

'Did she seem normal otherwise?' Lili had wanted to know.

'Yes,' I said, 'and that's just what made me feel so helpless. When her mind's wandering, it's easy enough to soothe her, but this was – I don't quite know how to describe it. Usually when she's alert, it makes her seem stronger physically too. Sort of as if she squares her shoulders and climbs back into her own body. You know what I mean?'

'I think so. She has more presence, and she even looks bigger.'

'Exactly. She was like that when I got her into bed. But later, when she rang, she just looked tiny and frail and boneless.' I told Lili what had happened. 'And after I left I'm sure she was crying.'

Lili nodded. 'Poor Tante Irène, it frightens her so. I never should have gone out and left her.'

I did not bother to refute that. 'What frightens her?'

'She hears – she says she hears sounds in the night outside her bedroom.'

'What kind of sounds?'

'All kinds, she says. Movement, footsteps, voices. Some aren't human. She calls those "spirit voices".' Lili pronounced the phrase with embarrassment. 'I asked her to describe them, and she talked of howls and moans. I suppose it might be a dog.'

'You haven't heard any of these sounds yourself, I gather.'

'No. You see, it only happens after we're in bed, and every time I answer her bell, the noises have stopped. That upsets Tante Irène even more – the fact that she's the only one to hear them. She's afraid I won't believe her.'

I studied Lili's young and troubled face. 'And you don't, entirely, do you?'

'We-e-ell. It's not that I doubt her word. But Tante Irène does get mixed up sometimes, so I can't help wondering if maybe – ' Lili chewed her lip, hesitating between loyalty and candour.

'Yes, I see. She might be alarmed at night by perfectly ordinary noises. Or she might even be imagining them.'

Lili nodded again. 'I'm careful not to suggest it to her. But I think she's starting to wonder herself whether she might be – losing her mind. And that, of course, frightens her most of all.'

Madame Isnard summoned Lili then, and Lew would soon be calling for me at Gran's house for our picnic, so the conversation ended. I did not think of Madame Isnard for the rest of Sunday morning, and by the afternoon I could think of nothing except Jay.

But now in the middle of the night, as I lay wakeful and worried, I reminded myself that Irène Isnard might be doing the same. I resolved to be more attentive to her, and helpful to Lili.

It would do me good to think at regular intervals of someone's problems other than my own.

117

SIX

Monday, 22 December

BY MORNING my anxiety over Jay was back at full strength.

Connie wasn't feeling too placid either, by the look of things. She criss-crossed the small apartment in a sustained burst of activity, yanking the curtains open, thumping cushions into shape, pulverising coffee beans in a hand-cranked grinder, pouring milk into a saucepan for our *café au lait* and into a bowl for the cat. All the while she muttered.

'. . . nine chances out of ten, catch the duty officer napping at his desk. Serve him right, too. If he can't do a simple favour for a colleague . . .' As soon as the coffee was brewed, she took her cup to the phone.

Finding a line open was no problem at that hour: even in Central America it was pushing midnight and respectable Washington had been asleep for hours. Connie got through directly to the right department, and within minutes to someone who knew who she was and what she wanted. She listened, apparently, to an apology and then to an update on the news from San José. Finally she hung up, saying, 'Thanks anyway.'

'Nothing?'

She shook her head. 'They didn't call me because they don't really know anything. All the lines are still down. Evidently our ambassador did contrive to get a message out – he went to the airport and buttonholed a pilot – but it was just a plea for various relief supplies. The people in Washington assume the Embassy's still standing, or he'd have mentioned it. Ditto on personnel. But they don't *know*.'

'Maybe the ambassador didn't either. He wouldn't have been able to check on all of his staff by then, would he?'

'I couldn't guess. I'm not even sure how many we have there right now.'

'So – there's nothing we can do except wait some more.'

'Afraid not.' Connie spread her hands. 'It'll be a while, too. It won't even be daylight in Costa Rica until it's dusk here. So there's no sense sitting around. I've got to go to work anyhow. What about you?'

With a sense of unreality I remembered that I had planned a full day's work in St Martin and in Grasse, before Jay had taken over all my thoughts.

Connie was right. It would be better to keep busy. We arranged that I would call her at intervals, but otherwise go on as planned with domestic chores and journalistic slogging.

Connie cleared away the breakfast dishes and put the cat out on the balcony while I stuffed my few things into my flight bag. In a couple of minutes we were on the street, climbing into our respective cars, waving cheerfully.

I watched Connie pull her Pontiac out into the early rush-hour traffic, then sat staring into the middle distance, ignition key in hand, until long after she was gone.

Up at the Eagle's Nest I parked in the same slot as before, right under Scotto's office window.

As a gesture of defiance it wasn't much. All the big black cars of Scotto's cronies were gone and Scotto's as well. In fact, the only vehicles besides my own were Jean-Marc's brown Rabbit, Régine's turquoise Fiat 127, and the furniture van from Vence delivering my new mattress, improbably, just when it was promised.

Two deliverymen were pounding Gran's brass door-knocker. I unlocked the house and directed them to put the mattress in the kitchen. It would have to be shifted later, when the living-room was less cumbered with plaster dust. In the meantime I was glad to see the manufacturer had sheathed it in airtight plastic.

119

The deliverymen had left the invoice in the truck, so I went back down the path with them and, leaning on the tailgate, wrote a cheque.

As they drove off, I frowned at the chequebook stub. The price, for a single-bed mattress, seemed king-sized. Like every college freshman, I had years ago learned the cost of bedclothes, but I had never yet bought an actual bed. I was staggered by the amount entered opposite *montant du cheque*. The bottom line, *nouveau solde*, was not much more cheering.

The roar of the furniture van died away and voices became audible. Two black-robed figures were descending the stone steps from Madame Isnard's house, gabbling like a pair of beldames. One, not surprisingly, was Mathilde in her standard black cotton dress, unrelieved now even by the white of an apron. The other, in black cassock and jaunty black beret, was the village priest. They halted when they reached me, but they did not stop talking.

'. . . such a comfort to her,' Mathilde was saying. 'I think what chafes poor Irène most about being housebound is not getting out to Mass.'

'We must pray she may again. I did think she was stronger today than on my last visit. Perhaps we shall see her among the congregation before many Sundays pass.'

Listening, I wondered whether some down-to-earth planning might not buttress the good curé's prayers and made a mental note.

'Until that time,' Monsieur le Curé went on, 'it rejoices me to be able to bring consolation to her. I only wish I might do as much for the unhappy lady who occupies her former place.' He sighed heavily and directed his gaze towards the broad stone façade of le Nid de l'Aigle, so I understood that he meant Madame Scotto.

It was hard not to laugh. For decades Irène Isnard had been the driving force behind the Eagle's Nest, running the kitchen, running the housekeeping staff, very nearly running Lucien Isnard. To compare her to Scotto's sequestered wife, who probably could not say how many rooms the place had, was a piece of innocence I did not think possible even in a priest. No, especially in a priest.

'Have you met Madame Scotto?' I asked without inflection.

'Not really. I saw her when she was first brought here, the day her husband took possession of the inn. But she was rather heavily sedated at the time – as she, um, as I am told she frequently is.'

Mathilde snorted. '*Fre*quently? She's doped up practically around the clock, from what I can tell. Whenever she comes out of it enough to set up a howl, Régine goes running, and it's quiet again in two shakes – and mind you, that only happens a couple of times a day.'

'Is that so?' The priest looked thoughtful. 'Does it happen regularly? I mean, at a set hour?'

'Indeed it does – praise be! At least we can have our meals in peace. It's after breakfast and dinner that she generally does it. If you want to hear her, in fact, you probably have only twenty minutes or so to wait.'

'Oh no, I don't want to hear her,' the curé said earnestly, 'I want to talk with her. Poor lady, she is cut off entirely from spiritual solace, and I think in such cases it is a great mistake. A diseased mind is the sign of a troubled soul. Medical science should not disdain our support in bringing the patient inner peace, since we are specialists.' Monsieur le Curé cleared his throat. 'It helps, however, if the patient is awake.'

Mathilde and I exchanged a speculative look.

'You want to see her now?' Mathilde said.

'I'd like to try, at least.'

'Well, I can let you in all right, and show you to her room. But I don't see how I can keep Régine away, and I don't suppose you want *her* around.'

'Absolutely not. You're sure there's nothing you can – '

Mathilde shook her head.

'An outside diversion, then? Perhaps a phone call.' Monsieur le Curé looked at me hopefully.

I could just hear myself, calling the inn from Madame Isnard's house and trying to tie up Régine long enough to give the curé some time. If I pretended to be French, I couldn't keep up the hoax for a minute, and Régine would hang up almost as quickly on a foreigner who was proving tiresome.

'No way. However,' I said, brandishing the chequebook I still held, 'I think I can keep her nailed to the desk for a while. I'll march up and say I want to pay my bill – that ought to rock her. If it isn't ready, she'll have to prepare it on the spot. And if it is, I'll go over every line of it, down to the last centime. If any of my dinners were charged to Jean-Marc, I'll insist they shouldn't be. *And* vice versa.'

Mathilde chuckled, but the priest merely said, 'Yes indeed, occupy Régine however you can, and when it is time for me to retreat, let me know by – by what means?'

We put our heads together and decided where Mathilde should be deployed to relay a signal. The plan satisfied Monsieur le Curé. He said:

'I'd rather not have to explain how I came into Madame's presence, but if I'm just seen strolling along a corridor, no one will question it.'

'Of course not, Father,' I agreed. 'Of all people, you have free access to any household in St Martin.'

The priest caught Mathilde's eye and gave a rueful laugh, the first break I had seen in his sobriety. Somehow my words had struck an ironic chord. 'God bless you, child, it's not since last century that a cassock was a *laissez-passer*. A good number of St Martin families would leave me standing on the doorstep if I came only as a cleric. No, it's *this* that's my passport to almost every house but yours.'

He lifted his briefcase, undid the buckle and took out a heavy black ledger.

'You see, I double as the village meter-reader.'

Psychologically, I found our enterprise unrewarding. I managed to carry off my own part of it well enough, but it required my leaving without talking to my co-conspirators. As long as Régine was there I had to stay away from the

Eagle's Nest. All I could do was go back to Gran's house and attack the accumulation of plaster dust.

It was, if anything, thicker than yesterday when the Gazagnaires' crew cleaned up. The dust-sheets had caught most of the mess then. But overnight all the particles floating in the two-storey unpartitioned space under my newly fixed roof had come to rest. Outside, the sun might be almost hot, but here indoors it looked like the traditional white Christmas.

It also looked as if an attempt to sweep it up would set it all in motion again. I wished for once that Gran had gone in for walls. Not to mention electricity. A vacuum-cleaner would have come in handy right now. I got out a bucket, sponges and floor cloths, and set to work. Luckily the supply of running water was unlimited. Luckily, too, Gran's taste in decorating favoured native handicrafts, which kept things simple. The tiled floors were dotted with woven rush mats. Almost everything was washable, and the rest easily portable. The only exception was the overstuffed chair – which I found myself thinking of, just as his dogs did, as Lew's. It would be nice if Lew himself happened down the mountain in the next few minutes. The chair was cumbersome, and I could use help getting it outside to beat it.

I got the help, but it came from Jean-Marc.

Watching him flail the powder-laden upholstery with a broom handle, I decided that American baseball had missed a great natural slugger in Jean-Marc Bertrand.

He had dropped by, he said between blows, to ask whether I might be free to dine with him. 'Not at the inn, of course, you wouldn't want to go back there. But anywhere else you'd like.'

'I'm sorry, Jean-Marc, I wish I could.' That was true on two counts, and Jean-Marc's personal charm at the moment counted second. Contrary to what he said, I wanted very much to go back to the Eagle's Nest, and the best way I could think of was under his aegis. 'But I'm busy tonight.'

'I see. I thought you might be, on such short notice, but since it was only a Monday . . . still, with all your old friends in the village. . . .'

The idea of my being the social lion of St-Martin-sur-Loup was a little inaccurate, but it did make me realise that Jean-Marc must be leading a rather lonely existence here.

'I'm hardly so much in demand,' I told him. 'Pick any other night from now till New Year, and I'll say yes cheerfully.'

'Can I pick all ten of them?'

'Don't be greedy. But I'll tell you what you *can* do. You can come along with me tonight if you like. It's just the opening of the art show at the château, and it'll be the usual mob scene, but you might enjoy it.'

'Isn't it by invitation only?'

'Sure, but if you say you know Rusty, it'll be all right. He organised practically the whole thing.'

'I wouldn't call Monsieur Traynor exactly a friend.'

'Oh, is that his name?' If Jean-Marc knew that much, he knew more about Rusty than I did.

'Russell Traynor,' he said. 'Russ T – *ergo* Rusty. But I thought you were a friend of his?'

'Only casually. Anyway, in that arty set last names are sort of out. Rusty's gang doesn't care for anything too conventional.'

'From what I've seen, some of them find personal grooming too conventional.' Jean-Marc administered a final series of thwacks with the broom handle to the overstuffed chair. 'On the subject of cleanliness, will that do?'

We got the chair back inside, and then I prevailed on Jean-Marc to help me put the new mattress on the day bed. Once its plastic cover was folded away for future mouse-proofing, and the bedspread in place, I could step back and regard the whole with satisfaction.

Jean-Marc was more critical. 'It isn't very wide.'

'It's the standard single-bed size.'

'My point exactly. I wish you'd shown more foresight.'

Instead of answering, I sprayed lemon oil on the dining table. Polishing, I resolutely avoided looking at Jean-Marc. I couldn't help hearing him, though. Those bedsprings always creaked, and they creaked now as Jean-Marc tested the new mattress.

'Small indeed,' he said, 'but *very* comfortable. Come and see.'

'Not with you there.' I kept polishing.

'How else? It's the only real test.'

I polished some more.

'Come on, Addie, I'm not a mad rapist.'

'No, at least you're not mad.'

'And you're not a prude. I know.' Jean-Marc's voice was so lazy, it even sounded horizontal.

The tabletop gleamed. I added more lemon oil and refolded the polishing cloth.

Behind me I heard Jean-Marc's sigh, and the creak of the bedsprings as he got up. Then I felt his arms around my waist, his hands moving upwards, his lips against my throat.

'Witch!' he said. 'You think your spells can ward me off, but you'll see they don't work after dark. I'll be back.'

His hands lingered for a moment, then slid away. One hand reappeared and laid an object before me on the mirror surface of the table.

'Your broomstick.'

My breathing got back to normal in a couple of minutes, but before I drove off to Grasse I spent another half hour with mop, pail and polishing cloths, getting my thoughts straightened out along with the house.

What I felt for Jean-Marc was easy enough to identify: sexual attraction first and maybe last. It didn't mean we were made for each other, or compatible, or even congenial, which we were. But ever since the first time we stood outside the Eagle's Nest watching the lights of St Martin below, and Jean-Marc embraced me, we could not be together without being aware of that special electricity.

It was healthy and normal, exhilarating – and finally frightening.

For I could no longer regard Jean-Marc objectively. His purely physical impact was too strong, stronger than any I

125

had ever felt. And it was all the more unsettling for being unwarranted. Now, if it were Lew . . .

But that opened up a whole new line of speculation, one I wasn't ready to pursue.

I pointed my battered 2CV westwards toward Grasse, taking the sharp curves less than sedately, letting the wind blast through the side window and blow the tangled thoughts from my head.

Digging up the story of the flower strike might be even harder than unravelling my own emotions. But it would make a welcome change.

At the time I couldn't know how important it was, but that was the day I met Flairaud.

Flairaud wasn't his real name, of course. When the secretary of the syndicate introduced us, he called him something quite ordinary like Jacques Dubois. But nobody else did. To everyone in Grasse and in the perfume business, he was simply Flairaud. The nickname referred to his nose. As nearly as I could make out, it translated as Sniffy – *flair* meant the sense of smell, though in animals rather than humans. Anyway, it was a compliment. Flairaud was renowned far and wide for the discernment of his nose.

For such an important organ, it was surprisingly modest. It was not notably long or wide or sharp. It did have, perhaps, a tendency to quiver when it was working, or even when it scented an interesting topic of conversation. But otherwise it looked unremarkable, like Flairaud himself.

His *métier* was the creation of new scents, and he had few peers around Grasse or around the world. The secretary of the perfume makers' syndicate told me, as we drove from Grasse to Flairaud's place some eight kilometres away near Valbonne, that in the decade since Flairaud and his backers had set up their own perfume works, he had built the business into a major success story.

'And I never even heard the name,' I said, feeling very provincial and un-chic.

'No reason you should. You never heard of these either.' He reeled off a half dozen other names. 'And they're all top firms. But you'll recognise the labels on their products – Dior, Patou, Chanel, Hermès, St Laurent. The great fashion houses contribute the lustre of their names and the power of their merchandising networks. Which is what we lack. Without them, even our best would go for bargain prices. With them, we can command as much for a few drams as the Saudis do for a barrel of – here we are.'

He pulled off the winding asphalt road on to a gravelled driveway and was halted immediately by a heavy wrought-iron gate set into gateposts of native stone. At one side stood a sentry box of the same material. The gatekeeper obviously knew the syndicate secretary well, and we were passed through with minimal delay, but even so, I could see how elaborate the security measures were. The fence that ran off through stands of scrub pine to right and left was electrified, with floodlights topping each stanchion, and the gate itself was opened by remote control from the sentry box. Inside the box, banks of levers and buttons were visible through thick barred windows of, I guessed, bulletproof glass.

It all seemed more appropriate to the Pentagon, I said, than to a little perfume works.

'Oho, don't let Flairaud hear you say that! Or indeed, do, if you want your ear filled. Which I suppose you do.' The secretary drew up on a loop of gravelled drive in front of a meandering one-storey building. 'Flairaud's a born talker, as I told you, so he ought to be just the man for your purposes.'

By the time we were out of the car, a middle-aged man in a crisp white lab coat had come to meet us, thumping the secretary on the back and shaking my hand enthusiastically.

'Well done, Léon.' He was addressing the secretary but looking at me. 'I'm sure we'll get on just fine. You go on about your other business and don't worry about Mademoiselle Forestier. I shall personally drive her back to Grasse for lunch.'

'But, Flairaud,' the secretary began. Finally he said lamely, 'Only last week you told me that you never lunch.'

'*Au contraire*! I said I never go to business lunches. Eating is an occasion for pleasure alone.' He squeezed my hand again, more warmly.

The secretary made another feeble protest, then left with a backward look that underscored his reluctance to abandon me. I wasn't worried, though. Flairaud's line of flattery was practised to the point of total reflex. He clearly didn't mind, or even notice, when I steered the conversation to solid matters.

First I asked him to show me around, since I had never seen a perfume works. 'Unless you count the guided tours through the Fragonard place in Grasse,' I added.

Flairaud pointedly ignored that. 'We're not really typical here,' he said, 'because we do comparatively little routine processing. We're more a research lab than a factory. But then, it's hard to say just what is typical in the industry. There are so many parts, and they're sometimes parcelled out in odd ways. Well, come and see what we've got.'

Flairaud's domain was housed in a sprawl of single-storey buildings all faced in the same glowing golden stone. It appeared that an original rectangular structure had, like Topsy, just 'growed'. Wings and ells jutted off at random angles, and the roofs of the components were at various levels, broken here and there by skylights or ventilator housings – but everything was linked. As we passed through a glassed-in covered passage, I could see that the additions came together in the rear to enclose a paved courtyard.

'Your layout reminds me of the Wild West,' I said, 'when the whole wagon train drew up in a circle for protection against the Redskins.'

'It's not Redskins we have to worry about. At least, not so far as . . .' Flairaud fell silent, frowning.

'Pardon?'

'Nothing. You're right, though, about our preoccupation with security. You noticed the boundary fence?'

I nodded.

'That's new this last year. Back in the old days we just had a pensioner as night watchman in this building, armed with a

128

telephone and a flashlight and a tape-recording of sirens that he could turn on to scare away prowlers. The occasional teenage vandal was the only trouble we expected. Except, of course, theft from inside.'

'Theft?' I echoed. 'You mean of the finished perfume, or of the – well, the attars or essences or whatever those expensive ingredients are?'

'Of neither. Even then, our inventory control was tight enough. I mean of something that could be carried away and still not missed – the formulae. A senior employee who found himself needing money could be bought by the competition.'

'Sure. Like a defence-plant engineer who sells blueprints of weapons to the Russians.'

'In a way. Stealing commercial secrets isn't quite on a par with treason, but,' Flairaud smiled, 'around here it runs a close second.'

He led the way through a series of buildings, each with its specialised function. Some had ultra-tight-fitting doors with airlocks between. All had highly sophisticated control panels for air-conditioning. I soon saw why. Flowers were being separated from their fragrances by just about every method known to medieval alchemy or modern science, and the resulting atmosphere was, to put it mildly, dizzying.

Halfway around the compound we reached a room devoted to distillations. We stood in the middle surrounded by vessels and tubes and coils and tubs, endless concatenations of copper and glass. Flairaud offered explanations he thought were simple, while I struggled to retrieve my memories of high-school chemistry, five years old and fading fast.

I was about to plead for mercy when a birdlike little woman burst into the room, her hennaed hair flying in all directions and her words tumbling before her.

'*There* you are, I've been looking all over, you'll have to come and talk to him because I can't follow a *thing* he says, he just talks lawyer-talk and besides he called PCV but I didn't dare hang up in case he might be on *our* side though I don't suppose he is because that sort never are and I don't think I can *stand* one more *thing*!!'

Flairaud got her calmed down and pointed her back towards the main building, with me in determined pursuit.

From the way he talked to her, I gathered she was his wife and he had dealt with her hysterics before. Still, his face showed agitation and so did his pace. He hurried us along, asking terse questions. When we were almost at his office, he remembered my presence.

'Mademoiselle Forestier, this is my wife,' he mumbled. 'Cécile, you'll take care of her.'

About that he was wrong. And not just slightly, as with my name. For the next half hour I was very busy taking care of Cécile. Her nerves were in shreds. She needed a safety vent. A priest, a psychiatrist – even me.

So I listened.

The journalist in me thought that was fine. I propped my steno pad on my knee below the level of her desk, trying to be unobtrusive, and hoped the scratch of my pencil and the flipping of pages would not distract her from her recital of worries.

The fellow-creature in me responded to her distress. It was not hard to find sympathetic phrases to keep her talking, for I sincerely meant each 'How upsetting' and 'What a nasty shock' and 'You must feel so helpless.'

Cécile had plenty to worry about. One misfortune after another had beset their company in recent months, and production was seriously disrupted. At hazard was the good name of her husband's business, and even its survival.

To her credit, Cécile was not one whit concerned for herself. Flairaud's talents would always be in demand, and they would eat. But the damage to his pride and self-confidence might be irreparable. 'And our employees – we have over twenty people depending on us for their livelihood, and I can't sleep nights for thinking about them.'

'If the worst came to the worst, couldn't they find work with other firms too?'

'Some, yes, the ones with special skills, but even those . . .' She sighed. 'You see, the perfume industry has been here since the Middle Ages and it's very paternalistic. There's a lot of tradition and company loyalty and family cohesiveness. Our key employees knew, right at the beginning when they came in with my husband, that they were abandoning safe jobs. And I mean safe for a lifetime, in some cases even *inherited*.

'These men came because they had faith. They felt they'd be building a new tradition, creating a heritage for their sons just as we were. So if the business fails – '

'It won't,' I said with assumed conviction. 'This run of bad luck is bound to end soon.'

'But that's just it! When the luck was good, I wouldn't even acknowledge it. All those years of steady building and finally our backers getting a decent return. Right up through the party last summer. God, it seems impossible it was so few months ago!' Cécile was starting to get hysterical again.

'What party was that?' I prompted.

'Our tenth anniversary. We had a big dinner – all our employees and stockholders and best customers and people from the perfumers' syndicate. There were toasts and congratulations, and my husband got up and said we owed half our success to our team of workers and the rest to our lucky stars. I told him he was talking nonsense. I told him his own talent and good management and hard work got us where we were.'

'And I'm sure you were right.'

'So why is everything suddenly going wrong? It's like a punishment for my scoffing – only dozens of innocent people are being punished along with me. It can't be just random bad luck. It's the gods visiting retribution!'

Flairaud shared his wife's doubts, if not her conclusion.

'It can't be just random bad luck,' he said over lunch. 'There's some pattern behind it. It may be aimed at more than my company, more even than the perfume industry, but there's *something*.'

Flairaud had driven me from Valbonne into Grasse, leaving a calmer Cécile at the plant. She wouldn't come with us. She said she was on a diet, but she was so thin already that I wondered. Maybe she thought they couldn't afford it.

When we had ordered, the *plat du jour* for both, I got Flairaud to confirm what Cécile had told me in her tumbled way. Then I asked:

'What about your competitors? Have they had problems like yours?'

'I wouldn't really know. Of course we've all had the same labour problems – union organisers coming around and trying to stir up trouble. But that's not what you meant, is it?'

'I mean the deliberate attacks. Attempts at sabotage, supplies that don't arrive, hijacked shipments.'

'Well, I have heard a couple of rumours. Misfortunes that have happened to other perfumers, small ones like myself. But we'd hardly tell such things to each other, you know, let alone to the press. We can't risk undermining confidence in our firms.' Flairaud looked across at me. 'By the way, you do understand – '

'Absolutely. I won't ever use your name if it could reflect poorly on you. But I can't help wondering – '

' – just how unique my troubles are?' Flairaud spread his hands. 'If my colleagues are being as close-mouthed with me as I am with them, who knows how bad it might be? I hope you'll be able to tell me.'

'So do I. Luckily, your syndicate secretary seems willing to open doors.'

Flairaud grinned. 'That's not luck. He's had a connoisseur's eye for the ladies ever since we were in school together. That's why he referred you first to me.'

I might have said something acerbic if the waiter hadn't brought our *civet de porcelet* just then, giving me a chance to think twice. After all, there were plenty of times in a journalist's career when it didn't exactly help to be a girl. I should welcome the compensation when it came. So I sighed and said, 'Here, I thought my incisive reportorial skills were doing it, and all along it was just my long legs and blonde hair. How deflating!'

132

'You can go ahead and be incisive if you want; I won't mind.' Flairaud filled my glass from the wine carafe. 'For starters, tell me what you make of our rash of troubles.'

'Okay. What strikes me, mostly, is that whoever is causing them has a very exact knowledge of what goes on at your plant. Either he works there, or he gets his information from someone who does.'

'Precisely. But I have a score of employees. How do I find out which one?'

I thought for a minute. 'You don't.'

'No?'

'At least not by going around asking pointed questions yourself. Or by bringing in the police either. You'd just destroy the feeling of one big family that you've worked so hard to build up. No, you'll have to turn that part over to somebody else.'

Flairaud's grin was positively wolfish now. 'I'm so glad you feel that way. It did occur to me you'd be – '

'Hey hey now, whoa! I'd love to help and all that, but I've already got enough to do to fill a ten-day week. Maybe when I've finished with your colleagues and the flower growers about this strike nonsense.'

'I thought you were interested in *any* abnormalities in the perfume industry.'

I was, and I had to admit it. Inasmuch as the industry had perked along for ages without a cloud on the horizon, and then was suddenly hit with labour unrest, growers' strikes and a whole raft of other simultaneous woes, the betting was that they were not unrelated. Which Flairaud would have figured out for himself.

I decided to give in gracefully. 'Then what do we tell people at your plant?'

'They already know you're a journalist. You might be putting together a feature article. No reason you actually couldn't, for that matter. We can say I've given you *carte blanche* to poke around and ask questions. That'll do, won't it? People hate to be interrogated but they love to be interviewed.'

133

'True. And since I'm a girl and a foreigner, it won't matter if some of my questions sound a little dumb.'

'Your words, remember, not mine,' Flairaud said. 'When are you starting? This afternoon?'

I dropped my fork on the plate and just stared at him.

'Anything wrong?' He was trying to look innocent.

'Oh no. Nothing, really,' I said sweetly. 'Between now and sundown I only have to interview two growers, one in Mougins and the other in Pégomas, and a perfumer in Roquefort and two more here in town, and telephone my lawyer and the Consulate in Nice, and get gas and buy groceries and a new typewriter ribbon, and somehow manage to keep watch on a certain postbox from half past three until it's collected. I already decided to forget doing my hair. So by all means, please expect me.'

Flairaud sighed. 'Then when *can* you come?'

'Maybe after Christmas. Half days anyway.'

'Hmm. Well, you can't be in two places at once, can you? It would be nice if – ' He stared off into space for a minute, absently tugging at his ear. Then he said, 'Listen. I've got an idea.'

Flairaud's 'idea' turned out to be six feet tall, with gangling limbs, knobbly wrists and a voice that had not yet decided how deep it was going to be. The boy looked a good deal like his father. He tried to act like him too, and though he hadn't quite mastered it, the attempt was nice to watch. His son's name, Flairaud said, was Théophile.

'But everybody calls me Théo,' the boy said quickly.

'And I'm called Addie. I'm really glad we'll be working together, Théo.'

I wondered for a moment whether I was overdoing the generation equality, but Théo swallowed it whole. He might be a good half dozen years younger than I, but he held his own in height.

It was Flairaud's plan that, until school recommenced, Théo should be my assistant – 'apprentice' was the term he used to the boy, 'dogsbody' to me – to take over some of my tasks and leave me more time for the one closest to Flairaud's own heart.

I was all for it.

So was Théo. Obviously he would do anything to help his father. Though we both told him he would be no more than an errand boy, his eyes already held starry dreams of daring and glorious deeds. Equally obviously, he didn't mind that the reporter he would be working for was a girl. The long blonde hair and long legs were not lost on him. Théo was Flairaud's son through and through.

I was to remark the fact again often in the coming days. Now, as we exchanged a few words and set off, Théo on shopping errands and I to my next appointment, I knew only that I had acquired an assistant who seemed a nice, steady boy, and I was content.

At six fifteen I was back in St Martin, in Gran's house, in the shower, when the doorknocker rapped hard enough for me to hear over the thrumming water.

I was reviewing the afternoon's progress (a fair amount, all considered) and wondering what one wore to a small-town *vernissage*, while I sluiced the shampoo out of my hair. Thanks to Théo, there had been time for this one personal indulgence. There hadn't been a chance, though, to catch Mathilde before the evening rush at the Eagle's Nest. I would have to wait a while longer to find out how Monsieur le Curé had fared this morning in his quest for Madame Scotto. There hadn't been a chance to call Connie again before five, either, by which time she had left the Consulate but was not yet home. And now here was Jean-Marc, a full fifteen minutes ahead of schedule, damn him!

I shut the water, gave my hair a quick wring, stepped from the tiled stall, and reached with one hand for the towel rack and with the other for the bathroom door. In the direction of the main door I shouted in French: 'A small moment, please.'

The voice that called back was not Jean-Marc's. It was

135

female and American and bouncy. 'Addie honey, did I catch you in the shower? Take your time. I'm just glad I found you here.'

'Connie! Come on in, make yourself at home. I'll be right out.'

Connie took me at my word. By the time I emerged to join her, swathed in towels, she had broken out a tray of icecubes, poured herself a Coke, and was hauling a jar of peanuts from my un-unpacked bag of groceries.

'Nice place,' she said. 'I can see why this Scotto creep wants to steal it from you.'

'Can you?' I took the peanut jar from her, emptied it into an oval bowl carved out of local olivewood, and set it on the divider counter. 'Then would you kindly explain one thing to me? How come Scotto's idea of home improvement is to bring on the wrecker's ball?'

'It does seem a little perverse. But that's progress for you.'

Connie moved around the divider and perched on a stool within easy reach of the peanuts. I went to the armoire and studied my meagre wardrobe for inspiration. Hauling out an ankle-length flounced skirt, I said over my shoulder:

'What are you doing here anyway? You didn't say anything about coming up when I talked to you at lunchtime.'

'At lunchtime I didn't know I was going to need company so much. But then I got home and looked at those four walls and at the phone I knew wasn't going to ring, and I decided tonight was your turn to put up with me.' Connie rattled the icecubes in her glass. 'I guess it wasn't such a great idea, though. You look like you've got a date or something.'

'Just an or-something. Jean-Marc and I were going to the art show at the château. Have I told you about Jean-Marc?' Connie said I hadn't, so I did. 'He'll be enchan*té* to have you join the party – a blonde on one arm and a brunette on the other. Come to think of it, the way he was acting this morning, it may be a good thing to have you along. He can stand some defusing.'

Connie laughed. 'You don't want me, you want a bomb squad.'

'Yeah, but you're what I've got.'

'I'll do my best. I'm afraid I'm not dressed to kill, though.' Connie looked down ruefully at her staid grey suit, tailored to banish sex from the office. 'You have anything that'll fit me?'

'Possible. Feel free.'

Connie narrowed the choice to two rustic print skirts, knee-length on me but easily mid-calf for her. While I rummaged to produce gold earrings and a gold belt, adjustable, she took off her suit to try on the skirts. And that was the state we were in – Connie down to blouse and slip, me in my terrycloth ensemble of turban and sarong – at half past six.

Punctual to the minute, Jean-Marc walked through the door.

After the initial consternation, everybody behaved very well. Jean-Marc apologised and claimed he had knocked, which both of us accepted without contradicting him. I performed introductions as though we were all fully dressed. Connie, instead of clamping one skirt frantically in front of her, simply held both up and asked Jean-Marc which he liked better. And I, with dignity and a small prayer that my towels wouldn't slip, brought Jean-Marc a drink and the bowl of peanuts before retreating to the bathroom with an armload of clothes, while Connie graciously undertook to entertain my guest.

With all that, it was some time until I could ask Connie the question that was nibbling at me.

We were walking down the hill from the Eagle's Nest, leaving all three of our cars in the parking lot. Between the *vernissage* and the Christmas-week influx, parking would be hopeless in the village. It wasn't really very chilly, so Connie and I were comfortable in light shawls. Jean-Marc, looking like a sober businessman flanked by a pair of gypsies, held the powerful new flashlight I'd had Théo buy in the afternoon. Concentrating on choosing sound footing for us, he was mostly silent. So was I. Connie chattered in bright bursts.

'Connie,' I asked in a pause, 'what did you mean when you

137

said the phone wasn't going to ring? Did Washington give you a time to phone them instead?'

'Oh no, it's business as usual. You know, "don't call us, we'll call you." But this time I'm afraid they really mean it. We could be in for a longish wait. Like, days anyhow.'

Connie's voice sounded almost normal, but beneath her determined buoyancy I heard a tiny note of anxiety, and it summoned an answering surge in me. I fought it down. Surely if Connie had any real news, she'd have told me right away. There was no reason to worry, no new reason at least.

'You talked to Washington? When?'

'Right before closing time. Morning back home, of course. They'd just heard from our ambassador in Costa Rica. He's a very resourceful fellow. I told you, didn't I, how he collared a pilot at the San José airport to get his first message out yesterday?' Connie knew she had; she didn't wait for an answer. 'Well, now he's put together a relay of ham radio operators to someplace where the phones are working, so he can get messages in *and* out. The folks at Foggy Bottom had a long chat with him.'

'That's swell, but what about Jay?'

'I'm getting to that now. The ambassador said there were no American fatalities reported so far. All embassy personnel in San José were present or accounted for. The only exceptions were one family who were driving down the Pan-American Highway to spend Christmas with friends in Colón. And a junior political officer named Jason Forrester who was also known to be south of San José, presumably on foot, somewhere between the Caribbean and the Pacific Ocean.'

'*Connie!!*'

'Now, Addie honey, don't get upset.' Connie came running around behind Jean-Marc and caught my hand in her own. 'I'm sorry if I sounded flip. Honest, nothing's changed. We still just have to wait until he can let us know he's okay.'

'What do you mean, nothing's changed? Not only don't I know how he is, now I don't even know *where* he is. And you expect me not to get upset?'

On my other side, Jean-Marc pressed my hand where it

138

rested in the crook of his elbow. He could not have understood all of Connie's staccato English – I hardly did – but he knew how upset I was and why. He shifted the flashlight and put his arm around my shoulders. The beam wavered, then steadied.

'But they do know where he is, sort of,' Connie said. 'According to the neighbours, Jay and a friend from the *barrio* called Joaquín set off early Saturday morning. They were going as far as they could by bus, then this Joaquín was going to guide them up a mountain track to his native village. There was also something about scenic waterfalls and cloud forests and teeming trout streams.'

I stuck to the main point. 'So once they find out where this Joaquín comes from –'

' – they'll know where to look for Jay. Right. But he may be stuck up there for a while. A lot of the roads must have been cut.'

The note of worry was gone from Connie's voice. I was picturing a Costa Rica marred by landslides, gaping fissures, rivers torn from their banks, fallen bridges and smashed buildings. Connie was thinking only of the lush beauty up in the Cordillera. She sounded completely cheerful again as she said:

'Really, when you think about it, it's typical of him. The whole city of San José is desolated by an earthquake, and where's Jason Forrester? He's gone fishin'.'

Sabine was more sympathetic. When I asked the others to stop at the Gazagnaire house on the way down so I could talk to Sabine for a minute, the first thing she wanted to know was whether I'd had news of Jay. But as before, she refused to believe he could be in any danger. Instead of hearing more of her sanguine reassurances, I changed the subject.

Sabine listened thoughtfully while I outlined my theory about giving Madame Isnard an occasional outing.

'You're right. We've all got into the habit of thinking she's bedridden, but she doesn't have to be, not any more. Maybe if we made a little more effort, she would too.'

'That's the idea – do her good physically and mentally both.'

'Well, I'll talk it over with Serge when he gets home. If he ever does. Honestly, you'd think he'd have more sense than to stay down at the café swilling *pastis* with the boys, tonight of all nights.'

'Why so?'

'Because at dawn tomorrow our hero, Serge Lucien Philippe Gazagnaire, bashful champion of the downtrodden flower growers, is driving a ten-ton truck full of violets straight through to Paris. *That's* why.'

'Oh? I gather you're not happy about it.'

'Hmmph!'

It was not hard to agree with Sabine. She couldn't see any logic whatever in the growers' strike. Even Serge was going along with it less from conviction than from a vague urge toward democracy and solidarity. It would have made more sense if somebody who was spearheading the protest, somebody like their neighbour René the Red, had been taking the truck up to Paris. But naturally it was Serge who got elected, because he was capable and steady and everybody trusted him.

'I'll look in at the Commerce on my way past,' I promised Sabine.

At the bottom of the hill I steered Connie and Jean-Marc, without any noticeable difficulty, into the Café du Commerce. Behind the counter Jacky's wife shuttled between the espresso machine and the *tabac* section while Jacky poured drinks non-stop with flourishes worthy of a Toscanini. At this hour all the business was inside. Every table was filled, and customers stood three deep at the bar. One of them, as Sabine had predicted, was Serge. And in his hand, also as predicted, was a milky glass of *pastis*.

'It's only my second,' he protested when I murmured Sabine's message to him. 'Most of the last couple of hours I've been arranging about the truck. You see, I'm going up to Paris tomorrow with – '

'I know, Sabine told us. It's quite an undertaking. I wish I could be there with you to see it all.'

140

I heard myself with surprise, and realised I was thinking out loud.

There was no denying that Serge's trip would make a great story. Trekking almost the length of France with a supremely perishable cargo, emerging from the dead of night into all the arc-lit turmoil of the Rungis wholesale markets, braving the commercial world for the first time against Paris's most expert hagglers, perhaps facing resistance or outright hostility – and doing it all on behalf of the entire village of St Martin – it was tailor-made for a feature article. I could see a colour photo of Serge with his partly unloaded truckful of violets, splashed across the front page of *Nice-Matin*.

'Who's going up with you?' I asked.

'Pierre. My cousin, you know, the one who was helping with your roof yesterday.'

I remembered Pierre, a hulking fellow with a beer belly and a bull neck. The thought of him handling flats of dainty violets presented a beguiling contrast.

'I see. Too bad, I was hoping there might be room for me to hop a ride with you, sort of as historian of the expedition. But with Pierre in the cab, two's already a crowd.'

'That's for sure. He can barely get behind the wheel. On that long a trip we'd all be too cramped. Now, if you wanted a ride on the way back, we could offer you a whole empty truck.'

'What's all this about?' Connie asked, turning back from the bar where Jean-Marc was trying to get drinks for us. 'Are you thinking of covering the great violet-vending caper?'

'That's right.' I introduced her to Serge. 'Do you think I'm crazy?'

'Not about that. I think it's a super idea. All you have to do is figure out how to get there.'

'Get where?' Jean-Marc wanted to know. He handed Connie and me each a glass of white wine.

'Paris.'

'Paris? That's the easiest place in France to get to.'

'Sure, if you don't mind throwing thousand-franc notes at the airline people. But even if I knew I could sell the story, I'd

141

wind up out of pocket. And hitchhiking's awfully chancy. I'd probably get there too late.'

'Why don't you drive, then?' Serge said. 'It'd only be one-way. We could piggyback your car on the return leg.'

'You've got to be kidding, Serge. Have you seen my old rattletrap? It's held together with spit and string. I wouldn't take that crate on a superhighway on a bet.'

Connie laughed. 'Now I *know* you're not crazy. So it looks like we'll have to take mine.'

'Yours? We?'

'Sure. It's too gruelling a drive for one person to do alone. Besides, you wouldn't accept the loan of my car unless I came along too, would you?'

'Well – no, but – '

'Then don't try to talk me out of it. It sounds like loads of fun. That market must be a fabulous sight just before Christmas. Suckling pigs, fat geese and guinea hens and pheasants, chestnuts by the ton.'

'Don't you have an office to go to?'

'No sweat. I've got some time off coming to me. And now that the boss is back, we're not shorthanded.'

'What about your cat?'

'My neighbour can take Minette in. She has a key. Hey, don't you *want* me to come?'

'Of course I do.'

'Then it's settled. At dawn the team of Ortiz and Forrester hits the road. What do you call the feminine version of knights-errant?'

'God only knows,' I said. 'Footloose females? Loose ladies? Wayward women?'

Connie sighed dramatically. 'I can see that this partnership is going to take a little polishing.'

Between us we managed to reduce Jean-Marc's annoyance somewhat by the time we reached the château. His nose was clearly out of joint all the time Connie and I were conferring with Serge at the café. So while we made our phone calls –

Connie to her boss at the Consulate, to her neighbour about the cat, to her friend Vincent at *Nice-Matin* about submitting my story; me to my new sidekick Théo about a whole slew of things – we made sure that the one who wasn't on the phone was batting her eyelashes at Jean-Marc in rapt attention.

When I hung up from talking with Théo, I watched Connie deploying her charms, and Jean-Marc opening up to it like a morning glory to the sun. I wondered if handling all men was so easy.

Then I spent a moment wondering if men thought the same about us. They must have compiled their own folk wisdom, their own set of proven methods for managing us females. Which probably worked about as often.

On the way to the château we talked about art.

Jean-Marc said he knew nothing about modern art, and the more he saw, the less he wanted to know.

Connie said she'd always had an interest in painting, but nowadays so much assorted junk was thrown on to canvases that sometimes you had trouble finding any paint there at all. And when there was paint, that looked as if it had been thrown on too.

I said it sounded like we were all in agreement, but it didn't matter because at a *vernissage* hardly anybody ever looked at the art on exhibit anyway. All we had to do was make a quick tour, admire Rusty's sculptures and whatever else wasn't too awful, and then stand around looking cultured until we felt like leaving. At which point we could whip around to the Pompeii and get one of their famous half-metre Four Seasons pizzas, guaranteed to delight the eye of anyone, even us philistines.

As it happened, we almost didn't get into the art show.

The ancient iron-banded oak doors of the château were thrown wide for the occasion, and a score of lamps designed to simulate flambeaux burned in sconces that ringed the cavernous stone-walled entrance and swept grandly up the curving stone staircase.

I had started to sweep grandly up the staircase myself when the way was barred by a wide woman in a grey silk blouse and a rather faded black floor-length skirt. She wore her steel-grey hair straight, her glasses on a grosgrain ribbon around her neck and, even with evening clothes, aggressively sensible shoes. She evinced no charm as she asked to see my invitation – but having had one look at her, I didn't expect any.

I produced my engraved card and a smile, and said, 'This gentleman and lady are my guests. Monsieur Bertrand is with –'

'Mademoiselle,' the woman in grey said firmly, 'I regret, but our invitation is valid only as formally issued, that is, for yourself. Accompanying persons may in no way be included.'

'I appreciate your position perfectly, madame, but in this case I feel sure the committee will –'

'There can unfortunately be no exceptions. I am desolated.'

Patently she wasn't, so I said clearly in English, 'Oh, stuff it!' I snatched my invitation back from her hand, gestured to Connie and Jean-Marc to wait, and ran up the staircase into the Great Hall.

In the milling horde of art lovers, there were familiar faces here and there. But despite my height and his, I could see Rusty nowhere. I did spot his friend Camille, elegant in a blue-and-gold caftan, holding court in the centre of the Hall, but although she was the nominal chairman of the exhibit, somehow I didn't think in view of our single chilly encounter that she was the right one to appeal to. I pushed on. Two smaller rooms later I found Rusty.

He was leaning negligently on a largish piece of smoothly sculpted limestone, talking with an American of about his own age. I didn't know the man, but while I waited I had a chance to examine the sculpture, labelled '*Oread*, Russell Traynor'. It didn't remind me much of a wood nymph, but whatever it was, it had nice lines. Rusty's work might have echoes of Maillol or Moore but, at least to my untutored eye, it was more than just derivative. I was pleased to see he had real talent. Pleased and, for some odd reason, relieved.

Finally Rusty turned, saw me, grinned.

'Help! Can you come with me for just a minute, Rusty?

There's this gorgon in grey on the staircase who won't let my guests come up with me, and I promise you they're dis*gust*ingly presentable, not at all freeloaders, so you'll straighten it out, won't you?'

I didn't give him time to protest, but dragged him out to the Great Hall and down the staircase, and plunged into introductions.

'Rusty, I'd like you to meet my good friend Consuelo Ortiz, an officer at the United States Consulate in Nice. Connie, this is Russell Traynor, the sculptor I've been telling you about.' I couldn't remember whether I actually had, but Connie would back me up. 'And I think you already know Jean-Marc Bertrand, of the Secretariat of State for Tourism.'

Put that way, the credentials sounded nicely impressive, hardly the sort of people one would turn away. So Rusty did just what I thought he would. He gave his arm to Connie and a quelling look to the grey gorgon, and escorted us upstairs.

'The weird part about Alice,' he told us, 'is that she isn't even French. She's been here a long time, though. If you're not careful, the rigidity can get contagious.'

That irritated Jean-Marc, I could tell. So I quickly said: 'Don't mind Rusty, he's from the West Coast. No Frenchman, or even New Yorker, can approach that studied casualness he approvingly calls laid-back.'

Rusty laughed. 'That's right. Your average Frenchie will never understand "mellow". Still, look at the things Californians live for – good food, fine wines, kinky sex, nude beaches – all imported from France. We borrowed just about everything from here except surfing and rock music.'

'And in the end,' Connie said, 'those may not make the all-time list of major advances in civilisation.'

'Please?' Jean-Marc was out of his depth.

'Only joking,' I said in French. 'Since we've got this far, why don't we have a look at the stuff on the walls?'

It was a strangely assorted mixture, somehow suggesting in its jumbled arrangement the bulletin board of a kindergarten. Unlike most group shows, where the exhibitors were linked by a style or subject matter or philosophy, these artists

145

only happened to live in the same town. Perhaps the organisers had chosen wisely in distributing the small groups of works for maximum contrast. At least no artist could feel he was deliberately placed in competition with his neighbour.

Some were quite good, but none were easy to see, the crowd was so thick.

Jean-Marc and Connie stuck together, two strangers to St Martin, and I tried to stay close as I greeted acquaintances from years past. These were mostly people I had not run into since my return. Unlike the 'real' villagers whom I saw at their daily routines – shopkeepers, men tending violet fields, housewives shopping – these were the artists, artisans and retired expatriates who formed the 'other' St Martin. Whether they lived in converted farmhouses or modern villas in the surrounding hills, or in the stone houses of the Vieux Village itself, they remained distinct from the old families, even after decades. The two groups maintained a symbiotic relationship that was cordial, but though they mixed they did not meld.

That was why I was surprised to find René Cordier standing in the middle of the Great Hall. Of all the villagers, this Bolshevik neighbour of Serge and Sabine was the last person I would have placed at a *vernissage*. He was there, he said, because his brother's oldest girl had married an artist and taken up painting herself, and he didn't like to refuse. But he was painfully out of place wearing his best suit and holding a glass of champagne in the middle of a couple of hundred people who were involved in the creation, criticism, and collection of works of art which must, he could scarcely doubt, reflect the worst excesses of bourgeois decadence.

He didn't say any of this, though. We talked instead for a minute about Serge's trip, and I left him looking somewhat less distressed.

The one 'real' villager whom I hoped to see, Monsieur le Curé, wasn't there.

Lew was, though. He came up the staircase ten minutes after we did. When I waved and beckoned, he fought his way across the Hall.

'Glad to see you're out partying,' he said. 'Does that mean you've heard from your brother?'

'I wish it did. It's the other way around. I'm trying to keep busy so I don't sit worrying.'

'Good girl. Chin up and all that. Shall I get you a glass of champagne anyway?'

'No, thanks. Come over here, there's somebody I want you to meet.' I gestured to the corner where Connie and Jean-Marc were inventing bizarre meanings for a series of particularly impenetrable abstracts.

Lew didn't quite frown. He had already met Jean-Marc and, his expression suggested, he wasn't too keen on pursuing the acquaintance. But he looked happier when I said: 'Lew, allow me to present my guardian angel Consuelo Ortiz. Connie, this is Llewellyn Rhys-Owen.'

Connie took Lew's hand and gave him her broadest and brightest smile.

'So you're Lew! I'm just delighted to meet you. Addie's told me *so* much about you.'

I almost choked.

Next I considered throttling Connie. Lew was looking at me quizzically, and Jean-Marc was glaring at Lew in pure hostility. But perky little Connie stood in our midst radiating innocence.

I wondered. Had I really talked to Connie so much about Lew? Whatever I said, had it sparked an interest of her own in him? Or convinced her of mine? Or, another possibility, was Connie simply being mischievous?

Clearing the air didn't look easy. So I decided to muddy the waters.

'Let's go and see Rusty's sculptures,' I said. 'I just had a quick look at them, but I thought they were awfully good.'

This had the desired effect of shifting the subject and the locus, but it didn't change the personnel. All it did was add Rusty. Which recreated the situation at my roof-raising yesterday, three warily circling males, multiplied by the female presence of Connie, and before long Rusty's friend Camille, who seemed to drift past with increasing frequency.

147

Luckily, I found a chance to sidestep it all. The American I had seen with Rusty earlier turned out to be the *Trib*'s Jeremy Arlington, so for the next half hour I talked journalism exclusively with him and incurred the resentment of none of my three 'admirers'.

At the end of the half hour I noticed why. My admirers were all admiring Connie.

I was piqued, then philosophical. Camille was regarding my abandonment with feline satisfaction. I moved closer to her and said with a friendly smile, 'They're all alike, aren't they? Do you suppose it's the artistic temperament? They can't resist showing off.'

Camille gave a rueful half-laugh. 'They're little boys, every one of them. And it's our fault. We encourage them.'

'I suppose we do.' I decided to try for further progress. 'That's a gorgeous caftan you're wearing. Did you get it in Morocco?'

'No. Rusty gave it to me,' Camille said meaningly. 'He has a friend who imports things from North Africa.'

"It's perfectly lovely. Usually that much embroidery makes them a little stiff, but yours moves just like chiffon.'

Camille's smile was not reluctant now. We talked only a minute more, but I thought she was no longer wary of me.

The crowd was starting to thin out. Rusty pressed us to join the artists afterwards at Camille's for their private bash – sort of like a Broadway opening-night cast party. Jean-Marc would have liked to go, I thought. Lew was indifferent. But the invitation was really for Connie and me, and we pleaded that we had to get up at an ungodly hour, so we simply couldn't.

Afterwards, when we had trudged up the hill, full of pizza, and convinced Lew and Jean-Marc that we were serious about going to bed early, Connie and I sat up for a few minutes talking by the light of a single gas lamp.

First we settled who would sleep where. Or Connie did.

'No way,' she said firmly. 'Did I give up my own bed for you last night? The sleeping bag is mine, and I'm using it.'

So I gave her the cushions from the day bed for a mattress, and we tackled more fascinating topics.

'Rusty's interested,' Connie judged. 'You could cut out Camille if you wanted.'

'Maybe. But I'd hate to have to rely on his attention span. Wouldn't you?'

'The here-today-gone-tomorrow type, you mean?'

'Probably also the harem type,' I said. 'What did you think of Lew?'

'The opposite. The hermit type. I'm not sure he could live with a harem of even one.'

'Oh, Connie, he's not *that* ascetic!'

'Well, he lives alone with just those two dogs.'

'You live alone with one cat, don't you?'

'Not halfway up a mountain without even a road.'

'So struggling writers can't afford the beachfront. At least he's sure he owns it – which is more than I can say about this place.'

'But this is a real house.'

'Lew's is too, now. He's done all sorts of clever things to it. It's truly a charming little house.'

Connie laughed merrily. 'Listen to you defending him! I thought there was a budding *tendresse* there.'

'Why shouldn't I defend Lew? I like him. And you're not being fair. You make him sound like some sort of anchorite. Really, he doesn't live like St Simeon Stylites.'

'I hope not. Simeon lived on top of a pillar. Or maybe you had some other saint in mind?'

'Now what's that supposed to mean?'

'It means that, unless I've forgotten, you never mentioned Lew actually making a pass at you.'

'Well, no, but –'

'I thought so. What was the title of that play? *No Sex Please, We're British.*'

'Come on, Connie, that doesn't prove anything. Lew and I've known each other less than a week.'

'I'll bet it didn't take Jean-Marc that long.'

'Jean-Marc's different.'

149

'That's for sure. Jean-Marc's the one we're supposed to have the language barrier with, but I understood him a lot better than Lew. Jean-Marc's up-front about everything. In a funny way he reminds me of Jay. Jean-Marc's sort of – physical.'

'Yes. Yes, he is.' I reached across to the lamp and turned off the gas. 'Very physical.'

The chimney dimmed gradually to extinction.

'Pleasant dreams, Connie,' I said. 'Your choice.'

SEVEN

IT WAS still pitch dark outside when I suddenly awoke. At first I blamed it on sleeping in another strange bed, my fourth in a week. But it wasn't that – the bed felt fine; Jean-Marc was right about how comfortable it was – and it wasn't sleeping in this house either. I had been doing that off and on for twenty years.

Then I figured it was because I knew I had to get up early. But my travel alarm was on the table beside me, and normally I would have stayed fast asleep until the moment it buzzed.

Finally I recognised what had wakened me, as a roll of thunder passed low over the hills. I could hear the insistent drumming of rain on the roof, louder on Serge's corrugated plastic patch job than on the original tiles.

The weather, I thought, had picked a rotten time to change, but at least I would find out right away how sound the roof repair was. I wiggled into my slippers, found the flashlight beside them on the floor, and pointed it up toward the loft.

Beside me Connie stirred. 'Mmmph. 'Stime to get up already?'

'Not really. You can stay in that sack another fifteen minutes. I'll take my turn in the bathroom first and then make the coffee.'

'Good. Until I get my morning coffee I'm a grumpy bear.'

'I noticed yesterday. Actually, you have two minor imperfections I know of. The other is, you snore.'

'Snore? I do not!'

'Somebody did, as soon as the lights went out. It was all quite refined and ladylike, but it wasn't just heavy breathing.'

151

'Funny. My sister never said anything, and we shared a room for years.'

'Maybe it was the champagne. Never mind, I won't tell anybody.'

'If you mean Jay,' Connie said, 'he's welcome to find out for himself.' She didn't sound grumpy at all. Wistful, though.

By the time I got my teeth brushed and the kettle on, Connie had rolled up her sleeping bag and was doing a series of toe touches and deep knee bends. She claimed to be un-depressed by the weather. When I asked if she still wanted to drive to Paris, she simply flung her arms wide and sang, in fair imitation of Al Jolson, '. . . it isn't raining rain, you know, it's raining vi-o-lets. . . .'

'Very clever. But it *is* raining rain, you know.'

'Maybe not for long – and maybe not for far, either. The weather in the rest of France is totally separate from ours.'

'Swell. So we may hit snow instead. According to the calendar, today is officially winter.'

'Hey, who's a bear in the morning? Smile!'

The only thing Connie was grumpy about, in fact, was the coffee itself. 'Instant?' she said. 'Addie, I'm surprised at you. No, correction, I'm appalled.'

'You're right, I should be shot at dawn. Except that we have to leave before then.'

'Seriously. Real coffee doesn't take much time.'

'No, but it takes equipment. At college I had a percolator that was turned on automatically by my clock-radio. But you won't find the luxury of electricity here. You won't even find a beat-up enamel coffee pot like cowboys use on the range. Gran drank tea.'

Connie managed half her mug, and poured the rest down the sink. 'Oh well, there's bound to be a decent cup of coffee somewhere between here and Paris.'

It wasn't at the Café du Commerce. Jacky put in a punishing day, certainly, but he was not open at 5 a.m.

Plenty of people were on hand, though, to see the flower truck off to Paris. Serge's and Pierre's wives, of course – Pierre's wife almost as corpulent as he, and easily rounder than Sabine without the excuse of being pregnant. There were violet growers, probably every last one who had contributed to the truckload. And there were the merely curious. Rusty and Camille and the artist crowd showed up soon after we did. They must have partied all night.

The loading was in the final stages, and I broke out my equipment to record it.

The light was a problem and it was difficult to get a good angle, so I didn't so much photographing. Paris was the place for that. Mostly I recorded man-in-the-street comments and dictated my own observations – some of them, anyway. I didn't put into words my misgivings, but I couldn't dispel a sinking feeling that the whole operation was on the amateurish side.

The truck itself was typical. Serge said they hadn't been able to rent a refrigerated truck on such short notice. Even if they could, it would have been too expensive. And probably too complicated to run. So they would make do with what they had – an inelegant vehicle the body of which looked like an oversized packing crate, with hand lettering on the sides proclaiming its cargo to be poultry feed. Serge had rigged some guy ropes that he thought would hold the flats fairly steady. As for keeping the flowers fresh, if the day started to get warm, they could dump a couple of tubs of ice into the truck now and then.

Dear God, I thought, if they stayed this insouciant when they got to Rungis, the buyers would eat them alive! If they got there at all. By now I wondered whether Serge or Pierre had even bothered to find out just where the wholesale flower markets were.

Never mind – it was Christmas time and Connie and I were going to Paris.

I flagged Connie across the street, where she stood talking with Sabine and René Cordier, and indicated I was going to stow my equipment in the car preparatory to departure. She

153

joined me right away. The violet truck was ready to roll, and so were we.

By French standards, I suppose, we got away fairly promptly. Serge and Pierre were kissed by their wives; that took no time at all. Then the two drivers had their hands shaken by each of the assembled violet growers; that took longer, as the French treat handshaking seriously. Next Monsieur le Curé appeared and blessed the enterprise. And finally, drivers and growers alike were regaled by 'a few words' from the mayor of St Martin. This worthy functionary climbed on to the tailgate of the violet truck and, as he promised, spoke only briefly. He spoke briefly about the origins of violet-culture in St Martin, briefly about the medieval heyday of perfumery in Grasse, briefly about the glories of Napoleon . . . right up to a brief justification of the present protest. Then he wish God-speed to the two warriors who bore the colours of St Martin (presumably violet) into battle.

Connie wished aloud that the mayor had talked a little longer. As Serge pulled the truck out, and we followed, Jacky finally opened the doors of the Café du Commerce and began dispensing coffee to everyone remaining in St-Martin-sur-Loup.

The rain had slackened during the mayor's valedictory, but it picked up again as we headed south to the coast and the autoroute. By the time we passed through the toll booths at Antibes, Connie had to switch the wipers up to high.

'That's the trouble with a subtropical winter,' she said. 'It never gets terribly cold, but it can get bone-soaking wet. This may sound odd coming from a Portorriqueña, but I was just a kid when we moved up to Ohio, and I learned to love a crisp white winter. Well, I suppose you do too.'

'I used to.'

Connie gave me a puzzled look. I knew my answer sounded curt, but I had to stare out of the window for a while before I could say more.

'It was in the middle of a blizzard, you see, when my

154

parents were killed in a car crash.' I told Connie what I knew about it, the other car skidding into theirs, knocking it off the icy bridge to plunge into the ravine. 'The guy had no business being out on a night like that without chains, without even snow tyres. But it was my parents who wound up dead. The stupid bastard who killed them got off with a broken wrist.'

Connie said nothing, but she made her sympathy felt. She seemed unexpectedly affected, in fact, until I realised she was thinking of the victims not as her new friend's parents, but as Jay's – as the couple who might even, had things gone differently, have become her in-laws.

I stared for a time at the wiper blades pushing aside endless sheets of water.

To stop brooding, I spent the next few minutes putting my equipment in order. First the tape-recorder needed attention. The cassette I had naïvely thought would carry us through arrival at Rungis was over half full with the parting remarks of the mayor of St Martin. My thumb almost punched the rewind button. Then I decided the speech was so pure an example of gas-filled Gallic officialese that it merited preservation. When we got home I would give it a proper hearing, and maybe even present it to the mayor – unless, of course, I ran short of tape in the meantime. So I filled in the label lightly in pencil and stuck a fresh reel in the machine.

Next I verified that there was most of a roll of film in the Hasselblad. If I had foreseen this trip to Paris, I would never have given Théo my Canon yesterday afternoon. That was the camera Dad said was ideal for news work, and always kept with him. So I kept it with me too, as a sort of ritual, ever since I inherited it – until impulse made me loan it to Théo.

With luck, though, Théo would make better use of it than I could. The Hasselblad was adequate for anything but the most rapid action shots. For portraiture and for the sort of landscape work I envisioned to go with my travel pieces, it was superb. At that price, it had better be. Even Dad could never have bought such a camera without a particularly generous gift from Gran who, one Christmas, had 'a bit more than usual left over'.

155

Top of the line it might be, but today I would have traded it for the Canon's handiness. I moved the focal length and shutter speed to middling settings. Habit only. There would be no need for the camera until we got to Rungis and plenty of time to set it up properly then. And that wouldn't be for another twelve or thirteen hours.

When we left the pitching-coins-into-hoppers stretch of the autoroute and stopped to collect our tickets for the Estérel section, the violet truck was just ahead of us in line. Pierre, taking advantage of the limited shelter, ran around the cab and climbed up to take Serge's place at the wheel. Connie followed the truck into position beside the ticket booth and said, 'Good idea. You may as well get your baptism of fire now. Slide over.'

She shoved the driver's seat all the way back on its runners, ducked out of the car, and reappeared on the passenger side with ticket in hand. Rather than let her stand there getting wet, I moved over obediently.

'Now then. The doohinkus for the seat adjustment is over there by your left foot. That's it. And the knob for the rake of the backrest is on this side. Comfortable? Let's go.'

'Wait a sec. What about the shift pattern?'

'Shift pattern? You put that selector thingie on D and drive. Like, the right pedal makes it go and the left pedal makes it stop. It's as easy as – instant coffee.'

I scowled. 'Connie, I *know* how to brew coffee. And I've driven a few cars, too, from my own dinky 2CV to a shiny red five-speed Ferrari. But I just don't happen to have driven any of these jumbo pushbutton non-cars.'

'No kidding? You never drove an automatic?'

'Nope.'

'Try it, you'll like it.'

I tried it, with an open mind. I couldn't say I liked it. There was an annoying lag in the engine's response to the accelerator. And the gear changes without warning were disconcerting. When Connie asked my reaction, I said it felt

156

as if I wasn't driving the car, it was driving me. 'But then,' I added, 'I don't like baking cakes from mixes either – and don't start again about the coffee!'

When we pulled within sight of the violet truck, I eased off the gas. It was agreed that unless we wanted to make an unscheduled stop, the truck would lead. In spite of the foul weather we were being passed by plenty of vehicles, cars and trucks both, as Pierre held to the moderate pace set by Serge.

I was watching the rest of the traffic, when my attention was yanked back by the sudden blaze of the violet truck's brake lights.

As Pierre braked, the truck slewed into the adjacent lane, almost sideswiping a passing car.

Pierre fought for control, getting off his brakes until he had the truck back in the slow lane. Then the rear of the truck lit up again, the red bank of lights flashing on and off, on and off, as Pierre tapped the brakes to grip the rain-slick pavement. Gradually he eased the truck on to the shoulder.

It took me longer to slow Connie's car. I wasn't sure how far to trust the Pontiac's brakes, and there was no manual transmission to put drag on the engine. So when I finally got us stopped on the shoulder, I had to back several hundred yards to the truck.

Serge was already out, standing by the right rear wheels, and Pierre was clambering down.

Connie stuck her umbrella through the open car door, raised it, and dashed back to join them. I did the same, pausing only to get my tape-recorder.

'I don't know,' Pierre was saying. 'We were going along just fine, no trouble whatsoever, and then all of a sudden there was this terrific screeching sound coming from the back of the truck. It sounded like – I can't describe it.'

Serge nodded. 'It sounded like metal scraping. Or like you'd jammed on the brakes, only you hadn't.'

'That's right. I was just driving.'

'We saw the truck skid into the other lane,' Connie said. 'Did that happen at the same time?'

157

Pierre shook his head. 'It's hard to remember, it was all so fast. For the first couple of seconds I couldn't do anything, with the noise coming like that. Then I hit the brakes and I think that's when we skidded. Maybe it was just because I hit the brakes so hard.'

'Or maybe,' Serge said, 'it came from whatever caused the noise. Some fault in the brakes, or in something else. What about the steering?'

Pierre thought. 'Apart from the skid, you mean? It seemed okay. Even when I was braking, afterwards. In fact, the brakes *and* the steering worked okay, as soon as I got over the first shock. But for a while there, the noise scared the hell out of me.'

'Did it keep up until you managed to stop the truck?' I asked.

'No, it didn't last that long. It seemed to get better as we slowed down. Wouldn't you say, Serge?'

'That's right. The lower you brought the speed, the less strident the noise was – kind of like an alarm clock running down. It stopped altogether when we were doing maybe forty, thirty-five.'

We all stood in the rain, staring blankly at each other and trying to make some sense of it. Connie and I were mere girls, but we probably had as much knowledge of automotive engineering as the violet farmers Serge and Pierre did – namely nil.

'Well, we can't just stand here,' I said. 'You set some warning markers back along the highway, and we'll call a mechanic from the next phone box. This truck have any flares or anything?'

Serge looked at Pierre. 'Probably, but we didn't think to ask.'

Connie said there was an emergency triangle in the boot of her car. I offered to get it; I could get my camera at the same time.

When I returned to the truck, the Hasselblad was strapped around my neck and nestled into my trenchcoat next to the tape-recorder, making me look only slightly more busty than

Mae West. As I walked I tried, umbrella clamped under arm, to unfold the luminous red triangle, but it was stiff and I was glad to hand it over to Connie.

Behind the violet truck, another vehicle had pulled up in my absence, a delivery van with no legend painted on the side. A small dark man in a black raincoat stood listening as Serge and Pierre repeated their account of the incident.

'. . . and when we got down to about 40 kph, the noise stopped,' Serge said.

'Could you tell exactly where it came from?' the dark man wanted to know.

Serge and Pierre compared impressions, and agreed it was the right rear corner.

'And you say it sounded like metal scraping? I wonder – wheel-bearings maybe.'

The dark man abruptly sat on the pavement and swung himself under the truck, apparently heedless of the mud. Twice he hitched himself further in along the axle. Then he slid out and stood, shaking his head.

'Sorry. Couldn't smell anything. Of course, with all this rain and wind, it'd dissipate fast.' The man gave a short laugh. 'Couldn't smell anything *wrong*, I mean. Whole truck smells like a flower garden. What you got in there anyway?'

'Violets,' Serge said.

'Yeah, I knew it had to be something like that. Jesus, you can't waste any time, then, can you? Somebody phoned for the breakdown service yet?'

Connie answered. 'We were about to go.'

'No need to bother, miss. I'll stop at the next call box. I just wish there was more I could do. Well, best of luck to you fellows.'

Our good Samaritan shook hands with the drivers and headed for his van. I trudged behind him carrying Connie's warning triangle, and continued a further thirty yards. By the time I had the triangle propped up on the shoulder, the van's motor had coughed and caught.

I hunched under my umbrella and set the focal length on

the Hasselblad for a long shot of the stranded violet truck. I didn't spare a thought for the aperture setting – the light had stayed at the same dismal level for the last hour and I didn't need a light meter to tell me so. I peered down into the finder and waited until the van pulled away.

One frame was enough, I decided – either the breakdown would prove minor, or it would kill the whole trip to Paris, and the story with it.

Anchoring the triangle with a stone from the roadside, I slogged back toward the truck. Wind-borne snatches of conversation drifted to me.

'. . . already about as wet as I'll ever . . .'

'. . . next rest stop, maybe we can use those hot-air hand-dryers to . . .'

'. . . what you like, but I'm waiting in the cab.'

'Too bad we didn't bring a thermos of hot . . .'

The world exploded then. A blast of air tore the umbrella from my grip and slammed me flat on the pavement. A wave of sound engulfed me, drowning the smaller sounds of wind and rain, expanding into a roar of impossible power.

A moment later I could distinguish one more sound, a cry of agony.

And then there was only a silent black void.

The rain on my face was already reviving me when I felt hands lifting my shoulders, cradling my head.

'*Etes-vous blessée, mademoiselle?*' a voice asked. Are you hurt, miss?

A second voice, sharper: 'Put her down, for God's sake! Don't move any of them. That's the first thing you're taught.'

And other voices.

'Don't look, Catherine. Just get back in the car. Drive up to the next phone post and call for the gendarmerie. Tell them to send an ambulance – no, two. Then wait there for me.'

'Quick, darling, bring our blanket from the back seat. Anybody else have blankets?'

160

'I saw it happen, I'm telling you, from half a kilometre back. It just blew up. Must have been the fuel tank.'

'Careful, don't get too close. There may be fumes.'

'Jesus Christ, did you ever see so many violets?'

'Hey, you there. Go back a way and try to do something with the traffic. Slow them down and move them to the outside lane. We've got enough casualties already.'

'We'll need flashlights to wave. Round up some flashlights.'

'My God, what a lot of blood!'

'Look here, there's another one under the violets! Help me shift these crates, quick!'

'Is she alive?'

'I don't know. I can't find a pulse.'

I fainted again.

The oscillating wail of sirens brought me fully back to consciousness, but I did not try to sit up. My ears told me as much as my eyes would have.

A Greek chorus of onlookers directed the ambulance crews to the casualties. Then the gendarmes chased the onlookers off the scene. The order boomed out, amplified, for everyone not a victim or close witness of the accident to leave immediately.

The blanket that covered me was peeled back and fingers were laid against my wrist and throat.

'I'm alive,' I whispered.

Two men bent over me, one in white and one in blue. The one in white said, 'Easy now. Tell me where you hurt.'

'I don't . . . feel too bad . . . little dizzy, maybe. Don't bother about me yet. Go and take care of the others, huh? Please?'

The medic pulled back my eyelids.

He nodded. 'This one's yours, officer. Keep her as warm and dry as you can. Don't grill her too hard. And call me if and when.'

The man in blue sat beside me on the pavement of the shoulder of the autoroute, sheltering both our heads under one large black umbrella. He was a big man, and his voice was deep and rough, but still he spoke gently.

'Do you feel you can answer a question or two?'

'Please, officer, tell me – the others, how bad – ?'

'Yes, well, that's the first thing I want to know, whether anybody's missing. Just who was here at the time of the accident?'

'The two drivers of the truck, and me and another American girl who were in the Pontiac.'

'That's something. At least nobody's buried in the wreckage. One of the men's pretty badly hurt, but as far as I know they're all alive.'

I closed my eyes and said a short but fervent prayer.

'Now then, about the accident, miss. How did it happen?'

'It wasn't an accident.'

'Pardon?'

'It – wasn't – an – accident,' I repeated. 'I don't know what it was, probably you have explosives experts who can tell you, but that truck didn't blow up by itself. It had help.'

The gendarme whistled. 'Sabotage? But nobody'd blow up a truck full of violets.'

'Obviously somebody would. Somebody did.'

'As you say. So underneath that innocent-looking load of violets there must have – '

'Listen!' I struggled up on to one elbow. 'Serge is an honest flower grower, with three children and a pregnant wife, and he's as nice a person as you'd ever hope to meet. Pierre's okay too. And they may be bleeding to death while you – '

'Gently, gently.' The gendarme forced me to lie back. 'You suggested sabotage. So something more than violets must be involved, no?'

'Sure. But you've got it backwards.'

'I don't have it any way at all yet,' the gendarme said patiently. 'I'll be glad to listen, though, if – '

A shriek, practically on top of us, swallowed his voice. The siren gained in force even as it became more distant, then gradually fell and receded.

162

'The first ambulance, taking the two men,' he told me. 'And now it's your turn.'

'Me? I don't need any – '

'Yes you do,' he said firmly.

Equally firmly two men in white positioned a stretcher on the pavement beside me and lifted me on to it.

'Hey!' I said weakly, clutching my bosom. 'Be careful. These things are my livelihood.'

The three men stared. One of the medics giggled nervously. Then the gendarme understood and reached for the straps around my neck. 'Here, let me check.'

He drew the Hasselblad out from the protection of my raincoat and examined it with respect. 'Quite a camera you have there. You're a photographer?'

'I'm a journalist.'

'Aha!' he said, as if that explained a lot. Maybe it did.

He pointed the Hasselblad in the general direction of the truck and tripped the shutter. Then he advanced the film and did it again. 'Your camera's fared pretty well. Cracked lens, that's all. Now for a look at the tape-recorder.'

The gendarme began pushing buttons. 'Rewinds all right. Let's try playing it.' The recorder whined up to speed, then emitted voices, none very distinct. A few phrases came through. '. . . anybody called the police yet? . . . should be here any minute . . . revolving lights coming now . . .' The tape clicked off.

'*Formidable!* Right up to our arrival. When does the reel start?'

It took me a minute to remember. 'As soon as Pierre pulled off the road. The truck was making an odd noise, so they stopped to see what it was.'

'And you got it all on tape – what a piece of luck for us.'

The gendarme popped open the little window to extract the cassette. I reached up and shut it again. 'Sorry. The tapes and films stay with me. You can have them later, but first I have to file my story.'

'Hmm. Where do you have to file?'

'With *Nice-Matin*.' Then I added, purely on hope, 'And the

163

International Herald-Tribune. Both are morning papers, so I have a little leeway, but not much.'

'If I came with you in the ambulance – '

'Absolutely not,' said the medic beside us. His partner had returned to their vehicle.

'I don't need any ambulance,' I said.

'Don't you want to be with your friend?'

Connie! I still didn't know how badly injured she was – of course I must go with her. As the medic and the gendarme brought my stretcher to the ambulance, I made myself think. Then I groped for the pocket of my trenchcoat.

'Maybe we can collaborate,' I told the gendarme. 'Here are the keys to my friend's car. As soon as you get things under control here, could you follow us to the hospital? By then, with any luck, I'll be discharged. You can drive me into Nice. You'll hear the background and the tape on the way, while I put my story together. That way, we'll both save time.'

'Fair enough.' The gendarme pocketed the keys. 'What name shall I ask for?'

'Forrester. Anne Forrester.'

It wasn't, I thought, an occasion for nicknames. But the gendarme seemed to think it appropriate for the whole French introduction ritual, or at least a shortened version suitable for minor disasters. He declared he was enchanted, he bowed over my hand (and the rest of me), and he produced with a flourish a card reading *Marcellin Morin, Adjudant-chef de Gendarmerie.*

I was boosted into the ambulance. I turned to the other stretcher and saw the medic bending over the still and silent form of Connie.

An hour later I was sitting beside her hospital bed in Brignoles. 'It's okay, really, Addie honey,' she said. 'You don't get a chance like this every day. Of course you have to go and file your story.'

'Still, I feel rotten leaving you alone.'

'If you stayed you'd just be bored too. God, what a drag! Twenty-four hours flat on my back. It isn't fair. I don't feel any worse than you do. We were both knocked out, that's all.'

'Sure, but you were out a little longer. Like, over half an hour. It's only natural they want to keep you under observation.'

'I know. And I didn't have anything else to do today – except go to Paris.' Connie sighed. 'Look, if you get time while you're in Nice, could you phone my boss and my pussy-cat?'

'Will do.' I reached for my bag and jotted down the numbers. 'Maybe at the Consulate they'll have heard from Jay.'

'I hope so. It's beginning to look like you Forresters have a magnetic attraction for crises. Earthquake, explosion – what are you going to come up with next?'

'Eviction, probably. That reminds me, I have to talk to Robert Mercier, or at least keep trying. Why didn't you tell me your lawyer friend never works during normal office hours?'

Connie laughed. 'Addie honey, didn't you know? That's the Mediterranean way. It's during office hours that nobody works. Outside of office hours, nobody's even *there*.'

I snapped my address book shut, dropped it in my bag, and took out brush and mirror. The brush confirmed what I already knew: the back of my head was swollen and tender. And the mirror confirmed that it didn't show under all that hair. In fact, I looked perfectly unmarked until I unbuttoned my shirt to examine the bruises made by the camera and tape-recorder as they slammed against me. Even this soon my upper chest was turning a mottled purple.

'Gross! Here, let me have that.' Connie reached for the mirror. She twisted to scrutinise the backs of her legs. 'Ouch!'

'Will you for pity's sake lie still? At least until the results of the X-rays come back.'

'The X-rays won't show anything – except that I've got a screw loose for voluntarily attending an explosion. But who'd ever expect to get clobbered by a bunch of violets?'

'Several bunches. With wooden boxes around them.'

'Lord, I'm going to be black and blue all over. I won't be able to wear a skirt for weeks.'

'So wear pants. One lucky thing, the bikini season's over.'

Adjudant-chef Marcellin Morin arrived as promised and got me sprung from the Brignoles emergency ward in about two minutes flat. He also got me the progress report that no amount of my patient persuasion would obtain. 'The Gendarmerie Nationale,' he told the admitting clerk sternly, 'wishes to know the condition of the accident victims Serge Gazagnaire and Pierre Pla.'

The admitting clerk scurried off and, fairly immediately, scurried back.

'Monsieur Pla has suffered a fractured pelvis and a number of broken ribs, one of which pierced the pleural cavity. The surgeons have been obliged to collapse the left lung. Further internal injuries, as yet undetermined, may have been incurred. Monsieur Gazagnaire has multiple fractures of both legs. He is now in surgery.'

I felt a rush of relief.

It might be mean of me, but when I heard Adjudant-chef Morin say one of the men was badly hurt, I desperately hoped it was not Serge. Not that I would wish ill on Pierre – but Serge was the one I knew, had known for twenty years, looked on almost as a cousin.

'Have their families been told? I asked.

'Mesdames Gazagnaire and Pla have been notified and are at this time *en route* to Brignoles.'

'Thanks,' said Adjudant-chef Morin. 'We'll be hitting the road ourselves.'

Marcellin Morin drove fast, too fast by any standards.

True, the rain had stopped, but he wasn't used to handling Connie's car, and probably he wasn't used to conducting

166

an investigation while at the wheel. But he didn't show any more prudence than I expected. Instead he drove like a cop.

There wasn't any point in worrying about it. I wasn't meant to die today, I figured, since the best opportunity had already been missed. If the choice was getting to Nice sooner or later, I'd take sooner.

Despite the rate we were clipping along at, we had the most pressing part of our business accomplished when we were still ten minutes west of Nice. I gave Marcellin Morin a thumbnail background of the perfumers-vs.-flower growers dispute. Then we listened to my tape with a few pauses for elaboration. Then I put a fresh cassette into the machine and began to dictate.

'*An enterprising journey by a pair of Provençal flower growers came to a near fatal end this morning on the rainswept Autoroute de l'Estérel as their truck full of violets, apparently the target of deliberate sabotage, was ripped by a savage explosion. . . .*'

Some fifty metres of tape later I rewound and played it through, changing a phrase here and there. The prose was a little purple, maybe, but that was intentional. *Nice-Matin* might prefer a more florid style than my father would have permitted. And at any paper, the rewrite people had their blue pencils poised. If they weren't given enough adjectives to cut, they might start axing the facts. So I told the story without repetitions, but I told it whole.

On the second replay I went more slowly, stopping every sentence or two to translate aloud into French.

This was partly for the benefit of Marcellin Morin – some points got clarified before he had to ask about them. But it worked the other way too, with the gendarme confirming or correcting my description of the post-explosion scene I had not so much seen as heard. And trying out my story on Morin gave me practice telling it in French, as I would have to do at *Nice-Matin*.

In fact, it was with the translating that Adjudant-chef Morin was most helpful, right from the time I said: '. . . *route mouillée* – no, what's a word that sounds wetter than that?'

'*Trempé, noyé*. Or you could say *les pistes pluvieuses*, that's a nice phrase.'

It was. Under the policeman's uniform beat the heart of a poet, or at any rate of a literate Frenchman. I took his advice on a number of stylistic points. We went along smoothly until I read: '. . . *secretary of the Syndicate of Perfumers, reached by telephone in Grasse, expressed his shock and outrage. He hoped that the regrettable climate of ill-feeling between his members and the flower growers would not be unjustly exacerbated, but that both parties would instead see the tragedy as an omen of the need to reconcile their differences.*'

Marcellin Morin whistled. 'When did he say that? Did you phone him from the hospital in Brignoles?'

'No. I'll call him from Nice.'

'You haven't even talked to him yet and you're quoting him?'

'I know the guy. I won't have to change five words, you'll see. Besides, if he doesn't say something conciliatory like that, I'll wring it out of him.'

'*That*'s reporting?' The gendarme dropped both hands from the wheel and turned to face me. Luckily it was a dead-straight stretch of road.

'I'd say so. By the way,' I said mildly, 'this car isn't totally automatic. It needs to be steered.'

Morin put his hands back on the wheel.

'You see, I believe there's more to a responsible press than mere accuracy. I could dig up all sorts of inflammatory comments, perfectly authentic, for the sake of a colourful story. But I know every flower grower in Provence reads *Nice-Matin*. If one of them got the wrong idea about who blew up that truck, and decided to retaliate tomorrow by blowing up a perfume factory, that would be my fault.'

'I suppose it might, if you put it that way. I'm all for crime prevention myself,' Marcellin Morin said. 'Then you don't think the perfumers could have had anything to do with it?'

'Of course not! Not as a group, anyway. They and the growers are in the same boat, watching their business go to hell. Something's causing it, but so far I can't find anybody who remembers exactly when and how it began.'

'Keep working on it. Maybe we'll meet in the middle.' The gendarme thought for a minute. 'What about those wholesalers who normally buy the violets?'

'As suspects? You tell me. Even if they knew about Serge and Pierre going to Paris, they could spike their sales attempts right at the market. They wouldn't have to blow up the truck.'

'Then who did do it?'

'Who knows?'

I resumed playing and translating my taped story. '*A police spokesman* – you don't mind being a police spokesman, do you, Adjudant-chef? – *said authorities were reluctant at this initial stage to place excessive credence in accusations against parties with conflicting interests, but would explore exhaustively all possibilities, from genuine accident to personal grudge. An expert team of investigators has been assigned to the case and early results are confidently expected.* How's that?'

Marcellin Morin threw back his head and guffawed. 'Perfect! It's bombastic, it's bureaucratic, and it doesn't say one damned thing. Where'd you pick that up?'

I shrugged modestly. 'It's the kind of thing police say in America, mostly. Don't they in France?'

'Naturally we do, all the time. Particularly when we haven't got a clue.'

Adjudant-chef Morin started remedying that the moment we got to *Nice-Matin*.

The building that housed the paper was inoffensively modern, a bronze-tinted glass and metal box sitting securely inside its metal fence in a new industrial zone beside the river. The sentry box was modern too, but the motorised gate through which we passed was apparently of white-painted wooden planks. It looked charmingly incongruous, a gate standing alone without its white picket fence, like a jump at a horse show.

We were waved right through, as Connie's contact Vincent had left word to expect us. That was a call I *had* made from the hospital in Brignoles.

Vincent seemed quite nice – he showed sincere concern about Connie, and even remembered to ask whether I'd heard from my brother – and he seemed efficient too. But neither Vincent nor his colleagues fell over themselves to get my story. They were too busy keeping up with the demands of Adjudant-chef Morin.

'Would you get this film processed on the double? And remember, two prints of each frame. . . .

'Would you get these tapes reproduced? Originals to me, copies to Mademoiselle Forrester. No legal value in voice prints, of course, but maybe for identification. . . .

'Would you get me a free desk and an outside telephone line?'

The gendarme's last request sounded like a good idea, so I asked for the same. All local calls, I promised, except to Grasse. I didn't promise they'd all be official calls, since nobody raised the question.

First I tried to get Jeremy Arlington, but he wasn't in. Neither was Robert Mercier, which at the moment bothered me less. So I started on the official calls after all.

I reached the secretary of the Perfumers' Syndicate, whose comments on the explosion were just what I'd predicted.

Next I phoned the mayor of St Martin, who said absolutely nothing, interminably.

René Cordier said plenty, but it was almost all, alas, unprintable. He vividly evoked the depravity of anyone who would commit such an attack. When he had also decried the concerted victimisation of the proletariat and linked the bombing to all the evils of the capitalist system, he got down to local news. He was stuck at home, he said, fixing lunch for his own brood while his wife Lucie was next door tending Sabine Gazagnaire's babies. It should have been Lili doing the babysitting, but as soon as Lili was told her brother Serge had been injured, she erupted into hysterics – something Sabine had not done – and was calmed only with difficulty.

170

Madame Isnard managed it in the end (a nicely ironic touch, I thought) and Lili stayed with her as before. Sabine and the wife of Pierre Pla had set out for Brignoles, perhaps had already reached the hospital, with Monsieur le Curé as chauffeur. Rene did not have to say what he thought of that arrangement; his anticlerical bias was built into his voice. He did relay what his fellow growers were saying, and it was uniformly ugly. Everything in the whole perfume and flower business stank.

I could not reach the wholesale flower mogul whose firm usually bought St Martin's violets. His assistant, in fluting tones, told me they had not received news of the mishap, but could frankly *not* be surprised if greenhorns who would even con*ceive* of transporting flowers by ordinary *truck* should come to. . . .

At that point I hung up.

Wanting to talk to somebody nicer, I called Connie's pussy-cat. The neighbour said Minette, though intermittently moping, was eating normally. Since the cat wasn't seriously distressed, Connie shouldn't be either. This cat's-eye view of the world left me a good deal refreshed.

At the Consulate the switchboard put me through to the Consul himself. He had a toned-down Midwestern voice, friendly but not blustery. It was friendly, at least, until I told him our trip had been cut short and Connie was now in the Brignoles hospital. This news provoked him to wonder aloud whether an involvement with the Forrester family was in the best interests of Miss Ortiz. I promised not to let her join in any more of my 'escapades'.

That brought me to my last call, to my *ad hoc* assistant, Flairaud's son Théo.

'Addie, hey, I'm glad you called. What's up? Did you think of something else I can do for you while you're in Paris?'

'No, not a thing. I just wanted to tell you I'm home sooner than we planned. Our expedition ran into some opposition.'

'Yeah? Like what?'

'Like sabotage. Somebody blew up the truck.' I heard Théo give a low whistle. 'It's a long story – which I'm in the

171

process of filing right now. You can read all about it in *Nice-Matin* tomorrow.'

'You didn't get hurt, did you?'

'No, I'm fine.' I thought about those who were lying in the hospital in Brignoles, but let the subject pass. 'What was it you wanted to talk to me about?'

'I was just thinking – when I go back to the post office today, I might stand a better chance of getting a line on that guy if I had another person working with me. Would it be okay if I got a friend to come and help me? I'd swear him to secrecy, of course.'

The youthful earnestness coming over the wire made me smile. 'You're the one who knows Grasse, Théo, do whatever you think best. When you want to report to me, call the number I gave you and tell Lili. But how you carry out a given assignment is up to you. By all means, use your own judgment.'

I meant only to inspire in Théo a little self-confidence. If I had dreamed how literally he would take what I said, I would have – no, on thinking back, I have to admit I wouldn't retract a single word.

The film came back from the photo lab, with the specified two sets of prints. Adjudant-chef Morin grabbed one. Vincent grabbed the other. Unless I wanted to squint through the strip of film, I was left to look over somebody's shoulder. Vincent was less burly, so I chose him.

'Superb, superb,' he said as he ranged the prints on his desk in a single row. Only half a dozen frames had been exposed – three in St Martin during the loading of the violets, one of the truck sitting at the side of the autoroute in the rain, and the pair that Adjudant-chef Morin had snapped when he was testing my camera for damage.

'Superb,' Vincent repeated. 'Before, during and after, it's all there. Of course, the last two are crooked and badly composed, they'll have to be cropped, but you did well to get them at all.'

I didn't contradict him. I just stared at the last two frames with their testament of awful, incongruous carnage. The back end of the truck largely blasted away, my friends lying injured and bloody among the débris – and over it all a soft mantle of tiny velvety violets.

'Superb,' Vincent said again. 'We'll print the whole series. Even that jagged streak across the last two frames is no problem. We'll just say in the caption that the lens was broken in the explosion. We'll turn it into a plus. Right, Addie?'

'Right,' I echoed dully.

'Wrong.' This was from Marcellin Morin. He reached between Vincent and me and with a flick of his thumbnail knocked the fourth photo out of the line. 'That one you can't print.'

'Okay,' Vincent said equably. 'It's the dullest one anyhow, just the truck sitting beside the highway, so we can do without it. But why?'

'If it was just of the truck, you could use it.'

I picked up the photo. 'You think it shows the van clearly enough to do you any good? He's already pulled out into the near lane and passed the truck. You can't even make out most of the licence plate.'

'But enough, maybe. Even a couple of digits are a big help.'

Vincent took the print from my hand. 'This van you're talking about, is that the guy who went to phone for a mechanic?'

The gendarme and I looked at each other.

'That's what my story, as filed, says he did,' I said. 'But the full version goes like this: he stopped and offered to help, he crawled under the truck to have a look, he drove away, and a few minutes later the truck blew up. Wouldn't *you* be suspicious?'

'Mmm. But how come the truck stopped in the first place?'

'That,' said the gendarme, 'is a very fine question. And the first person I'd like to ask is the driver of that van.'

'You mean if you could trace the van,' I asked, 'you'd pull in the owner?'

'What else?'

Morin's question was rhetorical, but that didn't stop me from answering it.

'Anything else. Tail him, tap his phone, trace his movements before and after the crime. Best of all, find out who he's working for – whether you can prove it in court or not.'

The gendarme sounded offended. 'Need I say we'd do all that before we arrested him? That's why you mustn't print that photo. We don't want him to think we have any clues.'

'But that's exactly why we *should* print it. Chances are, he was sharp enough to notice I had a camera. If we print an innocent picture with an innocent story, that just might make him think he's home free. Then he'll act normally instead of lying low.'

'If he thinks that photo is innocent, he's not as sharp as –'

Vincent shouted. 'I see it! An air-brush, no?'

I smiled.

'It'll be easy.' Vincent turned to the Adjudant-chef and explained eagerly. 'We can retouch the photo to obscure the licence plate, make it look like it was lost in a cloud of exhaust when the van drove off. It already was, halfway. We'll just finish the job.'

Morin was full of approval. He beamed most of it toward Vincent, but I didn't mind. I just wanted to be on my way, now that the story was filed. I asked Morin to give me back the keys to Connie's car.

'Soon,' he said. 'As soon as you drive me downtown to departmental headquarters and make a formal statement.'

'Come *on*! I already told you everything I know about the case – which is practically everything you know, too. And you already passed it all on to your superiors, I heard you.'

'Regulations.'

'Besides, there won't be anybody much there. At this hour the whole country's out to lunch. Which is where I plan to go. I'm starving.'

174

That, it seemed, touched Marcellin Morin on a sympathetic nerve. He was a big man who evidently enjoyed eating, and when I said I felt like more than a quick hamburger, he didn't argue. He just drove straight into Nice, parked (illegally, of course) alongside the port, and led me to a restaurant festooned with nets and dried starfish. It looked moderate to expensive, but since I had just sold my first French story I didn't care, if Morin didn't. Maybe when he travelled on duty he got a per diem. Or maybe, like cops in America, he knew where to go for a meal on the arm.

The proprietor rushed up and led us to a window table overlooking the port. 'Too long since we've seen you, Adjudant-chef. Always a pleasure. And with such a lovely companion.'

'Strictly business, Bruno.'

Actually, it was quite a cordial lunch. Marcellin Morin told me about his family, about life in a gendarmerie caserne, about his wife's feud with the major's wife next door. I told him about my family, about Gran's house, about my problems with the landgrabbing neighbour. We got to the Marcellin-and-Addie stage. We talked a lot about St Martin and the people who lived there – or I did. In fact, the meal was almost over before it hit me that I had done a good eighty per cent of the talking.

'I don't believe you, Marcellin! For the last hour you've actually interrogated me, at my own expense, and made me like it. You're amazing.'

Marcellin stirred sugar into his coffee. 'You thought reporters had a monopoly on those tactics? We can be disarming ourselves. And this is a lot more pleasant than dragging you to headquarters and firing questions.'

'Granted.'

'Also it was your own idea.'

'Also granted.' I scraped hopefully at the crust of the brie on my plate, but it was empty. 'So what do you need to know that you haven't already pried out of me?'

'Nothing, probably. I've heard about yourself and the

victims and their village, enough for background. You're a good observer, Addie, and very open. A policeman learns that everybody has something he wants to hide. But you seem quite forthright.'

I shrugged in embarrassment. 'I'm American. We're notorious for spilling our life story to total strangers.'

We drank our coffee. I stared out the window at the port, pretending an interest in a large vessel berthed just opposite us.

'She's a car ferry, the *Comté de Nice*,' Marcellin said. 'There are lots of crossings in summer time, from here and Toulon and Marseilles. Then they drop off, but they pick up again around now. Not for tourists so much, but for the Corsicans going home for the holidays.'

'Corsicans?'

'They're very clannish. They may come to the mainland to grub a living, as half of them do, but they go back for the important things. They're married there, and their children are born there, and they die there. With luck.'

'Small wonder. You call them "them", and so does every mainlander I've heard. They'll never be real Frenchmen.'

'It's their own doing. If you knew them, you'd understand.'

'Maybe. I only know one, my charming neighbour Scotto, and he's enough to turn me against the whole tribe.' I thought a few sour thoughts. 'Tell me, Marcellin, what percentage of Corsicans become honest policemen?'

He laughed. 'Let's say there are crooks who aren't Corsican, and Corsicans who aren't crooks, but the reputation came from somewhere. I take it you've heard of the Union Corse.'

'Are they really as bad as the Mafia are in Sicily?'

'I wouldn't know, but they're bad enough. Here in Nice and all down the coast, particularly in Marseilles. They run everything. Drugs, gambling, prostitution, protection rackets, car theft rings, smuggling, counterfeiting, you name it. And it's a rare day when one of them is put behind bars. They fight a lot among themselves, and kill each other off regularly. That helps.'

'Hmm.' I frowned. 'Are they into labour racketeering, the way the mobs are in the States?'

'I don't know anything about organised crime in America, except what's in the movies. Why do you ask?'

'Just a vague idea.'

It was vague enough. On the one end it went: Scotto, Corsican, automatic suspect. On the other end it went: bombing of violet truck, strife in perfume industry, Grasse. The only link was the post office box which Scotto, or Régine, had rented. Scotto might have any number of interests, legal or otherwise, centred in Grasse and requiring a message drop. But again, there might be more of a connection than just my wishful thinking.

I didn't tell any of this to Marcellin. I would have had to explain how I knew about the post office box and I wasn't quite up to that. He gave me credit for more forthrightness than I possessed just now.

When the bill came I tucked a hundred-franc note under the saucer and went to find a phone. This time Jeremy Arlington was in, so on our way to headquarters Marcellin and I made a slight detour to afford the *International Herald-Tribune* an opportunity to print my deathless prose.

When we got to gendarmerie headquarters, Marcellin abandoned me for another bout of telephoning. He talked at length with colleagues in Brignoles and, at least twice, in Toulon. Meanwhile I dictated my recollections of the morning's events to an ageing and bored clerk-typist. I had read through the typescript and signed it when Marcellin reappeared.

'I just called the hospital in Brignoles and talked to your friend Connie. She said she couldn't remember the numbers on the van's plate, but she's pretty sure the letters were SB.'

'Then we've got the whole last half, if we accept my impression that it was a local plate. Local for here, ending in 06, I mean, not local for Brignoles. What would that be?'

'Département of the Var, 83.'

177

'No. No, that wasn't it, I'm sure. Did you happen to find out how Connie's X-rays turned out?'

'All clear, no broken bones or anything. If her head feels normal between now and tomorrow morning, they'll let her go.'

'Super. What about the others?'

'Well – of course, you understand, they were much closer to the blast.' Marcellin seemed to be having trouble choosing his words. 'I gathered from what you told me, Addie, that you were quite fond of Serge?'

'Dear God, he isn't – ?'

'No, no. He's alive. But he was in surgery for rather a long time. Over four hours. The doctors think they've succeeded in saving his left leg.'

I looked at Marcellin Morin and waited for him to go on.

'There was nothing they could do for the right one. It's gone.'

Telling Lili was perhaps the hardest part of a hard day.

When I climbed the steps to Madame Isnard's house, I found the girl reading to her great-aunt, the old woman drowsing among her cushions. Her head lifted, though, when she heard me enter, and she greeted me with a firm voice. It didn't surprise me, then, that Madame Isnard took the news better. She turned even whiter than usual, but she said nothing. Lili gave a howl of anguish followed by a storm of sobs.

I had tried to break it gently and I was ready with words of comfort, all I could dream up during the forty-minute drive from Nice, but nothing I said could staunch the flow of lamentations.

Madame Isnard was the one who knew what to do. Already today she had seen Lili in hysterics. She gave the wailing a few minutes to spend its initial force, then she spoke to the girl sternly and without a trace of pity.

'Lili, take hold of yourself! You're carrying on as if your brother were dead. That's really quite enough. It might have been his life instead of a leg. You should get down on your own two perfectly good knees and thank God.'

The girl emitted one final feeble wail and subsided. She crept into the old woman's arms and laid her head on the blanket-swathed chest.

'I'm sorry, Tante Irène. But I love him so much.'

'Yes, darling, I know. Love is like that. We often have to pay in pain for the joy. But we'd be poor creatures if we refused the bargain, wouldn't we?'

Lili didn't answer, but lay quietly as her great-aunt's trembling hand moved to smooth her hair.

Irène Isnard, frail as she was, impressed me then as never before. A year ago on this date she had been making happy plans with Lucien at their hotel for the last Christmas they would know together. Now she wasted no tears on herself but worked to comfort Lili. As if to reinforce my thought, she lifted her eyes above the girl's dark head and looked across at me in the gathering dusk.

'It's been a bad week for brothers, hasn't it?' she said. 'Have you heard from Jay?'

'No, madame, but I'm trying not to worry.'

She nodded slightly. 'Don't you think, now that you're grown-up, you might call me Irène? It would please me if you pretended we were equals.'

I started to say the pretence was a stiff order, as she and my grandmother set a standard my generation wasn't likely to measure up to, but at that point the phone rang.

Lili jumped, dashed to the table by the hall door, and caught it on the second ring. Perhaps she thought it was young Marchetti, perhaps news from the hospital. Whatever her hopes, they were speedily dashed, and her voice fell to disappointment barely tempered by politeness.

'Hello? . . . yes, this is Lili . . . she's right here, would you like to speak with her? . . . no, it's quite easy to find . . . at the west end of town you take the Route de la Chapelle straight up to the inn called le Nid de l'Aigle and turn into the parking lot. We're just above. I'll leave the lights on over the steps . . . yes, I'll tell her to expect you.'

179

What stranger could be calling on Madame Isnard? Someone Lili didn't consider refusing. The police? But why? There was little time to wonder before Lili said:

'Addie, that was a boy called Théo who says he's your apprentice. What on earth does he mean by that? Anyway, he wants to see you and he'll be here, he says, in half an hour.'

That gave me an odd feeling which it took a minute to figure out. All my life my comings and goings had been regulated for the convenience of parents, teachers, camp counsellors, piano instructors, tennis coaches, professors. And when I was working, I did what any reporter does – go out after the story. But Théo was coming to see *me*, without questioning that this was the proper order of things. It was a tiny milestone.

On the way home I dropped into the Eagle's Nest to catch a word with Mathilde. She was rushed off her feet, she said, with no extra help for the holidays. I wound up trussing half a dozen chickens, but learned only that Monsieur le Curé had beat a quick retreat after our incursion yesterday morning and Mathilde hadn't seen him since. Whether he had in fact reached Madame Scotto, I would have to ask him myself.

Régine was behind the desk when I went back through the main hall. We traded barbed cordialities as usual.

In a flash of intuition I sensed that Régine's hostility was assumed, because her position with Scotto demanded it. But she played her rôle so well that the flash soon faded and my combativeness took over again.

Now I asked whether the inn was full yet for Christmas. Régine professed regret that they couldn't squeeze in one more table for Christmas dinner, much as she would like to have me join them. I said I would postpone the pleasure, as Mathilde cooked better when she was not overextended. My own guests would relax in my home over a traditional American Yuletide feast.

That part was pure invention, at least until Jean-Marc came in and overheard it. He slid an arm possessively around my waist.

'Baby, are you all right? Ever since I heard about the accident, I've been frantic. All they said on the radio was "four injured", so I knew it had to include you and Connie, but they didn't say how bad.'

'You heard it on the radio?'

'Sure. I mean, I heard about it first in a café in Grasse at noon, but after that I listened to the news every chance I got. Jesus, what a thing!'

Of all the thoughts I might have had then, the one that pushed foremost was not very noble. It was professional jealousy. My reportage in *Nice-Matin* would be unique, but with radio and television breaking the story first, it would be stale news. 'Not fair,' I said.

'Damn right it's not fair,' Jean-Marc agreed. 'Those two men had no business taking violets to Paris. They ought to have stayed at home growing them, instead of letting themselves be pawns in somebody else's power play. Your friend Serge, now, he didn't seem like the crusading type at all.'

'He's not. He only went because the others asked him, because they trusted him. And now –' I slumped suddenly in the circle of Jean-Marc's arm and buried my head against his shoulder ' – now he's had one leg amputated, and he may lose the other.'

'Jesus, what a thing,' Jean-Marc said again. 'And his wife, that was his wife there on Sunday, wasn't it, that pregnant girl with the sweet face?'

My voice was muffled by the fabric of Jean-Marc's suit. 'Yes. His wife's pregnant, and his children are just babies, and he's not even thirty yet, and he's crippled for life.'

Jean-Marc sighed. He said in a quiet voice, 'Régine, cognac.' He relaxed the arm that held me, lifted my chin until it came level, smiled encouragement, and turned me back toward the counter.

Régine was just turning too, a pair of snifters in her hands. She raised her eyes only enough to place the glasses squarely on the counter, then lowered them again. I wasn't seeing too accurately at that point, so I could have imagined it, but I thought I saw the glint of moisture on her lashes.

181

It was gone by the time Jean-Marc coaxed me into drinking my cognac and downed his own. Régine stood impassively behind the counter, her voice steady as she said what a shame it was. But there was an elusive expression in her eyes that might have been part regret. Something else, too. Fear?

'That's better,' Jean-Marc said heartily. 'Now that we've had our medicine, what about a real drink? I want to talk to you anyway, Addie.'

'Sorry, can't now.' I pushed back my cuff to look at my watch. 'I've got an appointment with somebody who should be arriving any minute. Business,' I added, to mollify Jean-Marc. That worked, but when I saw the fleeting spark of interest in Régine, I wondered whether it might have been wiser to let both of them think I just had a date.

'I'll walk you as far as –'

Régine gave a shout, almost a shriek. Before we could see why, she ducked out from behind the counter and ran towards the tower corridor.

Approaching her, on legs that were shaky but determined, was a gaunt female figure. She wore carpet slippers and a sloppily belted robe, but her face was gaudily made up and her hair, a reddish bramble thicket, was adorned if not contained by a gilt hoop that she had stuck in at the angle of a tiara.

'Régine, this cannot go on,' she said in a voice that was also shaky but determined. 'I must have clothes, proper clothes. He is right, I must make a beginning, or my life will never –'

'*Patrice!*' Régine was beside the apparition, taking her arm. 'Please be calm. You know what the doctor says about excitement.'

'The doctor!' The apparition laughed. It was a high silvery laugh, not the cackle or croak that witches are supposed to give. 'The doctor never listens. But God listens. Just today he told me . . . or was it yesterday . . . it's so hard to keep track. . . .'

I didn't wait for her to say more. Heaven knew what sort of disjointed interview Monsieur le Curé had with this weird

182

woman yesterday, but if I could, I wanted to stop her giving even a fragmented and fantasised account to Régine.

I dashed after the two women and took hold of the witch's other arm. Behind me I heard the footsteps of Jean-Marc. I looked into Régine's astonished face and quickly said, 'Let me help. I've had some experience.'

Régine didn't argue with me, or with Jean-Marc when he caught up. She directed all her persuasiveness at the witch, urging her to be good and return to her room. The witch was stubborn, though. She dug in her heels and insisted she was doing as God had told her.

'I must try . . . more every day . . . if I ask God, He will send me the strength. . . .'

She did not have the strength, however, to resist all three of us. Jean-Marc steered her steadily along the corridor, while Régine kept up a flow of little words of approval, as one might to a child or perhaps a dog. I held the witch's hand and said vaguely comforting things about trusting in God.

She turned and peered intently at my face. 'Who are you? Did God send you to help me?'

'He sends us all to help each other,' I said.

I was spared hearing any more of my own profundity. We reached the private quarters and Régine headed her charge through an open doorway. I had a glimpse of a frilly feminine room in considerable disarray, with tumbled bedclothes and a strewn floor. Régine dismissed us with a brief 'thank you, I can manage now', and Jean-Marc and I were left to stare at the closed door. We shrugged and went back to the main hall.

'Well now,' he said, 'that was entertaining. Not too enlightening, though. What do you make of our innkeeper's lady?'

'Patrice Scotto is markedly undernourished,' I pronounced.

'You're implying they starve her? That might account for the delusions. Where'd she get the idea God was broadcasting on her private frequency?'

'God knows.'

'Don't be funny. I think you do know. You fell in with the

183

whole charade without missing a beat. Have you been talking to Régine?'

'Don't *you* be funny.'

'Then how come?'

I considered. 'You're right, I wasn't all that surprised. I guess I assumed she'd seen the priest.'

'Priest?'

'He was up here yesterday visiting Madame Isnard. I talked to him in the parking lot and Madame Scotto could have seen him standing there. Maybe he even passed close to her window. Poor woman, if she's shut up alone all the time, no wonder it made her think she'd had a visitation.'

'Could be.' Jean-Marc frowned.

I picked up my bag from the counter. 'I really have to go now, Jean-Marc. But thanks for the moral support.'

'I've been supporting your *morals*? I must be losing my mind! Come on, I'll walk you home.'

At Gran's house – my house, I reminded myself – there was no sign of Théo, so I had no excuse to send Jean-Marc packing. He told me he wouldn't mind a beer, then went straight to the hearth and began laying a fire. As I watched him, I thought back to the night – was it less than a week ago? – when I had come home to find Lew lounging here before a roaring blaze, his dogs at his feet. When Jean-Marc got the fire going, would he sit in the overstuffed chair that was 'Lew's'? The thought made me somehow uncomfortable.

Instead he reclined like a patrician Roman on the day bed with its new mattress that was 'mine'. That made me feel uncomfortable too, in a different way. When he spoke, though, Jean-Marc didn't sound amorous; he sounded hurt.

'If you're having a Christmas dinner for all your friends, how come I'm not invited?'

'Aren't you going home? I thought your whole family was in Lyon.'

'It's too long a trip to be worth it. I'd have to start at dawn to make the midday banquet. And after my mother'd stuffed me full, it would be downright suicidal to drive back.'

'You only get the one day off?'

184

'My bosses are bureaucrats. They're not sentimental.'

'Then they're not Provençal either. You must be assigned out of Paris. Down here nobody even pretends to work for the last two weeks of December.' I paused. 'Of course, from what I've seen, it may be the same the other eleven months.'

Jean-Marc smiled. 'You're learning, baby.'

'Anyway, don't be insulted. I'd have invited you to my Christmas party if I happened to be giving one.'

'You said you were.'

'Only to Régine. Do I have to tell the truth to *her*?'

'What are your plans then?'

'Nothing much. Connie may be coming up if she feels okay. Frankly, I'm not in the mood for celebrating right now.'

'All the more reason. You shouldn't let yourself get beaten down. So what do you say, are you having a Christmas party after all? I'll bring the turkey.'

'No deal. I don't have the time to –'

'What else would you be doing Christmas morning?'

'Sleeping.'

'Cooking,' Jean-Marc said flatly. 'This is my first chance for a "traditional American Yuletide feast". I'll even do the shopping. You can't get a better deal than that.'

'If somebody else did the cooking, I could.'

'Ha! At least you're bargaining.' He reached for his suit jacket and pulled out a memo pad. 'Now then. Turkey – chestnuts – onions?'

'No, I have enough. Potatoes, please, sweet and white both. Apples. Parsley, sage. A package of that square sliced bread in Cellophane.'

'*Pain de mie?* But that's –'

' – dreadful stuff. I know. But since it's stale to start with, it's fine for the dressing. Chestnuts, yes. Walnuts, too. Cranberry sauce if you can find it. Grapes, they're in season, aren't they? Maybe a kiwi fruit if it's not over five francs.'

'Addie! Let me worry about the money, just this once.'

He took my wrist and pulled me down beside him on the day bed. My attempts to escape were expertly countered, and I wound up securely held with his face two inches from mine.

185

'You know what's the matter with you, baby? You're too independent by half. A little spunk in a woman is fine, but a man likes to feel like a man.'

'Does he have to act like a caveman to prove – '

Jean-Marc ended my protest by kissing me forcefully. I didn't struggle much, or at least it turned into something similar but nicer. After a while Jean-Marc let me catch my breath.

'I don't . . . know what you were . . . talking about,' I gasped. 'You certainly feel like a man to *me*.'

Jean-Marc set out to underscore the point when a loud knock came at the door. I untangled myself and straightened my clothes while he reached for his jacket in resignation. He walked with me to the door.

'I'll bring the groceries tomorrow at six. See whether you can't contrive to be alone for once, huh?'

I didn't answer. I wasn't sure I could. My hand was unsteady as I drew the latch to admit Théo.

'Sorry I'm late, Addie, I ran into – oh, excuse me!'

'That's all right, I was just going,' Jean-Marc told him. He turned to me with a lifted eyebrow. 'Business?'

I smiled and found my voice. 'What else? Don't you think I've had enough excitement for one day?'

There turned out to be more. Mercifully, several hours intervened.

Théo came into the house diffidently, holding a zippered canvas bag in one hand and a crash helmet in the other. He put them on the counter of the kitchen divider after a bit of hesitation, but he had more trouble deciding where to put himself. I steered him to the overstuffed chair and settled myself in Gran's rocker.

'You came all the way on your moto?'

'It's not so far. Cold out there, though. May go down to freezing tonight.'

'Oh, super! That's just what the violet growers need.'

Théo shrugged. 'Makes extra work, that's all. If they

186

spread plastic covers, the flowers are okay. It's the growers who freeze.'

'What about you? Are you okay?'

'I'm fine. That's a great fire you've got. It's made your face all red.'

I looked up sharply, but if Théo connected my flushed face with Jean-Marc, he didn't show it. Perhaps he was what he seemed, an old-fashioned innocent kid.

He was a sharp kid, that much was apparent as soon as he started telling me what he'd been up to.

' – if two were better than one, I figured, then a dozen would be better still. So I called a hasty meeting of my club.'

'What club is that?'

'Silver Strikers Football Club.' Théo frowned. 'To be honest, we don't win too often on the soccer field. But we have a lot of fun. We go camping together and enter gymkhanas and throw parties, you know. They're a good bunch of guys.'

'I don't doubt it. But what did you tell them? Surely not the truth.'

What I meant was, it would be unwise to share our purpose with so many others. Théo had a different slant.

'Heck, no, the truth wouldn't have kept them interested for ten minutes. I added a couple of embellishments. I said you were on the trail of a big Union Corse gangster who, for mysterious reasons, was behind the flower growers' holdout, and you wanted us to track the movements of his henchmen.'

I made a strangled sound which Théo took for approval. He went on.

'We had to do it ourselves, I told them, because there was a real chance of police corruption. Unless we got conclusive evidence and went straight to the magistrate, the police might tip off the mob, and we could find ourselves in hot water.'

I coughed. This was an angle I hadn't remotely considered. I decided Théo had a brilliant future as a scriptwriter of lurid television dramas.

187

'So I told them,' he concluded, 'we had to be omniscient, omnipresent and invisible.'

'Very sound in principle. How do you plan to be all those things?'

'Invisible's no problem. Who notices a gang of teenagers on bikes? Ditto for the omnipresent. We peel off from the pack when we need to, and join up again when we can.'

'And omniscient?'

'Yeah, I get to play God, of course, since it's my project. But everybody else has the fun parts, really. All I do is sit by the phone and keep track of things, starting tomorrow. The others get to play with their cameras and recorders and walkie-talkies and so on. I'd rather be with them in the field, to tell the truth.'

I had to try extra hard not to choke just then. Poor Théo, in his fifteenth year, already weighed down by the burdens of command! Still, it was a command he had assumed on my behalf, and it wouldn't hurt me to say he had done well.

He shrugged off my praise. 'We'll know in a few days whether we're wasting our time or not. By then we should be getting better at it. It'll be easier to report to you, too, when you're spending more of the day in Grasse.'

'Is that a hint?'

'Well, Dad did wonder whether your plans – '

I laughed. 'I thought so. Tell your father that as soon as Christmas is over, I'm his. Half days anyway.'

Théo reddened. He wasn't, I realised, totally innocent. He was just at that awkward age when everything was still theoretical – when the whole language was charged with *double entendres*, but a fellow didn't dare do anything beyond thinking about it.

'You didn't come all this way just for that, Théo. A phone call's a lot less trouble than an eighteen-kilometre bike ride.'

'Sure. But I thought you'd want these.'

Théo got up and fetched his zippered bag. First he handed me my Canon, the camera I'd wished I had this morning. 'There's still a full roll. I didn't have a chance to use it yesterday, as I told you. And today I got Dad's Nikon. Same with

188

the other guys. They have their own cameras, or their sister's or somebody's. Lots of other stuff too. One guy, his father's a doctor, he called a medical supply place and we're getting a dozen beepers in the morning. When you have a bunch of guys pooling ideas, it's amazing what you come up with.'

It amazed me, for one. I might be a child of the twentieth century, but Théo was born for the twenty-first.

'So when Charles turned up with a Polaroid, I stationed him with me for the first shot. He got two, actually, but this one's clearer. Does it tell you anything?'

The photo he handed me was shot from a distance, but the figure outside the Grasse post office was fully identifiable. It was the hulking creature Scotto employed, according to Jean-Marc, as a 'chauffeur', meaning bodyguard. He was also a mail collector, yesterday.

'Just the man I expected to see.' I tried to sound approving, not disappointed.

'But you'd rather know who was on the mailing end, right?'

'Naturally. I'd like to know what they're writing too.'

'Now *that* I can't promise.'

'You can't promise either one, as far as I can see.'

Théo waved a hand. 'I'll give it some thought.'

'For heaven's sake, be careful. The most important thing is not to get caught.' I stowed the Canon in my camera bag, and started to put away the Polaroid photo as well. Then I handed it back to Théo. 'Keep this. You'll want all your records together, I'm sure. I can consult them in Grasse, the same as the others.'

He returned the photo to his satchel and picked up his crash helmet. 'Phone me from Dad's place on Friday, okay? I'll try not to bother you before then. Merry Christmas!'

Belatedly I remembered the demands of hospitality. 'Théo, you're not leaving already! You've come all the way from Grasse, and you must have missed dinner at home. The least you can let me do is feed you.'

He protested, but I insisted.

'Besides, I need your help on the other project. I'd like you

189

to brief me as fully as you can on your father's plant – operations and personnel both. If I walk in blind, I'm apt to give myself away. But if I can whip through there sounding naïve and knowing what to look for, maybe, just maybe, I might turn up something.'

'If you put it that way – ' Théo set the helmet and bag down before I had to ask a second time. He even took off his windbreaker. 'Can I help with the meal?'

'You already did. You shopped for me yesterday.'

I busied myself lighting the oven, getting potato puffs from the freezer (in France, praise be, even frozen food is good), laying on the broiler pan the steaks I had thought Connie and I might eat tomorrow, slicing an onion, tearing a salad. When the onion was sizzling, I came around to set the table and saw what Théo was doing. I burst out laughing.

He turned, tongs in one hand and poker in the other, and said nervously, 'Did I do something wrong?'

'Not at all.' I kept on setting the table, and laughing.

'Please.'

'You probably can't help it, it's in the genes or something.' I folded the napkins and tucked them under the forks. 'Since I've been here, I've invited three men into my house, and every single one of you went right to the hearth and started practising some ancient fire ritual, as though a woman couldn't penetrate the mysteries. I mean, we've only been cooking on wood fires for about twenty thousand years!'

Théo laughed along with me now. 'Why don't you go back to the kitchen and cook on gas? That's something I can't do.'

I did. Théo was sounding suddenly buoyant, I thought, no longer defensive or insecure. The reason was not hard to find. I might have laughed at him, even criticised – but I had called him a man.

'Théo,' I said, 'the corkscrew's on the table. Would you open the wine?'

By the last of the firelight I read over my notes on what Théo had told me.

190

There was not much he didn't know about his father's perfume works. It was not surprising. Once Théo finished his university studies – probably in management more than in chemistry – he expected to join Flairaud in the business, and eventually to succeed him. But it was still impressive that he could cite each employee's name, duties, estimated salary, length of service, experience, strengths and weaknesses as well as the family connections with other perfume concerns.

I didn't ask anything, in fact, that Théo couldn't answer.

When I had straightened the kitchen a bit and taken a quick shower, I banked the fire and turned back the bedcovers. Setting the alarm clock meant balancing my priorities against Connie's; I compromised on seven o'clock. Then I decided to lay out everything ready for the morning. Tired as I was now, I might feel less energetic then. I moved the last of the dinner things to the counter, swept the table with my sleeve, and stacked on it my camera case, tape-recorder, clipboard and shoulder bag. On a chair beside the table I laid out clean clothes.

Finally, thankfully, I crawled into bed.

I must have slept less than an hour before I was awakened. Not gently, as last night, by rain on the roof. I was jerked into wakefulness by thudding fists on my door and a deep, insistent male voice.

'Mademoiselle! Come quickly, mademoiselle. You are wanted urgently on the telephone. Wake up, mademoiselle! Telephone!!'

I groped for the flashlight, found my robe and slippers, and headed for the door.

Still muzzy with sleep, I wondered who could be calling me at such an hour. I squinted at my watch and saw it was almost midnight. And why would anyone call me at the Eagle's Nest? The call must have come there, since it was a strange man who was summoning me. But Connie would have called Madame Isnard's. So would Adjudant-chef Marcellin Morin.

Jay! It was Jay calling me!! Of course it was – in Costa Rica

191

it was only afternoon, he had just got back to San José, he was calling to tell me he was all right.

'Coming!' I sang out.

Thank God, I said silently.

I belted my robe securely, wrenched the door open, and stepped out into the cold night air.

'Sorry to keep you waiting. I can't tell you how much I appreciate –'

That was all I had time for.

Something struck the back of my head and, for the third time in one day, I lost consciousness.

EIGHT

IT WAS the alarm clock, after all, that wakened me, right on time at seven.

I was in my bed exactly as I should be – nightgown to my ankles, covers to my chin, robe folded at the foot – but with no recollection of how I got there. Had I roused myself in the middle of the night and staggered to bed from wherever my assailant had left me? Had he carried me to bed unconscious and arranged my clothes and covers?

I didn't want to think about it, not yet. I didn't even want to light the lamp or open the shutters. All I wanted was to sink back into oblivion.

Something wouldn't let me, though, some nagging pull on my senses. A smell. A smell that reminded me of – school? High school. Biology lab, that was it. The lingering odour in the air was chloroform.

My assailant had made sure I stayed unconscious quite a while, then. Long enough for what?

I hadn't been assaulted physically, I thought. Not in the euphemistic sense, that is. I had certainly been knocked on the head. Below the lump remaining from when the truck blew up, there was a fresh one, just as large and much more tender.

I forced myself to get up and light the lamp.

The house didn't look ransacked. At first glance it didn't even look touched. If it weren't for the lingering odour, and my throbbing head, I might think I had had an ordinary nightmare.

In slippers and robe I went first to check the door. It was pulled shut, the snap-lock engaged. When my assailant was

193

through with me and my house he had made sure no chance prowler could get in. Did he mean to be chivalrous?

Silly thought. I must be punchy. He meant no help to reach me by chance before I was able to summon any.

I put on the kettle. The kitchen looked normal.

I brushed my teeth. The bathroom looked normal too.

The living-room didn't look quite as it should.

Apart from the evident meddling with my professional gear on the table, the signs were subtle. The intruder had left the same amount of casual disorder as he had found. But though I might be a little messy, I had acquired the visual memory of a photographer. I knew when things were moved. All the obvious hiding places had been tested – under cushions, behind books on the shelves, among the stacks of sheets and towels, beneath the clothes in their drawers. The rugs had been turned back and the pictures on the walls looked behind. Nothing was taken, though, because there was nothing to be found there.

The missing items were all from the table. While the Canon and the Hasselblad were there, they were both conspicuously empty of film. So was the camera bag. The cassette I had left in the tape-recorder was gone along with all the other tapes, whether labelled or blank. And from my clipboard the sheets with writing on them had been removed. The intruder had made a clean sweep.

Or so he thought –

I began to smile. If the intruder wanted to deprive me of my files and find out where my investigations had led me, he had drawn a gaping blank.

The film was worthless. None of it was even exposed, except for one roll of glorious full-colour horticulture, shot on Saturday as I visited various flower growers. Thank heavens I hadn't kept the photo Théo had brought me last night showing Scotto's chauffeur at the post office – that would really have torn it! As for the film of the sabotaged truck, it was safely in the hands of *Nice-Matin* and the police.

So was the tape. True, I had a copy, but the saboteur knew what was on it already because he had been there. And he wouldn't learn anything from the reel I had dictated on the way back to Nice either, that he couldn't read this very minute at any corner news-stand. The only tape that was at all unique, in fact, was the one made yesterday before dawn while the violet truck was loading – a few minutes of the local growers' homespun sagacity, followed by the mayor's 'brief' speech. I was almost sorry to lose that gem, but the loss was repaid by the thought of the thief listening doggedly through the whole thing.

The sheets on the clipboard were no loss at all.

One was my photo log of frames shot. One contained addresses of perfumers I intended to visit, which I could always get from the secretary again. And one was my list of standard questions about the unrest and how it began – specific enough, but no news to anyone following my doings. They didn't want to know what I was asking, they wanted to know the answers I got. And the answers were hidden in a place most men would never look.

If I had planned it, I could never have hit on such a hiding place.

All I was trying to do was store my notes fairly method-ically. As it happened, the only ring binder in the house was Gran's looseleaf recipe book. Some of the dividers held quite thick sections – Fish, Poultry, Meat, Cakes, Pastries – but other dividers were entryless, being British terms Gran didn't think in. So I had stowed my notes on flower growers under Savouries, my notes on perfume manufacturers under Con-fectionery, and everything about Flairaud's problems under Steamed Puddings. It didn't have to make sense to anybody but me.

I pictured the intruder riffling through linen and turning back rugs while, all along, the notes sat on the kitchen counter like Poe's purloined letter.

After I had dressed, I leaned on the divider over a mug of coffee and did some thinking. It made me angry.

My assailant knew or had learned enough about me to know the telephone ploy would work. I had sailed into the trap, joyously on my way to talk to Jay. It wasn't the bump on the head that bothered me. It wasn't the manhandling of my body, the rifling of my house, the theft of my belongings. What angered me was the deception. To let me think I was hearing from Jay was cruel.

As I stalked down the path, I felt in my coat pocket for the keys to Connie's car. At least the intruder had left those. I wouldn't have liked explaining to Connie the misplacing of her Pontiac.

However, I had better start explaining things pretty quickly to the police. Since I had Marcellin Morin's private number, that would be the best place to start.

If I thought Régine was up, I would call from the Eagle's Nest. It would be worth entering the lion's den to watch her face as I reported assault and robbery. But she never worked the desk before eight.

The nearest alternative, Madame Isnard's, was more promising. Lights burned in several windows, so I climbed the steps and Lili let me in. She didn't ask me what I wanted. She simply thrust a copy of the morning paper into my hands and burst into tears.

Quickly I searched the headlines to see what fresh grief had struck. But I found only standard news – more deaths in Poland, more births in India, Mitterrand announcing more austerity measures – and my own story. It got a prominent box on the front page and almost an entire inside page, between text and photographs.

I had no chance to savour the feeling, though, with Lili weeping over my shoulder.

'You didn't,' she gulped, 'you didn't tell me . . . how bad it was.' She pointed jerkily to the colour photographs of the wreckage, and wept louder still.

I ignored her and scanned the text for accuracy until Madame Isnard's voice, thin and unsteady this morning, called, 'Lili! What's going on?'

Lili was clearly not good for much now, so I put down the paper and went into the bedroom. 'It's me, Irène. I'm disturbing you again, I'm afraid. Did you manage to get any sleep?'

196

'Some, dear, thank you,' she began bravely, then added, 'but not a lot. So much worry and turmoil yesterday. And last night – ' She sounded embarrassed.

'Those noises again?'

She gave a little nod.

'It was a bad night for us both, then. You don't suppose this hill is haunted by evil spirits?'

Madame Isnard looked at me uncertainly, but decided I was not making fun of her. 'I never believed in evil spirits. Not while Lucien was alive, at least.'

'These would have shown up later. Within the last six months.'

'Oh. You mean, perhaps, imported from Corsica?'

'Exactly.'

'I prefer mine imported from Scotland.' Irène Isnard smiled modestly at her own joke. 'The Corsicans were never noted for wine *or* spirits.'

I dropped a kiss on her cheek. 'You can stop worrying about your mind, Irène, there's nothing wrong with it. Is it okay if I use your phone to call the police?'

'My dear! What's happened?'

'It was a bad night, like I said. I got knocked out and my house burgled.'

She moaned faintly.

'Nothing serious,' I assured her. 'I'm still here and so is the house. Really, they didn't get anything much.'

'Anne's silver candlesticks? And those wonderful Buffet lithographs?'

'No, no. They just took some stuff that was on the table.'

That was literally true. However, I didn't know how much had been taken from the table until I went to the phone to call Marcellin Morin. When I reached into my bag for my new address book, I found it wasn't there.

' – *and* my passport *and* my driver's licence *and* my chequebooks *and* my credit cards. Even my Social Security card, which says right on the front it isn't for identification. I

197

don't have one damn thing left that has so much as my name on it!'

Adjudant-chef Marcellin Morin grinned. 'If you just want something with your name on it, I can give you a summons for driving without a licence.'

'Go to hell.'

Morin turned to his colleagues. 'Didn't I tell you what a sweet girl Addie was?'

We were at the gendarmerie post in Brignoles and it was already after nine o'clock. Marcellin had phoned Connie and told her I would be late getting to the hospital, but official business or no, Connie would be fuming.

'Look,' I said, 'it doesn't take guessing games to figure out their message. They took my film but not the cameras, my tapes but not the recorder – and my papers but not the whole wallet. They're sending loud and clear. Neither I nor my investigations are welcome here. It's a classic case of Yankee Go Home.' I stood and slipped my bag on to my shoulder.

'Where do you think you're going?'

'Home.'

'To America?!'

'Not on your life. To St-Martin-sur-Loup. That house is mine, and I have no intention of being forced out.'

'Sit down.'

Marcellin Morin's voice was unemphatic, but I gathered he meant it. I sat.

'First, about your house.' He picked up the phone and asked for the gendarmerie post in Vence, then covered the mouthpiece and said, 'I hope you remembered to leave a key for them.'

I told him I had left the key to the padlock with Lili next door. I also told him I wouldn't mind if the gendarmes arrived in several cars, with a pair of police dogs, and sirens screaming. The neighbours were welcome to know I had allies.

When that was arranged, more or less, Morin said, 'Next, about your personal safety. I know I'd be wasting my breath if I – '

'You are now.'

198

He sighed. 'Just let me add a personal plea, then. The world already has too few good-looking girls, so don't do anything irreversibly stupid.'

I promised solemnly to keep all my stupidity flexible.

'And now, about the incident yesterday on the autoroute. We've been busy — our explosives experts whom you so rightly suggested, and others as well. There was definitely a charge of *plastique* attached to the axle at the indicated point. But there was something else interesting in the wreckage. A rather large and cheap alarm clock, almost intact.'

'Alarm clock? You mean, like the kind terrorists are always using to set off time bombs?'

'Just so.'

'But — but that's weird.'

'What's weird?' Marcellin Morin sounded less interested than encouraging, like a conscientious schoolteacher.

'It only took three or four minutes for the *plastique* to explode after that fellow crawled under the truck. I would have thought he used a straight fuse. And even if he was crazy enough to use a timer and cut it that fine, wouldn't the clock have been blown to smithereens?'

Morin turned again to his colleagues. 'Not sweet, maybe, but she is bright, isn't she? Edouard, tell her just how you found the clock.'

A lean gendarme scarcely half Morin's size stirred importantly in his chair.

'It was not blown to bits, to answer mademoiselle's question, because it was not sufficiently near the charge. While it was also located in the right rear quadrant, it was inside the body of the truck. We owe its recovery to its fortuitous placement next to one of the sidewall supports. The hands on the dial were stopped at the exact time of the explosion.'

'Big surprise,' I said. 'How was it wired?'

Marcellin Morin answered. 'That *was* a big surprise. It wasn't.'

'No wires at all?' I chewed my lip and thought. 'What about the alarm, then?'

199

'Good girl. Edouard?'

'The alarm indicator pointed perhaps a quarter-hour before the explosion. Of course, with these cheap models, one cannot be exact. Nor can we be sure that we found it in the same state as before the explosion. But when we found it, the alarm button was pulled out and the spring quite without tension.'

'In other words, it rang until it ran down. Serge had it right.'

'Serge?' asked Morin.

'You heard the tape, remember when he said the screeching started suddenly, then diminished as they lowered their speed, like an alarm clock running down?'

'Yes. He knew unconsciously what the noise was, but he dismissed it – we all did – because it made no sense.'

'It does now. The screeching alarm was just to make them pull off. Which anyone would. And the anonymous fellow in the van was hanging back waiting for it to happen. When they were off the road, he could stop to offer help, and blow up the whole works.'

'But why a two-part operation?' Marcellin Morin went on. 'That's the question. Why not let the truck blow up on the highway?'

Edouard, the lean gendarme, cleared his throat. 'Maybe the saboteurs were afraid of a major highway catastrophe which would attract extra police attention.'

'They got plenty of attention as it is,' Morin said.

'Just the amount they wanted,' I said with sudden conviction. 'They did it that way so nobody could think it *was* an accident. A police investigation doesn't bother them – they figure it'll hit a dead end in two days and get filed. But the people in St Martin and Grasse will know it was a deliberate attack, and they won't forget.'

'Then if we accept your theory that it's part of a broadside assault on the perfume industry –'

'Well, don't you?'

'Say we do. We still have only two leads to whoever's behind it. The man who planted the *plastique* and, if it's a separate person, the one who planted the clock.'

200

'They're separate. I can't say who was at the violet-loading, but the fellow in the van wasn't. I'd have recognised him.'

'Would you again? Say, from a series of photographs?'

'You want me to look at a rogues' gallery?'

'Later, maybe, if we come up empty-handed. It's like looking for a needle in a haystack. The fellow may not even be from the Midi.'

'Too bad I didn't get a snap of him. The one of his van hasn't been much use.'

'It may.'

'Couldn't we try to make one? A picture of him. Back home they use a thing called Identi-kit to get a composite they can show around.'

Marcellin Morin smiled tolerantly. 'Here in the remote wastelands of Europe, child, we also have such things. But I think we'll postpone the services of the police artist until we can get all four of you witnesses together in Nice, and that may take a while. The Gazagnaires are being transferred to St Roch Hospital this afternoon by ambulance, but the doctors won't consider letting Pierre Pla be moved before the weekend.'

'What do you mean, "the Gazagnaires"? You mean Sabine is being allowed to ride along with Serge, don't you? The way you said it, it sounded like – '

'No, Addie,' the big gendarme said gently. 'I mean she is a patient too. I'm sorry to give you bad news again. You must have left St Martin before the family heard. Last evening, after she visited her husband, Sabine Gazagnaire suffered a miscarriage.'

' – lucky she was right here in the hospital, was what the matron said.' Monsieur le Curé's skirts rustled in brisk indignation as he led me to Sabine's room. 'Nothing lucky about it, I told her. If evil men had not maimed Sabine's husband, it would never have happened. She would be at home now, safe and happy and still pregnant. If the men who did it

201

thought they escaped with no deaths on their souls, God knows better.'

The curé stopped at the door of the Obstetrics and Gynaecology ward. 'Shall I come in with you?'

'No need, Father.' I smiled and settled the sheaf of tulips I carried into the crook of my elbow. 'Even a priest can stand to be let off once in a while.'

I was back in the corridor scarcely five minutes later. The tulips were still in my arm.

'Here, *you* get rid of these,' I told the curé, offloading them on to him. 'Sabine said the doctors would be letting her join Serge in a couple of hours, so I should give the flowers to somebody who really needed cheering up. Can you believe it?'

'Sabine's a remarkable girl. I remember the day I married that pair. I thought her far too young and fragile for the responsibilities of marriage.' Monsieur le Curé smiled deprecatingly. 'Well, God may be omniscient, but His priests occasionally fall an inch or two short.'

'She keeps surprising us all. Just now when I said how sorry I was about Serge's leg, she said what hurt her most was watching him being so brave and not being able to help him bear the pain. But that's just what she's doing, as much as any other person can.'

'She's helping with the bravery all round, I'd say.'

'Yes. She said that after they'd adjusted to the news, they talked it over and realised how much worse it could have been. If he had to lose something, he could spare a leg sooner than an arm, or his hearing, or his – '

' – or his sight, or his life,' the priest concluded. 'I know, she used the same words to me.'

'And then about her miscarriage, she admitted she'd cried for a while, but pretty soon she recognised that God wasn't adding to her burdens, He was easing them. Serge would be needing her more this coming year, and they could always have other babies. They can, by the way, can't they?'

'As far as I know. Right now, for Sabine,' the curé went on, 'the best therapy will be the regular care of her own children.

But she can't resume that for several days, and it will be longer before Serge is at home. Meanwhile, Addie, do you think you could find a couple of hours tomorrow to – '

'Please, Father!' I held up my hands in protest. 'Another piece of Christian charity? Lili and I are already going to make up to Madame Isnard for what Serge and Sabine promised. Are you trying to sink my entire Noël without a trace?'

'Addie.' The priest sounded altogether reasonable. 'Just listen.'

I could not refuse to listen. And, listening, I could not refuse.

'You sure you feel up to driving?'

'I could drive a team of mules from here to Nice. Honestly, Addie, you're as bad as the doctors. I feel fine.'

'Good. In that case, you wouldn't mind going by way of Grasse, would you? It's not much further.'

Connie laughed. 'Oho! I thought the tender solicitude was too good to be true. What's in Grasse?'

'Théo's in Grasse. And after what happened last night, I want to make sure he and his juvenile accomplices don't do anything that's, in Marcellin Morin's words, irreversibly stupid.'

Connie knew what I meant. In the half-hour since we left the hospital in Brignoles, I had brought her up to date.

She slid the Pontiac into the right lane and slowed for the exit. 'You want to go into Cannes and see if the *Trib*'s on the stands yet?'

'Thanks, but it'll probably get to St Martin just as early. Anyway, I'm a big girl, I can wait.'

'I should hope so. That thing there,' she gestured at the full-colour spread in *Nice-Matin* on the floor between us, 'ought to hold you for a while. It's enough to give anybody a swelled head.'

'My head can do without any more swellings, thanks. You bear left here.'

When we got to Grasse, I called Théo for permission to

203

visit his command centre, and Connie said she could just as happily kill an hour shopping here as in Nice.

Théo was in fine spirits. Though he had no more photographs for me, he said one of his club members was setting up a darkroom of their own. And the rest of his 'men' were deployed about the area, recording the likenesses, names if obtainable, addresses, licence numbers, and movements of Scotto's chauffeur and anyone he came into more than casual contact with. 'Like tracing the strands of a spider's web,' he said with the air of someone producing an original simile.

'Swell. Just remember this spider's a tarantula.'

I delivered my planned warning but Théo was predictably unimpressed. Danger was something which affected girls. He was chagrined, though, that he had not saved me from my assailant. 'Just think, he may have been lurking right there in the garden when I left. If I'd known, I might have seen him.'

That wasn't the possibility that concerned me. 'Do you think he might have seen you?'

'If he was in the – oh, you mean really *seen*? I doubt it. The moon was out so I didn't have to use my flashlight. And I hadn't brought my bike right up. Lili said the path was pretty badly overgrown, so I wheeled it inside the hedge at their place, where nobody'd be apt to see it. Actually, the path looked wide enough to me, but maybe she thought I had a heavy motorcycle.'

Now that Théo mentioned it, I had dimly noted in the last twenty-four hours a perceptible improvement in the grounds-keeping at Gran's house. Some good fairy had heard my resolve to hack back the weeds and done it for me. An agreeable mystery to lighten more sober questions, and one which I guessed could be resolved in two seconds flat.

' – wouldn't have connected it even now, but it must have had something to do with it,' Théo was saying. 'After all, it was right next door, and close to the same time. But I figured what I was hearing was just Lili's own dog. All the sounds were sort of muted – whines and growls and moans – like you hear from a dog that's muzzled and chained, and not happy about it.'

'Where did you hear this, Théo?'

'Like I said, at your neighbour Lili's.'

'No, I mean *where*.'

'Gee, Addie, it was dark when I got there, so all I know is the path to your house and the stone staircase Lili came down. I guess the sounds were somewhere up the steps. Not way up behind the house, just partway, as if somebody was holding his dog there waiting until – did the man who attacked you have a dog?'

'He had a blunt instrument, that's all I can tell you.'

'Anyway, just as I was coming up, a light went on in Lili's house, and the sounds stopped.'

Funny, I thought idly, how Théo kept referring to the Isnard place as Lili's house. He was still child enough to associate a house with the young people who lived there.

I had one other thought, not so idle.

Théo had heard the sounds which plagued Madame Isnard in the night. They weren't all in her head, after all.

The secretary of the Perfumers' Syndicate clearly wondered how I could have mislaid the list he had given me, but he replaced it without comment. Then he asked how I was getting along.

'Spottily. Every grower says the same thing – he can't remember who first aired the idea that their flowers were going too cheap, but by the time he heard about it, his neighbours were pretty well unanimous. Sounds like somebody did a thorough selling job on a prepared opinion.'

'Elementary mob psychology. If you want to command a majority, the first step is to say you do.'

'It worked here. I just wish I could find out where it all started.'

'I'm more interested in where it will all end.'

I stared at the secretary as though he had just said something brilliant. 'Good God, you're right, I've been going at

205

things backwards. I should be trying to find out where it's *meant* to end!'

'Pardon?'

'Listen.' I was excited now. 'People keep talking of a grower-perfumer confrontation, as though two sides were marching into battle, but that's wrong. Sure, the flower growers have been whipped up, by themselves or somebody else, but the manufacturers have never wanted a fight. They don't want the labour unrest that's been brewing either, or any of the other recent problems I've been hearing about. They aren't slitting their own throats, it's being done for them.'

I had the secretary's full attention and sympathies.

'So if this goes on much longer, if the flower growers won't settle, just how badly do the perfume makers stand to suffer?'

'Depends.' The secretary thought for a bit. 'The bigger firms might even welcome it. They can shut down, do plant overhaul, sell off surpluses that piled up while the economy was sluggish. But for some of the smaller operations that have had to borrow heavily, even a month's layoff could be fatal.'

'You mean they'd go bankrupt?'

'Essentially, yes.'

'Then the plant would be closed, the owners broke, and the employees out of a job.'

'Well – not necessarily. The owners would lose control of course, but in most cases refinancing could be arranged, because the failure would have resulted from mismanagement or undercapitalisation. As a whole the industry is basically healthy.'

'I see. So there's no trouble finding new investors?'

'Quite the contrary. In the last couple of months I'd say there's been a definite surge of interest. A number of members have mentioned being approached by lawyers with feelers about buying in, or even taking over outright.'

'Who are the principals, do you know?'

The secretary shrugged. 'Germans, Italians? We've had increasing foreign investment in Grasse over the last decade or two, so it could be them. But with lawyers fronting – who can say?'

'No, you can't see until tomorrow.' Connie set her shopping bag behind the driver's seat of the Pontiac and pointedly heaped her raincoat over it. The coat, barely adequate when we set out yesterday on our aborted trip to Paris, was decided overkill for a sunny noon on the south coast. As we headed east out of Grasse, Connie rolled down the windows.

'I wouldn't have asked you if I thought you'd go out buying things.'

'You'd have asked me,' Connie rejoined, 'if I'd been encumbered with twenty Afghan refugees. You *claim* you need me to protect you from Jean-Marc.'

'You've never been alone with him; you don't know.'

'I still can't see it as a fate worse than death. Did you invite Lew?'

'You think I should?'

'Why not? We make a nice prickly foursome.'

'I don't think Jean-Marc is Lew's favourite person.'

'Mutual, no doubt, and for one good reason. Believe me, Lew would rather be present than not. Particularly when Jean-Marc is.'

I decided to change the subject. 'How soon can you get me a new passport?'

'Monday. Just give me the photos.'

'Photos,' I repeated. Then I started to laugh. With all the cameras at my disposal and Théo's, and even a darkroom, it had not occurred to me to turn them on myself.

'Don't tell me, you don't have any.'

'I'll get some. At least I'm restocked with film. Lord, I lost a small fortune last night. That SOB didn't stop to notice it was mostly unexposed. It wouldn't have hurt him to leave it.'

'What about insurance?'

'I'll check, but they're sure to say I'm not covered. After all, I opened the door to the guy.'

'Rubbish. A clear case of breaking and entering.'

'How do you figure that?'

'He broke your head. And he entered.'

Connie drove me up the Route de la Chapelle to the gates of the inn, and departed for a reunion with her pussy-cat. I got my key from Lili, together with the information that the gendarmes had stayed about half an hour and left as noisily as they had arrived. That was fine by me – I did not ask stealth or even discretion – but Lili thought they might have shown some consideration for the neighbours.

'If you mean me,' Madame Isnard said, 'you can save your concern. I watched them coming and going from my window, and I was glad of the entertainment. High time we had some harmless excitement around here.'

'It wasn't harmless, Tante Irène. Addie was hurt and robbed.'

'Oh, but that was already done.' Irène Isnard was putting on a determined show of pluck today. She turned to me. 'I hope you don't find the house a shambles, dear. Those policemen may have gone through like bulls in a china shop.'

It wasn't as bad as that, but they had left more evidence of their passage than the thief did.

'I didn't mind the fingerprint dust,' I told Madame Isnard on my way back an hour later. 'It's no different from plaster dust, and heaven knows I've wiped up enough of that in the last week. But it would have been nice if they'd made use of the doormat.'

'Men don't,' Irène Isnard said imperturbably. 'Lili, what can we offer Addie for lunch?'

'Thanks, no. I had something at home. I'm off to do some shooting while the light lasts – it's such a radiant gold now. But I just remembered, I wanted to tell you something.'

Irène Isnard's eyes were alert. I could not help thinking how different she was now from the maundering sunken shell I had first seen, and how quickly she could slip back into it. While I told her what Théo had heard, she was almost holding her breath.

208

'He described the sounds much the way you did, and he placed them just outside the house, partway up the steps. Unfortunately, they stopped as he came close, and he saw nothing. But maybe another night we'll find out more.'

Lili started asking a whole lot of questions, but Irène Isnard silenced her. She beckoned me forward and kissed me on the cheek.

'My dear,' she said softly, 'I think you know you've just given me a lovely Christmas present.'

I shot half a roll before I got down the Route de la Chapelle. All the intriguing angles and compelling colour fields that my subconscious had been marking for some future day leaped clamouring to my attention. The steep descent was not much more than a kilometre, but it took me and wheezing Peu Belle an hour.

The light was at its peak when I reached the chapel and I did a couple of exteriors in the glorious lambent glow of the Provençal afternoon. It seemed a shame to go indoors then, but the clouds gathering over the Courmettes told me we would have no more sunshine today at least. More important, this was the time to photograph the chapel, with the parish women's holiday decorations providing a perfect counterpoint to the almost pagan quality of the primitive murals. I was glad my wide-angle lens had survived the vicissitudes of yesterday.

The last frame had taken me on to a hummock from which the chapel dominated the rooftops of the Vieux Village. As I scrambled down, well pleased, the chapel door opened and Rusty Traynor came out. I started to hail him but was stopped by a feeling akin to *déjà-vu*. This had happened last Friday.

Did Rusty come here regularly? If so, I didn't think it was out of piety. He might just like the place, as I did, out of wacky artistic taste.

I pushed through the rude wooden door into the dim

interior. With Rusty gone, holy Martin looked down from his flaking murals on to an empty shrine.

A sudden impulse urged me to light a candle, say a prayer, do some special thing that would make Martin feel less neglected. But I was a non-Catholic, untrained in pleasing saints. So I got out my camera as intended. Photographing the murals might satisfy him and induce him to remain my personal protector. I could surely use his patronage: like Christopher, Martin specialised in wayfarers.

The altar did not merit photographing, so I concentrated on the primitive paintings. I had worked myself around to a position on the back wall when the door suddenly swung open. Even before I could see her, I knew the click of heels for Régine's.

It really was Friday over again.

This time, though, I did not care to encounter Régine and be dispossessed. As she advanced down the aisle, I retreated along the back wall until I could slip behind the hinged panels that partitioned off a corner. I'd always assumed the space was a confessional; now I found it was a broom closet. I pulled my foot back smartly to avoid kicking a galvanised bucket.

Watching through a slit between the panels, I was conscious of irony. If Régine knew I was watching, she would think I was spying on her. The only way I could forestall that was actually to do so.

Pretty soon, too, I admitted I was curious.

Régine went almost to the front of the chapel and took an aisle seat. She rested her clasped hands on the chair-back in front of her, bowed her forehead on to them, and remained that way for several minutes. Then she lifted her gaze to the crucifix over the altar. I could see her lips moving. In the sober black and white she habitually wore, she looked very much like a *réligieuse*. Her devout expression was not assumed; Régine clearly believed.

Equally clearly, she was deeply troubled.

Presently she squared her shoulders and rose. Bending her knee towards the altar, she turned to leave. Halfway up the

210

aisle she passed from my field of vision, but I could hear the steady click of her heels. Then at the back of the chapel the footsteps halted, only a couple of yards away.

I had to twist awkwardly to shift my line of sight without upsetting the mops and brooms surrounding me. When I could see Régine again, she was kneeling before the bottom shelf of an open bookcase that ran along the other half of the back wall.

The bookcase had never excited my notice before. It contained the expected items, a mildewed stack of catechism aids here, a yellowing stack of parish bulletins there. But now I saw it was a repository for other things – a paper-wrapped parcel that looked like somebody's laundry, a coil of stout rope, an old-fashioned lantern, and a rucksack I was pretty sure was Lew's. Apparently people used the chapel as a way-station.

Régine did. In one hand she held up a corner of the shelf paper that covered the rough plank. In the other hand she held an envelope.

I could not tell whether she was sliding it under the shelf paper or taking it out, for she wheeled and rose and shut the flap of her bulky black shoulder bag in one hasty sequence, and moved an innocent distance away from the bookcase. The cause of her haste was plain to hear, and right outside the chapel. The rumble of a heavy diesel engine and the squeal of brakes were followed by the babble of several dozen package-tourist voices.

I willed Régine to leave quickly so I could have just a minute alone in the chapel. But now she moved with calm deliberation. She was barely out the chapel door and I out from behind the panelled screen when the horde of sightseers entered.

They paid me no heed, elbowing me aside as they elbowed each other, taking me for one of themselves.

For some reason this infuriated me. The only thing I had in common with these pasty-faced, flabby, dowdy, sheep-like, name-badged Belgian bus riders was that we all toted cameras. And even there I could legitimately claim

211

superiority. I decided to ignore them and go right ahead with my search for Régine's envelope.

Just then, however, their tour director planted himself on the corner of the bookcase, notes in hand, and, having reminded his flock that the bus would leave in exactly one hour, called their attention to the fresco on the east wall.

I left – for exactly one hour.

Around the square the food shops were not yet open, but in the Vieux Village all the ateliers of the artisans displayed their wares. The Grand'rue, alive with tourists drawn to the Côte d'Azur for the holidays, was one long curving cobble-stoned bazaar.

I browsed in the shops of the weavers and potters for a gift for Connie. At the olivewood carver's I almost settled on a cheeseboard and knife, adorned with a winsome wooden mouse – if Connie didn't like the mouse she could always give it to Minette to play with. The silverworker had some pretty jewellery, but nothing I could afford. The leather crafter's things were too lumpen for sprightly Connie. And then I found myself outside a gallery named simply RussT.

It surprised me to realise I had been back in St Martin eight whole days without yet penetrating to this most central and charming part of the Old Village. Here the ancient stone houses with their red tile roofs rose in steep tiers under the brow of the château. Shops and galleries occupied many of the ground floors, while the windows of the dwellings above were alternately enlivened with gay boxes of geraniums, over-laden racks of multicoloured laundry and roosting pigeons. Any one of the three was apt to sprinkle the heads of passers-by, but that was generally accepted as part of the scene.

When I entered Rusty's gallery, the door chimes sounded and a voice called from the back, 'Coming!' For the next few minutes I was alone, unless I counted the five elongated nudes in polished white stone who sported together under a central spotlight. I was looking over the smaller pieces on glass shelves set into the stone walls when Rusty appeared.

'Gorgeous! Am I believing my eyes? You finally came to see the old sweatshop.'

212

'Scold me, Russ, I deserve it. I've been charging all over two départements, but it's taken me till now to come halfway across our own village.'

'I guess little old St Martin's too tame for you. I've been reading the papers.' He gestured toward the desk at the back of the gallery. I could see the garish red and purple heads of *Nice-Matin*. 'Don't you think you're mixing in some kind of heavy action?'

'Could be. Tell you what I'll do, I'll take the day off tomorrow and stay strictly out of trouble.'

'Big of you. Still, twenty-four hours is better than nothing. So tell me, are you just slumming, or can I do something for you?'

'You mean am I a customer? Probably not. Don't let me keep you if you were working.'

Rusty laughed. 'Sculpting? I don't even *try* to do that in the daytime any more. Somebody's always asking me to play Mr Fixit instead.'

'And you find that a terrible drag.'

'Okay, it's a turn-on, I admit it. Now which of my, uh – lines were you interested in?'

'Actually, I wanted a Christmas present for Connie.'

'Connie?'

'My friend from Nice, the one you met Monday. You found her quite captivating, in fact, or so it seemed to Camille and me.'

Rusty's face hardened. 'Look, I do not play Mary to Camille's little lamb, got it?'

'Sure, Rusty.' I turned away and resumed examining the small pieces on the glass shelves. 'Anyway, Connie really liked your work, so I thought maybe I'd get her a table model. But I'm afraid the numbers on your stickers are a bit up-market for me.'

'Don't let those put you off, they're for strangers and suckers. Real collectors get a reasonable price. And friends are in the half-price-and-under category. How much do you want to spring?'

I hesitated. 'A hundred francs?'

213

'Take your choice. Any item up to twelve inches.'

'A cat then.' I didn't hesitate any longer. 'This cat here, it reminds me of Connie's. Could you inscribe "Minette" on the underside?'

'Minette?!'

'Sorry about that.' Minette, a diminutive of Minou, meant kittycat, more or less. 'Probably she was already named when Connie got her.'

While Rusty was inscribing and wrapping the stone cat, I said casually, 'Glorious day for photographing. I shot half a roll at the chapel inside and out. I have a thing about that place. Well, you must too – I've seen you coming out of there more than once.'

'Not because I think it's the Sistine Chapel, let me tell you. It's probably months since I looked at those murals.'

'Why do you go then? Meditation?'

Rusty's laugh was ironic. 'I tried transcendental meditation back when everybody else did, but I don't guess I'm the spiritual type. I go to the chapel to pick up my laundry. The lady who washes for me lives up your road, and it makes a convenient drop.'

'That's not so bad. As my grandmother always said, cleanliness is next to Godliness.'

I pulled out my wallet, and that reminded me of something else. 'Rusty, would you do me a favour?' I put the Canon on the counter beside him. 'Stand me in front of this blank wall and shoot me. I need a passport photo.'

'You just got here. How come your passport's expiring?'

'It isn't. It's lost, strayed, or stolen.'

Rusty looked up from his gift-wrapping. He wasn't very good at tying bows. 'Stolen, huh? Outasight.'

'No problem. Connie works at the Consulate. She can get me another one.'

Rusty said nothing more until he had finished the wrapping and taken the pictures I wanted. When he did speak, he sounded diffident.

'Look, I don't mean to butt into what isn't my business. But some of us have been talking, and we're wondering if you

214

know what you're messing with. Like, we're getting a little concerned.'

'Don't worry about me, I'm not fragile.'

'I'm serious, this may be just a local war, but it's already taken casualties.'

'And those casualties are my friends. I'm sticking.'

Rusty sighed. 'Well, if you won't listen to reason, will you at least promise me something? If things get too dicey, don't try to go it alone. Call me.'

'Sure, Russ. If I need your help, I'll ask.'

'I wish you'd say it like you meant it.'

I smiled and put the Canon back in its case, along with the gift-wrapped sculpture. Rusty went to the desk at the rear of the gallery and brought back a handful of newspapers. 'You want these? I thought you might like extras, to send to folks in the States or something.'

'Gee, thanks, I could use – hey, is that the *Trib*? Is it in there too?'

'You mean you don't know?'

'I've been kind of busy today. There wasn't time to get to the news-vendor before noon.' I scanned the headlines and found the story on page two, under the caption 'US Diplomat Injured in Provence Strike Violence'. It was a slant I wouldn't have thought of. The story was cut to ribbons, but that was expected. *Nice-Matin*'s beat was the Riviera; the *International Herald-Tribune* covered the world.

'No byline,' Rusty pointed out.

'In the *Trib*? I'm lucky to get a paragraph printed there. Believe me, Russell old buddy, I ain't complainin'.'

'I thought all you newshounds were in it just to see your name in lights. But you, you're so modest you don't even check to see whether you're in print. Why *are* you a reporter?'

It took me about one second to answer. 'Heredity.'

After I fought my way through the *mercerie* and the baker's, I gave up trying to do any more shopping. I didn't even stop

215

for my own copies of the papers. The shops were just too crowded.

The Chapelle St-Martin wasn't empty, either. Several schoolgirls were clustered around the altar doing something with a great number of candles. I did not wait to see if the result would be artistic, but headed straight for the bookcase and commenced an obvious search. If anyone wondered, I had lost a film wrapper.

I didn't find one. I also didn't find the envelope that had been in Régine's hand an hour ago. Either she was taking it away with her then, or it had been collected since. The mildewed papers were still on the shelves, and the rope and the lantern. The laundry bundle was gone. So was Lew's rucksack.

Peu Belle mounted the Route de la Chapelle at her own plodding pace. I thought I might overtake Lew and save myself a twilight climb, but it was a forlorn hope. I ought to have found out whether he received messages at the Commerce, or mail at Poste Restante, but I hadn't.

At the house I dumped my bag and camera case and changed into my running shoes. I was out the door and snapping the padlock when I remembered to go back and get the big flashlight. It wouldn't stay light over half an hour more, even this far above the village. And the climb to Lew's cabin had always taken fifteen minutes, even when I was a teenager bursting with energy. Nowadays I would have to allow time to stop and pant. I decided to clock it.

Fifteen minutes later I was there, not in the least winded. Maybe my strides were longer now. I felt obscurely pleased, like a matron looking for new wrinkles and finding none.

After all that uphill plodding, I didn't find Lew either. Though a bit of light showed at the windows, there was no answer to my shout, and no barking. I gave it a minute in case I had caught Lew bathing or something, then pushed on the door.

It opened easily. Probably it was never locked. There was a screen in front of the fire. The screen confirmed that Lew was out. The fire confirmed that he hadn't gone far.

I looked for a clue to where he might be, but everything was as it had been before, except for a wicker basket on the floor in front of the bookcases. This held wrapped packages. The largest was tagged 'Best Love, Gwennie'. Another said 'Lew from Grandma and Grandda'. Then I saw the tag floating from a slim package reading, 'For Addie with warmest wishes of the season, Lew'.

Suddenly I was sorry I had come in. It didn't feel like trespassing before. But now I had intruded on Lew's privacy, and in the process deprived myself of what should have been a surprise.

Pulling the door firmly shut, I set off to find Lew. A minute of circling the house and calling in all directions brought no response. I tried another tactic. Pitching my voice higher, I called, 'Dylan, Caitlin!' and whistled. This time there were answering barks.

A little way up the path toward the waterfall, I saw a new branch path, clearly of Lew's cutting, leading in the direction from which the barks had come. A couple of minutes more and the terriers were with me, leading me to Lew.

He stood on the edge of a sharp drop, beside a sort of derrick that held an inch-thick rope on a series of pulleys. As he worked a large crank, the rope moved uphill and over the pulleys, then back down where it had come from. Lew did not turn but said in a voice strained with exertion, 'Hi. Be with you in a minute. Ruddy thing's almost up.'

Presently I saw what the 'ruddy thing' was. It was a platform, a simple flatbed suspended by the corners from a ring, which in turn hung from another pulley-like gadget. On the flatbed were a couple of cardboard cartons, a butane bottle, and a fifty-kilo sack of dry dog food.

As the flatbed cleared the lip of the precipice, Lew reached out to steady it with his free hand, then secured it with a hooked metal rod attached to a ring set into the concrete base of the derrick. He took a few seconds to catch his breath before unhooking the elastic straps that held the cargo in place.

'What do you think of my goods lift? Elegant, no?'

217

'Reminds me of a Model T Ford. How does it work?'

'You ski, don't you? Just like a cablecar. There are five pylons running downhill to a point just off the Chemin du Baou. One of these days when I'm feeling rich, I'll get a secondhand donkey engine to run it. Meanwhile the engine is me.'

'It's still a lot better than carrying everything up the mountainside like a Sherpa porter. What can I take?'

'Not the beer. That's weatherproof; it can wait till tomorrow along with the bottled gas. If you can manage the dog food, we can get the rest in one trip.'

Lew helped me lift the sack and settle it on top of my head. 'Most fetching Sherpa porter I ever did see,' he said. 'You go ahead and I'll shine the torch on your feet.'

We didn't talk on the way back to the cabin. It was all I could do not to lose my footing, particularly with the dogs bounding around me the whole way. Probably they knew what was in the sack. A classic case of what Gran used to call cupboard love.

When we were sitting before the fire with a pot of tea – good Keemun tea carefully brewed, not the murky battery acid I had encountered daily on my one trip to England – Lew said, 'You're back early, aren't you? I didn't expect you so soon.'

'Back from where?' I hadn't a clue what he was talking about.

'Why, back from Paris, of course.'

I looked at him in stupefaction. Was it conceivable that anyone in St Martin could fail to know of the sabotage of the violet truck?

Llewellyn Rhys-Owen could. He read not *Nice-Matin* but the *Daily Telegraph* a day old. When he listened to the radio, it was the BBC World Service or RMC Classique. He didn't even go into the village every day. With his books, reading and writing, he lived in another world.

Finally I said simply, 'We didn't go after all. It's a long story. But that isn't what I came about.'

'What does bring you away up here at twilight?'

218

'A last-minute invitation. I've been bludgeoned into cooking a turkey dinner tomorrow, and I wondered – I know it's awfully short notice, but – Connie and I thought if you weren't committed to somebody else's turkey, maybe you'd come and help us eat it.'

Lew looked almost shy. 'Thank you, I'd like to. May I bring something?'

'I can't think what.'

'Nor can I.' Lew grinned suddenly, himself again. 'But whatever it is, there's a lot of it. Gwennie's package weighs eight pounds, and the customs declaration reads "Food". It's bound to be seasonal. Why don't I bring it along in its wrappings, and we'll all take pot luck? Together we can eat it, or feed it to the pups.'

'Splendid idea. Come at noon, or earlier if you want to catch us with aprons on and flour in our hair.' I set down my teacup and reached for my coat.

'Must you leave already?'

'I have to be home when the groceries are delivered.'

With a twinge I realised I had said it that way on purpose, so Lew would think I meant a delivery boy and not Jean-Marc or some other potential rival. My subconscious was doing unaccountable things lately.

I said, 'I came for one other thing. I wanted to thank you for my Christmas present.'

'But I haven't –'

'Yes you have. It was you who clipped back my weed-grown path. It was either you or the fairies. And while I know every Britisher is born with gardening tools in his hands, deep down I really don't believe in fairies.'

Jean-Marc was prompt to the minute, at least with the first load. After that his arrivals were more erratic. He had quite a few of the supermarket's little plastic bags to bring in, and he didn't seem any more efficient at carrying them than he had been at filling them. Items from the cooler and dry boxed staples were dumped together on top of produce. But he had forgotten nothing I had asked for, and added a few grace notes of his own.

'God, it's cold in here,' he said after the last trip.

'Sorry, I just got home myself. You lay a fire and I'll mix you a drink. Fair enough?'

'If you don't put any ice cubes in it.' He crumpled paper and heaped on wood while I finished stowing the perishables. A lighted match was already in his hand when he said, 'By the way, you *are* staying home for the rest of the night?'

'Sure. I mean, I'm going to midnight Mass, but apart from that –'

'You're having dinner here?'

'Uh-huh.'

'Enough for two?'

'Two? Not really.' I could hardly offer Jean-Marc the bacon and eggs I planned to feed myself.

Jean-Marc swore and dropped the burning match on to the bare bricks of the hearth floor. Perhaps he had singed his fingers. Perhaps he was simply exasperated.

He picked up his coat, and mine. 'Come on. Mathilde will feed you, or it's the fourteenth month of the year. And I've got a perfectly drinkable bottle of cognac in my room. Much as I adore your company, I don't see any need to undergo medieval tortures to get it.'

'Yes, Jean-Marc,' I said meekly. I wondered what that signified. I had never been meek to any man, not even my father. Did that mean in Jean-Marc I had met my lord and master? Or simply that we could never last?

At the Eagle's Nest, Jean-Marc went into the kitchen for a minute to tell Mathilde that one more serving would be needed. Then he came back, ready to whisk me off to his room. I didn't know what he planned, except that it wasn't medieval tortures, and I wasn't totally reluctant to find out. The fact that the evening got ruined then wasn't Jean-Marc's fault or mine.

The first contribution came from Régine. She was behind the desk when we got there, and as Jean-Marc rejoined us, she brought a package out from under the counter.

'This came for you today,' she told me. 'In view of the date, I accepted delivery and paid the postman the usual charges. I thought you'd want it for Christmas.'

My eyes were fixed on the printing on the brown paper wrapping as I thanked her, but still I could feel her watching me with a strange intensity. She must have known what my reaction would be, so what was she looking for? Did she want perversely to savour my pain?

And then Joseph Scotto came along the tower corridor, walking smoothly, smiling smoothly, speaking smoothly.

'Ah, my dear Miss Forrester, how happy I am to see you among us for the holidays. I do hope things have been going well for you?' He didn't wait for an answer; his sort seldom did. 'Have you by chance heard from your brother yet? It would be so nice to have everything settled before the turn of the year.'

I opened my mouth but no words came out. I looked down at the package in my hands, at the rows of gaily coloured stamps, at the profusion of stickers, at the San José postmark with its date ten days ago, before I had even arrived here. I looked at Jay's strong square printing.

I pulled the package to my chest and, right there in front of Joseph Scotto, I started to cry.

NINE

Thursday, 25 December

CONNIE ARRIVED, accompanied by Minette, just at nine on Christmas morning. She wouldn't let me open the big beribboned box she brought, but she insisted that I open Jay's present the minute the turkey was in the oven.

'The longer you stare at the wrapping, the more you'll imagine dreadful things. Go ahead and find out what he's sent you. It's bound to make you feel better.'

As usual, Connie was right. When I had the package open and the skirt Jay had sent me spread on my lap, I could picture him shopping for it in the bazaars of San José, moving from stall to stall, a blond giant among the dark *josefinos*. I dwelt on the image, and the conviction grew again in me that he must be all right.

'It's magnificent. Try it on,' Connie urged.

I found a red pullover to go with the skirt and put them on. The skirt was a peasant weave, its gathered wool soft but its pattern a bold mixture of red and white, black and green. Surveying myself in the mirror of the armoire, I thought I looked unquestionably Christmassy.

That was how Lew found me, not in an apron with flour in my hair, when he showed up at eleven.

I was glad to see him. So was Connie, she said. Minette, however, took one look at Dylan and Caitlin and streaked straight up the ladder to the loft. Connie coaxed her down by noon, and the terriers were models of amity, but she continued to give them a wide berth. On balance, even after I gave her the whole turkey liver, I think Minette would have preferred to stay home in Connie's empty apartment.

222

Besides Dylan and Caitlin, and the promised package from sister Gwennie, Lew brought a bulging sack. With his nose red from the chill mountain air and a tasselled knitted cap pulled over his ears, Connie told him he looked like Santa Claus. He dumped the sack outside the door, shifted Gran's knick-knacks from the mantelpiece on to a bookcase, and began carrying in armloads of greenery.

'You inspired me,' he said. 'I've been for a tramp in the woods.'

Connie and I were both busy in the kitchen, so we let him have his head decorating the mantel. First he laid down a bed of pine boughs complete with cones. Next came garlands of ivy. Finally he added sprigs of shiny red-berried holly.

'Got any red ribbon?' he asked.

I hadn't, but I found a ball of ropey red yarn in Gran's knitting basket, and contributed a box of candles. By the time Connie and I were finished in the kitchen, Lew had done the mantel and a table centrepiece as well. Connie went up into the loft to pacify Minette, and I stood with Lew before the hearth expressing my admiration of his handiwork. It was a talent I hadn't expected in him. Having seen what tasteful things he did to his own house, though, I shouldn't have been surprised.

'Now I need a drawing pin,' he told me.

This mystified me, but translated from British to French back to American proved to be a thumbtack, which I could provide.

'Close your eyes and come where I lead you,' he ordered. I obeyed. I heard the door open and close, then a chair scrape close by, then Lew saying, 'Look over your head.'

I saw the mistletoe a half second before Lew hastily claimed his kiss. 'Merry Christmas,' he said.

I looked up into his blue eyes, now shy again, and replied softly, 'Merry Christmas. It's a lovely big bunch of mistletoe. Don't you think it earns a bigger kiss?'

Lew complied, more wholeheartedly than I had intended. He might wait to be invited, but then he accepted without reservation. After a couple of silent but eventful minutes, I was relieved to hear Connie descending the ladder and saying, 'What's going on down there? Break it up!'

Connie claimed her own kiss, a friendly smack. At that point Jean-Marc arrived and the cycle was completed. His kiss for me was considerably brief but quite personal. And Connie's didn't look too frosty either.

'Where'd you get the *gui*?' he asked. 'This isn't prime Druid country.'

'Uphill.' Lew gestured. 'Quite a way up.'

'That's powerful magic stuff. Provided you cut it properly, that is. But I don't suppose you happened to be carrying a golden sickle for the occasion.'

'Golden sickle? You don't cut mistletoe, ever. It's got to be shot down cleanly, with arrows or stones. Every Welshman knows that.'

A heated dispute brewed between the Gaulish and Welsh branches of Druidism. Connie tried waving a bottle of champagne between the two men, but that didn't work. So I got Gran's copy of *The Golden Bough* and invoked Frazer's authority. We all learned more than we needed to know on the subject.

Mistletoe, gathered the right way, cures epilepsy.

Mistletoe, gathered another right way, is an antidote to poisons.

Mistletoe aids barren women to conceive.

Mistletoe, given to the first cow who calves in the New Year, grants fecundity to the herd. In general it brings good crops.

'Quite right. "No mistletoe, no luck",' Lew quoted.

Mistletoe, hung in the house, protects against lightning, at least in the Scandinavian and Baltic countries.

'I've heard that one,' I said. 'My other grandmother, the Swedish one, used to say it was proof against lightning and all sorts of fire.'

'Too bad you didn't have any here during that thunderstorm last month,' Connie said. 'You might still have had a roof.'

224

'Well, as they say, better late than never. Won't *somebody* open the champagne?'

We opened the champagne, and the package from Gwennie, and the rest of the presents too.

Except for Connie's. That one she insisted on holding back until after dinner, and when I was finally instructed to pull on the pompom that topped the big box, I saw why. I withdrew a ribbon with stages of the gift fastened along its length. First a package of paper coffee filters emerged, then a plastic filter cone, then a bag of coffee beans, high-roasted but not ground, and finally a marvellous antique wood-and-brass hand grinder. So we were able to finish our feast with coffee that for once was up to Connie's standards.

Of the packages we opened with the champagne before dinner, Gwennie's came first. This was fortunate, as it included a plum pudding which Lew declared had to be put up to steam for an hour, and must be served with a hard sauce he would himself confect. Personally I thought the mince pie Connie already had in the oven would be enough, but the majority ruled for gluttony.

Since Jean-Marc seemed chagrined not to have brought me a gift-wrapped offering like the others, I made a point of thanking him for everything we were about to consume, from bird to brandy. And I gave him his gift first.

It was only a box of three handkerchiefs, but to let him know he wasn't being slighted, I said, 'I'm afraid the monograms aren't too perfectly stitched. We girls aren't schooled now the way we used to be.'

In fact the monogramming had mostly been done under the courtesy light of Peu Belle, with the heater running, while I waited for Lili and Irène Isnard to attend midnight Mass. I'd have stayed for the service myself, after depositing Madame in her reserved place at the front, if I hadn't seen I'd have to stand. Getting the stricken woman down the steps from her house had taken effort, and I was saving all the rest of my energy for carrying her back up bodily. But she was so grateful to be able to attend, and to pray for Serge and Sabine, that I couldn't begrudge an ounce of exertion. And since I hadn't planned ahead, I'd have been awake anyway, stitching away on Jean-Marc's gift.

'Just what I needed,' he said gallantly. 'How did you know?'

'I know because when Peu Belle wouldn't go and you fixed her, you got your handkerchief hopelessly grease-stained. I'm glad I can atone.' I turned to Connie, 'Here, this one is yours.'

Connie seemed delighted by the stone cat. Lew and Jean-Marc both looked less than pleased that I had singled out Rusty's work for patronage. Minette was unmoved.

Lew and I, naturally, exchanged books.

Not only was mine a volume of Lew's stories, which I had hoped it would be, but on the flyleaf under the heading 'For Addie' were two dozen lines of my very own Christmas ode. I was sure Lew could tell how pleased I was, but all I managed to say was, 'I'm terrible at reading poetry out loud. Could I just keep this for myself?'

Lew seemed even more unsettled by his gift than I was, but I soon figured out why. The book, Waverley Root's supremely literate volume entitled *Food*, was patently the most expensive item in the lot. To ease his embarrassment I said:

'It's only secondhand, Lew. But I've seen your library, and I think it'll find a place. This is the book I gave to Gran the last Christmas she was alive. It's had some experience being a Christmas present.'

'It won't be passed along again soon, I promise you. This is a real treasure. It makes you hungry just looking at it.'

'Swell, because we've got a *lot* of food,' Connie said, 'and the banquet starts right now.'

When we were grouped around the fire relaxing with our coffee and brandy and listening to a tape of Corelli's Christmas concerto that Lew had brought, Connie paused in

226

her rocking in Gran's chair and said, 'You wouldn't have a Bible, would you, Addie?'

I got up and lifted Gran's big old leatherbound Bible, the Lowell family Bible, from its shelf.

'I was just thinking,' Connie went on, 'now that we've done all the pagan things, holly and ivy, mistletoe, plum pudding, it might be nice to read the Nativity story.'

The Bible fell open at the Book of Esther. There was an envelope stuck between the pages, and I knew the story was one Gran read often. Other places fell into natural breaks with markers too – the last psalms, Ecclesiastes, a passage in First Corinthians – and one of these was the beginning of the Gospel According to St Luke. Idly I unfolded the paper tucked into the pages and saw it was Gran's *permis de séjour*, her residence permit for France. Gran had odd ideas about what constituted a bookmark.

I passed the open volume to Connie, and for the next few minutes we listened to her reading the familiar story in the majestic English of the King James version. Familiar to Lew and me, that is. Jean-Marc had never heard it in English, so he found it totally fresh. Besides, as he said, Catholics hardly ever read the Bible.

After I put the book back on its shelf, we relapsed into a stuffed lethargy. Then suddenly there was a knock at the door and Rusty appeared. He sniffed the air and said his timing could have been better, so we took pity on him and gave him dessert.

He had brought me a showy poinsettia. 'A potted plant. Or as the British say, a pot plant. I'd have brought you one of *those*, but I wasn't sure of your tastes.'

I thanked him simply for the pretty flower.

We sat over coffee and brandy for a while longer, but Rusty's addition had thrown our little group out of harmony, and it wasn't long before the party broke up. Jean-Marc said he was going to sleep off the meal, and Lew to work it off, while Connie and I were both heading down to Nice.

Lew was still outside, playing with the terriers, when I left. 'Sorry I have to dash now,' I said. 'I'd meant to catch you up on the Perils of Pauline, but – never mind, it probably doesn't make the best Christmas hearing anyway. You be around tomorrow?'

Lew smiled gently. 'I'm not the one who's forever darting off in all directions. I'll be around.'

When I called for Lili I took a platter of holiday treats with me to the Isnard house. Irène said she appreciated the thought but not the food, having just been regaled with Mathilde's sublime feast sent across from the inn. I had to admit I was outclassed, particularly as Mathilde was sitting right there.

'Who would have thought we'd be spending Christmas afternoon this way?' Lili said as we drove down the hill. 'Or that we'd be glad to be able to do it?'

At the Gazagnaire house an exhausted Lucie Cordier turned over the three children to their Aunt Lili. The twins were bursting with mischief, and as Lili shooed them into the back seat of the 2CV and climbed in between them holding the baby, I knew that my task as chauffeur was far the easier.

At the hospital in Nice, we learned that the regulations had been bent and Serge and Sabine were permitted to share a room. When Lili put the baby in her sister-in-law's arms, there was no doubt that seeing her children was the only present Sabine wanted.

I had to restrain the twins. 'No, you mustn't climb on Papa's bed. Papa's been hurt. You can climb on Mama's bed if you don't bounce.'

'Papa's hurt? Where?'

Sabine explained, in three-year-old language, likening Serge's injury to a broken doll. Serge picked up the analogy.

'They're going to make a new leg for me, just like a doll's leg. It won't be alive like the old one. But I'll be able to stand and walk on it. And that's what legs are for.'

Lili jammed her fist to her mouth and turned quickly so the others would not see her face. I know what she was remembering.

Serge, his cap turned backwards, hunching over the handlebars of his Peugeot racer. Serge, brilliant at midfield for the St Martin football club. Serge, who never walked anywhere but ran for the sheer joy of it.

He might minimise his loss now, but his brave words held a powerful understatement.

'Whew, am I frazzled!' Lili said when we had returned the children to Lucie Cordier. 'I guess Sabine's used to it, but those twins don't just make double trouble. The mischief gets worse geometrically.'

'You'd better cross your fingers that Lucie holds up until Sabine's home. Otherwise you'll get them full-time.'

'Please God, no!'

We swung under the wrought-iron arch of le Nid de l'Aigle. At the far end of the car park a horn hooted twice, but now at dusk the feasting was long over and the lot almost empty. I parked Peu Belle in the slot closest to Irène Isnard's steps. Lili really did look wrung out.

'I'll call you in the morning and give you the number where I am,' I told her. 'Meanwhile I'll be at home.'

Lili didn't ask why I mentioned it. She had just seen her brother, and she knew how anxious I was to have mine tell me he was at least alive.

'You'll hear from him soon. I have a strong feeling – Addie! Isn't that an awful lot of smoke coming out of your chimney?'

It took one look through the treetops to send me sprinting down the path. Lili was with me by the time I had the padlock undone.

I opened the door, choked, pulled it shut. 'Quick, the fire brigade!'

Lili raced off.

For long seconds I stood staring at the door in the dreadful certainty that the firemen would never arrive in time. The nearest station was in Vence. And they might not even respond right away. On Christmas they would likely be undermanned. Calling them could well prove useless.

Finally I shook myself into action.

At the back of the house I heaved the garden hose off its

229

stanchion and screwed it on to the outside tap. I started dragging it forward, then stopped. Even if it reached to the door and through to the fire, I would not be able to see to direct it. The fire was just on the other side of this wall. What I needed was somehow to break through a window and – of course! The trick window, I could open that from the outside.

As I worked on it, I could hear shouting from the direction of the inn, and Lili's slight voice straining for volume as she cried, 'Help, help, fire!'

The window came free. I went back and turned the water on. Just as I was steeling myself to crawl over the sill, a hand closed over mine on the nozzle.

'Addie no! You can't go in there. Let me have it.'

'Rusty?'

'Let *go*, I said. Where's it burning, do you know?'

'I couldn't see. Too much smoke. Around the fireplace, I guess.'

Rusty climbed on to the sill.

'Wait!' I dragged my scarf from my pocket, thrust it under the nozzle and wrung it out. 'Tie this across your face.'

Rusty was inside about a minute, then he was back, doubled over the windowsill. He breathed in great panting gulps as the smoke poured out over his head. A minute of breathing, and he went back into the smoke.

The third time he came back he said, when he was able to speak, 'Open the door. And any other window you can reach.'

'The flames are out?'

'I think. Won't know until we can see.'

I went through the door and, when I had the first window open, followed Rusty's example by hanging over the sill for breathable air. Then I opened the remaining windows. The smoke cleared enough for me to find my big flashlight and inspect the chaos.

Outside there was a babble of voices, and heads poked through the windows. Mathilde was there, and Lili, and Régine, and Jean-Marc with his coat pulled crookedly over what looked like a pyjama top.

Inside there was a sodden and sooty mess before the

fireplace. A good proportion of it was Lew's greenery; the mantelpiece was now bare. A couple of the rush floor mats were gone, and though Gran's rocker was hardly singed, the overstuffed chair that had become Lew's was badly burned and still smouldering.

Jean-Marc helped me get the chair out of the house. 'At least this is the last time you'll be asked to lug this old thing,' I said. I started to laugh nervously, reaction setting in. Jean-Marc grasped my shoulders firmly until it subsided.

Then we all waited for the *pompiers* to show up and tell us the fire was out.

Meanwhile, we tried to figure how it might have started. Rusty thought the candles in the mantelpiece decorations could have been to blame, but Jean-Marc was sure they had been safely placed and carefully blown out. And I was positive the fire had been well banked before we left, and the gas lamps properly turned off.

When the firemen came, they had no further ideas. They did say it was all right to swamp the mess out, so I found a sheet of oilcloth and shovelled the sludge on to it, and Rusty and Jean-Marc carried two corners each.

Everybody wanted to know what he or she could do to help me.

Mathilde said the tower room at the Eagle's Nest was mine if I wanted it, and Régine hastily seconded the offer.

Lili said I had my own bed at their house, and Madame Isnard would be offended if I went anywhere else.

Jean-Marc thought I should go to his place and work on his bottle of brandy. Although that was his prescription for everything, it did sound unusually tempting now.

Rusty felt it would be kinder for everyone to leave me in peace. However, if I could manage to stay intact until Saturday, he proposed to take me to a party down on the coast where I would meet the Riviera's leading literary and journalistic lights. This would keep me out of trouble for a few hours at least. I rejected the imputation, but accepted the date.

Neither Rusty nor Jean-Marc seemed willing to leave me alone, even to walk as far as Madame Isnard's house.

231

I asked them to wait outside while I changed. My clothes reeked of smoke, giving me an excuse for privacy while I packed an overnight bag. The first item in, without hesitation, was my sheaf of notes on Flairaud's plant filed in Gran's looseleaf recipe book. Only then came fresh underclothes, jeans, a couple of shirts and sweaters, and my nightwear and toothbrush.

After giving the floor a summary swabbing, I hooked the louvered shutters and passed my luggage out the door. Rusty took the camera case and recorder, Jean-Marc the overnight bag.

'All secure?' Jean-Marc asked.

'Not half,' I said with determined jauntiness. 'Behind the shutters the windows are wide open so the place can air out. But what the heck, this house has weathered a bashed roof and a robbery and a fire. I figure she's determined to stand.' I pulled the door to, and snapped the padlock through the hasp.

When I tugged the lock to be sure it had caught, I felt the hasp give. I brought the flashlight up and found the screws on the left-hand plate were a good centimetre loose. I stood looking at it for a minute, then said evenly, 'That's funny, I could have sworn that door jamb was solid. I'll have to get some plastic wood tomorrow.'

Beside me I heard Jean-Marc say, almost inaudibly, 'I salute you. Anyone else would have broken long ago.'

Lili and I were nibbling at leftover turkey and Madame Isnard, older and wiser, was having only tea, when the curé came in. He apologised for making his visit a brief and late one ('Christmas is high on my list of working days') but said he had stopped by to say how glad he was to see Madame Isnard among the congregation again. Also he wanted the latest news on Serge and Sabine.

'Walk down with me, Addie,' he said on his way out. 'I want to talk to you.'

I went with him to the Eagle's Nest parking lot. His little black Simca was parked next to Peu Belle, but he continued walking across the gravelled courtyard.

232

'What was it you wanted to talk to me about, Father?'

'I don't. I want to talk to Madame Scotto.'

I halted on the spot. 'Oh no! Not if you're mixing me up in it, you don't. Wild horses wouldn't drag me back into that place. And I think you ought to stay clear, too. The last I knew, Scotto was there.'

That stopped the priest. 'Maybe you're right. Still, I told the poor woman I would come back soon. If I hadn't been so long in Brignoles – you think her husband will be in her room with her?'

'What's that got to do with it?'

'Will he?'

'Not likely, but – '

'Then come along and show me which is her window.'

I tried to talk Monsieur le Curé out of it, but he was adamant, so against my better judgment I led him to the barred window at the end of the east wing. The window was just out of his reach. He went forward into the garden and came back with a bamboo wand which he tapped gently against the glass.

'Patrice,' he intoned in his best pulpit voice. 'Patrice, my child, are you there?'

I was afraid the voice was too loud, that it would cause some other window to spring open or would frighten the woman. But the curtains parted swiftly, and the window swung wide.

'Lord, you've come back!' Patrice Scotto sounded as if she verged on hysteria.

'Yes, my daughter, just as I promised.' The curé stepped back so that he could see and be seen from the window. I thought I was deep enough in the shadows, but apparently Madame Scotto could see me too.

'And you've brought the blonde angel with you!'

This gave the priest a second's pause, but he recovered, and beckoned me to stand beside him. 'The angel's name is Addie. She helps me quite a lot. You can trust her.' The curé continued, 'How are you, Patrice? Have you been feeling better?'

'I'm trying, God, I'm trying very hard. I stay out of bed

233

and walk back and forth, back and forth. But it's so hard, with the medicine. . . .'

'I know, my daughter. But you must be strong. Have faith, and pray, and I will come to help you.'

'Yes, please, Lord, I need so much help, I've been weak for so – '

'*Patrice!*' Régine cried.

Madame Scotto whirled and spread her arms, facing into the room. I dived for the *mas* wall and slid quickly around the corner, with Monsieur le Curé right after me. Régine's voice followed us.

'Come away from that window instantly. You'll make yourself ill again. Who were you talking to?'

'N-nobody, Régine.'

'Don't lie to me, Patrice. I heard you talking.'

'But you won't believe me when I tell you.'

'What's going on here?' This voice was stern and male.

'Oh, Joseph, she thinks she's been talking with God again. Honestly, I have *no* idea – ' Régine's words were cut off by the closing of the window.

I tugged the priest's sleeve and we recrossed the car park as quietly as we could. At the bottom of the steps I told him I thought he had better come up to the door with me. Then I would turn on the lights and call goodbye to him as he went down, so the sound of his car leaving would be associated with a visit to the Isnard house.

I found Lili idly leafing through a magazine and her great-aunt snoozing. After the priest's visit, Lili said, Madame Isnard had reminisced a bit. She talked of last Christmas, Lucien and herself presiding over the big family table after the guests were fed and dispersed, Mathilde bringing out the family's platters and sitting down with them. 'Then suddenly she was off into the past again, talking as though Uncle Lucien were still alive. It's so unsettling. One minute I think she's tracking perfectly, and the next, she has everything muddled.'

'But does she really, Lili? I mean, I know the present sometimes feels so full of loss and pain that she just slips out into a prettier time. But she doesn't stay away for long, at

234

least not since I've seen her. And when she *is* in the present, she's not in the least mixed up. Or no more than you and I.'

'Yes, I see. She doesn't mix up the two. She just switches sometimes from now to not-now, when she has to.'

'Exactly. I wish I'd understood that, the first time I heard about the weird noises in the night. I might have believed a little sooner.'

'Were they there tonight?' Lili asked in alarm.

'No.'

'You know, I think that was the best part about last night, going to Mass and all, that after we got home there weren't any of those noises.'

'I can imagine. Somehow I don't think there'll be any tonight either.'

'No, really?'

'Really. I've left the outside lights on, and I have an idea the spirit voices won't like that. Let's get Irène into bed, and all have a good night's sleep.'

We did. But before I climbed into the bed across from Lili's, I stood at the window for a minute looking down over the inn to the village, and wondering what this Christmas Day would have been like if Lucien Isnard had lived another year.

As it was, the Eagle's Nest had gone from surrogate home to uncertain host, from good neighbour to encroacher, from haven to threat.

I remembered the first time the inn had earned inclusion in the Guide Michelin, that universal bible of the traveller, and how Lucien Isnard had held the new year's edition in his hands, smelling the fresh ink, savouring the crisp black type that commended his inn to the world's attention – crisp black except for the red symbol of tranquillity, the little bird with a rocker underneath.

The solid stone walls, the round tower, the tile roofs of the *mas* were just as before, I knew, as I turned from the window and crawled into bed. But the Eagle's Nest no longer rated a red rockingbird.

If the inspectors from Michelin awarded such a symbol, I thought, a mockingbird might do.

TEN

Friday, 26 December

THE DAY after Christmas seemed, later, only a blink long from start to sundown. Maybe that was because what happened in the evening was so much more important to me. Or maybe because I had determined to attack matters more directly from now on.

I started practising the directness first thing in the morning with Madame Isnard. The old woman was awake early, saying she had slept wonderfully well and asking how I had managed to exorcise her ghost voices.

'I haven't yet, not permanently. But it seems they don't like too much company. Meanwhile, you may be able to help me with a problem of my own.' I told her, without prettying up the story, of my troubles with Scotto.

'So that's what all those veiled references were about. I did wonder, though I didn't want to pry.'

'I ought to have come to you straight off, Irène, but Mathilde felt nobody should tell you anything distressing.'

'What nonsense! If people try to keep me from worrying, they just make me worry about what it is they're keeping from me. Oh dear, was that too garbled?'

'Not a bit. Funny how I'm suddenly treated like an adult and you're not. It must feel awfully insulting.'

Irène Isnard smiled gently. 'People mean well. How is it you think I can help, dear?'

'Well, the *notaire* LeClerc handled everything for Gran and he's in jail, and my own lawyer isn't breaking records getting things traced. I wondered whether your papers might include a copy of the sale to Gran.'

236

'I'm sorry, Addie, but that land was in Lucien's name, not mine, and when he died it was LeClerc who went through all his papers. So you're back where you started.'

'Looks like it.' I grimaced. 'If I could even be sure Scotto wasn't right – '

'Oh, but he's not,' Irène Isnard said vigorously. 'I remember the circumstances very clearly. There had to be two separate conveyances, because when the sale first went through, it turned out the property line wasn't where we thought it was. Scotto had that part right. But then Lucien sold your grandmother the rest of her property for something like one franc, just to make it legal. I'd be perfectly willing to give a sworn statement to that effect, if it would be of use.'

Irène Isnard must have seen my reaction, though I tried not to show it. She sighed softly.

'No, I don't suppose it would. I wouldn't be regarded as a very reliable witness, now, would I?'

I decided on directness at Flairaud's plant too. The charade of interviewing all the employees would only waste time. Théo's briefing was so thorough that it wouldn't take me long to identify the breach in Flairaud's security. He probably could have done it himself if he weren't reluctant to suspect any of his own workers.

The family were just finishing breakfast when I got to their house in Grasse. Flairaud was anxious to be off to the plant, but I prevailed on Cécile to wait and drive out with me, as soon as I had received the report of my lieutenant Théo.

Théo had plenty to report. He and his pals had done an impressive job of sleuthing, even putting a watch on the letter slot outside the main post office. 'Charles had the idea of leaning his bike against the wall so the handlebar mirror pointed up. Even if a letter was put in the slot face down, he could see if it was addressed to the Régine postbox. We must have missed some, of course, but we identified five.'

Next he showed me elaborate charts of the movements of the individuals under surveillance, designated by number and cross-referenced, with a dossier for each. The photos varied in quality but, though none were quite mug-shots, most were usable for identification.

'Do you have duplicates of these?' I asked.

Théo handed me an envelope. 'I had the darkroom print some extra sets. Let me know if you need more.'

'Théo, believe me, if I need *any*thing, I can be sure you'll have thought of it before I do.'

Théo was gratified by the praise, and his mother even more so. On the way to the perfume works she tried to live up to the example set by her son. She didn't just answer my questions literally, but stopped to think exactly what I was driving at. Before we reached the plant, we were in agreement.

'Then it has to be someone who works right in the office,' she said.

'If you and your husband have the only keys, it does. Nobody else could come in during office hours and systematically copy the files without being noticed. Nobody except the office staff, in fact, would know where to look.'

The process of elimination was equally swift. There were only four in the office, three not counting Cécile, all women. One was Flairaud's maiden aunt, a woman so efficient and upright she could never have been suspected even without family ties. A second was also unlikely, since she was the wife of the chief chemist, who had a financial stake in the firm – and she was also Cécile's best friend.

Which left Yvette.

Yvette did the routine typing and filing and, significantly, the photocopying. She had only been with the firm for six months, but already Cécile was looking forward to the day when the girl would snaffle some equally brainless young man and leave to get married. Meanwhile, she was not quite bad enough to fire.

Cécile loaned me her private office to interview the girl. I began by asking whether she liked her employers.

'Oh yes! My uncle told me Flairaud was a good man to work for. My uncle runs the stockroom here, you know.' That explained how she got her job.

'Then you wouldn't knowingly do anything to harm them?'

'Of course not!'

'Yvette,' I said, 'surely you can't imagine that what you are doing could *help* them?'

'I'm not doing – '

'You are. And you have for several months.'

'I don't know what you're talking about.' Her voice was now a trifle uncertain.

'Don't you? Someone is passing information outside this plant. And that someone is you.'

The girl glared at me defiantly now. 'What right do you have, a foreigner, coming in here and accusing innocent people of – '

'Every right. Your employers chose to call in me, rather than the police. If you think about it,' I gave her a chance to, 'I'm sure you too will prefer me to talk to.'

The girl looked down at her hands. They were covered with gaudy rings, and the fingernails were too long for typing and too painted for good taste.

'He – he promised it wouldn't hurt them,' she mumbled.

'He?'

She still avoided my eyes. 'The fellow who asked me to give him the papers.'

I let that go for the moment. 'And you believed him?'

'Well, sure. He said he worked for somebody who sold supplies to places like this. If his boss knew what Flairaud's orders were, in and out, he could undersell the competition and get the account. With the papers from me, he wouldn't cut his prices more than he had to, but Flairaud would still save money, and I'd get something to spend on myself.' She looked up sullenly. 'They don't really pay me very much, you know.'

I could imagine. She was probably paid only double what she was worth.

'What else can you tell me about him?'

Yvette knew the man only as Albert, and she always gave him the photocopied orders at the same discothèque where she had first met him. Her powers of observation and description were nil. She could not guess his age or even remember the colour of his eyes.

'All right, Yvette, I want you to look at these photographs. Some are just of people who live in Grasse, but some might be this Albert and his friends. Tell me if you recognise anyone.'

It was the first look through the photos for me as well as for Yvette. Interestingly, we managed between us to identify about a third of them. Some Yvette knew as local Grassois. Some I recognised as the cronies Scotto had convened at the Eagle's Nest. Of these, to my relief, Yvette named one as her contact Albert. But there were two other photographs in Théo's gallery that were of infinitely greater interest.

One, I was sure, was the man in the black coat who had followed the violet truck in his van and planted the *plastique* that blew it up.

And one, sharply focused and full-face, was Jean-Marc Bertrand.

Marcellin Morin came straight to Grasse when I phoned. I had forgotten how fast he drove. He reached Flairaud's plant moments after Théo – who only had to call off his cohorts, gather up his records, and come eight kilometres by moto.

In the interim, Flairaud, Cécile and I conferred, and sent the girl Yvette home with orders to stay there. She would be told after the weekend whether she could keep her job. Meanwhile she was under no circumstances to see or speak to Albert, and if he telephoned, she was to say she was ill.

Actually we wanted to get her away from the plant before any police, even Adjudant-chef Morin in mufti, showed up – as long as the stupid girl didn't know an official investigation was underway, she couldn't let it slip to Albert before the police were ready to make arrests.

When I introduced Flairaud and his family to Marcellin, I gave Théo a good build-up so Marcellin would grant him an attentive hearing. Once he did, things took care of themselves, and the boy and the gendarme got along famously.

240

After listening to us all for almost an hour and struggling to fit together our overlapping stories, Adjudant-chef Morin protested that he was outnumbered and convoyed us to the headquarters of the gendarmerie company in Grasse. There, in the forbiddingly military surroundings of the Caserne Kellerman, it was we who were outnumbered. Flairaud and Cécile found themselves closeted with a pair of gendarmes for hours going over the incidents of hijacking, theft and sabotage that had plagued them. And Théo and I got the attention of a whole troop of Marcellin's colleagues. Trouble in the perfume industry was not news to them, it seemed, though our effort to link it all to Scotto was. By the end of the afternoon, when we were dismissed, we were sagging.

'At least you can go home now to a quiet apéro and dinner,' Marcellin Morin said. 'Our work's just beginning – identifying those photos, taking them around to the other manufacturers, and the growers.' He turned to Théo. 'Well, I don't have to tell you about footslogging police work. You and your friends have been ranging the countryside these last few days like the Marshals of the Ancien Régime.'

Théo said modestly, 'I thought of us more as the boys in Baker Street who ran errands for Sherlock Holmes.'

The gendarme grinned and handed the boy a recruiting brochure. 'If you should ever decide you'd prefer police work to perfume, you can count on a strong recommendation from me.'

We were on our way out the door when Morin called us back. 'Addie! Phone for you.'

I frowned at the receiver in puzzlement. '*Allo, oui?*'

'Addie? Are you all right, honey?'

'Sure, Connie, I'm fine. Why?'

'Because I just tracked you down at a gendarmerie fortress when I thought you were safely playing in a perfume factory. Considering your recent misadventures, you can understand how this might worry me.'

'Don't let it. We had a breakthrough today. With a little luck we just might nail Scotto's hide to the wall.'

'That's nice. Now listen to *my* news. I just got a message

241

from Stateside. Let me read it to you. "IN RE YOUR QUERY OUR CENTRAL AMERICAN DESK, PLEASE CHECK WITH PAN-AM ON ARRIVAL FIVE THIRTY FLIGHT FROM NEW YORK." I don't know what it means, but I'm off to the airport as fast as my hot little Pontiac will take me. Can you meet me there?'

'*Can* I? I'm not even going to ask my buddies here for a motorcycle escort. They wouldn't be able to keep up.'

In fact it took an excruciatingly long time to get there. The general direction from Grasse to Nice-Côte d'Azur Airport was downhill, but the road through Roquefort was a constantly twisting one, and I was stuck behind a fuel oil delivery truck for kilometres. Then in Cagnes it was rush hour, with traffic backed up more than usual by the holiday influx from Paris and elsewhere. Finally the bridge over the Var was cut to one lane by a breakdown. When I got to the airport I didn't bother to park Peu Belle legally. I just pulled her up to the curb in front of the arrivals section and left her.

Inside, the arrivals board said the flight had been down for twenty-five minutes. It took me another couple of minutes to find the Pan-Am desk. As I fought through the crowds towards it, I heard Connie's voice calling, 'Addie! Over here, Addie!'

The scene when I turned was more beautiful to me than any of the splendours nature provided on this celebrated coast.

There, standing half a head taller than anyone around him, his blond hair like a golden halo, a grin on his tanned face, one arm encased in plaster and the other holding Connie, was my big brother Jay.

In the car Jay caught me up on what he had already told Connie. The drive to St Martin, in fact, took much longer than the few minutes he'd had with Connie at the airport, but the telling also took longer because, as Jay informed me with one of his sunny grins, Connie was a marvellous listener who didn't keep interrupting him all the time with questions.

'But of course I have to know every little thing,' I protested. 'I care a lot about you.'

'Yeah? As far as that goes, Connie put on a pretty good imitation when she met me.'

He sounded halfway smug, and I felt wholly jealous, at least for a few seconds. Then I let myself be glad for Connie that she'd had first chance at him. When my turn came, the welcome he got was maybe tumultuous, but hardly a surprise.

Connie's Pontiac was just behind us now. She'd tried, sincerely, to leave us together at the airport and go back to Nice. But she was so obviously glad to see Jay, and she'd suffered so long with me, that we both insisted she come up for the evening.

Jay wouldn't tell me any more than he'd already told Connie, he said. Then he'd have to tell every story twice. So I only heard the dramatic highlights of his trek up into the Cordillera, his arrival at Joaquín's village, the sudden shock of the earthquake, the illiterate medicine man who had placed his broken arm in a mysterious poultice of soaked leaves before splinting it, and the wait at the bottom of the mountain for the fallen bridge to receive a temporary rope replacement.

'So when did you finally get back to San José?'

'Christmas Eve. But I didn't wait around. People were still lined up six deep for doctors, and all I had was a broken arm. It was a lot harder to get into a hospital than to get out of the country. Relief planes were leaving empty every hour. I got the arm set at an Air Force base in south Texas. Then they dumped me on the next flight for Andrews. I didn't care as long as they kept sending me somewhere in the direction of France.'

'How come you didn't call us?'

'Baby, you've got to be kidding! Getting a phone call through to France at Christmas is like winning the lottery. And telegrams aren't even accepted. It was a major coup just getting through to Zuckerman in Springfield.'

'Who's he?'

'The lawyer who has Gran's papers. Or had. I got him to air-express them down to Kennedy so I could bring them with me. He sounded a little testy about my interrupting his holiday.'

'Tough. So you just picked up the papers and flew on here?'

'Sure. One thing you *can* do at Christmas is find an empty seat on a plane. So I signalled Foggy Bottom to signal Connie and I took off. Now please tell me from the top, what's all this crap about somebody named Scotto claiming our house?'

That part of the story lasted until we got to the Eagle's Nest. Connie pulled up beside us and we all went along the path to Gran's house. The house smelled a little smoky, but it was still standing. Jay, male-fashion, immediately began to lay a fire, one-armed. Connie helped. And I got the lamps lighted and opened my day's mail.

It wasn't mail brought by the postman. It was a manila envelope tied to my doorknob and addressed to A. A. Forrester in the bold hand I recognised as Lew's. There was a sort of chromium pipe inside, and a note that said:

Just now catching up on your exploits; I've not been unsympathetic, only ignorant. Crave audience. If granted, kindly blow on enclosed Horn of Roland. Wee beasts will hear and summon me.

Yours, Lew.

I put the pipe to my mouth and blew tentatively. It didn't make any sound. I stood in the doorway and blew harder. Still no sound. I tried it backwards and upside down, and again the original way with all my lung power.

Then I started to laugh. The thing was evidently a dog whistle, pitched too high for the human ear to hear. The way I'd been calling them, Dylan and Caitlin must have thought I was Gabriel blowing the Last Trumpet. So it was no surprise when Lew showed up just ten minutes later.

At this point Connie was prospecting in the refrigerator, Jay was unloading a basket of logs into the wood hatch, and I was trying to explain how I had been careless enough to let the house catch fire.

I heard the dogs before the doorknocker, and Lew was talking the moment I pulled the latch.

'Addie, why didn't you tell me all these dreadful things? It was only this morning that I even heard about the lorry being blown up, let alone your getting coshed and robbed and – '

Behind me I heard Jay shout, 'What?!' and Connie say, 'We've had a couple earthquakes of our own here. Tell you later,' and Jay ask, 'Who's this?' and Connie say, 'Her boyfriend, or one of them. The frontrunner, I think,' and meanwhile Lew was still talking.

' – but if I'd known, I'd never have gone off and left you alone in this house. If you even had Dylan and Caitlin to stay with you – '

Jay was beside me then, his good arm around me. 'She won't be alone any more. Now that I'm here, I intend to stay until things are cleared up.'

For a moment Lew felt rebuffed, and it showed in his eyes. Then suddenly his whole face lit up. 'You must be the brother. By God, am I glad to see you!'

It was then, I could tell, that Jay decided he was prepared to like Lew.

Connie did the introductions. We moved into the living-room.

'Hey, where's my chair?' Lew said. When he heard how that sounded, he looked sidelong at Jay.

'Your mistletoe didn't work too well,' I told him.

'What are you talking about?'

'As fire prevention. We had a little excitement here late yesterday afternoon.' I gave him an abbreviated account. 'Luckily, it didn't seem to have been burning long before I got home.'

'It couldn't have been,' Lew said. 'After everybody else left, I pottered outside here for an hour or so, clearing weeds from the flagstones and doing some pruning.' Again he glanced at my brother in apology for sounding possessive. 'So the start of the fire got delayed at least that long.'

'Do you mean what I think you mean?' Jay demanded.

'I do. It looks like we add arson to the list.'

Jay was silent for a minute. Then he turned to me. 'If it's not asking too much, sis, could you for once begin at the beginning?'

The telling took a while. I talked and Jay listened. Lew tended the fire and made drinks. Connie, across the kitchen divider, contributed to the episodes she'd taken part in. The story continued over the dinner table. Connie had whipped up an *arroz con pollo* which everyone agreed was delicious. I didn't think it was Lew or me she was trying to impress.

Lew left right after dinner, saying he'd intruded on family matters long enough.

Connie left too, but first she offered Jay the use of her sleeping bag, which was still in the trunk of the Pontiac, until the loft could be turned back into a usable bedroom. Jay accepted, with a murmured remark to Connie that made her turn a very pretty shade of pink.

When Jay came back and dumped the sleeping bag on the floor, I expected him to dive into it within sixty seconds. He couldn't have had a decent night's sleep in a week. Instead he added a couple of hand-width oak logs to the fire and said:

'Okay, baby sister. That was a nicely told string of colour pieces. But now that the others have gone, how about the hard news analysis?'

'What's to analyse?'

'The motives of friend Scotto, that's what.'

'You mean why he's been stirring up the flower growers and sabotaging trucks and wrecking Flairaud's business? If I knew, I'd have spent the day with the editor of *Nice-Matin* instead of with a whole company of gendarmes.'

'I'm not talking about what he's doing in Grasse. I'm talking about what he's doing in St Martin, right here at the top of the Route de la Chapelle.'

'Well, it's pretty clear he doesn't want any neighbours, us *or* Irène.'

'What's he done to Madame Isnard?'

I told him about the noises Irène Isnard heard in the

246

night. 'He bought her house *en viager*, you see, and she hasn't obliged him by dying promptly. I'll bet he arranged those noises to frighten her into moving out.'

'Or frighten her to death,' Jay said, only half joking.

'She's tougher than she looks. And he's not going to frighten me out either. Too bad if I spoiled his plans by showing up when I did. Nobody'd been here for two years, so he probably thought he could get away with anything he wanted. He almost did. Just think, Jay, if I'd come even one month later – '

'Yeah. You'd have found a vacant lot. We could have taken him to court, but that wouldn't give us back this house.'

'You love this place the same as me, don't you?'

'No. I love you *much* more than this place.'

'Seriously, though – '

'I am being serious. This is only a house, Addie. It's already put you in danger more than once. And it doesn't seem as attractive as it did, with Scotto for a neighbour. Maybe we shouldn't buck him.'

'Come on, Jay! You'd let that Corsican parvenu run us off?'

'I'd rather lose the house than my sister.'

'You're not going to lose either,' I said. 'And with luck we may not have Scotto for a neighbour much longer. He may go to join LeClerc in jail where he belongs. Even if the police don't pin anything on him, he may resell the inn if he can't make the alterations he wants. Irène might live a long time, the way she's going. And he's not going to get our property either, now that we know his story about the boundary line won't hold water.'

'Won't it?'

'I told you what Irène said about the second sale, didn't I? The one that gave Gran what she thought she'd bought in the first place.'

'Sure, but she doesn't have any proof, does she?'

'Well, no,' I admitted.

'Scotto may have a case after all. On the flight over, I went through the papers Zuckerman sent me, all the papers Dad brought back with him after Gran died. And there was one, just one, deed to this property. If Irène Isnard has no proof the line was redrawn, neither do we.'

I sat staring into the fire and trying not to feel down. We might not be able to prove that our house was ours, but my brother and I were together. I could hear him singing lustily from the shower.

I had to laugh when he came out, he looked so *outré* dressed in pyjama bottoms and a bright blue plastic garbage bag taped over his plaster cast. He extended the arm for me to de-bag it. Then he stood in front of the fire drying off.

'In the morning,' he said, 'I think I'll see what I can find out about Madame Isnard's ghost voices.'

'Fine. Then you can come to Grasse with me. I promised Marcellin Morin I'd bring him the notes from my interviews with the growers.' I got up and went into the kitchen.

'If you're getting a snack, bring me one too.'

'Jay! I saw how much of Connie's dinner you ate. You can't be serious.' I opened Gran's recipe binder on the divider and began taking out looseleaf sheets.

Jay chuckled. 'That's what you call a filing system? Keeping your interview notes in a cookbook?'

'Must be a trait I get from Gran. She had some peculiar ideas about filing. I found her *permis de séjour* under Luke 1:28.'

I went on removing notes from the ring binder. My own words did not register on me, but they did on Jay.

He lunged for the bookcase that held the big old leather-bound Lowell family Bible and, with his one good arm, carried it to the dining table. Laboriously he fanned the pages and amassed a small heap of papers, snapshots, yellowed newspaper cuttings, envelopes with faded ink. 'If this is where Gran tucked her treasures,' he explained, 'it's our best hope. Dad would have cleared out her desk. If it's anywhere –'

I came to help immediately. Hampered by his cast, Jay limited himself to preliminary sorting and left the unfolding of papers to me. We worked steadily, pausing only once for a few seconds when Jay came across Gran's sepia-coloured wedding portrait, taken the year the Great War ended. Then Jay put that too aside.

There was a flash of hope when I unfolded a bill of sale for a piece of property, signed by Lucien Isnard. But Jay looked it over and said the date and other particulars corresponded to the deed he already had, so it came from the original, incomplete sale.

We worked on, and the pile of discards mounted.

Almost at the end Jay stopped suddenly and sat looking at the envelope on top of the small stack remaining before him. Then he picked it up and, holding it in the fingers that protruded from his plaster cast, took out the piece of paper inside. This too he opened himself. He held it up so we both could see.

We read it through three times before we let ourselves believe it. Then Jay wrapped me in a crushing hug, plaster cast and all.

I could barely speak for laughing. 'You did it, Jay, you found it! All we have to do is bring this to the lawyer and our trouble with Scotto is over.'

In that happy belief, we settled down for a long and peaceful night's sleep.

ELEVEN

SHORTLY BEFORE noon, at the gendarmerie caserne in Grasse, Marcellin Morin listened to Jay's tale of his search for Madame Isnard's ghosts.

'There weren't any wires that I could see, anywhere on that wall, or along the foundation either. After I spent some time looking through the shrubbery, I began to question whether those weird noises were really a tape-recording at all.'

'Sounds like the most reasonable theory.'

'But not if somebody had to sneak up under her bedroom window every night. It would only make sense to work it by remote control – which would mean an auxiliary speaker on a long lead. And I couldn't find the lead.'

'Did you decide there were no noises, then?' Morin asked. 'Or simply no wires?'

'Exactly. I stopped thinking how I'd have done it myself, and started figuring how somebody with other resources might do it. That made me focus on the window itself. Which I should have done in the first place.'

'What was it? False lintel? Something under the sill?'

'The outside of the shutters. Diagonal struts had been added. It was a good job, symmetrical, with the wood almost matching, and anyway nobody'd see because in daytime that side is pinned back to the wall. But one of the struts sounded hollow when I knocked. I thought I'd better leave it to you to dismantle, but my guess is you'll find the speaker.'

'And a battery-powered radio receiver, eh?'

'I'd say so. And if you check which rooms at the inn have a good enough view of Madame Isnard's room and Lili's to see when the lights go on and off, you'll shorten your search for the transmitter.'

Marcellin Morin cleared his throat. 'Yes, well, it may be some time before we're ready to go bursting into le Nid de l'Aigle with a search warrant. There's still a lot of preliminary work. Your sister's given us a good deal to think about.'

'I'll bet.' Jay punched my shoulder affectionately. 'Addie's been stirring up hornets' nests ever since she was six. Amazing how seldom she gets stung, considering.'

'Don't stir up this one any more.' Morin turned to face me. 'I mean it, young lady. Forget the investigative reporting and stick to flower photography until this is over. Don't do anything that might goad Scotto.'

I raised a hand. 'Worry not. I'd like Scotto to forget I exist.'

'Me too,' Jay agreed. 'I'm not even sure I want him to hear *I'm* in town.'

'Right,' I said.

'Wrong,' said Marcellin Morin in a tone I knew. 'Avoid him by all means, Mr Forrester, but it might be helpful if he learned you were here. You can manage that?'

'Addie can. Can't you, sis?'

'I could let it slip to Régine, I suppose.'

Marcellin Morin nodded. 'Good. Then Scotto will be more inclined to keep his hands off.'

After lunch I took the drive from Grasse to Nice at a relaxed speed. Yesterday I had been tearing headlong for the airport and news of Jay; today he sat beside me. Though the air was chill and the sky an ominous overcast, I was in a sunny mood.

Jay said, 'I hope you don't think it's cowardice.'

'What is?'

'My avoiding Scotto.'

'Anybody in his right mind would avoid Scotto.'

'I could handle talking to him, it's not that. In the diplomatic corps, you spend half your time smiling politely at people you know are knifing you in the back. You get used to it.'

251

'What then?'

Jay gave one of his engaging grins. 'I'd rather he didn't know my sister's dauntless protector is a one-armed invalid.'

'You don't look so harmless, even in a cast,' I told him. 'Anyway, our protection is that paper in your pocket, and the faster we get it into Robert Mercier's hands, the better I'll feel.'

The lawyer was just unlocking the door of his firm's offices when we arrived at three. Our footsteps echoed in the empty reception room as he led us to his private office.

After I introduced Jay, I said, 'It's awfully nice of you to come in on Saturday afternoon. We appreciate it.'

'I'm a very philanthropic fellow,' the lawyer said. 'For instance, I didn't call you on Wednesday when I might have. The answer to my query came back then, but I decided not to spoil your Christmas. So I was glad to hear you say you've got good news.'

'What was it you found? These?' Jay handed Mercier the bill of sale and deed from the original transaction between Lucien Isnard and Gran.

The lawyer flipped through them. 'That's right. And if you've examined them closely, you'll know they support Scotto's contention straight down the line.'

'Luckily, the widow of Lucien Isnard remembered there was more to it than that. Tell him, sis.'

I recounted Irène Isnard's story about the second sale, and our ultimately successful search for proof.

Jay laid before Robert Mercier the printed form, filled in by typewriter, naming LeClerc as the *notaire*, and signed by Lucien Isnard as vendor and Gran as buyer.

'What puzzles me,' he said, 'is why it doesn't have a deed to go with it, like the other one.'

Mercier scanned the form and began to laugh. 'No mystery, no mystery at all.'

We waited for him to share the joke.

'In France, you see, there are two branches of the legal profession. My own, the *avocats*, are of course uniformly honourable and high-minded gentlemen who regard the defence of the law as a sacred calling.' He looked up archly.

'But the *notaires* too often see the law simply as a means to make money. For instance, every time property is sold, the new title must be drawn up by a *notaire*, who receives for his pains the exorbitant sum of ten per cent of the purchase price. In the original sale, that is, LeClerc got four thousand francs merely for preparing this.' The lawyer picked up the cardboard folder containing the deed. 'And even then it wasn't done correctly. When the buyer and seller discovered the error and went to him to put it right, he let them sign this.' Now Mercier picked up the second agreement to sell. 'But that's all he did. Preparing another deed would have meant getting the pink sheet from the tax people, and official stamps, and processing charges, altogether several hours of work – for which he would be entitled to ten per cent of the nominal purchase price of one franc.'

'So he simply filed it and forgot it?' I asked.

'Evidently.'

'And then when Scotto came along, the two of them put their heads together and tore up that inconvenient piece of paper. Some people just brim with integrity, don't they,' Jay said. 'So how do we stand now?'

'Solidly, I'd say. I'll petition the court on Monday. Normally this paper alone might not guarantee our winning, but the fact that LeClerc is already in jail for some other bit of creative law practice doesn't exactly hurt. I'll keep you informed.'

While Robert Mercier put the precious paper in his wall safe, Jay used his phone to see whether Connie was at home. Fifteen minutes later we were in her apartment.

'That's fabulous!' She hugged and kissed us both. 'It calls for a super-special celebration. Can I take you guys someplace fancy for dinner? Tell you what, we'll go to Monte Carlo. Okay?'

Jay was all for it. So was I.

'I'll have to go home and change,' I said. 'But that's okay, it'll give me a chance to plant the word at the Eagle's Nest about your arrival, Jay. You can stay here. I'll only be – oh *shoot!*'

253

'What's wrong?'

'I forgot I have a date for tonight. Never mind, I can break it. Connie, where's your phone book?'

'You don't have to cancel, sis,' Jay said. 'We can celebrate another night. I'm not leaving soon.'

'Who's the date with?' Connie wanted to know.

I told them about the party Rusty had invited me to.

'But, Addie honey, if it's Jeremy Arlington's crowd, all the journalists up and down the coast will be there. You'd make all sorts of professional contacts. Don't you think you ought to go?'

'Weren't you looking forward to it, sis?'

'Well, yes,' I admitted.

The pair of them urged me not to change my plans just for them. Jay said he could take Connie out here in Nice tonight, and we'd all go to Monte Carlo tomorrow. The look on Connie's face when he said that settled the issue. If I made it a threesome, I'd feel mean about it all evening. Then Jay had an afterthought.

'What about this Rusty? Is he okay? He's not a friend of Scotto or anything?'

I laughed. 'Hardly. I don't think Californians and Corsicans mix. Not that Rusty's a goody-goody. I'd lay odds he's the local dope dealer. But he does that for the same reason he does other things – he likes being the leader of the gang and having people come to him for favours. It's his form of stroking. I think he's basically harmless.'

'All right. But remember, go to the inn first thing and do what the gendarme said. And if you can, try to get someone to walk over to the house with you.'

'Jay! I'm a big girl.'

He kissed me. 'I know. Big and brash. I'll be home tonight before you are. In the meantime, *try* to stay out of trouble.'

The electric Christmas stars and comets' tails blazed against the solidly dark sky over St Martin as I crawled to a halt in front of the square. The invariable backup of traffic seemed

254

worse than ever. Part of the reason was clear to see. The western half of the square was barricaded off, and before Marchetti's grocery several men worked at erecting a large platform. It looked like the one used last week for the violet growers' rally.

A hand rapped on Peu Belle's fender and René Cordier motioned me to pull over. I did, intensifying the bottleneck, and flipped up my window.

'Did you get to the hospital today?' he asked.

'Yes, for a few minutes. Serge is looking a lot better. Sabine wants to stay with him through tomorrow, but she'll be home Monday morning.'

'It can't be any too soon. Lucie's a wreck. I used to think our own kids were monsters.'

I nodded. 'What's the platform for? You planning a rally every Saturday?'

'*Merde*, I hope not. But after what happened this week, we've got to get together and decide something, don't we?'

'When is it?'

'Hour from now. You coming? You could cover it for your paper and give us a sympathetic write-up.'

'Can't say, René. I'll have to see.'

The car behind me honked. I moved my 2CV forwards the few yards possible and eventually made it through the village.

As I crossed the bridge and swung up the Route de la Chapelle, I weighed the possibility of attending the rally. True, Adjudant-chef Morin had forbidden me to do any more reporting. But just standing in the square with everyone else in the village – surely that didn't count? Anyway, my date with Rusty wasn't until seven. If I arranged to meet him at the Commerce, then got there early and sat outside listening to what went on across the road –

The debate resolved itself within half a kilometre.

The Route de la Chapelle was poorly surfaced to start with, and Peu Belle never took it smoothly, but suddenly I could feel her limping badly. Poor two-horse, I thought, she's thrown a shoe. Sure enough, when I got out to look, the left rear tyre was flat.

It was no place to change a wheel. The road was narrow and steep and dimly lighted. So I got back into Peu Belle, put one foot on the clutch and the other on the brake, and rolled her downhill as far as the chapel. There I took the 2CV manual from the glove compartment and was looking for the tyre-changing instructions when I belatedly woke up.

Rusty expected, no doubt, to go to this party in my car. So why not let Rusty change the tyre?

I locked Peu Belle and slogged up the hill, wishing I were more warmly dressed. But with all my 2CV's faults, her heater worked, so I'd worn only a light sweater when Jay and I left this morning. Now there was a distinctly wintery nip to the air. If this had been Massachusetts, instead of the Mediterranean coast, I would have said I smelled snow.

Still, the exertion of the climb warmed me. And if I had underdressed, at least I had sensibly worn Adidas instead of high-heeled boots.

As I finally turned through the wrought-iron gates of le Nid de l'Aigle, I began to relax. Another couple of minutes and I would give Régine and Scotto the vital news that Jay was here, and invoke Rusty's help.

It worked out a little differently.

As I walked into the parking lot, I saw the wild figure of Patrice Scotto standing behind the bars of her brightly lighted window. She saw me just as soon.

'Angel!' she called in a high, carrying voice. 'Angel Addie! I knew you'd come when I asked. Be quick, angel!'

My first impulse was to hurry away. But the deranged woman would only call louder, I was sure. So I hurried forwards instead, imploring her to be quiet.

She had to talk to me, she insisted; they were going to do terrible things and I had to help her. There was no time to lose. Her voice rose again alarmingly.

'Yes, Patrice, I'll help. But shut the window right away, and draw the curtain. You don't want them to hear, do you? I'll talk to God and come back to you as soon as I can.'

256

This seemed to calm her, and she did as I said.

Heaven knew how long she would stay calm, though. Somehow I must get hold of Monsieur le Curé. If he had a plan for handling this tornado he had unleashed, he had not told me what it might be.

Maybe Mathilde knew. I went down the garden steps and around the curving flagstone walk to the kitchen. But although several cauldrons simmered on the big stove, Mathilde wasn't there.

I went through into the dining-room. Again no Mathilde.

The glass doors to the main hall stood open, and I was about to seek Régine there when I heard two voices. They rose together, Régine's in agitation and Rusty's in anger.

'Are you crazy?' she said. 'I told you never to come here.'

'Sweetheart, you're through telling me anything. Tonight I'm doing the telling, and you'd better listen hard. There won't be any more favours, or any routine business either. Our relationship is over, finished, broken, terminated.'

Régine's voice went flat. 'You think it's that simple?'

'I know it is. It may take a while, but I'll find a supplier who can provide the same quality for my clients without the weird side orders you and your friends add on. I deal, sure, but I don't do arson and bombings and –'

'It wasn't a bomb, I swear it wasn't! I told you –'

'Yeah, and I believed you. It was just a package. If I put it in the violet truck, somebody'd pick it up in Paris. Of course I figured it for coke at least or maybe smack. But it was just a simple favour – until the truck blew up. Even the next day I believed you when you said it wasn't connected. But after the fire, how could I swallow anything you said?'

'You know yourself we had to look for her papers. That girl was poking into all kinds of things, and if she got on to the drugs, we were in trouble.'

'You didn't find anything, though, did you? I told you, I dropped a couple of hints and she wasn't interested.'

'But we had to be sure. If you'd gone in yourself the way I asked you –'

'I don't do housebreaks either. And I wouldn't even have

257

stood lookout for you and honked when she came back if I'd known you were going to cap it by setting the place on fire. What did you do that for? Pure spite?'

'I didn't do it. It was an accident.'

'Like the truck blowing up. And now you want me to deliver Addie in person to your tender mercies. Frankly, I'd as soon drop her in a pool full of piranhas.'

'Scotto only wants to have a talk with her.'

'Yeah, sure. Let him find her himself then.'

'Rusty.' Régine's voice was icy cold. 'You don't have any choice.'

'You coming blackmail at me, sweetheart? You've got it backwards. I'm the little fish. If I nail you, they let me off. And if you nail Scotto, *you* get off. If I were in your shoes, I'd give it some thought.'

Rusty laughed, a slightly unpleasant sound. 'As for me, sweetheart, it's time to grab my stash and bail.'

After the big main doors banged shut behind Rusty, I stood motionless in the empty dining-room until I heard the sound of Régine dialling at the switchboard. Then I slipped back into the kitchen and out to the garden.

Telling Régine of Jay's arrival was nothing I wanted to do any more, certainly not alone – except perhaps by telephone. In fact, a telephone was what I wanted most now, for it would get me the advice, and perhaps the physical protection, of Marcellin Morin and his gendarme colleagues. And the way to the nearest phone was across the garden, through the cypresses, over Gran's wall and around the path to Madame Isnard's.

I moved cautiously along the flagstoned path towards the west end of the inn, keeping to the shadows.

For a minute I felt foolish and melodramatic. Surely there was no real danger – Rusty had just told off Régine and gotten away with it. She could do nothing without Scotto. And even Scotto was no menace unless I was alone. He was capable of any coldblooded action, but he avoided witnesses. And anyway he wasn't here.

258

Then suddenly he was.

A car roared into the parking lot, its headlights raking the cypresses that bordered the garden. I shrank back against the west wall of the *mas*. Two more cars followed the first. Tyres chewed gravel, doors slammed, footsteps crunched. Then Régine's heels clicked down the steps.

'Oh, Joseph, thank heavens you've come! I've just been trying to phone –'

'Where is she?'

'I don't know. She wasn't home fifteen minutes ago. And now Rusty's just refused to help –'

Scotto interrupted her again, this time with a short string of curses followed by brisk orders. 'Blacky, J-J, go and bring back that red-haired American, the man we passed on the way up. He hadn't gone far, you can catch him before the crossroads.'

Then he resumed swearing.

He said the idea of involving Rusty was a stupid one. He said Régine was altogether a stupid bitch. He said it was stupid for a man to depend on any woman for anything but – here he used a vulgar phrase I had not heard before – and that included Régine, and his own wedded helpmate Patrice, and Albert's incredibly witless accomplice Yvette in Grasse, and most of all the tall blonde American whose legs weren't half as long as her nose.

'What – what's happened?' Régine managed to ask.

'Plenty. The Forrester girl somehow got wind of the Flairaud business, and pried out of Yvette everything she knew. Yvette won't do any more talking, Albert's seen to that. But the Forrester girl apparently was flashing dozens of photos, a lot of them of ourselves. So you can see – even with your limited mental powers, my dear Régine – that we have to get to her before she takes her patchwork of facts and guesses and runs off again to that tabloid in Nice.'

'Yes, Joseph,' Régine said submissively. 'It won't be long now. She expects Rusty to call for her at seven, so she'll have to come back to St Martin by then.'

'Don't you know anything? She is in St Martin.'

259

'Is she? She's not here. I went to her house, and I phoned Madame Isnard's too.'

'Her car's at the chapel. I left Tonio and Roger there to intercept her if she didn't head uphill.'

'She must be back early for the rally then. The violet growers are meeting again tonight.'

'Like Pavlov's dogs – good. When?'

'Six.'

Scotto sighed. 'Be too big a crowd already. We'll have to wait for her to come up.'

'What will you – say to her?' Régine asked hesitantly.

'That I don't like being harassed. That she can be on a plane for New York tomorrow, with my cheque in hand. Or,' Scotto sounded smug now, 'I can interfere with her business as she has with mine.'

'You think she'll see reason?'

'She'd better. Otherwise she'll have a mysterious accident tonight. And it's not long enough since the last one.' Scotto banged his hands together. 'Maybe we can make it look like a case of exposure. A night like this, anyone caught outside could freeze to death. Come on, Albert, let's go in and get some coffee.'

Footsteps crunched, then Scotto's voice came again more distantly. 'Jacques, cover the gates with Luc. And Raoul, you stay by the path below the old woman's steps. She can't pass any other way.'

The main doors thunked shut. I huddled beside the west wall of the *mas*, contemplating the bleak truth of Scotto's words. He intended to catch me coming up to the Eagle's Nest, while what I needed was to get down from above. But either way, he was right. I couldn't pass.

Could I wait them out?

No. When seven o'clock came and went, they would not leave. They would summon more men and search in earnest.

Should I walk in innocently and accept Scotto's offer?

Yes, if it would buy me tonight, for tomorrow Jay would be with me.

No, because once Scotto had me, he would never allow

me a minute of freedom, let alone a night. And Jay, thinking Scotto was neutralised, would instead walk into an army.

Somehow I had to get down to the village before Jay passed through it, if it took the whole six hours from now until midnight.

And it might. The way to Madame Isnard's, with the only telephone above the inn, was blocked. Scotto had nine men along the road from the inn to the chapel, and on this side of the mountain there was no other way down. Gran's garden, like the inn's, ended at a sheer rock face that I knew I could never descend in the dark even if I had a hundred metres of stout rope, which I didn't. The precipice, which we had always valued for the security and privacy it gave us, had become a prison wall.

The only way down, I realised, was up.

I would have to climb the path above Gran's house at least as far as Lew's. From there, there must be some way down another face of the mountain. Lew could tell me, even guide me. The ghastly possibility that he might not be at home occurred to me, but I pushed it firmly out of mind.

Before I could get to Lew's house I had to get to my own. The only gap I knew of in the cypresses between the inn's garden and Gran's was beside the parking lot. Here near the west wall the trees grew in a solid phalanx, their trunks only two feet apart. I would have to force my way through by main strength.

In the dim light reflected from the parking lot I chose a spot where the branches seemed to grow less thickly. Past the feathery leaves and hard little cones I could feel the low stone wall on Gran's side. I pushed my bag through, and was about to follow head first, when powerful hands seized me from behind.

I struggled only a moment, then went limp. There was no sense fighting a grip as strong as Jean-Marc's.

Or was it Jean-Marc?

A week ago, when I stood outside this same building and

261

strong hands covered my mouth and held me the same way, Jean-Marc was protecting me from discovery by Scotto. But if Jean-Marc was here now, he must have come with Scotto, must be working with him.

If so, there was nothing I could do but go gracefully, and try to buy time.

I tapped gently on the hand that covered my mouth, to indicate I would be docile. The grip relaxed. I turned to face –

Patrice Scotto.

Even in the dim light I could see the crazed look in her eyes. No wonder I thought it was Jean-Marc holding me – she had the strength of a madwoman. Now her hands tightened on my shoulders and she brought her head next to mine.

'You must take me away, now,' she whispered. 'Joseph is going to move me to another place, I heard him tell Régine, and even God won't be able to find me. And I won't have a way to get out, either, the way I did here. Joseph has come, angel. You must take me away with you.'

I knew with an awful sinking certainty that she was right.

Not necessarily for the reason she stated, of course. The threat of Scotto locking her away thoroughly might exist only in her deranged mind, though it had the ring of reality. But even if she was in no danger, I had to help her for my own safety. To let them recapture her was to risk her telling them she had seen me.

Now that I had to keep Patrice with me, the problem of getting up the mountain to Lew's cabin was not only greatly compounded, it was suddenly urgent. For if Scotto would only start wondering where I was after seven, he might discover Patrice's absence at any time.

'Listen!' I whispered into her ear. 'We have to go through the trees here. You'll be scraped and hurt by the branches, but you must make *no* sound. Understand?'

Patrice nodded, and placed a solemn finger across her lips.

In this I thought she would obey me. She might be nine-tenths unhinged, but a psychotic's monomania could serve us now. I wanted Patrice to fasten singlemindedly on the need for silence.

'I'll go first,' I told her, 'and try to hold the branches for you.'

I put one arm across my eyes and used the other to haul me through the cypresses and over the wall. Patrice came right behind me, without the least whimper.

Just when I was starting to feel better about our chances, Patrice's hand closed on my arm.

'I've lost a slipper,' she whispered.

I closed my eyes and for a long moment said nothing. There was no point in scolding Patrice. She was doing the best she could. So I dropped to my knees and felt the ground all around her. But the one slipper she wore was the only one there.

There was no choice, I had to go back and find it. Once Patrice was missed they would search for her. They would concentrate the search inside the Eagle's Nest – unless the dropped slipper pointed them outside.

A minute later I had wriggled through the hedge and found the slipper. But when I put it on Patrice's foot, I had a sobering realisation.

Patrice was dressed for a boudoir. And it was not just starting to rain. It was pelting down real hail.

I put a finger on Patrice's lips again, then tugged her through the rosebushes to the back of Gran's house. Of all places it was, ironically, safest for a few minutes, because Scotto was quite sure I wasn't there. I would not risk the noise of the padlock and the front door, though. I would use the trick window. I just had to be careful not to let the latch on the shutters swing over.

When I was inside, I passed a footstool through the window so Patrice could follow me. Obviously we couldn't go up the mountain in this weather dressed as we were. And with the window closed again, we could talk softly as we changed.

Patrice was afraid to say a word. The total darkness dis-oriented her, and I would not light even a candle, so she

263

stayed rooted just inside the window. As I brought her items of clothing, however, she helped me put them on her. Her frilly robe was replaced by a turtleneck pullover, a flannel shirt, and a Yale sweatshirt. For pants I gave her the bottom of my jogging suit, turned over twice at the waist. The top I put on myself, along with Jay's old sweater and my trench-coat.

A raincoat for Patrice was something of a problem. In the end I groped under the sink for the box of lawn-and-leaf bags, and poked head and arm holes to form a rudimentary plastic poncho.

For her feet I could do nothing but give her two pairs of socks. My own footgear was miles too large. Patrice would have to make it up the mountain in her shaggy pink bedroom slippers.

Thus attired, we climbed back out the window.

It gave a touch of comic relief to consider how odd we must look. But every bit of ill-assorted clothing was welcome, for, though the hail had stopped, I felt on my face a soft wetness that wasn't rain. My New England weather sense had been right. The French Riviera was in the middle of a snowstorm.

The snow didn't have to pose more problems, but it posed different ones. And they changed depending on how much it snowed.

Light was one. Without snow, we would get some reflection from the parking lot on the first part of our climb. In a blizzard we could use my giant flashlight freely. But in this moderately gentle swirl of fat wet flakes, we had to do without either. And it was a good long way until the path shelved and turned so we could confidently use light without being visible from the Route de la Chapelle.

Footprints were another problem. So far the snow was not sticking. But the temperature felt well below freezing. At the rate we could climb in the dark, it would not be long before we were leaving a plain trail. And it was a matter of luck how soon Scotto's men might be looking for one.

There was a sudden blaze of arc lights in the parking lot, floodlights in the garden, interior lights everywhere in the inn straight up to the tower suite. They already knew Patrice was missing.

Whether this was good luck or bad I couldn't quite decide.

We had stumbled a pitifully short way. Now with our eyes acquiring night vision, the extra light meant we could triple our rate of climb. It was still a halting, stumbling progress, but at least we could tell roughly where the path lay and concentrate on our footing.

Patrice's arm tightened around my waist.

'They're looking for me, angel, aren't they?' she asked.

'Yes, Patrice, but don't worry. They'll never think of going up, the way angels do.'

The answer seemed to satisfy her. She plodded beside me, going where my arm guided her. Ten more minutes and we reached the bend where the lights of le Nid de l'Aigle, even the tower suite I had occupied ten days ago, were no longer visible.

Now I switched on the flashlight we so desperately needed.

Patrice climbed faster, almost half as fast as I would have alone. We were doing splendidly. We would reach Lew's place in no time.

We would have, if Patrice hadn't just then cried out and sunk to the ground, clutching her ankle.

She believed me when I said it wasn't broken – she seemed to think all angels were also nurses – but no amount of reassurance would enable her to stand on it. The pain was obviously severe, and already I could feel the swelling.

Again, there was no point in blaming Patrice. More likely the fault was mine for setting too fast a pace.

I mentally inventoried the contents of my shoulder bag, trying to think of something to make her more comfortable while I went on alone to Lew's. But I had nothing in the medical line except Dramamine and a couple of Bandaids. The best I could do was fold my scarf for padding, and criss-cross her ankle tightly with the belt of my trenchcoat.

265

When I told her I would leave her for a few minutes to bring back help, she fastened on my arm with renewed strength, and howled as she had not from physical pain. A sharp reminder that Joseph might hear brought down her volume, but she blubbered on, half incoherent with fear.

'No! Joseph will find me and take me away. And nobody will help me any more, not even Albert. I have to stay with you, angel! If you abandon me, I'm lost for good.'

Reasoning with her was hopeless.

We tried going on together but, even tightly bound, the ankle would take no weight at all. And I could not carry Patrice Scotto up a mountain as I had carried Irène Isnard up a flight of stairs. I had to get help. Every time I tried to break away from her, though, Patrice howled louder. I was afraid if I did succeed in leaving her alone, she would summon Scotto and his entire army.

How much further was it to Lew's? I wondered. Could I risk whistling and calling to Dylan and Caitlin? Or would Scotto's men hear what the dogs, shut up indoors, could not? If the wind carried –

Of course!

My left hand groped in my trenchcoat pocket. Nothing. My other arm, with Patrice clinging to it like a leech, moved more slowly, but I searched the right pocket too. Again no result.

It took some persuasion, but Patrice finally sat down and let me go through my shoulder bag. She held the flashlight while item after item came out of the leather bag and on to my lap. I began to think I must have left it on the kitchen counter, or even given it back to Lew, when my hand finally closed on the little chromium pipe.

I put it to my lips and blew with all my might, once, twice, three times. I waited half a minute and blew two more blasts. After another thirty seconds I tried a series of short, sharp notes, erratically timed.

The whistle was silent, and for a crawlingly long time, so was the hillside above us. But then Patrice clutched my arm again.

'Dogs!' she whispered in terror. 'They've set dogs to track us!'

'No, Patrice,' I told her. 'Joseph has no dogs. I called these dogs from above to help us.'

'Oh.' She nodded her comprehension. 'I didn't know you had dogs there, but I suppose they go to heaven the same as anybody.'

There was a temptation to explain that these dogs came not from heaven but from Wales. But Lew would probably have contested the distinction. And anyway, if ever dogs were heaven-sent, Dylan and Caitlin were now.

My lap was barely cleared of the contents of my bag before the terriers were into it, climbing to lick my face. And Lew was only seconds after them. He must have come down at break-neck speed through the swirling snow. He called anxiously, 'Addie? Are you there, Addie? For God's sake, tell me you're all right!'

I pushed the dogs off my lap and rose to meet him.

'What is it, love, what's happened?' He held me so tightly I could barely answer.

'Madame Scotto and I have run away together and now she's sprained her ankle. Scotto knows she's gone, though he may not think I'm with her, and he may not think she's come this way. We have to get her to shelter, then go for help.'

Lew accepted this without asking for elaboration. He turned and calmly regarded the weird spectre of Patrice Scotto. Looking into her wild eyes he said formally, 'At your service, madame.'

'Patrice,' I told her, 'this is a friend of mine. He's one of the angels too, and his name is Louis.'

Lew didn't even blink at that. He just helped Patrice Scotto to her feet – or her one usable foot.

He was prepared to carry her up himself, but I suggested we might do it together, and showed him how to form the hands-on-elbows chair seat I remembered from Scout days. The path was wide enough, if only barely, so it was easier on everyone. It did mean entrusting a flashlight to Patrice, but when I explained that she would have to be our guiding star and light our feet, she fulfilled her role perfectly. Over our

267

clasped arms she sat erect and allowed herself to be borne up the mountain with the air of an oriental empress.

When we got her to Lew's cabin, he pulled a wing chair closer to the fire and installed her in it.

'Here we are, Patrice. We must warm you up first thing – except for your ankle, of course. I haven't any ice for it, but tonight I can offer you plenty of snow.'

He went outside with a basin, then packed snow into plastic bags while I removed the larger bag that still encased Patrice.

Even without her makeshift poncho, she looked bizarre, from the gold circlet that somehow lodged in her tangled hair through the Yale sweatshirt and the jogging pants to the single sodden pink slipper. But on her trip up the mountain she had become familiar with Lew, and with the terriers as well. Though she was in a strange house, her face was more relaxed, more sane, than I had yet seen it.

When Lew propped her foot on a hassock and surrounded it with snow packs, she actually smiled. 'Thank you, Louis, that feels much better.'

Lew set me to making tea next, while he filled hot-water bottles to tuck around Patrice. Being British, he owned at least three. Over the shared kettle, we talked softly in English.

'What did you mean about going for help?' he asked.

'I meant getting downhill and phoning the gendarmes. Like, PDQ.' I told Lew what I had heard at the Eagle's Nest, and how Patrice's flight had attached itself to my own. 'Scotto could already muster nine men when we left. God knows how many he has now, or when he'll send a party up.'

'And nobody below has any idea? Where's Jay?'

I told Lew that too, and why, according to Marcellin Morin, it was safe for me to come back alone.

'My arse!' he said. 'Frigging police are worth damn-all!' He had never sworn that way, as far as I could remember. 'You're right, somebody's got to get down bloody quick. And it had better be me.'

'Why, Lew? It's true I'm the one Patrice knows, and you're

268

the one who knows the mountain. But once I got to a phone, I'd get quicker results out of the police. And we need to turn out every caserne from Nice to Grasse. From the look of it, you can handle Patrice. Just point me down a path and give me a couple of landmarks, and I'll be fine.'

Lew scowled. 'Addie, how much have you climbed on this mountain?'

'Well, mostly just here or to the waterfall. Jay and I went all the way up to the ridge once, maybe twice.'

'Then you know it's a four-hour climb before you can even start down the Tourrettes side. And on this side it sheers off everywhere the way it does below your own garden. The whole face is a collection of mini-*baous*.'

'You mean –'

'I mean that, apart from the path you came up, there *is* no way off the mountain.'

Lew brought Patrice hot-water bottles and snow packs for her ankle. I brought us all cups of tea. In between, Lew and I talked over the problem.

Lew still thought, after looking at it from every angle, that he should be the one to go.

'I'll march down the mountain as though I own it, which I partly do. When I get to your house I'll pound on the door and call your name. If anyone's about I'll ask whether they've seen you. And then I'll walk on innocently into the village.'

'And if they don't let you pass?'

'They will.'

I sighed, wishing I could share his confidence. 'Remember last Sunday? We were kidding about your having a telephone put in by the pool. Tonight it isn't funny any more.'

'Life's little ironies,' Lew agreed. 'I contrived it so I can get anything I want up the mountain, never dreaming I'd need to get a message down. I could so easily have strung wires on the pylons and put in a –'

I cried out in excitement.

'What is it, love?' he said.

'That's the answer! The thing holds fifty-kilo sacks of dog food, and full butane bottles. So it's bound to hold me, isn't it?'

'The goods lift?'

'Sure. I'll ride the thing down and call for help, and you'll still be here with Patrice to hide her if they come looking. It's perfect. And it can't be any slower than going down on foot.'

'No, much faster. Also much too dangerous. It's out of the question.'

'So is staying here any longer. So we'll have to trust the contraption. Come on, I'm willing, and it's my neck.'

I put my coat back on, found my bag and flashlight, and retrieved my scarf from beside Patrice's footstool.

'Listen, Patrice,' I said calmly. 'Louis and I are going out now to call some more angels. You stay here by the fire with the doggies. Louis will be back in just a few minutes, and I'll bring the other angels a little later.'

Lew continued to protest as he followed me to the door. 'It's a crazy notion, Addie. The thing's not designed for safety. The lines could foul, and you'd be stranded twenty feet up in the air.'

'Better lend me a twenty-foot rope, then, in case.'

'Or they could snap completely.'

'Um – a parachute?'

'I'm not joking, you could get killed!'

I stopped with my hand on the latch and met Lew's eyes. 'I know that, Lew. And if I don't go now, we could all get killed, very soon, because Scotto isn't joking either.'

He glanced at Patrice, watching us anxiously from the fireside, and made himself smile reassurance at her.

His voice was quiet again as he said, 'All right, love. You'll want gloves for holding the guy ropes. Take these, they're fur-lined. And you'd best have my umbrella.'

It was I who couldn't speak normally then. With a jaunty wave to Patrice, I ducked out the door into the quickening swirl of snow.

The giant flashlight, lashed to the derrick, sent its beam

through the snowflakes around us and over the precipice into the void below.

Lew held me a final moment. I could feel his heart racing like mine. Then he released me and caught my hands instead. Though there was no one to hear, he whispered as he said:

'Go now, love, but come back safe and soon.'

He helped me on to the platform of the lift. I knelt on one knee, centring my weight, each hand grasping a pair of guy ropes.

I opened my mouth twice before any words came out. 'All right, Lew. You can start it down now.'

Lew unhooked the platform from the steel bar. Though he restrained its swing as much as he could, the sudden lurch, and then the pendulum swing over empty space, resonated in my already queasy stomach. I reminded myself that, except when it passed the pylons, the actual ride would be smoother.

I was glad Lew had not insisted on my facing downhill, but had compromised on sideways. That way I could glance occasionally at the lights of St Martin when they came into view, but otherwise try not to think how long a stretch of Mediterranean coast must be visible once I got below the snow line from this dizzying height. Mostly I intended to look uphill. Lew would be cut off from sight as soon as he started working the crank, but I would know he was there.

When it came, the movement wasn't frightening after all.

It was exhilarating, in fact. Though my senses told me I was dropping, the platform felt unexpectedly steady. I actually wished for more speed, for I knew the descent was bringing me closer to St Martin and help. Even when the lift passed under the first pylon, the sudden bumps were no shock. My ears, used to the sound of ski lifts, must have warned me.

I shifted my weight experimentally. The platform continued to feel stable.

Slowly I let go of one pair of guy ropes and took my flashlight from my pocket. The succession of snow-mantled trees, then brush, then bare rock, then black void skimming in turn past the lip of the platform was a heady sight.

271

The second pylon came, and the third. The snow became wetter, then turned to rain.

Halfway down, I thought, maybe more.

Just past the fourth pylon, the rhythm altered.

My stately progress, until now broken only by the passage of the pylons, became jerky. The platform began to rock fore and aft. The jerks seemed to come at regular intervals, every so many metres. But they were not regular in time. The time between jerks, in fact, was getting perceptibly shorter.

Something had gone wrong above. In the maze of wheels and pulleys that fed into Lew's hand crank, some governor must have cracked and spun off the line.

The jerks came faster.

I turned the flashlight downhill. I don't know what I was looking for – perhaps a clump of bushes or a scrub pine I could jump into. But all I saw was rock. And another pylon.

What I did next could not have come from conscious thought.

I wrapped the arm that held the flashlight, the downhill arm, around the guy ropes. With the other hand I snatched up the umbrella and, as the platform jerked its way past the pylon, I hooked the handle around an upright.

How I managed to hold on I will never understand. If madness gave Patrice Scotto a man's strength, perhaps fear gave it to me. I only knew that if I did not check the lift now, it would crash out of control at the bottom.

The platform, its momentum arrested, tilted almost vertical. My right foot slid to the rim and lodged there jarringly. From wrist to shoulder my right arm screamed with the pain of holding the platform's weight and my own. Through Lew's fur-lined glove I could feel my hand slipping along the shaft of the umbrella.

Then it was gone.

The platform rocked wildly. I scrambled for balance, catching a guy rope with my right hand, but losing the flashlight over the side. My fear surged higher yet. The lift would tear the rest of the way down the mountain now.

It didn't, though. It stayed miraculously just where it was.

When it did move, it was a cautious foot or two – uphill! The little respite I had given Lew must have been enough.

I said a wordless prayer of thanksgiving. Among the fears flashing through my head and clutching at my heart, I recognised, not the smallest was for Lew. I had pictured him knocked senseless. Worse, mangled by runaway machinery. But he was in control again now.

I crouched on the platform ready for the descent to resume. Below me, improbably still burning where it had fallen, the flashlight threw its beam obliquely through the pylon and uphill in the direction I had come.

Why was Lew waiting? Was he working on some repair? Was the lift perhaps beyond fixing? Did he expect me to climb down the pylon and go the rest of the way on foot? I began judging the feasibility of that. I would have to work my way hand over hand along the rope for a few metres, but it could be done. And this pylon was the last before the bottom and the Chemin du Baou leading into the village. There must be some way, with the aid of the flashlight, for me to scramble down.

I was about to try it when the lift began moving, again uphill. It went slowly for perhaps thirty seconds, stopped, and, with little jerks, started down.

It came opposite the pylon. If I wanted to get off, now was the time.

I would trust Lew. I would stay on.

Three minutes later I was on the ground, on the Chemin du Baou, running toward St Martin.

Jacky was alone at the Commerce. Everyone else in town was across the road in the square at the growers' rally.

They were making so much noise that I asked Jacky to close the door while I was on the phone. I didn't care whether he stayed inside or out – and since I had arrived at a dead run, dirty, dishevelled and gasping, I wasn't surprised that he gave up listening to the growers in favour of eavesdropping on me. Jacky could sense a vintage item of news, and it would be all over town before morning anyway, so he was welcome to break it.

He didn't even stay to listen to it.

He just heard me get through to Caserne Kellerman in Grasse and to Adjudant-chef Marcellin Morin, and tell the gendarme that Scotto was trying to capture me with murderous intent because I had found out he was behind the trouble between the flower growers and the perfumers. . . .

Jacky was out the door, running faster than I had. He was back before I hung up, and René Cordier was with him.

They both listened uncomprehending as I told Marcellin Morin that I had taken Patrice Scotto up to Lew's place, and described how to get there. When I was off the phone, René demanded the whole story, instantly.

I gave him the short version, instantly. 'Anything more you want to know? I have time. I'm under orders to stay by this phone until the *flics* get here.'

René asked a couple of questions, then he too was off at a run.

The crowd parted for him and hands helped him up on to the platform. He raised his arms, and under a sea of umbrellas the villagers fell silent, waiting for his words.

René was in a blazing fury. The legitimate struggle of the working class had once again been perverted, used as a blind for the base motives of rapacious individuals. But somewhere under the indignation I could sense that René was gratified too. The villains were the parvenu Scotto and his gangster minions of the Union Corse. And to René the Red, organised crime was the most right-wing institution of all.

That René was an orator I knew, but now I found that his talent verged on demagoguery. In no time flat he transmitted all his fury and turned the crowd into a mob.

'Up that hill are the wolves who robbed us of our livelihood, our independence and our honour! Up that hill are the swine who put Serge Gazagnaire and Pierre Pla at the brink of death!

'They may yet do more harm before the police arrive.

'*Alors, des gars!* Let's give the men in blue a hand. Let's show them what the men of St Martin are made of!'

TWELVE

'AT WHICH point the crowd split in two and charged up the hill,' I told Jay. 'The men who came by the Ruelle des Violettes waited at the junction for the main body climbing the Route de la Chapelle. Most of the growers live on one road or the other anyway. And as they reached their houses they'd dash inside and come out with a rifle or a shotgun. Everybody here hunts, you know. So they made a pretty formidable mob.'

We were sitting around the fire in Gran's house, six of us, or eight counting the terriers. It was perhaps an hour past midnight.

'I wish I'd seen it.' Jay reached for Connie's hand. 'Looks like we missed all the excitement, doll.'

Connie nodded. Her face plainly said, though, that of the eight hours she had just spent alone with Jay, she wouldn't trade a single minute.

'I almost missed it myself,' I said. 'But then Marcellin and his troops roared in like the US Cavalry and brought me up the hill with them. I was beginning to think there wouldn't be any action left.'

Marcellin chuckled. 'That's not what *we* were worried about. We were afraid there wouldn't be anything left of Joseph Scotto. Those peaceful violet growers had turned into a real vigilante mob. But luckily the French don't think in terms of hanging, and they didn't have a guillotine handy.'

'They gave us more resistance than Scotto and his men did,' Jean-Marc pointed out.

He sat across from me on a straight-backed chair, looking

275

terribly official. I still wasn't used to the sight of him in his uniform, but I had to admit it looked splendid on him.

'Scotto's type never resist,' Marcellin said. 'They wait for their lawyers to spring them. Still, between what Addie's given us and what your branch has come up with, I think we may put Scotto away yet.'

'Now let me get this straight,' Jay said. 'Do I understand that the gendarmes were already investigating Scotto for a month before Addie got here?'

'Not us.' Marcellin jerked a thumb in Jean-Marc's direction. 'Him.'

'I was doing undercover work for the narcotics bureau,' Jean-Marc explained. 'That's separate from the Gendarmerie.'

'We're part of the Ministry of Defence,' Marcellin Morin said. 'And his service are *douaniers*, under the Treasury. A vital difference.'

'But the most important distinction,' Jean-Marc went on, 'is that they wear black stripes down their trouser seams, while ours are red.'

The two policemen shared a comradely grin.

Lew asked, 'Whose lot was it, then, that descended on my place?'

'His,' Jean-Marc said. 'Right now I'm just liaising.'

Lew picked up the story at that point for the benefit of Jay and Connie, recounting what had happened after he sent me downhill on the goods lift.

'Towards the bottom it started going out of control. I probably wouldn't have been able to hold it if Addie hadn't understood and contrived to give me some help. Normally, you see, a downhill load is only twenty or thirty pounds, perhaps a dustbin and an empty butane bottle, and the counterweight is set accordingly. If I'd known how much you weighed, love,' Lew turned to me with an affectionate smile, 'I'd never have tried it at all.'

For answer I stuck out my tongue at him.

'Then I went back to the house and, except for the odd word of reassurance to Patrice, I stayed outside listening. After ten or fifteen minutes, a great roar went up from the village, and I thought I could hear it coming closer. At the same time I saw lights on the path just below my house. I went inside and was about to hide Patrice when suddenly there was the most godawful racket. I was frankly startled witless, but Patrice didn't turn a hair. She said, "That'll be the other angels. How modern you are, using helicopters nowadays."'

'Modern indeed,' Marcellin agreed. 'That's our new six-man Ecureuil. It'll cruise for four hours at 250 kph.'

'It wasn't cruising, it was buzzing my house. So I opened all the shutters and went out with my torch and waved it down. Made a mess of my cabbage patch. And then Patrice refused to get into the thing. She didn't mind the idea of a helicopter. But she wouldn't believe angels ever wore police uniforms.'

'Very narrow-minded of her,' Jean-Marc said.

'Inconvenient too,' Marcellin added. 'We had to send the helicopter to fetch Addie up from the Eagle's Nest, and she was already busy there dealing with another balky female.'

'Lord, yes,' I laughed. 'Scotto and his men surrendered without a peep, but Régine barricaded herself into the tower suite. She was convinced the mob was going to lynch them all. And she wouldn't listen to any stranger who said otherwise. She listened to me, though. I told her Rusty was talking his way out of a jail term and she ought to do the same.'

'She sang like a bird,' Marcellin said. 'I wonder whether she would have, if she knew Rusty wasn't here at all.'

'Rusty got away?' Connie asked him.

'Scotto's men never caught up with him. Slippery character, that one. We found the wall safe at his studio open and empty. No point putting out a bulletin on him. From here it's only an hour or two to the border.'

In a way I was rather glad. Rusty wasn't innocent, but he was in way over his head. I wished he'd tried to warn me before he cut out; it would have been a nice gesture. Under the circumstances, though, it wouldn't have done any good.

'Anyway we don't need his testimony, with Régine's.' I turned. 'One thing she said will interest you, Jay. Remember

Mathilde told me my first day here that this roof was hit by lightning in November? Well, Régine had a different version. Scotto waited for a thunderstorm all right. But then he helped the storm along with a bundle of dynamite on the roof.'

'Neighbourly of him,' Jay said mildly.

'Régine was full of little stories like that. I didn't get to hear most of them, because I had to go up and take care of Patrice. The ride in the helicopter was fun – after the goods lift, nothing could scare me. And Monsieur le Curé had shown up, so I dragged him along and he was the one who went with Patrice to the hospital. Lew and I were glad to walk back down here. We were a little tired of playing angels.'

'What was the matter with Madame Scotto?' Connie asked.

Lew answered. 'I didn't talk to her that much, and she wasn't too coherent, but from what I could piece together, it all dates back twenty years or more. She'd have left Scotto soon after they were married, but they had a child, and she knew he'd never let her keep the boy. So she stayed, never enquiring too closely into what her husband's business was, trying to raise the boy decently. And then a few months ago, when Albert was through school and university and she thought she had him safely headed for medical school, Albert announced that he planned to go into business with his father.'

'And that was when her mind snapped?'

'Apparently. About the next part I'm only guessing. I think the way they've restrained and sedated her isn't on the advice of any reputable doctor. I think Patrice Scotto threatened to keep Albert from his father's influence any way she could, including sending Joseph to jail. And Joseph was afraid she could do it.'

'So they kept her drugged?' Connie asked. 'Her own husband and son? Nice people.'

'Drugs is their stock in trade,' Jean-Marc said. 'So Scotto moved her to a strange place, installed his mistress as watch-dog and kept her doped up. He probably wouldn't have been even that humane if he'd been more sure of Albert.'

I quoted, ' "How sharper than a serpent's tooth – " ' then I

278

sneezed violently three times. It was only an hour since I had managed to get out of my sodden clothes.

Connie said, 'Bless you.' Jay brought me a lap rug. Jean-Marc jumped up to get me a glass of brandy – his answer to everything. And Lew handed me a packet of tissues.

'Would you rather use this?' Jean-Marc asked, offering me the handkerchief in his pocket. 'First-quality, hand embroidered – with someone else's initials. It'll make a unique souvenir of my time as Jean-Marc Bertrand.'

I knew now that his full name was Jean-Marc Bertrand Claude Pascal Jarricot. 'Shall I embroider another set for you?' I asked. 'No, maybe better not. It might be awkward explaining it to your wife.'

Jean-Marc met my eyes with a level gaze. 'I'm not married,' he said quietly. 'Do you think I'd lie about that, baby? There's a difference between undercover and underhanded.'

I was careful not to show any reaction. In the first place, I knew Lew was watching, though he seemed not to be. Besides, why should I have any interest in, let alone be fishing for, information about Jean-Marc's civil status? He was just a physically attractive Frenchman about whom I was no longer sure I knew anything. Still –

'Tell me something, Lieutenant Jarricot,' Jay said. He didn't seem to have noticed the by-play. Perhaps right now he could think of romance only in terms of Connie and himself. Which was fine by me.

'Yes, Mr Forrester?'

Jean-Marc was being deliberately formal with my brother, perhaps to place himself in contrast with Lew, who claimed every ounce of familiarity he could without looking blatant. Clearly, the game was on again.

'What was it, Lieutenant, that brought you to le Nid de l'Aigle six weeks ago?'

Jean-Marc straightened a little inside his uniform. 'My service became interested in Scotto some time ago. And in the summer, when he left Marseilles, our interest sharpened. You see, the drug trade there, the so-called French Connection, was getting progressively unlinked. In a sense, we were too

279

successful in breaking up the importers and refiners. Some went to jail, some prudently retired – and others left Marseilles. But if we only broke up the drug trade geographically, we hadn't broken it at all. So when a pivotal figure left, we followed if we could. In the case of Scotto, I followed. And when he bought a public inn, I found it easier than usual to establish myself close to him. But even before I moved in last month, we'd learned a good deal about his nosings about the area, and his particular interest in Grasse and the perfume industry.'

'I should think so,' Connie said. 'It's pretty obvious.'

'Obvious?' This from Jay. 'What's obvious?'

'Why Scotto wanted a perfume factory,' Connie said patiently.

'For refining heroin?'

'It's made to order. A perfume factory is just a series of chemistry labs designed for extraction and refinement processes. You could go right on with business as usual. Except that every weekend the "specialists" in Research and Development who were supposed to be working on a new perfume would be whipping up a batch of pure white powder instead. Once you got the operation underway, it could go on for years without anybody suspecting. It wouldn't even look odd if you added a twenty-foot wall and a battalion of armed guards. With all the hush-hush development projects and secret formulae, the perfume industry is very high on security.'

'Hmm. Makes sense,' Jay said. 'But if Scotto wanted a perfume factory, why didn't he just build one?'

'That *would* have looked odd, since he had no way to assemble a team of trained perfumers. They're a tight fraternity. All he could plausibly do was buy into an established firm.'

'Okay, so he went to all that trouble for months, organising strikes and sabotage and general chaos in the industry. What was the point? To keep it up until some company was forced to sell out?'

'Sure,' Connie said.

280

'But isn't that overkill? I mean, Scotto would still have to pay a hefty purchase price for the factory. I thought most drug refiners worked on a shoestring.'

'That's true,' said Jean-Marc Bertrand – no, Jarricot. 'They usually choose an unprepossessing building in a remote spot, and use a homemade still that can be put together and knocked down pretty quickly. They prefer a mobile operation, and very little cash outlay except for the raw heroin base.'

'Then why didn't Scotto settle for a shack in the hills like everybody else?' Jay asked.

'That's a good question.' Jean-Marc turned to Connie. 'Why didn't he?'

'But that's what's so obvious! For himself a shack in the hills would have done fine. For himself he didn't need a legitimate company with an established name and a shiny modern factory. But Joseph Scotto was setting his son up in business. The factory was a present for Albert.'

Jean-Marc Jarricot nodded slowly. 'Of course. Albert.'

Jay nodded too. Then he grinned his wonderful grin. 'Connie, I think you'd better marry me. I'm clearly much too naïve to get through life without you.'

Connie didn't answer. She didn't have to.

It was Lew who spoke next. 'It all has a nice internal consistency – the idea of using a perfume factory to refine heroin. The real perfumers extract the essence of orange blossoms or rose petals or violet leaves. Scotto's raw material would have come from flowers too. Only his were the opium poppy.'

'Hey, that's good!' I dived for my clipboard. 'Mind if I steal the line?'

'Be my guest.' Lew smiled tolerantly.

I scribbled, paused, scribbled some more. I glanced at my watch. 'Darn! Too late to call anybody now. But I can leave a message at *Nice-Matin* and find out what time they start work in the morning. Marcellin, Jean-Marc, where are you going to be for the next few hours? I'll want you to go over my copy and check what I'm allowed to print. Now where did I put those blank tapes? Jay, would you – '

'Addie!' Jean-Marc exclaimed. 'Are you out of your mind, baby? You can't start writing –'

Lew turned from stoking the fire. 'You're coming down with a cold, love. This is no time to –'

Jean-Marc stood, placing himself between Lew and me. 'It's almost two o'clock. After all you've been through, baby –'

Lew moved forward, resting his arm on the back of my rocking chair. 'You've been out four hours in the snow and the rain, love. What you want is a hot bath and –'

' – and a stiff shot of brandy,' said Jean-Marc.

I looked at Jean-Marc. I looked at Lew. I looked for a while at my feet.

Then I looked up sidelong at Jay.

His face was almost impassive. Only the slightest curve of his lip, the slightest crinkle around his eyes, the least lift of one eyebrow, told me he was an inch away from outright laughter.

I got up, walked between Lew and Jean-Marc to the dining table, and put a fresh cassette in the tape-recorder.

Of course I would stay up all night, and all tomorrow too. The story had to be written in English and French and filed with two papers. Then there were the follow-up pieces. Jean-Marc could help me talk Marcellin into protecting my exclusive. Thank heavens Lew had no interest in doing non-fiction. Now, if Flairaud would approve the magazine piece –

Did neither Lew nor Jean-Marc understand anything?

Of course I had to start writing right now.